The shining splendor of our Zebra Lovegram logo on the cover of this book reflects the glittering excellence of the story inside. Look for the Zebra Lovegram whenever you buy a historical romance. It's a trademark that guarantees the very best in quality and reading entertainment.

SURRENDER TO TEMPTATION . . .

"I want you out of here," Cassandra snapped as the man who called himself Trane Taggart pressed her back into the softness of her featherbed.

"I'm going nowhere, Cassandra. You need me."

"I need the devil about as much as I need you!"

"We'll call a truce," he whispered.

"I don't bargain with the devil."

His body shifted. She sensed his face near hers, she could hear his breathing, and then his voice came at her in the dark, "Then you can go to the devil *with* me," and his mouth closed over hers before she could protest.

Soft, angry kisses, insistent, demanding . . . these were the kisses of a man who wanted the sensual life of the woman he held in his arms. This was a man demanding everything—her desire, her soul, her complete capitulation—and she didn't know it was hers to give. She didn't know how to give. . . .

How could he do this to her, her demon, her savior—she didn't know which; she couldn't think . . . she could only *feel*. . . .

THE BEST IN HISTORICAL ROMANCES

TIME-KEPT PROMISES   (2422, $3.95)
by Constance O'Day Flannery
Sean O'Mara froze when he saw his wife Christina standing before him. She had vanished and the news had been written about in all of the papers—he had even been charged with her murder! But now he had living proof of his innocence, and Sean was not about to let her get away. No matter that the woman was claiming to be someone named Kristine; she still caused his blood to boil.

PASSION'S PRISONER   (2573, $3.95)
by Casey Stewart
When Cassandra Lansing put on men's clothing and entered the Rawlings saloon she didn't expect to lose anything—in fact she was sure that she would win back her prized horse Rapscallion that her grandfather lost in a card game. She almost got a smug satisfaction at the thought of fooling the gamblers into believing that she was a man. But once she caught a glimpse of the virile Josh Rawlings, Cassandra wanted to be the woman in his embrace!

ANGEL HEART   (2426, $3.95)
by Victoria Thompson
Ever since Angelica's father died, Harlan Snyder had been angling to get his hands on her ranch, the Diamond R. And now, just when she had an important government contract to fulfill, she couldn't find a single cowhand to hire—all because of Snyder's threats. It was only a matter of time before the legendary gunfighter Kid Collins turned up on her doorstep, badly wounded. Angelica assessed his firmly muscled physique and stared into his startling blue eyes. Beneath all that blood and dirt he was the handsomest man she had ever seen, and the one person who could help beat Snyder at his own game.

Available wherever paperbacks are sold, or order direct from the Publisher. Send cover price plus 50¢ per copy for mailing and handling to Zebra Books, Dept. 3266, 475 Park Avenue South, New York, N.Y. 10016. Residents of New York, New Jersey and Pennsylvania must include sales tax. DO NOT SEND CASH.

SOUTHERN SEDUCTION
THEA DEVINE

ZEBRA BOOKS
KENSINGTON PUBLISHING CORP.

In loving memory of my two dear fathers

My gratitude to:
Susan Sackett, for teaching me what it means to persevere
Pat Nemser, with love
Betina Krahn, for asking why they loved each other

And, as always, to John

ZEBRA BOOKS

are published by

Kensington Publishing Corp.
475 Park Avenue South
New York, NY 10016

First printing: January, 1991

Printed in the United States of America

Prologue

I am free . . .

Startled, she lifted her head for a moment. It was the first time the thought had consciously formed in her mind since Jesse's death. She bent her head again, savoring it.

I am free.

A hand on her shoulder offered sympathy. It slipped around her, offering support she did not want. She sniffed ever so slightly, as if she had been crying. The hand squeezed her arm lightly. The minister droned on, oblivious to the restlessness of the small group of mourners.

I am free.

The day was one of those March days that seemed headed into spring; there was a lively snap in the air that was belied by a calm, warm breeze.

Though it was overcast, there was a sense that the sun might pop through the clouds at any moment. But there was also the sense that the mourners had better things to do than listen to the eulogizing of Jesse Taggart by his graveside for an hour.

She knew it. She had prepared very thoroughly to play the part of the bereaved widow. No one would be able to say she hadn't been utterly grief-stricken.

She looked around surreptitiously before she slipped her handkerchief into her reticule where she carried a small

5

cupful of water. It was enough, just enough, to wet the handkerchief, which she then held to her face under the veil so she could blot the wetness on her cheeks.

And then she lifted her veiled face to the sky, as though the minister had said something profound, and the wafting breeze flattened the black net against her dampened cheeks, just as she intended.

The mourners murmured commiseratingly at this evidence of her grief, and she bowed her head again, a small triumphant smile on her lips.

I am free.

She could not get the thought out of her mind. She let her shoulders shake a little, as though she were crying, and took a deep, shuddering breath. Free.

The places she could go, the things she could do . . . she could leave the sweat of the field in someone else's hands . . . she could . . . She was sick to death of being the one who pushed for things to get done at Riveland, sick to death of the isolation and the loneliness, sick to death of working hard—

She wouldn't think about it. She didn't have to do anything she didn't want to do . . . now. She slipped her hand into the reticule once again to soak her handkerchief so she could apply more moisture to her face.

The minister appeared to be winding down. He motioned to the man standing nearest to the grave, a man she did not know, but someone obviously a friend of Jesse's, indicating to him that he was to throw the first shovelful of dirt onto the casket.

"No," she heard herself say with some authority, startling the minister. "I will do it."

The man hesitated, his dark eyes sweeping her mourning dress, trying to see through the blessed opaqueness of the veil, trying to decide how hard he ought to object. Jesse's wife . . . the poor thing—really!

But she held out her hand. She very definitely wanted to be the one who wielded the first shovelful of the arid soil that would finally and completely bury Jesse Taggart.

6

She held her body defiantly, she dared the stranger to deny her the right to see Jesse in hell. He had no rights whatsoever; she had all the right in the world and she challenged him to deprive her.

But he wasn't a relative; Jesse had no relatives: he was only a friend, some lifelong neighbor whom Jesse had known and she had not, and after another moment, he handed her the shovel without a word.

She hefted it with the assurance of someone who was familiar with tools, and dug into the pile of soil on her side of the open grave.

The soil hit the casket with a vengeful thunk. *Yes,* she thought, heaving another shovelful over the side, and another, and another. *Yes, yes, yes, you deserved it, you deserve it, I'll bury you with it, I won't stop—I won't . . . I won't—*

Someone grasped her arm before she could dig into the dirt pile again, and she relinquished the shovel dazedly.

It was the stranger who took it from her and laid it aside, and then offered her his arm.

Her chin lifted as she accepted, and he turned her from the grave and led her away.

Belatedly she wondered if that shovel were the very one with which she had killed Jesse Taggart.

Chapter One

And she wasn't done yet wearing widow's weeds. There was still the lawyer, and it worried her because it was a name she did not know and he was coming from Atlanta. He was not one of Jesse's cronies from the social clubs of Carthage, and he surely was not someone who would have protected her interests.

He was just a name on a piece of paper she had found among Jesse's effects; she had written to him to inform him of Jesse's death and he had acquiesced to the day she had proposed as being the most convenient for him to see her.

As soon as possible.

Did she *look* like a widow? The velvet-trimmed shiny black bombazine dress took all the color from her face, and that was good. She had managed, with no little difficulty, to scrape her golden curls back from her face and into a neat widow-ish bun at the nape of her neck, and this threw her finely modeled cheekbones and green eyes into high relief against the deadly black. She looked as if she were playing grown-up, she thought, fussing with one unruly curl. She looked all of sixteen. She still looked young.

She settled her face into a mask of sadness. There, just so — pull in the cheeks, purse the lips, look tormented.

She had been tormented, but he didn't need to know that. She would arrange to meet him in the small parlor at the back of the house. The windows there overlooked the garden, and the light in the morning was strong and glaring.

She called Ojim from the barn to help her rearrange the small mirror-backed loveseat so that it was against the window, and she settled herself into it, folding her icy cold hands into her lap and squaring her shoulders.

Her widow's face would not be pinpointed in the streaming morning light, and she would be able to see his cleanly and clearly. A Mr. James Greve. A man she had never heard of, who now held all of Jesse's secrets and her future in his hands.

Warily, she waited.

At ten o'clock promptly, Sully, the major domo, opened the door and announced Mr. James Greve.

Cassandra Coburne Taggart took a deep, sharp breath as the lawyer entered the room and stopped short at the sight of her.

"Miz Taggart?" he asked uncertainly.

"I am," she said firmly. "Mr. Greve?"

"I believe I am," he murmured, moving forward again. She was so young! Jesse Taggart had been sixty if he had been a day. She could not be more than twenty-one or -two. Or -three. At the most. He felt off balance and a little resentful that Jesse had not prepared him for this.

"Please be seated," Cassandra said, motioning to one of the two chairs opposite her.

Her voice was cool and dispassionate and her face was sweet — and sad. Her eyes, a true leaf-green, were guarded. She didn't know what to expect, he thought. But then, neither had he.

"My wife is trying to kill me." Jesse Taggart's first words to him as he barged into his office in Atlanta were not mitigated by James Greve's first sight of Cassandra Taggart.

But he had thought . . . Jesse had led him to believe . . .

"We interred Mr. Taggart three days ago," Cassandra said.

9

He nodded. He hadn't expected to be invited to the funeral, and he was beginning to see now that Jesse had sought him out solely because he wanted no quibbles about his suppositions or the disposal of his estate.

"My wife is trying to kill me."

And with that, Jesse Taggart had cut a vindictive swath through all the legal paperwork, and left him with the unpleasant task of informing the young and beautiful Mrs. Taggart just what he had left in store for her.

His duty was to Jesse, as his executor, and he could not let himself be swayed by Cassandra Taggart's circumstances. Not one bit.

He opened a leather case and retrieved a thick handful of dreadful-looking papers, and then rummaged around for his eyeglasses while the tension heightened to an almost unbearable point.

"Mr. Greve," Cassandra ground out, almost at the end of her patience.

"Miz Taggart . . ."

He was taking forever to organize his papers and his thoughts to get to whatever he wanted to tell her. There was only one thing she wanted to hear: that Riveland was hers fully and unconditionally and that Jesse's accounts were enriched by the last crop he had delivered to Savannah and she could finally feel secure and at peace.

He pushed his glasses up closer to his eyes. He really was a most disarming-looking man, she thought. He had a very open face and she almost had the feeling she could trust him. He was a large man, heavy-set; he had the look, but not the personality, of the kind of man Jesse habitually dealt with.

He looked like the last man Jesse would have hired as his lawyer, and what she did not like most about him was his air of distress. He pored over the papers and it almost seemed to her that he was wavering back and forth about what to present to her and how to do it.

"Riveland passes to you," he said finally. "Of course Mr. Taggart could do no less."

10

The words sent a knifeprick of terror through her. But he would not have left her destitute; he had been very conscious about the look of things, no matter what their marriage had come to after all those years. But still . . . a man could wreak havoc from beyond the grave—and Mr. Greve's impassive expression, along with the ominous rustling of all those papers, did not reassure her at all.

"I visited the coroner, of course," he went on.

She stiffened. "And why did you?" she asked carefully.

"It was incumbent on me, by the terms of the will, to be sure that Jesse Taggart did not die in any way that could be construed as questionable."

Questionable. Another shock wave. How did a lawyer define questionable in terms of death? "Mr. Taggart's death was an accident," she finally managed to say.

"Indeed," Mr. Greve said, still shuffling papers and not looking at her.

She knew what he would have seen had he glanced up for just that fleeting moment.

Fear.

She bit her lip. She didn't want to ask. Whatever the reason, it was pure Jesse Taggart. She couldn't keep herself from asking, "Why is it relevant?"

Because he thought you were trying to kill him. He almost said it. He couldn't look at her. That young, beautiful woman. That calcified Jesse Taggart—it *was* possible, but he hadn't cared until he came face to face with Cassandra Taggart.

And he had to tell her.

"I'm getting to that, Miz Taggart. Just be patient. There is a clause, one among several, in fact, which are severely restrictive. Mr. Taggart had reasons for the way he allotted the estate, you must understand. Nonetheless, all the strictures devolve on you and you must agree to all of them. The first of them is that if Mr. Taggart had died of unnatural causes"—he adjusted his glasses again as he scanned a page he had removed from the pile he was holding—"everything is to go to his issue. *Everything,* Mrs. Taggart, and there is

11

no provision at all for you in that event—no home, no annuity . . . only to the children."

Cassandra's face drained of color. *"Why?"*

He was a little taken aback by her direct question, and his first impulse was to say: Mr. Taggart thought you were trying to kill him, and he wanted to punish you for it. But the whole will was a punishment, designed, he had thought, to avenge a lifetime of ills with a woman that Jesse Taggart had hated, someone his own age, someone able to battle his vindictiveness or to somehow work around that awful clause by the grace of her offspring.

"He felt his life was in danger," Greve said finally.

"From *me?*" It was so ludicrous she wanted to laugh. What if she said to him now that Jesse had been trying to kill *her?* What if he knew that Jesse had hated her, had despised her barrenness, had wanted to remarry and could not divorce her? What could he do? What would he say?

"He obviously thought so," Greve said reluctantly.

"There are no children, Mr. Greve," she said quietly, relishing the final irony.

"No—children?" He felt as if he had been toppled upside down. "I truly don't understand this, Mrs. Taggart. He obviously meant future children. After all, there is always hope . . ."

"No children," she said again, and there was just the faint pulsing of anguish within her. Not Jesse's children.

"His first wife perhaps . . . ?" he asked delicately, his eyes still on the papers and not on her face.

So he knew that much as well.

"I don't know," she said stiffly, but something flashed behind her eyes, some memory of her mother talking about Jesse's first wife. But it was buried with the wash of her mother's demand that she marry Jesse and what an opportunity it was—for both of them. A home, money, servants . . . her duty—

To bear sons for Jesse—her duty . . .

"I see," he said, and he didn't see at all.

"I trust you were satisfied that Mr. Taggart's death was

12

an accident," she went on, diving into the silence to catch him off guard. He didn't know about there being no children; he was obviously perplexed, trying to rewrite it in context so that it made some sense to him. But did Jesse's death make sense to him?

She held her breath as he considered his answer.

"He slipped from the ladder in the hayloft," he said. "Mr. Terhune, the coroner, mentioned it was a rickety affair, most unsafe for a man of Mr. Taggart's size and weight. A support beam broke his fall; the injury killed him, although the knife he was carrying went through his heart and he had broken bones and ribs. It was a hard fall, Mr. Terhune tells me. Nothing questionable. You found him?"

"Yes," she said, willing that one word to be strong, clear, without doubt.

"And no children," he muttered. "Even knowing that, he . . ."

"No," Cassandra said sharply, "we don't know. We don't *know* what he meant or intended—or anything, Mr. Greve. Nor have I a legion of friends and family to attest to the fact that I was a loyal and dutiful wife to Mr. Taggart since the age of sixteen."

Eight years, she thought. A prison. A lifetime. And it hadn't been enough. He had wanted to get rid of her. Or punish her.

"Finish the accounting, Mr. Greve. I can't tell you how distressed I am by the implications of this."

"Then let me warn you—you will find the rest as painful."

She didn't care. Questionable death. Issue. Hell on earth. What else could he do to her?

"Everything passes to you—house, slaves, some cash for living expenses—but be aware, Mrs. Taggart, everything is tied up in the plantation."

"I am very aware of that," Cassandra said tartly. "Please—"

"By the provisions of the will, Mrs. Taggart, you are restricted from marrying, *if* you wish to continue to live and

13

draw your income from Riveland."

She thought she might die then. No hope, no hope—how stupid she had been. She barely caught what Greve was saying next.

"Mr. Taggart specifically stated he did not want Riveland to pass into any other male hands under the *femme couvert*."

"And what a choice plum I would be, owning Riveland," Cassandra added acidly. "Not a man buck in the whole of Carthage who wouldn't want to legally take control of Riveland." And me, she thought, fighting the sinking feeling within her. And there was still more: she could see in his face that he was waiting to deliver the final blow.

"Now, if you decide to live elsewhere, you forfeit Riveland. You cannot give the estate into the hands of an overseer and live in Savannah, for example. Mr. Taggart was very specific on that: you are to make your home on Riveland full-time or give up your rights to the plantation."

"I see." She didn't see. What would the difference have been to Jesse—in death?

Her heart pounded painfully she awaited what he would say next.

"And finally, you must secure good advice in the management of the estate, and you are directed to provide the executor with proof that this provision is being carried out. Now, Mrs. Taggart—"

She didn't even hear him.

Free . . . how could she have dreamed of such a thing. Jesse Taggart had, with his conditions and provisions, managed to bury her at Riveland as completely and deeply as she had buried his body three days before. He wanted her to be a widow forever, and he had arranged it so neatly and incontrovertibly that she herself might just as well be dead.

"I beg your pardon, Mr. Greve?" She came back from the grave in which she had immured herself in her thoughts.

"Are you all right?"

"No, I am not," she said sharply, and then got a grip on herself at his shocked expression. Mr. Greve obviously never dealt with females who spoke their mind, she thought, but there was no sense her losing control in front of a stranger who could not change the matter anyway. He hadn't known her; he hadn't needed to protect her rights. He was Jesse's lawyer, sworn to uphold Jesse's last wishes, and he was not here to help her.

She needed to think. She needed to find some way around the impossible conditions of the will. She needed to negate that awful finger-pointing questionable death clause. *He felt his life was in danger.* The perfidy of the man, when he came at her with words, with knives, with brutal abuse, with betrayals, and finally—that awful afternoon—with intent to kill.

Could she ever forget it? He felt *his* life was in danger. In other words, he thought his wife was trying to kill him. Questionable death—no inheritance.

Otherwise, if she behaved herself and abided by his wishes, she would have security and a home for the rest of her awful, long, isolated, lonely life.

She was only twenty-four.

She mentally shook herself, trying to quell her fear and her rage that Jesse had done this to her.

But he had always been a vengeful and vindictive man. She had hated him—God, she had hated him. One minute after her mother had forced her to marry him, she had begun to hate him with all her heart, and only her mother vied with him as the target of her hate.

But even that was nothing compared to how much she despised him now. She felt as if she could tear apart the house beam by beam, brick by brick; she felt like firing up the cotton fields and letting them burn to a blessed useless cinder, irreparable, unplantable. She wanted to destroy Jesse's legacy utterly, so no one would ever know Riveland had existed, in reality or imagination.

And she could do none of it. There were no heirs—but

15

then to whom did she forfeit if she did not uphold the conditions of the will? He hadn't said. There *were* no other heirs except her, his first wife had died. She had no family—at least that Cassandra knew of. God, this was so twisted, so perverse. And then the question of issue . . . damn Jesse, *damn* him.

She could not destroy what was rightfully hers.

Nor did she know what she could do to save herself.

"If I remarry . . ." she began tentatively, not sure exactly what question she was asking.

"You lose everything," Mr. Greve said bluntly.

"To *whom?*" Now she was thinking, now she needed further answers, further evidence of Jesse's perfidy. Everything she had suffered at his hands had come to this; who took precedence over her in this burial ground of a will.

"Oh yes . . . did I not say?" Mr. Greve consulted his papers. "Yes. Jesse has a brother, Jackman, whereabouts at this point unknown. If you were to give up your rights to Riveland, they would pass to him or his heirs. I assume Mr. Taggart was reasonably sure that you would accept your inheritance and not dispute it. I think, Miz Taggart, a court would find it very hard to find in your favor when you have been given all any widow could expect and under certain reasonable conditions. The remarriage clause, well—I don't know how much leeway you have there. Mr. Taggart seemed sure that remarriage would not necessarily be a consideration with you, given your . . . circumstances."

Cassandra flinched. "And what were my circumstances?" she asked softly, dangerously.

Mr. Greve had the grace to look embarrassed. "Your inability to conceive," he said finally.

"Or Jesse's," Cassandra snapped. "He had no right to determine that about me—not at all."

"But the facts . . ."

"The facts are that there are no children, and in all of his whoring around, he did not produce any children either, Mr. Greve."

"I cannot comment. You must decide whether you will

16

contest any of the conditions of the will," Mr. Greve said stiffly.

She took a deep breath to deflate her anger. Her sole enemies then were mythical: a brother she had never known Jesse had, and his "issue"—whatever *that* meant. There were no children. None.

"All right then, let me see if I clearly understand *everything*," she said temperately.

"Certainly, Miz Taggart," he murmured, but he looked wary.

"There is no question that Mr. Taggart died of unnatural causes?"

Right to the gut; she did not beat her way around any questions whatsoever.

Mr. Greve was not sure he appreciated such forthrightness. He did not like being continually caught off guard. He in fact did not like speaking to the heart of any matter if he could get around it by invoking high-flown lawyer phrases.

He cleared his throat. "I am empowered to go by the facts as the coroner stated them in his report and on the certificate, Miz Taggart. You may rest easy on that score."

She bowed her head. "Thank you." She knew the relief washed her face in telling color, but she couldn't help it. She *had* to know. "So the question of issue becomes negligible."

He was silent for a long moment. "It troubles me."

"And me," Cassandra added sharply.

"It is negligible in the sense that you mean."

"Thank you again, Mr. Greve." She let out her breath this time. Could he see the monstrous relief in her face and the lessening of tension in the grip of her hands on her lap? She hadn't moved for at least the fifteen minutes since he had walked in the door. And now . . . and now—

"Riveland is mine then under these several conditions: I am not to remarry . . ."

"Then too," Mr. Greve interrupted hastily, "if you had been nearer in age to Mr. Taggart, as I had supposed, this

17

would not seem so—"

"Limiting?" Cassandra suggested. "How could you have known, Mr. Greve? In any event, not only may I not remarry, I also may not live away from Riveland. . . . Is it specified how many months in the year I must maintain residence here?"

Again he was caught short. He hadn't thought of it either. "No—only that you are not to live away and still derive income by virtue of overseer management."

Horrible, wretched man to do this to her. He couldn't kill her one way: he had planned completely and cunningly to do it the other.

"You may know I have been running the business of the plantation for the past five years. Are you still telling me that I must acquire an advisor?"

"I did not know," Mr. Greve said defensively. This was not the poor bereft widow he had envisioned dealing with. This was a young woman in full control of her senses, her grief, her expectations. She would not accept calmly everything Jesse Taggart had chosen to do to her. Oh no, the questions she asked were all cool, self-directed, self-motivated; there wasn't even room for him to get a toehold here, and he had counted on it, absolutely counted on it.

A grieving widow of waning years—he had been prepared for that; he had been willing to offer his services as well, including the magnanimous inconvenience of relocating to Carthage to help her maintain her inheritance.

But this . . . "I assumed it was a reasonable condition, Miz Taggart. Most women cannot—and do not wish to—manage such a large estate on their own; usually there is someone in the family who steps in, of course. You would be the exception, and I truly assumed Mr. Taggart had your best interests at heart and sought to relieve you of the burden of daily decisions."

She felt like throwing something at him for his sanctimonious recitation. It was utter nonsense. She didn't say it. It really had been that *she* had relieved Jesse of the daily burdens while he forged a trail of lust from the slave cabins of

18

Riveland to the whorehouses of the Savannah docks.

And she had hated it so much, and she was so good at it. Now it was to become her life, no matter what she wanted.

On the other hand—she had a thought.

"We have now determined what I cannot do, Mr. Greve. What *can* I do? May I travel?"

He felt as if the ground had been pulled from beneath him. He didn't know—and he cast his mind furiously over the circumlocutory phrases of the will for some reference. . . . "There is nothing about that, except that if you were to be away from Riveland for an appreciable amount of time, which would mean putting the business into the hands of your overseer . . ."

"However, that provision specifically states that I must not 'live away' from Riveland. The question, Mr. Lawyer, is what constitutes living away—and does one taking a trip 'live away' from home? Perhaps we need a judge to make a ruling on that?"

She was a whip, he thought agitatedly; she would beat every last nuance of the will into the ground and shape it, somehow, the way she wanted it. "That is left to my discretion," he said stonily. "Is there anything else, Miz Taggart?"

She pounced on it. *"Your* discretion, Mr. Greve?" Worse and worse.

"Mine. Final arbiter of any questions that should arise, Miz Taggart."

She heard a threat there; she heard something that made her back up a pace— another, another—back into the shell of the grieving widow. He expected to see it, she thought. He was leery of her. Her questions disrupted everything. Her *appearance* disquieted him. He needed time to back away and consider the ramifications of her age and the provisions as Jesse meant them.

"I see," she said meekly—well, just a little more respectfully. Jesse had well and truly cornered her, and given her a jailer as well. She saw immediately that he expected that she would turn to him for all things, and she couldn't conceive that Jesse had meant that as well.

19

If Mr. Greve wanted anything from this windfall that had burst into his office, he could not count on having her—unless he knew of a way to negate the marriage provision.

"One more question?" she asked.

"More than one," he said genially. He, too, had reassessed his position. Her fool questions were meaningless, after all. She really had no one to turn to but him; he was the only one who was fully aware of Jesse Taggart's state of mind and the intent of the will. Perhaps he had even skewed it slightly so that he could benefit as well. Taggart had obviously been wealthy and his young wife, treacherous though she might be, looked like a luscious handful.

He could handle her. "Ask away, Miz Taggart."

She lowered her eyes demurely. "Of course Riveland is a big responsibility, Mr. Greve, and my husband has now left it that I am sole legatee. I merely wish to know if there is any question about how I may dispose of the estate in *my* will?"

He almost fell off the chair. He hadn't expected that, not so soon after everything. Not *ever.* The indelicacy of it! The sheer gall of her!

Jesse Taggart had thought of everything—except *that.*

Damn and blast.

What was on her mind?

"No," he said reluctantly, as the silence between them widened into something ugly and suspicious. "No. You may do as you like."

She smiled grimly, and he didn't like the smile either—like a cat who had just lapped up a surprise treat of clotted cream.

He didn't like it, and he wanted out of that room as soon as possible so he could study the will and find a way to control her impulses.

But she was satisfied now. Her smile had faded; her eyes were properly downcast and her hands came to rest once again on her lap.

"Thank you, Mr. Greve." Her voice was calm, accepting. He thought she might even be verging on tears. And well she should, being handed something like Riveland virtually on a silver platter. She had a home and security for the rest of her life, he thought, as he gathered up the papers and tucked them back into his briefcase.

What more could any woman want?

Chapter Two

There wasn't a room in the whole first floor of Riveland that could contain her fury.

She felt fragile as glass, that she would *shatter* if anyone so much as said a word to her. Oh, but glass was strong too, and it could take a lot of wear, a lot of abuse before a fine crack-line appeared.

She wondered how much more abuse she could take.

There had to be some way around those impossible conditions in Jesse's will. There *had* to be.

She didn't know which one enraged her the most; there was absolutely no comfort in knowing that she could remain on Riveland for the rest of her natural life — alone, isolated, unloved, unmarried.

Oh damn the soul of the man, how could he have done this to her?

But she knew . . . she knew: he had made a bargain with her mother and she had turned out to be the devil.

Oh mother, she thought, *how happy you would have been to see me come to this. All you ever cared about was living well, and you would have paid any price to accomplish it — even sell your own daughter. Well, I'm enslaved forever now, dear mother, and we can live happily ever after, you and I. And when we're gone, the land will remain, and that was all Jesse wanted anyway.*

Oh God . . .

She felt dead already. Her worst enemy could not have avenged himself on her any more thoroughly and completely than Jesse, and her worst enemy had died five years before.

She had nothing, nothing: her home was a prison, she had no freedom, no pretension to any sort of life beyond that of maintaining Riveland—with *help,* damn him . . . *male* help—he had sealed her in a wall without breathing space because he had been sure he would kill her eventually just as he intended.

Oh, Jesse—you won't break my spirit, even in death, you bastard, she vowed to the hills outside the parlor window where he was buried. *I'll get around this, I'll find a way out, somehow, and damn your lawyer and his* discretion.

She had to think—but her all-enveloping wrath overset everything; she couldn't think, she could only curse the fates that had put her in the depraved hands of Jesse Taggart.

She paced the high-ceilinged rooms of the lower floor of Riveland furiously, in thrall to her anger and her feeling of helplessness.

And that stupid lawyer had expected her to fall down on her knees in gratitude! She should have kicked him in the knees instead. She should have thrown something. She should have killed Jesse before he made his last trip to Savannah . . .

Oh, she had wanted to, especially after the last time and Jesse's impatience: "You sure you ain't carryin', girl? You dead sure, or you keepin' secrets, and just gonna go to that backwoods lady and get rid of it anyway? Maybe you been doin' that all along, pretty lady—ummm? Maybe I ain't never gonna get a son off of you, Cassandra Co-burne barren bitch . . ."

He watched her calendar as if it were the crown jewels. He wanted that son the way he had wanted a young and malleable wife, someone who wouldn't back-chat him, someone who would do exactly as he wanted, someone he could dominate and reward. Someone with no appreciable family of her own who would care about what was going on in the rural Georgia countryside. Someone with a greedy and impoverished mother who had social ambitions for her only remaining daughter. Her baby. Someone who was so young, she could do no less than try to please her mother, particularly after her older sister, Linnea, had upped and married a British nobleman and abandoned them to go live in England.

Cassandra Coburne had been that someone, ripe and ready to be plucked out of poverty along with her avaricious mother who had pushed her right into Jesse Taggart's lap the day he happened into their boardinghouse in Atlanta.

He was in town on business; he wanted a home-like atmosphere for the several days he would be in town. He wanted to be fussed over by a pair of women who needed his money, and Raylene Coburne knew just how to oblige.

Her own husband had been moderately wealthy at one time, but she was disobliged to talk about how she and her two daughters had wound up in such dreary circumstances.

Later, of course, Cassandra knew why. Raylene had cleverly imparted the information that they were genteel poor because Raylene could sniff out matrimonial interest like a hound tracking a fox. And she knew, within moments, that Jesse Taggart hadn't just "happened" on their quaint little boardinghouse.

He had come to look over Cassandra Coburne, who was young, moldable and marriageable.

And Raylene was going to make sure that Jesse got exactly what he wanted.

It wasn't that she had been perfectly amenable.

In point of fact, she had never been amenable to anything, and Raylene knew it well.

"Momma, he is so old." Yes, she remembered saying that over and over. "I don't like the way he looks at me . . . he ought to be thinking about courting *you*, Momma."

"Nonsense, girl. I'm too old for him; I can't bear him children. He wants sons. It's perfectly obvious to me, Cassandra. He wants a young wife who has lots of childbearing

24

years ahead of her. Every man wants a *young* wife, and the fact that you are beautiful as well does a lot of mitigate the fact that we are in straitened circumstances."

"I don't understand you." But she understood too well.

"You be nice to him."

"I don't want to."

"You *have* to. I can't *bear* living my life this way. And then what would happen when I'm gone, Cassandra Coburne? What would happen to you? You know very well: you would become a governess, not eligible to men of our class. No matter how low *I* must sink, I cannot leave you to that fate. Therefore, my girl, you will go out to the parlor and make a little conversation with that very interested gentleman, and hope that he covets your beauty and youth more than youth and a dowry. Oh, and can't I wait to thumb my nose at your unseemly and ungrateful sister! Mistress of Riveland Plantation—think of it, Cassandra, think of me . . ."

And she went, resentfully, sulkily, and for some reason, Jesse Taggart seemed charmed by her pouts and her skewing looks at his thick, large frame that utterly repelled her.

He knew she had no choice. But she didn't know that—not at that point.

"Now where's that delicious Cassandra daughter of yours, Raylene?" he would boom as he entered the house.

"I believe she is upstairs resting," Raylene would say, even if she knew Cassandra was in the kitchen peeling potatoes for the evening meal. After all, she was the daughter of a plantation owner herself; Mr. Taggart mustn't be led to believe that Cassandra performed any mundane household tasks at all.

"Call her on down here," Jesse would say. "I can't wait to refresh my eyes."

Raylene thought it was intensely romantic how Jesse just reveled in her daughter's youth and beauty. But invariably, after Jesse had subtly made his intentions known, she would never find Cassandra exactly where she expected her to be.

"I want you to be waiting for Mr. Taggart when he arrives. Have you noticed, my girl, that now he is sending advance word when to expect him?"

"I don't care."

"You had better care, my dear. I do not intend to run a boardinghouse for the rest of my life and see you marry into penury. What use is that? One does not marry for love, Cassandra. One marries for position and wealth, and you have an unparalleled opportunity to secure both while you are young. Be thankful that Mr. Taggart is only interested in your youth and not what property you could bring to a marriage with him."

But even she could see that had not interested Cassandra at all.

"And just think," she had added craftily, "since he *is* so much older than you . . . how long—*really*—can he live?"

"Long enough," Cassandra muttered. "So what?"

"I won't allow this rebellion, Cassandra. All you need do is be nice to him."

She didn't like being nice to him, but then, she didn't like working like a slave in her mother's boardinghouse when even she could remember the better times, when her father was alive, before he had gambled everything away and died of an alcohol-sodden broken heart.

She stoically resolved to keep Mr. Taggart company. Really she hoped that he would invite them to live at Riveland but without the complication of his marrying her.

False hope.

She was almost sixteen that year, old enough to be bedded, and Raylene was being both blunt and subtle about it. "You give that man sons, Cassandra, and he will give you the earth."

"I don't want the earth. I want everyone to leave me alone!"

"Very well, Cassandra. You don't want the earth. How about just a little piece of it—one where your every desire is fulfilled and you have personal servants to tend to all those tasks that you complain you must do here and now. How about beautiful clothing and elegant surroundings and bountiful dinners and a lovely home that you can call yours? How about all that? Would you not trade your rags for that? Would you not trade this broken-down old building for that? *Wouldn't* you? For *me?*"

Raylene had grabbed her shoulders. "For *me,* Cassandra? What about me?"

Cassandra had stared into her mother's fleshy face and seen the reflection of her own, the same green eyes, the same flawless skin but now wrinkled with years of discontent, the body no longer slender with its protruding belly that was ill-disguised by the drab hooped skirt of the housedress she wore. Her mother. And her years of travail—she was not to forget about that, obviously. She was to take into account that it was up to her to make it better: she read it all in the downturn of Raylene's finely modeled mouth (her mouth), the angry frown, the tension in Raylene's hands as if she could squeeze Cassandra's shoulders into submission.

She understood then, and a tremor of horror shot through her body. She read it all in her mother's blurring features and thickening body and hands: it was killing Raylene that she was no longer young, no longer beautiful, that her husband had died—the ultimate abandonment; that her elder daughter Linnea had run off with an Englishman without thinking for one minute about her mother's comfort.

It was killing Raylene that she was forced into the most menial work of all, caring for other people's comfort; and it would utterly destroy her if Mr. Taggart came to heel and offered marriage and her stupid rebellious daughter turned him down.

Because he would never offer for Raylene, and she was very well aware of it, and the knowledge of *that* was killing her too.

Chapter Three

Mr. Taggart had been smart enough to negotiate the marriage with Raylene; he had never even asked Cassandra directly to be his wife.

"We have come to terms," Raylene announced one afternoon after Mr. Taggart left on one of his trips back to Riveland, "and we will make preparations for you and Mr. Taggart to be married when he returns."

"I will *not*," Cassandra muttered. She hadn't even reached her sixteenth birthday, but she realized her mother had plotted so that she would have just turned by the time the wedding took place.

She hated her mother.

"You *will*," Raylene told her forcefully. "Listen . . . damn you, *listen*. He is giving us *everything*, my girl—do you *understand*? *Everything!* A home, respectability, position in society, *money*—clothes . . . a plantation home, beautifully maintained and lovingly cared for. A retinue of servants to take care of us . . . do you *hear* me, my girl?"

Cassandra turned away. Raylene's voice followed her. "*Everything* we had, everything we could wish for. And all for the paltry price of a son. I tell you, Cassandra, men are so stupid about the things they value: he wants a son, another son. He had a son—Cassandra—are you listening?"

"I won't marry that man," she shouted, hardly hearing a word Raylene had said.

Raylene ignored her. "Yes, they say he had a son, a long

time ago with his first wife, and they say he ran away and never came back. Cassandra, are you listening?"

"*I'll* run away and never come back. I will not marry that pig-man."

"That man has a will of iron. They say he disowned the boy—Coltrane his name was—and they say you'd never know he existed."

"I wish I didn't exist," Cassandra moaned. "I wish I were dead."

"You stupid girl. So what. A man wants sons, a smart woman gives him sons and takes everything she can get."

"You marry him."

"He doesn't want *me*," Raylene said bitterly. "He wants a *young* wife, and you had better believe I checked everything out about him."

"You *what?*"

"I checked everything. I used Mr. Wiltshire's money. Do you think I would let you marry someone who *said* he was rich without finding out if it were true? Do you think I would risk everything and give up this small measure of security on the say-so of a man like Mr. Taggart who would not normally frequent a small boardinghouse like ours? Oh no, my girl. That son is presumed dead, his first wife is gone, and he has been alone for these ten or fifteen years and he sees himself getting older and older with no one to whom to pass on his land and possessions."

"I don't want them," Cassandra said violently. "How could you do this to me?"

"I wish your father could see us now, recouping our fortune and setting ourselves up in the best possible way, with a man of wealth and power—and *no debts*. I feel ten years younger just thinking about it."

"And I feel twenty years older," Cassandra muttered divisively.

"Be quiet, my girl. You are *not* going to spoil this for me. You are going to tell Mr. Taggart when he comes that you are honored by his proposal and you gratefully accept. And you *will* gratefully accept, Cassandra—for both of us."

Cassandra felt a frisson of foreboding squiggle down her spine. "What do you mean, mother?"

"What do you mean, what do I mean? It's perfectly clear: you will marry Mr. Taggart, and we will both go to Riveland."

They were married two weeks later. Mr. Taggart had even provided the dresses, a pretty white satin and lace confection for his young and virginal bride, and a suitably elegant watered-silk dress for her girlish mother.

This hiatus, and the succeeding week after the wedding when Mr. Taggart installed his new bride in the most expensive suite in Atlanta's most distinguished hotel, gave Raylene the time she needed to make arrangements to sell her boardinghouse and to gather herself up a suitable wardrobe for the mother of the mistress of Riveland.

And it gave Jesse Taggart a suitable amount of time to initiate his trembling young bride into the mysteries of marriage; he did this with great enthusiasm and no great concern for delicacy or pleasing her. He had only one objective in mind and he kept Cassandra behind closed doors for the entire week with that clear purpose in exercise of his marital rights.

And when they arrived at Riveland, Cassandra could only see the rabbity, scared expression on the faces of the house servants, and Raylene only saw the surroundings of luxury, freshly updated to suit her taste.

Raylene had ignored the bruise marks too, and the haunted look in Cassandra's dulled green gaze. "Mr. Taggart is obviously keeping you busy," was her only comment. She only saw that she had arrived at the pinnacle of her dreams, back where she belonged, and somewhere in the secret recesses of her mind, she was the mistress of Jesse Taggart's house and not her fertile, childish, ungrateful wretch of a daughter.

Six months later, Cassandra had still not conceived and Jesse was in a rage. "What'd I buy you for, girl? I want that

30

son, you hear? We're gonna work on it some more, pretty girl. We're gonna make that boy baby because I want that more than anything in the world. Even you."

That scared her. If she didn't conceive, he would get rid of her.

Raylene went into a royal snit. "What's wrong with you, girl? That man has ridden you long and hard and nothing has come of it yet? Are you crazy?"

"I hope he throws us out."

"He'll kill you," Raylene told her prophetically.

But he did worse than that: he strutted his manhood all over Carthage and three counties beyond, and she couldn't do a thing about it.

A year later: "Well, pretty girl?"

She shook her head, ducking at the brutal assault of his words. But he let her alone this time. He let her muse on the error of her ways and think hard about getting him a son, as if her very thoughts could conceive the reality.

Three months later, he took her again in endless violent assaults to prove his manhood, and his fertility, and nothing happened.

Except that Cassandra got a little older and a little wiser. She learned how to parry his words, to slough off the hurt, to find the pride that would not let this man destroy her soul. When Jesse's frustration turned to violence, she could not escape it. When he began to leave her alone, she understood why: there was another, better woman available to him, right in his very own home.

When she was unable to give him his dearest desire, he tired of her, too, and sought solace elsewhere.

When Raylene became sick, Cassandra nursed her out of sight. "He doesn't like sickly souls," Raylene would tell her as the disease wasted her body and her memories. "Strong men don't, you know. They feel it saps the life from them, too."

"A man is not strong by virtue of how hard he wields his whip," Cassandra told her stolidly, but when Raylene, loyal to Jesse to the last, died, she did not mourn.

31

She had left her daughter a legacy of violence that Jesse would perpetrate now that Raylene was a buffer between them no more.

"Gotta get me a new wife," he would say over and over. "Can't divorce you, pretty girl. Gotta get rid of you. And I will, I will. Ain't no one gonna look for you. I'm gonna put you right next to that conniving mother of yours, see if I don't."

She locked her doors, she locked him out. She marveled at the strength she found in herself, the determination not to let him defeat her. She disguised herself and stole his guns in order to teach herself to shoot. She armed herself with a knife, with words, with the knowledge that somewhere in the eight years they had been married, she had become strong and outspoken and absolutely consumed with a rage to live.

"Gonna get you, pretty girl. Need me a new woman. Need me a son before I die, you hear? You had your chance. Your greedy momma had her chance and what'd she do but go die on me. You're bad stock, Cassandra Coburne. You lured me on with your innocence, but the proof's in the showing: no babies, no future here, pretty girl. Bred or dead, and that's it: if you ain't one, you're the other, you hear?"

They stalked each other for a year, ever vigilant, ever wary, sleepless, restless, haunted. He locked her away when he conceived the notion that she and his overseer Daggett were meeting secretly. He locked her away when he went on his mysterious trips to Atlanta. And he locked her away when he was foraging in the cathouses in town and the slave quarters a hundred yards away.

And it finally came down to one bleak winter day when he caught her unaware in the stables, and came after her with a knife, forced her to the hayloft where her hand grabbed a fortuitous weapon, a shovel, and in a blind fight for her life, she thrust it at him as he climbed up toward her, and thrust it at him, and shoved it into his gut with every last ounce of her strength and the overwhelming force of her fear. Horrified, she saw the ladder heave backward as he lost his balance; his arms flailed wildly and the weight of his body carried him downward, falling, falling . . .

She saw his head strike the support beam as he landed on the stable floor with a sickening thud, the ladder crashing on top of his chest, the knife protruding like a signpost from his ribcage.

She saw him buried three days later.

And three days after that, she saw his last will and testament bury *her*.

She had to think. Surely Mr. Greve didn't expect her to sort things out immediately. Surely she would have several days, a week — a month, perhaps?

It wasn't easy to distill eight years of a hellish marriage into a coherent decision that would affect the rest of her life.

What life?

How many sleepless nights would she devote to the torturous negatives of any decision she might make?

There had been no life with Jesse. There had been master and servant: he took, she gave, without choice, without free will.

She felt a thousand years older than the child Jesse had brought back with him to Riveland, with her childish little trunk all packed up with the pranks and costumes she used to escape reality.

She felt that tingling little quirk of fear that every last thing Jesse had said about her might be true: she had been a goddess and a whore both. An innocent and a wanton, and in the end, barren as a desert, dry as dust above, moist and secret down to the core.

She had labored long and hard over the burden of what use she would be if she could not bear sons, but in the end, after Raylene died and Jesse's abuses began, she hadn't wanted to bring a child into a world that *he* inhabited. She never wanted a child after that who would call Jesse Tag-

33

gart his father.

Sometimes, near the end, she had been grateful that no child had been conceived.

And yet, if she could not bear sons, no man would want her, not even for the price of Riveland in his name. Jesse had been a saint to bear up with her. Jesse had been fascinated by the femininity that could not cradle a seed. Jesse had been sick with it, had tormented her with it.

No, she did not want marriage, not ever again. Cohabitation was vile, man was vile, his instincts were primal and wild, violent. Even if she had been strong enough to defend her childlessness by pushing some blame onto Jesse, she knew the truth: something in her could not connect with him, and every man deserved sons to carry on his name.

The marriage clause would cause her no sleepless nights at all, she thought deep into another night in which she could find no rest.

But all she had ever thought about was leaving Riveland. She hated Riveland, hated the mantle of responsibility that Jesse had allowed to fall onto her slender shoulders as he pursued his relentlessly lusty path to forbidden pleasures. In this last year, he had cared nothing for planting, harvesting, shipping his goods; nothing about the farm, the food, the care and feeding of his retinue of slaves. She had undertaken that, had been handling the various and sundry duties connected with the farm for more than a year until she noticed other things were being let slide, and she stepped in and took over.

"Damned unladylike, my lady wife sittin' in the overseer's cabin readin' the accounts," Jesse grumbled testily at first, and then with a repressed anger that she was capable of doing it, and not other things.

"And who will do it, Mr. Taggart? Big Jake? Ojim? Daggett?"

"You got your momma to take care of. That's what ladies do. They take care of people and house things. They don't go in the fields. My wife don't go in the fields."

"I won't go in the fields," she promised, but in the end,

34

she and Daggett went to the fields when Jesse was not around.

She hated the dispirited look of Jesse's workers. She hated the downcast eyes of the house servants and the particular reluctant step with which they walked.

They hated Jesse.

And now he was gone, she wondered if they hated her as well. The situation was ripe for violence and she knew she could never depend on the good will of the overseer Daggett to protect her: he had hated Jesse too. She was aware he saw Jesse's death as an opportunity to plot a takeover of Riveland, because he saw her as utterly useless in spite of her business sense. He knew nothing of the will, and she wondered how long he would stay on after he learned its immutable details.

Nonetheless, she was the one who had to cope with her servants and the workers, and there she saw a distinct disadvantage to the provisions of the will. A husband would have strengthened her own position, would have been a figure of authority that she could not present.

A husband . . . she shuddered. She would have to be her own figure of authority. She would have to get everyone on her side; she couldn't afford not to. She couldn't afford anything, not even the chance to run away.

And how had Jesse known she yearned to leave Riveland forever? How clever he was, circumventing her neatly, forbidding any pleasure at all except the pure respite at the end of a day's work.

Oh Jesse, how perfectly you cloistered me here! All she needed were prayers and incantations and a bell to sound the stations of her day.

She didn't have to accept those terms.

And yet, what else was there? If she left Riveland, she would be cast out into a world from which she had already been sequestered these last eight years.

What could be out there for her if she weren't seeking a husband, if she had no money to support herself, if she couldn't visit relatives indefinitely as some widows and

35

spinsters were wont to do? On the other hand, she had no doubt that if she had an aunt, a cousin, a sister-in-law, she would be welcomed into the family fold and given the task of caring for the children she could not have. Which was a double-edged sword to be sure: she would then be at the mercy of and a burden on a cadre of loving relations whose sole interest was to relinquish parental responsibility and simultaneously censure the caretaker who had not achieved the ultimate goal—marriage and children.

Linnea, even if she were not in England, would have been of no possible help. Nor could she see herself traveling to London to beg sanctuary from the sister who had not even bothered to respond to her letter detailing Raylene's death.

It was perfectly obvious she really did not have choices unless she wished to give up Riveland and become a beggar.

It was also obvious that Mr. Greve would soon come to visit her to discuss these matters with her when she had had a day or two to mull them over.

He was inconsiderate enough to come on the succeeding day.

Sully announced him. "Mr. Greve done come, ma'am."

"He done come too soon," she muttered and then looked up at the aged butler whose eyes, as usual, were downcast as he ushered in Mr. Greve. She moved away from the window where she had been staring out at the garden.

"Mr. Greve."

"I hope I haven't returned too soon."

But you did, she thought, and said, almost as if her mouth were connected to her thoughts: "I had hoped for several more days to consider this matter."

"I thought you might want to have someone to discuss your thoughts with," he said, ignoring that, and with very bad manners, not offering to return another time.

"My thoughts have been totally chaotic, Mr. Greve. Surely you can appreciate that it will take time for me to sort out the intent of Jesse's bequest."

"I do, truly I do, Miz Taggart, but I have to assume that

36

you are going to comply with the provisions."

"Why is that, Mr. Greve?" she asked silkily. She still had not asked him to be seated. She wasn't sure she was going to.

He smiled a rueful little smile and waved his hand self-deprecatingly. "What else can you do, Miz Taggart?"

"I was hoping to think of something," she murmured, but in truth, she knew that was exactly the case. What else could she do? And in point of fact, if at any time she really wanted to relinquish Riveland, she had only to violate one of the stringent conditions, and Mr. Greve would see that she was removed as expeditiously as possible. She saw it all very clearly in that instant. There were two ways to look at it: Jesse had bound her up and immured her forever, or—she could choose the conditions until she elected to void them, whenever it suited her purpose. And if that were true, the only thing she would have to contend with was secreting enough money to support herself if she ever made such a decision.

It was like a light flooding the room: her perceptions changed and instantly everything looked possible, instead of nothing. She only hoped it didn't show in her face.

"Sit down, Mr. Greve," she said finally as he hovered edgily near a chair.

"Thank you, Miz Taggart." He sank heavily onto a balloon-back side chair that looked as if it might collapse under his weight.

She took a similar chair from behind a table and pulled it close to his and sat down beside him. "Now, Mr. Greve. You were saying?"

For one moment he thought she was being deliberately obtuse. But he couldn't afford to get angry or to let any feelings get in the way of his true purpose. He took a long breath and let it out to calm himself. "I said, what else can you do, Miz Taggart."

"Oh yes. Indeed, what else?" she agreed with a touch of irony.

"So I may presume you accept the terms of the will?"

"When I *do* accept the terms of the will, what will happen?"

He almost bit his lip in frustration. "There will be papers to sign, of course, and then everything will pass to you, Miz Taggart. Am I to assume that you will sign the papers?"

She shook her head. "There is the question of the 'advisor,' Mr. Greve. There is no simple solution, no immediate relatives or friends upon whom I may call—and it rankles me that I must be made to do so."

The opening, he thought. "I understand that, Miz Taggart. You want some more time to consider this decision."

"I do. Unless there is a specified time in which I must make a decision. Or a reason I must do it immediately?"

He backed off. "Not in the least, Miz Taggart. If you are well in your mind as far as the other conditions go, you should take all the time you need to choose your advisor." He got up from his chair and she did the same.

"I would like to suggest, if I may, that it might be beneficial to name your lawyer as your advisor."

"*Are* you my lawyer, Mr. Greve?"

"I believe I have your best interests at heart, Miz Taggart," he said stiffly.

"But you know nothing about Riveland, Mr. Greve."

"I was talking purely for the purposes of satisfying the will," he said, and he could not keep the edge out of his voice. She could not possibly have misunderstood him, but he was at a loss to define why she did not immediately leap upon his offer with great gratitude.

She stood very still for a moment, heeding a faint tingling sensation deep within her, and then she nodded. "Yes, I can see that might be advantageous indeed, Mr. Greve, but permit me—I really must think about it."

He raised his hand, as much to stop the flow of words that were forming on his lips, as to say to her, enough. "It was only a suggestion, Miz Taggart. You are under no obligation to even consider it."

She smiled faintly. "But my husband chose you for this most important legal work of his life, Mr. Greve. The suggestion has merit, and I will consider it."

"Thank you," he said. "I will see myself out."

She watched him negotiate the room, her emotions roiling. She hadn't expected this pressure, this insidious prizing into her life by a stranger. She understood now — everything with him would have to be put into writing, every condition she agreed to, every discreet decision he made in her favor — except she didn't think now there would be any favors granted at all if she did not name him as her advisor. Blackmail, pure and simple, and she wondered if that had been on Jesse's mind as well, as they two wrote out the terms of the will.

But what possible reason could she give him for not asking him to be her advisor?

Damn Jesse for binding her hands on this as well; she would have to accept help and have no choice in the matter either.

She shook her head. There had to be a way; there had to be something that took precedence over the oh-so-helpful Mr. James Greve, who knew she lacked friends and family to assist her in this situation.

Friends and family . . .

Would that Jesse had had friends. He had had business associates only, and a paltry lot of them if the attendance at his funeral were anything to judge by.

Once Mr. Greve had gone, she paced the rooms of Riveland once again, railing against Jesse and his vindictiveness. Friends . . . family . . .

Mr. Greve certainly could not argue a family member as her advisor.

She rubbed her eyes.

The mysterious brother she had never heard of, who would inherit everything should she choose to give it up.

A brother whom nobody knew would do nicely.

She thought about that. He could have heard about Jesse's death and gotten in touch with her. No, yes — but — if he were anything like Jesse, he would be very interested in seeing her fail because he would then take possession of Riveland—and very likely make her leave.

No. Damn, a brother would have been wonderful. How could Mr. Greve dispute the fact that this Jackman had consented to help her—long distance? If only the man didn't have a personal stake in her success. If only she could count on his never turning up.

But she knew she couldn't count on anything except her own wits. A brother explicitly named in a will just would not do. But the idea was the right track.

She wished there were some other far-off relative that she could conjure up—fast.

Like a son.

A son . . . ?

Where did that idea come from, a son?

They say Jesse had a son . . .

Somewhere in her mind, she heard the words, or she imagined she had heard them. Who had said that? Or no one had said that, but it was something that came up from deep inside her and she was sure in that instant it was exactly the right solution to her problem.

Jesse's son. He had been away, he had only just heard of his father's death. He had been to sea. Perfect. For years and years. Jesse had disowned him. Wonderful. He had wanted his son to take over Riveland and his son had run away. Who wouldn't? She could just imagine Jesse with a son, hounding him, abusing verbally and maybe even physically. Poor son-that-never-was. She could feel it in her bones. He had gone because Jesse was a bastard and he hated Riveland—then.

Maybe he didn't now. Maybe Jesse's death would make a difference. Of course Jesse never talked about him: he had wiped every trace of him out of existence. It was exactly as if he had never had a son.

. . . Issue . . .

The troublesome phrase popped right into her head and she rubbed her hands gleefully. An invented son would put to rest that troubling clause as well. An invented son would get Mr. Greve out of her life altogether.

So . . . she had to get this story straight: Jesse had wiped away all trace of his son, never spoke about him, had been deeply disappointed in him. And that was why she did not know about him either. He would never admit that kind of defeat to his second wife on whom he had placed the burden of bearing his *perfect* son.

It made lovely, lovely sense. She would write the letters, she would show Mr. Greve the ongoing correspondence and Mr. Greve would just pack up, go away and leave her alone.

She sat down at her desk in the bedroom to write out the entire life history of Jesse's son-who-never-existed so that Mr. Greve could not trip her up when he questioned her closely—as he was sure to do.

But the fictional son of Jesse Taggart would not stay a character on a piece of paper; he had a history, as she wrote long and hard into the afternoon and early evening, and oh, such a romantic history she gave him. It was perfect, it really was.

He would not know that Jesse had died; he would write to him—from Boston, she thought, or maybe even New York or Portsmouth, New Hampshire, and he would write because he wanted to finally and after all this time mend the rift between them. Yes, that was good. He would have been to sea at least . . . Oh Lord, now how old *was* he going to be? If she was twenty-four, she would have to make him at least . . . thirty. That was good. He had gone when he was fifteen, well before his mother had gone on, and *years* before she had been approached by Jesse.

Yes. Good. That would be very strong because then he would have to be sensitive to her widow's needs and he would not come barging in on her grief, and that would explain that situation very nicely.

And then she in turn would tell him the terms and provisions of the will and ask if he would be kind enough to lend her assistance periodically if she wrote to him.

And he of course would be very happy to.

And that, she thought triumphantly, should keep Mr. Greve satisfied. Jesse's invented son was going to be very busy with shipping business in Boston or Baltimore or somewhere far away and he wouldn't have time to visit her anytime soon. He would be very very regretful about that, and equally glad to be able to help her. He would remember Riveland very well, and he would be such a success in the shipping business that his sole concern would be to see that she made a success of Riveland too—for her own sake.

What a nice man, she thought, as she sat back to contemplate the fiction she had just composed. He would be a very nice man.

Maybe he would even hope that his father's second marriage had tempered his attitude and that all had gone well with it. Yes, that would be a nice touch. He obviously would not have known about another marriage.

Business definitely would keep him up north for a good long time.

Maybe . . . oh, wonderful idea . . . he had a family up north: he was married and had . . . oh, six children at least.

She smiled at that. She surely would like her creation to be nice and have a family. It pleased her enormously.

But I need a name, he whispered to her out of the closely written pages of his life story.

Yes, he needed a name, she thought. A strong name for a strong nice man. "What shall I name you?" she wondered idly.

But she knew his name. His name was Coltrane, and they called him Trane. Trane Taggart.

Chapter Four

She was very happy with the way she engineered things so that she didn't introduce the existence of Jesse's son so soon that Mr. Greve became suspicious.

On the other hand, he wasn't too happy about the delay. "Really, Miz Taggart, I don't understand why so much time is necessary to contemplate this one decision. I don't see that you have much of a field from which to make a selection."

"This is true," she agreed calmly, "but there are one or two of Jesse's business associates who might wish to render me this service and I have written to ask if I may call on them." Of course she hadn't, but she needed to buy time, and she was willing to invent still more to make that possible. She went on, "Still and all, there are several things that we need to discuss aside from the question of an advisor, the principal thing being the amount of time I may remove myself from Riveland and not be in violation of the will."

That would keep them busy, she thought, as she introduced the topic. They would negotiate it, and she would see that the sessions would not be daily, that they would take two weeks at least, and more if she could possibly stretch it out further, and then and only then would she present him with the sudden shocking announcement that she had a letter from Jesse's son.

"The marriage provision does not trouble me nearly as

43

much," she added. "I truly had not contemplated remarrying after Mr. Taggart's death. But I do need to know that I have some freedom to attend to my own needs. It's not uncommon for families to remove to Charleston or take themselves to White Sulphur Springs during the summer, as you very well know. I certainly should be able to do the same without disinheriting myself."

"But they are gone for *months,*" Mr. Greve objected.

"And I am—and will be—a woman alone. I recognize the fact that the family standard does not hold for me. But surely I should not be denied a respite; I will be working as hard as any man. I surely won't be a lady of leisure. I need to know how much leeway I have to leave Riveland and return."

"Your husband did not specify."

"Then you must, Mr. Greve."

"I have to think about it."

"Most assuredly you do," she agreed, and she knew he would take just as long thinking about that as she had about her advisor.

All to the good. The more time that elapsed between his proposal and her receiving a letter from Jesse's long-gone newly invented son the better.

"I feel that perhaps we should not meet again until you have thought about it in great depth, Mr. Greve."

He ground his teeth. Lord, he had not expected her to be so obstinate and unyielding, and yet everything she said had merit, and she was not hard with him, nor was she subtle. She was plainspoken, and in a way he was not used to. He wished she would not say exactly what she meant, so that he did not have to pressure her. He wanted her to come to a decision all by herself on the basis of his proximity and availability, and he did not want to have to threaten her with what she could or could not do—by his discretion.

Nonetheless, the threat was there, reedy and ensnaring, and he knew she was aware of it, and that perhaps his determination about her time off of Riveland would be based solely on her affirmative answer.

"These . . . um . . . friends of Jesse's . . ."

"Business associates," she interpolated. "I don't know when or if they will respond. You must know that my husband was not a popular man either socially or with his associates. However, some of them held him in esteem for the way he conducted his business, and I am hoping they will be willing to help me."

He turned away to hide the flash of anger in his eyes.

But she caught it and she said gently, "After all, Mr. Greve, you cannot want to remain forever in Carthage when your own business must be taken care of in Atlanta."

He bowed. "As you say, Miz Taggart. It certainly would be to my benefit if I could return to Atlanta." But he was not going to return to Atlanta, he was certain of that. However, that was something she did not need to know—yet. He still had the implicit threat on his side, and even her own sense of justice. He *should* be rewarded for writing such a scurrilous document, he thought.

Jesse had paid him well for his services with one hand, and opened the door of opportunity with the other, and no matter what the fractious Miz Taggart said or did, he was going to take advantage of it.

The frustrating thing was, *she* never sent for *him*. He felt at a distinct disadvantage every time he turned up at her door without advance notice. He had the passing thought she was doing it deliberately, but he could not for the life of him see what it would gain her. And he felt thwarted because he could not check on these associates of Jesse's whom she claimed to have written, to find out where they stood on the matter of assisting her.

The most he could do was stay away, and he hated that because every day they did not talk was a day he did not know what the future would bring.

But he saw staying away as a punishment, because he

45

was certain Cassandra Taggart was as eager to settle the terms of the will as he, and he did not know why she was being so strong-willed in the matter of who would be her advisor.

"But you must understand, Mr. Greve. A man such as yourself has great expertise in handling legal affairs and all, but you know nothing about planting cotton and handling the workers," she told him roundly one afternoon two weeks later. "You must understand, I have been managing everything for these five years, and I will not gracefully hand over the reins to someone with less competence in the matter than I myself."

Oh damn, now she had done it. She had told him plainly what her objection was and he looked taken aback and just a little annoyed. But what could she do with him when he pointed out she had as little choice in this matter as she did in accepting all the terms of the will?

She sighed. She would have to dredge up some flattery to soothe his wounded pride, but still and all, the facts were the facts. He was not equipped to advise her about running Riveland.

"You would be very unhappy, Mr. Greve, to have me run rampant over your head every time you had mandated something and I disagreed with it."

"We would work in tandem," Mr. Greve said tightly. "I would never jeopardize the welfare of Riveland or its productivity. I felt I was candid with you at the outset: this would be solely to abide by the terms of the will. I certainly would not push my way into an area I know little about. But I would welcome the opportunity to learn."

"Thank you, Mr. Greve; that much relieves my mind," Cassandra said, but something in the tone of her voice made him look at her warily. "When we come to terms on this, as we will, I would like to have our agreement set out in writing so that neither of us can misconstrue what was said."

Oh, he hated her. He had never dealt with a woman like this, who did not depend upon a man's honor to protect her and to see that all would be as she wished. This kind of clear thinking was an unwelcome and most unfeminine trait in her, and it underscored her lack of trust in a most unflattering way.

And he would make her pay for that, too, he thought. She was not in control here, *he* was, by virtue of Jesse's will.

He just wished he had known when he had drawn it up how young and beautiful the intractable Miz Taggart was. He would have done things very differently. Very differently. At the least there never would have been a clause forbidding her remarriage.

But he couldn't change that now. Cassandra Taggart would ultimately bend to his wishes; she *had* to, and then—well, there were ways to nullify the provisions of wills.

He would find one, he was sure of it.

Her frankness had chased him away, she thought in satisfaction, but that was short-lived. She knew she was walking a fine line with him and she had almost stepped over the edge: he did not like his capabilities questioned, and she did not like his assumption that she would throw herself on his breast and beg him to take over her life.

He had better reconcile with that, she thought, because she had other things to worry about. She had allowed herself the luxury of seclusion these two weeks and more, but now, with the onset of the season to recultivate the fields, she knew she had to take a stand with Daggett and exercise her authority over her workers.

"I ain't takin' orders from no woman," Daggett told her when she called him in to discuss the matter.

"You have been taking orders from a woman for these last years," Cassandra pointed out acidly.

"But they was backed up by Mr. Jesse. This is different, and them bucks don't like it neither."

"Very well. Then you are dismissed, Mr. Daggett, and I will find an overseer who *can* work with a woman."

"Now wait a minute . . ."

She turned away from him. She hated him too; he was a short, squat, beetle-browed little man who swaggered and misused his power, sometimes. She supposed he was better than some, and no worse than most. But she was in a precarious position: she was a woman alone on a plantation of thousands of acres and a hundred strapping men all of whom had resented Jesse and, by extension, Daggett and her.

She could not depend on loyalty to thwart an insurrection, nor invoking the power of Jesse's name.

She felt a distinct sense of helplessness, as if she were teetering on the edge of an abyss where one misstep would send her plunging into nothingness.

"Excuse me, Mr. Daggett?"

"I wasn't talkin' leavin'," he growled.

"I must have misunderstood. Just what did you mean?" she asked, pivoting around to face him again, wondering if this little man thought that somehow he held her life in his hands or that he could blackmail her. It was amusing, as far as it went. But he knew nothing of Jesse's will. And soon he would.

"I was talkin' about me runnin' things—in the field, I mean."

"So how would that be different from when Mr. Taggart was alive?"

"It would be *me* runnin' it, Miz Taggart. See, when Mr. Taggart was alive, he was *there*. There wasn't none of 'em that didn't know Mr. Taggart was in charge. He was *there*, even if you and me was walkin' the fields. Now they know he ain't there, and they ain't gonna respect me nohow if they don't know *I'm* in charge."

"I see," she said slowly. "Yes, it is important for the

man to be in charge, isn't it? Well, let me tell you, Mr. Daggett. Those fields have to be cultivated and we have to get our next crop in and right now *I'm* in charge."

"They won't go for it."

"They've gone for it, Mr. Daggett. The only difference is I will not do things the way Mr. Taggart did."

"They ain't gonna go for it. You can't get 'em to work sometimes if you don't know how to handle them," he warned her.

"You will have to do it my way, Mr. Daggett, because there is no way I will give you full control."

"I can't promise that, Miz Taggart. *You* have to back *me* up."

"No, Mr. Daggett. *You* have to follow *my* orders, otherwise we can sever this connection. Perhaps you would like to think about it."

"Yeah," he muttered, "yeah. I would like to think about it. But you ain't got that much time for thinkin', Miz Taggart."

"I'm aware of that, Mr. Daggett. If we are a week late with the planting, or a month, then that is how it will be. I won't tolerate disloyalty from you or my workers, and I intend to make things at least palatable so that they are more willing to cooperate with whoever oversees the next crop."

He didn't like that insinuation one bit. It sounded like she was after making them comfortable, and everyone knew a slave who got comfortable was a slave who got uppity. Mr. Jesse knew that. Men who feared worked harder, men who had nothing always strived for something—even against impossible odds and the hardest taskmaster.

But it was always the way when women got their hands on things that were meant to be the sole province of men. And Miz Taggart looked determined. Hell, she looked downright resolute, and he just knew she was fixing to interfere somehow in some no-good way.

49

"You can't rock the boat . . ." he began in a reasonable voice, but she interrupted him.

"I can do what I want, Mr. Daggett, and you would do well to think on that. Think hard, Mr. Daggett, and we'll talk again."

And he did not like being dismissed like a hired hand in that smug, inflexible tone of voice of hers, but he had no choice after all but to leave the tight, closed-in little office where they always conducted business and which was always filled with the cloying scent of a woman who did not know her place and wouldn't let well enough alone.

Cassandra watched him broodingly from the window as he mounted his huge black stallion and raced off toward the fields, and a futile rage engulfed her—again.

It struck her that she had spent these last couple of weeks in an ongoing fury, fending off *men* whose sole desire was to take everything away from her, and she did not understand that. But no matter: she would take control now, she thought; it was time. She had only to write the letter, the one that would introduce the very fictional, very married and extraordinarily busy Coltrane Taggart, the one who would with grace and good humor give her everything back.

She wrote the first letter very carefully that night. There was no room for mistakes; she could not give Mr. James Greve an inch of room to question anything about Coltrane Taggart.

She listed all the facts first and then wrote a rough draft of the letter, and rewrote and crossed out and rewrote it again until she had simplified it and made it sound as plausible as possible.

She disguised her handwriting on the final copy, slanting the paper in the direction opposite her normal script, and then, with uncharacteristic caution, she put the letter away for a day, two—and then took it out and read it again to see how it sounded to her.

When she was finally satisfied with it, she folded it up many times, stepped on it to give it the appearance of having been in transit, "aged" the fold lines with tea, tore one of the edges, and dampened the center of the letter with water which she allowed to dry overnight.

She was pleased with the end result: her letter looked as if it had been in the hands of some scruffy messenger for at least three months. And of course the envelope had fallen to pieces—there was just that little bit of it, with Jesse's name on it and instructions as to the location of Riveland. Yes, that would work, she thought, as she slathered dirt on the printing on the ostensible front of the envelope. And she was sure Mr. Greve would want to see it. She would lay money on it.

And that was the easy part. The hardest thing she had to do was focus on her note to Mr. Greve, which had to sound properly appalled at the unexpected appearance of a missive that both announced Jesse's supposedly long-lost son and brought to light the fact that Jesse had lied to her. That was a very good tack to take, she thought: Jesse had lied to her and she was prostrate at the thought of it, and would Mr. Greve be so kind as to come so that they could discuss this shocking turn of events.

Just the right note there. Just how he expected her to sound. God, she hated it. She folded the note and sent for Sully, sure that Mr. Greve would attend to her that very afternoon.

There was a little velvet one-armed sofa in the library which Ojim obligingly brought into the parlor for her so that she could arrange herself to the best effect to await Mr. Greve's arrival.

He came within three hours of receiving her note, but then it was raining and the roads were muddy and slow.

"My dear Miz Taggart," he exclaimed, rushing into the room to grasp her outstretched hands. "I don't understand."

"Nor do I," she said faintly. "I'm glad you could come so quickly."

"Your note was incoherent, Miz Taggart."

She knew it hadn't been, but of course he would say so. "I stated the facts exactly," she began heatedly and then pulled back at the expression in his eyes. "I received . . . no, Mr. Taggart received a letter today, Mr. Greve, and I truly don't know what to make of it. You see, on the one hand, it means that my husband lied to me, and that distresses me greatly. And yet, on the other, it seems I have a stepson who perhaps might be the answer to my problems . . ."

She caught his disapproving frown just in time. Slow down, she thought; she could not introduce that notion until he had accepted the premise of the letter.

"But why don't you read the letter, Mr. Greve, and tell me what *you* think." She reached toward the small side table next to the sofa, opened its drawer, and removed the torn envelope with the letter which she had artfully arranged within.

He examined the envelope very carefully, as she had known he would, and then took out the letter and smoothed its creases painstakingly before he began to read it, silently.

She could not tell from the expression on his face what he was thinking; it was obvious he was rereading it and reading it still again, and that he probably didn't want to tell her what he thought. He probably wanted to consign the thing to the flames in the fireplace and pretend it didn't exist.

"Well," he said finally, heavily, after a good fifteen minutes had passed. "This is very convenient." Did he sound petulant?

"I don't know what you mean," Cassandra said tightly,

taking offense instantly, defensively.

He lifted his head to look at her and she consciously stiffened, smoothing her face into a mask of indifference, hiding her hope. He must not think she understood him or that she knew the letter wasn't real. She had to believe it with all her heart or it would never work, *never;* she was counting on it working.

"I find it hard to credit that a letter arrives out of the blue from someone claiming to be Jesse Taggart's son and you, my dear Miz Taggart, never knew of his existence."

She drew herself up. "Why is that so strange, Mr. Greve? I was all of sixteen at the time. Did you think Mr. Taggart told me anything of his business or his previous marriage? Or do you think there were relics of that life, that time, around Riveland when I arrived? No, he cleaned out the whole house, had it fitted out especially to suit my mother and myself just as we wanted. If he had a son, he never told me. If there is a trace of him in this house, it is buried. We never socialized, and no one ever told me. Jesse Taggart kept to himself at all times, and he kept his personal life close on Riveland. It was no one's business, *no one's.* And I had no reason to be suspicious of anything, even if he was inordinately anxious to conceive a son. Most men are, as you yourself must know, Mr. Greve, and I'm deeply distressed that by your statement you are accusing *me* of deceit when it is Jesse Taggart who has been deceitful—to us both."

There! It was a good speech, one that had him properly mortified as well as including him in the ruse.

Mr. Greve scanned the letter again. "He says he wants to mend the rift with his family. I can't believe you don't know anything about this."

"I do not know anything about this," she said staunchly.

"He's waiting to hear from his father . . . an address in Baltimore, and you must assume he has no knowledge of the death of his mother either."

"I can't imagine what his history is, Mr. Greve. Perhaps he went away when his mother died. But we have no way of knowing, do we?"

He looked at her closely. "No, we don't," he said at length. "A son who has gone to sea after an estrangement with his father suddenly returns and begs forgiveness — but not to return to the family fold, because he has made a success of his chosen field and hopes his father will feel some pride in that accomplishment . . ." He shook his head. "I don't know. I don't know. He has a family; he has settled in Baltimore, he says, and still does not wish to return to the Riveland of his youth even though he treasures its memories more than his father would have ever thought possible. He seeks only to be reunited with his family, and begs his father to send word that he is amenable. I don't know . . . I don't know . . . I suppose it *is* possible."

"I must write to him," Cassandra said firmly, knowing that Mr. Greve was about to make that offer himself. "Truly, Mr. Greve, it will be better coming from me that his father and his mother are now gone. He must be invited here nevertheless, and I must invite him, and then we will see where we stand with this mysterious son whom no one has ever heard of. I will devise some test to verify his identity, and then . . . well, then we'll proceed from there."

Mr. Greve was not a happy man. Cassandra had just handed him Coltrane Taggart's response to her condolence letter and it seemed to him, as he scanned its contents, that his well-ordered plans were slowly being torn to shreds before his very eyes. And Miz Cassandra Taggart was being inordinately helpful as she pointed out to him that Mr. Taggart had passed her every test.

"I fail to see *what* you tested," he said irritably. "He is deeply grieved to learn of his parents' deaths, and assures

54

you that you may call upon him for any assistance whatsoever, even though he has no plans to travel to Georgia any time soon."

"Go on," Cassandra prompted, hoping the eagerness in her voice escaped his notice.

Mr. Greve took a humphing breath and read further. "Oh, of course—all his boyhood reminiscences . . . really, Miz Taggart—"

"But you see—he *knows* Riveland like no one else upon whom I could depend. Look, right there, he talks about how he and his father always fought about his having to pay endless close attention to the planting and cultivation of the seeds and how when he was growing up, his father wanted him to train to do the seed selection for the succeeding year's planting. And here, sometimes when they ride the country in and around Baltimore, how the scent of the cultivation brings sharply to mind early March days and the planting of the corn on Riveland. Now, Mr. Greve, what you do not know is that we are engaged in doing just that thing as we speak—and here, this man, this stranger, mentions it because he *knows*—even as far away as he has been—*he* has been a part of the cycle here in a way no one else has, and you must credit that, Mr. Greve, and allow me to avail myself of his expertise."

She was an actress truly, she thought. In another life, she could have mounted a stage and made speeches to an audience, because she could see that though Mr. Greve was highly unwilling to concede her argument, he almost knew he had no choice if the writer of the letter were who he claimed to be.

But she needed to push him an inch more. "Come with me, Mr. Greve. I don't believe we have toured Riveland yet. When we do, you will see plainly what I mean."

She snapped her fingers as they entered the vestibule, and Sully appeared. "Order out the gig for us, please. Mr. Greve would like to see all of Riveland today."

He marveled at the dispatch with which the conveyance

appeared, with Ojim at the reins. He had already admired the approach to the house, which was a mile-long drive up a canopy of hundred-year-old oak trees, but he had never seen the vista which she presented to him now: a sweep of side lawn of about ten acres, dotted with oak and magnolia trees, that rolled gently down to the banks of the Little Midway River; lacy cast-iron benches situated invitingly under several particularly shady trees; a play of light and shadow that gave an altogether fairy tale quality to the scene which he coveted immediately.

This extension of the main driveway wound around the side of the house, past a small veranda, out toward the back and the fields. Here, attached to the house by a covered walkway, was the brick-built kitchen, the dairy, the smokehouse, and a small storage house.

Beyond that, ranging downward again toward the river, beyond a stand of trees and a line of cabins reaching back in the opposite direction to the horizon, lay the endless grids of the cotton fields where gangs of workers, looking like miniature mechanized people, moved torpidly through a square dance of tasks in the early morning heat.

Still more buildings edged one end of the farthest field, and far and away in the distance, they could see Mr. Daggett silhouetted against the sun, riding high on his stallion, pointing his crop, shouting directions that echoed back against the sky like a primitive chant.

"There is the work of Riveland," Cassandra said, her voice a flat monotone. Everything depended on her performance now. Mr. Greve could insist or desist, depending on how convincing she was, how much she could scare him. Just this one act she had to perform now, and then she could allow herself to unwind, to *feel*. "Can you tell me, Mr. Greve, which of the fields need manuring, and which need drainage? Can you walk into the field and tell me when we should hoe and when we should track, when to pick and when to clean, when to whip and when to mote and when it will be ready to bale? Yes," she interpolated tensely as he looked at her askance, "I know the vocabulary and Mr. Daggett knows the when and why of it, but still—there has to be a firm hand who can guide the rest—someone who knows the risks—and the fragility of this kind of crop. Someone who knows Riveland, Mr. Greve—otherwise everything could go under. *Everything.*"

He refused to hear her. "Nonsense. Between you and Mr. Daggett everything will go just fine, just as it has been. You've been at great pains to tell me so, haven't you, Miz Taggart?"

She stiffened. Stupid of her to boast—had it been boasting or mere pride in her accomplishment that was about to be overset by Jesse's demands beyond the grave? Nevertheless, she *had* given him the lever with which he was hoisting her words right back at her.

"It isn't as simple as it sounds, Mr. Greve. Only today, Mr. Daggett was demanding that he have full and equal charge of my workers in order for Riveland to maintain productivity. Here is a touchy subject for your consideration: Riveland's field hands have answered to no one but my husband and Mr. Daggett, and Mr. Daggett at this moment has strict control—but no authority. Nor will I relinquish it to him."

She paused in her recitation and slanted a look at him. He was staring off into the distance, his mouth a down-turned line, as he gave her his full attention. She could almost see his mind busily working out the scenario that would be his best answer to the problem, the one that would cause her to demand that he become her savior.

How well she had learned her lessons under Jesse's tutelage: she could outmaneuver any man most adroitly with words, and Mr. Greve was surely a man of many words.

"Mr. Daggett will not work for a woman," she went on, "and under his influence, perhaps neither will my workers. I have suggested he might leave if he cannot tolerate this condition—"

"But you have no right . . ." he burst out in protest.

"Of course I have the right," she said blandly, and continued, "Now you can see, Mr. Greve, just how someone unfamiliar with the conditions at Riveland might blunder into a situation and, without understanding the subtleties, enter into a disagreement with the one who does. My workers are answerable to me as they were to my husband, and I need no outside source to confirm the extent of my obligation to them or theirs to me. Now you see, Mr. Greve—as you noted so wisely earlier on, a family member who would customarily undertake this role would be well aware of these delicate matters."

"I—"

"Of course you would," she cut him off neatly. "But you understand the necessity now of my writing to Mr. Taggart and asking for the help and counsel that he so generously offered, do you not, Mr. Greve?"

Lord, the man was obtuse—or he was after something himself? But there was nothing for him to have; Jesse had tied her up too thoroughly, and she could not allow him to look too closely into the matter of Jesse's fictional son, or he would discover her ruse.

She had to get rid of him and get out from under Jesse's impossible strictures. "Yes, she said thoughtfully, "I'll write to him tonight. With any luck, we should have an answer within"—oh, she could *not* be in a hurry, but still—"two weeks."

"Miz Taggart . . ."

"I can't think about anything else, Mr. Greve," she said sharply, as she signalled Ojim to set the gig in motion. "Mr. Taggart's lies, his keeping this secret from me, are just bales on the boat now. He can't undo it, and he can't redress the wrong, and all we can do is go ahead with the work of Riveland for which I need Mr. Taggart's good counsel. And that is *all*."

But she knew it wasn't all; the very look on his face told her that Mr. Greve would not let go the reins easily, not at all. She would have to make sure she covered every objection, every question that he could raise, in this next succeeding letter, and then finally he would go back to Atlanta and administer Jesse's estate from there, and she would never have to see him again.

Chapter Five

The waiting was impossible: she was alone on Riveland for the first time in eight years—really alone, with the knowledge that there was no one watching her, no one to criticize, no one to prevent her ordering a carriage to take her to town, no one to keep her out of the fields or out of the way, no one to rescind her orders or countermand them. No one to interfere in any way—except the barbarous Mr. Greve, who finally had the good grace to stay away until she sent for him.

She felt a pure wave of terror sweep over her.

She had never been *alone* before, with sole responsibility for everything resting squarely on her shaking shoulders. She had never been at a place where she didn't need some kind of artifice to escape the control of someone else.

She almost wanted to slip into another persona just to escape the onus of being Jesse's widow.

. . . God, Jesse's *widow* . . .

The house felt more like a prison than ever, like a cage. She wanted to rattle the bars, she wanted something, someone to rail against because she didn't, for all her bravado with Mr. Greve, really know how to be on her own.

But she had learned a lot from Jesse. She *had*. It was only that she had to have that immovable wall against which to test her mettle.

Because Jesse had taught her so well.

So well that she never wanted another man to touch her again. So well that she would never trust that another human being knew more than she herself knew from instinct or experience. So well that she knew the very words to handle his hate and his justifications when he lashed out at her for stealing his manhood and paying his bills. Oh, so well that she knew tricks to use to escape him and gloried in the power she felt when she successfully eluded him incognito and he passed her by as if she didn't exist.

Yes, she had learned from Jesse.

Being Jesse Taggart's wife had been akin to being a puny mortal climbing a steep, steep mountain and finding nothing to support her but the odd toehold here and there, and at the end only a sheer fall to nothingness.

She felt it keenly, the nothingness. He had left her nowhere to go, nothing to do but sink her life into Riveland, into its fertile productive life, so much the opposite of hers.

How ironic that she should have invented a son for Jesse, and what a lovely touch it was that in her fiction, she made sure he had hated Riveland as much as she. The emotions there were real: she felt them too.

Riveland forever.

Forever . . .

She couldn't grasp it as she wandered its rooms in the succeeding days and tried to galvanize herself into some kind of constructive action. She had to deal with Daggett; she had to find a position of strength with him and her slaves, and she didn't quite know what to do.

But—did it matter?

Really? Forever . . . ?

They could all rise up and murder her and no one would know the difference. Maybe Jesse had been counting on that; they had hated him, they still hated him and she, by extension, *was* Jesse. The house servants still cowered, still did her bidding with a wary fear in their eyes and a reluctance in their hearts, and she did not know how to combat that either.

She had to do something.

It was time to set in the potatoes and the corn, time to check the first blow of cotton, time for too much as April waned and May seemed to be coming too fast with nothing settled except the fact that Cassandra Taggart was depressingly *unsettled*.

One day, about two weeks later, she called for Ojim. "What are they doing now?" she asked him briskly, to show him she was taking full control as of that moment; she had only to present the same unvaried face to Daggett when she encountered him in the field and he would understand exactly who was in command from now on.

"Dey's plantin' de back half o' de corn, ma'am. An' dey cultivatin' de potato fields now fo' first plantin' end o' de month," Ojim told her respectfully, but he wouldn't look her in the eye.

"And the first show of last year's crop? Has Mr. Daggett done anything yet?"

"He ain't tol' me, ma'am; don't know what he 'tends to do 'bout dat."

"Then we'll find out," Cassandra said authoritatively. "Bring 'round the gig, please."

"Yes, ma'am," he said obediently, yet something flashed in his eyes, and she caught it—just a momentary eye contact, a comment—but on what she did not know.

She had not resolved her problem with Daggett; if anything, the problem had expanded because of the necessity of selecting an advisor. But that solution was almost at hand, and she could use it to fight off Daggett and his attempt to take control of Riveland.

How could she have just sat back and not even checked on his day-to-day activities, she wondered, as the gig bumped down the long gravelly track to the fields. Useless to berate herself now. Another woman would be prostrate with the burden and the restrictions.

But not she. *She* would find a way around things. She

would make it work for her. She would make Daggett work for her, too, or she would send him right out to pasture with no hesitation whatsoever.

She understood the look in Ojim's eyes as they came within viewing distance of Daggett and the gang of workers seeding the hillocks of the back field.

He sat high on his stallion, shouting imprecations, exhorting the line to move faster, smashing his crop against his boot threateningly.

"Mr. Daggett."

He did not respond to her icy tone; he didn't turn. It was almost as if he willed her away: if he didn't see her, she wasn't there.

"Mr. Daggett."

Louder this time, authoritative, firm.

"Ma'am?" His voice came out of the side of his mouth, reluctantly, with just the faintest condescension to a situation in which he wanted to be as rude as possible to reinforce his dominance.

The workers kept moving, their eyes down, their arms moving rhythmically as though someone were counting beats and they had to be on time with each handful of seeds they sowed in the ground.

She felt a thick wave of revulsion and she wasn't sure whether it was she or the feeling of hate that surrounded Daggett like an aura.

"I'll expect you, Mr. Daggett," she said finally, pulling back on her feelings and her urge to say more. She didn't need to undermine him. She needed to make him understand who had control now, and that it was not he.

"Take me to the cotton field, Ojim." She made sure Daggett heard that, too, above Ojim's clucking to the horse, above the crusty sound of the wheels on gravel as they turned and veered off in a different direction.

There was activity everywhere. From late March through the early spring all hands were in the fields, cultivating, hoeing, hauling manure, building up the hilly little ridges in which a battalion of workers would drill seed holes and plant the fragile cotton seed. Far and away in the next field, the first show of the previous year's planting would be opening: the bolls closest to the stalks would be picked and the seeds harvested for the succeeding year's crop.

This was to be Ojim's specialty, this was the test of the quality of the cotton produced at Riveland. And now she understood, as the gig bumped its way down the wagon track, she had to be taught these things too.

Her heart sank. If her knowledge of Riveland became so deeply rooted in its soil, she might never be able to leave it, ever, in spite of Jesse's will, and what an incongruity that would be.

She would be buried here too, figuratively and literally; she felt the power of Riveland taking hold of her. She could feel a nature in herself she had not known existed that wanted the substance and permanence of Riveland, and she could feel herself resisting it with all her might.

If she came to love it, how would she give it up willingly?

And if she didn't, and if she nurtured every stalk and boll of cotton in spite of that, how could she let it all go—willingly?

The baby stalks of the next year's crop that were just starting to shoot out from the heated soil touched her heart. The fragility of it, the vastness of nature and the elements that conspired to bring forth this elegant spurt of life that had nothing to do with humanness and everything to do with supporting humanity.

Two or three leaves danced on each tender stalk. There were still many weeks to go before they could begin the first hoeing to tear away encroaching grasses and loosen the soil. And eighteen months to harvest, each crop overlapping the preceding one, with the first bloom of the boll harvested for seeds and to test the quality of each year's crop.

It was an unending circle of cultivating, planting, harvesting, testing and planting again. And Jesse had sown as well two yields of potatoes and one of corn in the early spring, and they fed on the ears and used the dried leaves for fodder and the withering stalks to support the vines of climbing vegetables after the corn had been stripped away. These, along with peas and beans, were their staple vegetables, and she wondered why, as the gig crunched its way down the criss-crossed tracks of the cotton fields, they couldn't do more.

They could have a garden and raise common vegetables too: carrots and cabbage, tomatoes, beets, cucumber; fruits—apples, figs, strawberries, oranges; maybe grain, wheat—her mind ran riot.

All Jesse had ever cared about was providing the minimum for the sustenance of the workers on Riveland, and himself, and pocketing the revenue from his most profitable crop.

Jesse had allowed no one but himself, to have anything—not his wife, not his slaves. She had lived in stark luxury and abject fear, and they lived in strongly built utilitarian cabins and their fear had been every bit as encompassing as hers, and they had nothing and she had everything—including the power over their lives.

It was almost laughable when she hardly had power over her own.

Yet something elemental caught at her as the gig topped a small undulating rise and began its downward glide toward the fields sprawled out in a great, symmetrical, white-topped green grid as far as her eye could see: the tall, lengthening, hardy stalks and the budding bolls, tightly compressed by tenuous green fingers peeking white, flecked the field like a length of dotted swiss voile.

This was *hers* and she was bound to it as tightly as with baling wire, and she hated it and wished she had an ax so she could chop it all away and free herself. Whatever Jesse had been thinking, he could not have been counting on her determination. He had either wanted to imprison her at Riveland or make her go away altogether: either decision would have been a punishment, but as she stepped out of the gig and knelt to examine the tender bolls of the previous year's seeding, she felt only the desire to meet the challenge—and to win.

She made two decisions as Ojim drove her back to the house. It was imperative that she erase the fear and loathing of the mistress from her workers' minds and hearts, and it was equally important that she lay to rest the final condition of Jesse's will.

When Mr. Daggett reluctantly joined her later that afternoon, she saw immediately that he was predisposed not to agree with one thing she wanted, and she would have to be rooted and firm with him.

"I am making these changes," she informed him from her seat behind her walnut double-pedestal desk in the office, disregarding the instant shifting of his stance from deferential to defiant. "I will have a detail of workers to lay out a garden behind the kitchen. It will be substantial, Mr. Daggett, and it will require several women to maintain it and that will be their regular duty. I will oversee this. Now—did you say something, Mr. Daggett?"

"Don't see no need, ma'am," he muttered.

"No, I didn't think you would," she retorted. "However, that is what I want. I also want Saturday and Sunday free for the workers, starting this week. This weekend, they will mark out garden plots for themselves, and begin cultivating their own gardens. If their yield is bountiful, they will be free to sell their produce, although I reserve the right to buy with first offer, and I reserve the privilege of harvesting their blades if they grow corn. Is *that* clear, Mr. Daggett?"

He stared at her stonily. "You gonna spoil them blacks, Miz Taggart, and you are gonna be damned sorry."

66

"Or perhaps I'm going to make life here a little more tolerable so that someone doesn't take in his head to rise up some night and kill us both, Mr. Daggett—or hadn't you even thought that was possible?"

"Wasn't possible when Mr. Taggart was in the fields," Daggett snapped.

"Mr. Taggart is no longer in the fields, Mr. Daggett, and you are. In addition to that, I want Ojim with the last year's crop for harvesting—when do you think that will be?"

"Better toward the end of the month, ma'am."

Again that hesitation, that unwillingness to share information with her—things she knew already, but only from the chair of her desk where she arranged shipping the crop and dealt with the factor in Savannah, paid the bills, ordered the supplies and made sure that Jesse's excesses didn't put them in debt. Well, she was out to learn it all now, and if Daggett didn't like it, she would dismiss him.

"Ain't no lady planters, ma'am," he added belligerently.

That angered her. She stood up abruptly and slammed the flat of her hand against her account book. "Then *I* am the first, Mr. Daggett."

"It's against nature," he shot back.

"Nature doesn't provide your living, Mr. Daggett."

"But you don't understand, ma'am; she does. And she's mighty finicky, mighty quirky." He slanted a wary look at her to see if she got his meaning. Her face was composed, still. She wasn't biting. He went on, "A little too much rain, a little too little—a cold spell, well . . . I'm at the mercy of nature, Miz Taggart, and so is Riveland's yield, and so is its mistress."

Her mouth tightened; he was a stubborn little man and she meant to make very clear to him who had control over whom. She needed him still—just for a time until she learned it all, and after that . . . Her insides recoiled. She didn't want to learn it all, nor did she want to dictate to anyone. She wanted to run away.

67

"Let me make this clearer, Mr. Daggett. You are at the mercy of the plantation mistress, and if nature destroys my crop, then I will destroy *you*."

She waited a long moment in the thick tense silence to let her meaning sink in, and then she sat down again. "You will call the workers together, tonight, within my hearing, and you will detail to them what I have told you. The square beyond the kitchen will do very nicely. At seven o'clock, Mr. Daggett. I bid you good day."

He stalked out of the room, a man in a fury, slapping his riding crop against his thigh with the same vehemence he wanted to smash it into the lady mistress's smug face. He hated her. He *hated* her. For all these years, his job had been to accompany the hard-riding, hard-driving Jesse Taggart; he was Jesse's man, he had acted on Jesse's wishes, spoken Jesse's thoughts, carried out Jesse's demands.

And now—now he was nothing, a puppet in the lily hands of a bitch-lady mistress he longed to tell to go to hell.

He had nothing. *Nothing.*

And worse than that, he had nowhere else to go.

Two days later, Mr. Greve sat in her parlor once again, his face a pained mask as he tentatively took the folded piece of paper from Cassandra's hands.

"He was prompt," he said, his voice neutral, some little vein of iron in him willing him to remain composed and accepting even though he too would have liked to throw something into Cassandra's face.

"He is most accommodating," Cassandra murmured, clamping down on her excitement that the thing was almost, finally over. "Please read what he says."

Mr. Greve had no choice then but to unfold the letter, but his reluctance was palpable, and he knew it. He scanned it quickly, his frown deepening.

"I presented him with a problem," Cassandra interpolated.

"So I see. That was a little presumptuous," Mr. Greve said disparagingly, his eyes still on the words. He didn't know how he was going to combat this usurper, and he cursed the fates that he hadn't thought to demand an address so he could write to him and forestall this frustrating turn of events.

It wouldn't alter the fact that Coltrane Taggart had more claim on Riveland than he, but by God, he could have bought the man off—something. He felt a mounting fury as he registered exactly what Cassandra Taggart had demanded of the man and his precise instructions in response.

"What made you so sure he had been aware of the situation with the slaves here?" he asked pettishly.

She shrugged. "My husband was that kind of man, Mr. Greve; perhaps it was not obvious to you. But for the eight years I have lived here, things have always been the same, and now that Mr. Taggart is gone, I'm in a position to be more aware of the . . . problem. And after all, Mr. Greve, Riveland is now my sole livelihood—and theirs. I need their loyalty and they need mine."

He hated that too; he despised when she talked mannishly. It desexed her, and he felt almost as if he could not deal with her because he did not know what he was dealing with—woman or man.

He read on. "Well, you put it very prettily, I must say: you are *immediately* going to take him up on his kind offer, and beg to invade his store of knowledge about Riveland—which he considers no invasion whatsoever. *And* you had the temerity to ask him whether the rift between him and Mr. Taggart was of a nature that would cause him to rescind his offer. Really, Miz Taggart."

"Well, he says not," Cassandra said spiritedly. "You can see—Mr. Taggart wanted him to stay on Riveland and he wanted to go to sea, and that was the end of it. He went, and my husband remarried to get the son who would stay. And now it's too late, and Mr. Taggart is willing to provide me with whatever guidance I require, and that should be the end of the matter, Mr. Greve."

She thought she phrased that very well. She was never going to need anyone's guidance ever again, but Mr. Greve did not need to know that.

"Mmmm," Mr. Greve said, reading on. "Well, yes, I see. He thinks giving your workers some small incentive is a very good idea. The weekending days—are you *sure,* Miz Taggart?"

"My husband worked his men too hard, Mr. Greve; it isn't necessary for productivity. Even Mr. Taggart says so. You see—there's a place where he mentions something that happened when he was a boy—where it turned him against the life on the plantation for one of those very same reasons. But you see, he is not loath to speak of these things, and this is further proof he is Mr. Taggart's son, painful as that is for me. I can do nothing to change the past, Mr. Greve. I can only make do with what I have been given in the present."

"That is so," he agreed slowly, folding the letter with stiff fingers. He could not quarrel with any of it; he couldn't fight it because he would risk too much.

"I trust you feel I have satisfied the final condition of the will," Cassandra said softly, crossing her fingers in the pockets of her skirt that he would concede and sign whatever was necessary and tell her he was leaving town within the week.

"Yes, of course," he murmured abstractedly.

"And so we may sign the necessary papers and you will return to Atlanta—when, Mr. Greve?"

He smiled at her, a kind of quick, abashed little smile that was very out of character for him, and he handed her back the letter.

"Oh, my dear Miz Taggart. I knew there was something I neglected to mention. I've decided that in order to oversee things as effectively as possible, I should relocate to Carthage. I've opened an office at the Riversgate Hotel. We'll be seeing each other quite often, Mrs. Taggart, I intend to be vigilant in protecting your husband's estate, and of course, you will regularly submit to me the letters and advice you receive from Mr. Taggart. I truly will need to know that all is in order, Miz Taggart, and I'm just delighted with the town, just delighted. . . ."

The shock almost sent her through the floor but she recovered; she was good at recovering, and now she knew she could not be soft with him. He was after something— Riveland most likely—and he thought he had a better chance by staying around than by just signing over what was her just due and disappearing from her life.

He was a damned interfering man, and she was going to make him pay for it.

"How nice," she murmured. "You'll be so nearby that we can conclude this portion of our business with dispatch. I'm so happy."

"I appreciate your good wishes."

"Well then, we now come to the problem of how much time constitutes time away from Riveland," she said softly, gouging deep. "I need a figure, Mr. Greve, and please do not insult me by offering me a week when you know as well as I that planter families spend months away from the plantation and everyone survives very nicely."

"I haven't thought about it," he said reluctantly.

"You must think about it now, Mr. Greve."

Damned man-woman.

"Two weeks then," he said firmly.

"Ridiculous. Think again, Mr. Greve."

Outrageous demanding woman. What could she do to him after all if he made that a condition of the bequest? "Two weeks is adequate."

"Two months is civilized," she spat, well aware that she had nothing with which to compromise him. *Nothing.* Did she? "I'm sure Mr. Taggart would agree; after all, he spent

71

fourteen years here, fourteen seasons and cycles of planting and harvesting. Yes, another question for Mr. Taggart"—a phrase came to her mind and she almost choked—"who is the sole issue of my husband."

She almost whooped when she saw a tiny frisson of fear slither across Mr. Greve's face. Sons had rights that wives didn't? she wondered. There was a toehold here that had nothing to do with her or Jesse's will, but something to do with Jesse's son who never was? What could such a son do that she couldn't and Mr. Greve knew that could break Mr. Greve's desire to cage her at Riveland just as Jesse desired?

She pushed it. "Three months, Mr. Greve."

"Impossible. That *would* require turning the running of Riveland over to Mr. Daggett." He rose because he needed to move, to leave her presence quickly before he overstepped his bounds. "Three weeks, Miz Taggart."

"Barely time to travel, Mr. Greve."

"And where would you go, Miz Taggart?"

"White Sulphur Springs, Saratoga, Boston—who knows, Mr. Greve? A season in Charleston might be nice, but the season only begins after three weeks, I'm told." Well, she hadn't been told; she didn't know anything about it. She was making it up as she went along, and she could see he was thinking, wavering, assessing. "Two months, Mr. Greve."

"You can't be gone that long, Miz Taggart."

"I'll accept nothing less."

"We will both think on it tonight and I will return tomorrow if I may."

"Certainly."

"Good day, Miz Taggart."

"Good day, Mr. Greve." She swung the door closed behind him and leaned her back against it heavily as if it were the only thing that could support her body now.

She had pulled it off—Jesse's fictional son her savior and her confidant. It was almost over; she was almost free. For whatever reason, Mr. Greve would come to terms with her, she felt it in her bones. She was almost there. She had to remain strong and, no matter what happened afterward, she herself would be free.

"A month plus two intermittent weeks," Mr. Greve said the next morning as he settled himself once more into his habitual chair in the parlor.

"Three weeks," Cassandra shot back.

"I've weighed this carefully, Miz Taggart, and I think my offer is fair."

"There is no offer relevant to this will that is fair, Mr. Greve, especially the part about the details to be worked out at your discretion."

"I grant you that."

"Then *you* must be fair to me," Cassandra said, "since you recognize that fact and agree with me. Isn't it enough I may not marry and I must beg for counsel? Please . . . three weeks, and you may add the condition that I may not take the succeeding week after New Year's should I desire to travel during the month of December. That way you have control—and I have some control."

He studied her face for a moment: here, she was being reasonable, arguing as persuasively as a man for her side, conceding as well as making demands, garnering his sympathy and presenting him with a result that he could not dispute, and which he would have reached himself if she would have given him just that little bit more time.

He hated encroaching women.

"Three weeks, one of which you must spend either in Savannah or Charleston, whichever you desire. You will need that much time to settle with Riveland's factor at any rate, Miz Taggart, and of course you will want to shop and replenish supplies."

"A week is hardly time enough to accomplish all that, Mr. Greve," she said tartly. "I will take an additional week then, if you must limit me to either of those two cities, to make a total of eight weeks: four at a time, two intermittent, two in either Savannah or Charleston in a joint business and pleasure trip. That should satisfy *you*."

He had corraled her at last. No more than six weeks of freedom away from Riveland—away from where he could keep an eye on her. The two other weeks—he was going to be sure he was on the scene in any case, drumming up new business or acting as her agent, he didn't know which. But this was enough.

"All right," he said grudgingly, "that is acceptable." He reached for his briefcase. "However, you must inform me of when you leave and what your destination will be." He opened it and withdrew a sheaf of papers. "In addition, every fortnight, I will require to see evidence that you have been regularly consulting Mr. Taggart on matters of Riveland."

"Every month; it takes a week for a letter to travel to Baltimore."

"Three days, Miz Taggart."

"Mr. Greve, I do have better things to do than bother Mr. Taggart every week with minor irritations."

"Three weeks, then."

"A month."

"Three weeks, Miz Taggart; I'm truly not sure this long-distance management will be beneficial to you or to Riveland."

"Once it is signed, how can it be arranged otherwise?"

"We'll put in a provision," Mr. Greve said, drawing a small nearby table close to him.

"Oh," Cassandra murmured, "a provision." Yes, a provision. Something that could be changed or covered or otherwise rearranged. Precisely.

"Well, after we attend to the provision, Mr. Greve, you will be so kind as to draw up my will."

"Miz Taggart?" He was shocked, even though she had mentioned it before; he had just put it out of his mind,

74

and now he did not have time to present her with any choices, and his brain worked furiously trying to find a way to stave her off.

"Yes. In the event of my death, Riveland goes to my sister, Linnea, who resides in England now, Mr. Greve. No one else. Nowhere else. And I expect to sign the papers today."

Chapter Six

There wasn't a landmark along the road to Carthage that looked familiar to him. But then, when a man had been away a long time, there wasn't any which way that had value; he just went the way of least resistance.

When he got tired and he felt like putting down roots, he found the likeliest place. If something seemed attractive, he followed the lure of it, simple as that. If it didn't work out, a man cut his losses and moved on.

He knew a lot about that. He had followed a lot of lures and lost more than he had ever gained, but he had the sure feeling that he really was the richer for it.

And he had learned something too: he knew how to ride the road and make it over the mountain, and if he knew nothing else, he supposed that was as good a thing to know as any.

The trouble was, though, sometimes a man had to ask directions and then he never was certain he wasn't getting things from the wrong perspective. Sometimes it was just better to nose the thing out, no matter where it led you.

It had been an excruciatingly long trip on horseback, and he wasn't sure yet it was worth it. There was just this palpable urge inside him, underpinned by the nuances of life itself which, even after thirty-plus years, he was not used to dealing with. He had had too much wanderlust, a healthy overdose of pure lust, and a couple of decades of responsibility to no one but himself.

And even this misbegotten journey could have been said to be a totally selfish undertaking: he had any number of good reasons, but the only justification that stuck was that he had made a promise, and he intended to keep it.

Nonetheless, the road to Carthage did not lay out exactly as he had expected and he found himself faintly amused at his naivete. He knew better than anyone how things changed, moved, rearranged, transformed themselves—a landscape was the least of things that would stand still in a dozen years or more.

But still, the expectation was, somehow, a disappointment, as if he had been led to believe one thing and quite another had transpired. He had wanted some substance of a golden memory to be a reality still, but he knew he should have anticipated that nothing would be the same; memory was a great enhancer.

And so was a man's thinking mind, the part that wanted to convince a man to undertake a fool's journey.

But promises made were promises met.

He bunked down for this night in the town ten miles to the south of Carthage, knowing he was that close to his goal, and that finally it was time to ask the questions to which he truly needed the answers.

"Where you headed, stranger?"

He was seated by a window in the dining room of the hotel, poring over a handwritten map, when the waiter approached him.

"Carthage," he said, not looking up. "I figure I've got about ten more miles here right along the river."

"You got that right. River Road'll take you right into the heart of town."

"Sounds good." He wrapped up his crude map and looked up at the man with a faint smile. "Cup of coffee and some eggs would do me fine this morning."

77

The waiter hesitated a moment; they didn't often see the likes of this kind of man around Eden County. He didn't look barely as if he could pay for a meal. "Sure enough, stranger," he said, finally making up his mind.

Well, that was part and parcel of what he had expected. Everyone in this part of the country judged a man by how he appeared, but there wasn't much he could do about that now; at least he hadn't slept in his clothes—in the hotel.

The coffee was damned hot and revivifying, the eggs didn't much matter. They filled his belly and a half dollar on the table paid the fare; another dollar and two bits tidied up the room rent.

He left before the bells tolled for church. Sunday was as good a time as any to get into town early, and Carthage was no exception. The road ran straight, just as the waiter had said, and by nine o'clock of a hot June morning he was nudging his tired mount toward the center square of town.

He felt a supreme sense of disorientation. He had a map—a different map—one that laid out the streets and buildings as they were a decade or more ago, a map made out of memory, just like errant dreams. It was meaningless here and he was grossly out of place.

At that moment, he didn't know quite what he needed except to go back where he came from and forget promises and history.

But as the church bells tolled in Carthage, he knew he had to be faithful to the promise, and that was the only thing he would allow to matter.

The Riversgate Hotel was a large white clapboarded building with a wraparound veranda that overlooked the river, and this was the hotel recomended to him by the minister at the church. Not that he was a churchgoing man. He prided himself on knowing just where to go to get information. And the town minister didn't ask questions, didn't look down on him, didn't do anything but offer his help to someone who looked as though he needed it.

"It's all right, Reverend," he had to assure the man. "I've got all I need and the Riversgate will suit me just fine, if you think they'll take me in."

"Your money's as good as anyone else's," the reverend said drily. "But you come to me if there is a problem."

"Much obliged," he murmured, shaking the reverend's hand and taking his leave. That was one thing about small towns, he thought—there was always someone to lend a hand; there wasn't a man who'd let another man down if he could help it.

The desk man at the hotel wasn't any too pleased, however. "How long?" he asked disdainfully.

"I don't rightly know. A week will do fine."

The desk man looked him up and down. "I need the week's rent in advance."

He withdrew a roll of bills. "How much?"

He hadn't counted on making such an ostentatious appearance, nor had he thought to draw so much attention. But he was so damned out of place amidst the formal broadcloth and muslin and crinoline that it was almost ludicrous; he was a caricature of himself, and Carthaginians were damned nosy. Someone was bound to ask questions. And someone did.

"So where you heading, stranger?" Another curious voice at the bar that evening.

"Figure to head out to Riveland, why?"

"Hope you don't have business there, is why. Ol' Jesse Taggart died about two months ago, or didn't you know that? His baby bride's runnin' the place now, with the lawyer hangin' over her shoulder and operatin' a business right out of the hotel here."

"That right?" He forced himself to sound bored. Baby bride? Jesse dead? Hell and damnation. Jesse dead . . .

79

He got out of the room as fast as he could.

The next morning he headed over to the bank. "I need a strongbox," he told the first person he saw.

"Of course you do." No nonsense in Carthage. Everyone needed a strongbox, even a stranger.

He signed papers, he paid out money and he handed the clerk a piece of paper which he deposited in the box with the reverence of a priest.

"There you go, sir, safe and sound." The clerk picked up the receipt. "Mr. . . . Mr.? I can't make out the name here. Now, I've got to get the name exactly right for when you come back to retrieve that precious piece of paper."

He flinched. "The name is Trager—Cole Trager." He watched the man write it down, printing it, spelling it exactly as he dictated, and he watched him carefully tear the receipt in two and hand him one half.

"There you go, Mr. Trager. Just you bring that back when you want access to your strongbox, hear? Don't forget the receipt."

"I won't forget."

"I never forget a name, Mr. Trager."

" 'Preciate it."

"Or a face," the clerk called after him, but the stranger didn't hear him. "Mr. Trager," he murmured to himself as he took the box back into the vault. "The stranger, Mr. Trager . . ."

During those same two weeks, Cassandra had never been happier in her life. She didn't think it was an exaggeration: she was virtually free of restraints, since she didn't count the ubiquitous Mr. Greve as a restraint; he was more like a bothersome gnat she had to swat every time he showed his face—and she was running things *her* way, despite the disgruntled Mr. Daggett, and she had the backup letters of Mr. Coltrane Taggart to attest to the soundness of her judgment. What could be better?

She could do whatever she wanted to do, or she could do nothing if that were her wont. She spent some time in the field with Daggett and Ojim, both, as May shimmered into June.

She saw the tension in the faces of her workers and she knew they still felt that flay of fear under Daggett's heavy hand. She had to get rid of Daggett—but she couldn't afford to fire him before the harvest was brought in. She was seeing productivity increase, and she saw the cornstalks in the gardens of her workers climb toward the sky and felt as though she had made several long strides away from Jesse Taggart.

She felt Zilpha's concern now, Zilpha, who had served her so dispassionately since she had arrived at Riveland had never shown her an inkling of emotion; she had done what she was told and that was all, and yet now occasionally there was a glimmer of gratitude, a nod, a faint smile, an odd word where before she had not spoken at all.

From the little gig, she watched the hoe-down of the potato patch and the slips cut to be planted for the second yield, and she took some and had Leola, one of the kitchen girls, plant them in *her* garden.

All around her she saw fertility and opportunity, and she felt a racing in her blood that it was all in her hands and sensed that the tentacles of responsibility were winding tighter and tighter around her and she might never get away.

She carried on. "We need more cows," she told Mr. Greve one day. "I wrote to Mr. Taggart about it, and he agrees wholeheartedly. It's not only the milk, you know. It's the manure. You see the pile of it up by the barn for the growing field? We had to supplement it this year. Mr. Taggart concurs with me about the cows. We'll construct transportable fences so that whenever we need to lay in manure before planting, all we have to do is let the herd loose for several weeks field by field and then turn it

81

under."

Mr. Greve could not disagree with that.

"Now here, Mr. Taggart advises us to revise our work system. Years ago there used to be the task system; now it's just workers in gangs sent out wherever Mr. Daggett deems necessary. If we assign by task, we can distribute the work more efficiently and we won't force those into the fields who for health or age reasons can't work the fields. Everyone is assigned a stake and a man knows beforehand exactly what the expectations are for his workday. What do you think, Mr. Greve? Do you know anything about it?" she asked craftily.

"No, but obviously you do," he retorted. "And what does Mr. Daggett say?"

"Mr. Daggett likes to use the whip, Mr. Greve, and I will not tolerate that. And of course Mr. Taggart agrees with me."

"Of course," Mr. Greve said drily.

Another time: "Ojim must go to the fields and pick the best bolls to harvest for next year's crop. Mr. Taggart has detailed exactly what we must look for, and he cautions us to beware of the rain and check for rusting daily if we have to. Would you care to come, Mr. Greve?"

"I would *not*."

And again: "Mr. Taggart says it is fine for me to barter for the cull of the workers' corn crop; he suggests sugar, coffee, molasses, and we might consider allowing them to raise chickens. In fact, I don't know why *we* are not raising chickens and geese—or sheep. You know, that is a question I would like to put to Mr. Taggart in my next letter . . . "

"Do you not feel you are overdoing it, Miz Taggart?"

She looked at him in surprise. "Why no, Mr. Greve. I only meant to comply with this provision of the will, to your satisfaction."

"I appreciate the fact," he muttered, but he didn't appreciate at all that she chose topics of which he had no

82

knowledge whatsoever. It put him in the peculiar position of having to defend her counselor and agree that she could not question him often enough to make sure that things ran smoothly at Riveland.

And yet, she knew so much herself.

Even Daggett complained to him. "She's pokin' her nose where no rightful lady has a mind to put it: in the fields and with that buck, Ojim. It ain't right, and she ain't leavin' the decisions to me, where they belong. You watch out. She's gonna run the place to the ground with that goddamn task business. You tell her."

But he couldn't tell her, because Taggart had told her differently, and he didn't know himself.

"But you don't need to know," she pointed out. "Daggett knows, and Mr. Taggart and I will keep him in line."

"I can't agree about that, Miz Taggart. Mr. Daggett is right on the scene and Mr. Taggart is hundreds of miles away."

"And you have never been in charge of a plantation, Mr. Greve, and Mr. Daggett will never be in a position to do so; he is my employee now, and if he dislikes my methods so much, he is free to leave, and so I have told him."

"I ain't leavin' that lady-bitch," Daggett said vehemently in private to Mr. Greve. "She ain't gettin' the best of me, and I don't believe all that crap about no letters from Baltimore."

Mr. Greve was puzzled. "But surely you *knew* Mr. Taggart's son?"

"Nah . . . none of us knew what happened before we got here. He brung us on to Riveland a coupla months before he went up to Atlanta to marry my lady up there, slaves and all. Ain't no one here from before, but we been here long enough to know how things has to go, and she ain't doin' no one no favors with her newfangled ideas and ways of ruinin' everything. You tell my lady up there in the big house that she ain't yet got her hands dirty enough to tell Daggett what to do, you hear? You tell her."

But he couldn't tell her, he thought caustically; she would write a goddamned letter to Mr. Taggart the young and come back with some hell-for-leather advice that she would be sure to carry out.

"Mr. Taggart says he hopes that we have not neglected the good fishing on the river," she told him calmly. "There's mullet and trout and in April and later on, bass. I didn't know. My husband never fished—never for food, certainly not for sport—but Mr. Taggart says he remembers what great sport it was in early spring. And there is most likely shellfish. We could send the boys down to rake the river bottom by the shore and . . ."

"Miz Taggart—"

"But this is wonderful. There are things Mr. Taggart never thought of doing. We have so much, and we never put to use a tenth of what's available to us here on Riveland."

"How supportive of Mr. Taggart junior to relay this information to you," Mr. Greve muttered, grasping at the letter so he could read through this gratuitous and welcome advice. Oh, and it was all there, couched in that tiresomely helpful tone the young Mr. Taggart always affected in his letters, along with his dozenth refusal to come visit the home of his childhood.

"My husband was right: I know everything I need to know to ready our cotton crop for market, and I know how to deal with our factor in Savannah; I can order supplies and pay bills as well as the next man, Mr. Greve. But I didn't know how to judge my crop and how to make use of my land in any other way but that which I saw Mr. Taggart do. This is—a revelation."

But it was a revelation to him, too. Above and beyond the complexities she had pointed out to him, there were layers and levels of cultivating the land that were a science in themselves, and yet she—through the necessity of these letters—was fair to becoming an expert in these matters.

It had to follow that he, too, could become knowledgeable in this area. He would spend a week or two researching it, and he would return to Riveland as knowledgeable as she, without any damned Coltrane Taggart over his shoulder feeding his mind. He couldn't wait to leave, and so he did not see the evident relief in her eyes as she bid him good-bye.

He visited too frequently, she thought, and she wondered why he did not have enough business to keep him busy in town, and why she felt she must provide herself with a backlog of letters in order to prove she was complying with the dictates of the will.

She knew now why she had not yet gone to town: she had been scared of running into Mr. Greve, or any of those who frequented the hotel. His presence there had to have given rise to much overt speculation. By now everyone in Carthage had to know he was Jesse's lawyer and what his purpose had been in coming to Carthage.

She felt mortified that her distress was probably common knowledge, and comforted that Riveland was so far removed from town; it was like living in a dream world that had nothing to do with Mr. Greve or letters or even Jesse Taggart.

She never would have believed that she would be willing to stay on Riveland more than an hour after Jesse's death, and yet here she was, step by step moving into possession of the land and into the land's possession of *her*.

Yet, with any luck, she might be able to plan a trip away from Riveland for the month of July—the hottest part of the growing season—to take advantage of her agreement with Mr. Greve.

Because she had that to look forward to, she did not feel trapped; she felt liberated, and not even Mr. Greve's stifling presence could put a damper on that.

It truly was as she had thought: she was free, and she had outwitted Mr. Greve and Jesse both, and now no one could tell her what to do.

Two weeks later, Ojim told her it was time to harvest the best bolls of the previous year's seed.

"I'll come with you," she said immediately. "Zilpha, lay out my calico. It's too hot for black, anyway. You wait right here, Ojim. Now, does Mr. Daggett know?"

"He done sent me, ma'am."

"I'll be back in a moment." She raced upstairs, unhooking as many of the pesky fastenings of her mourning dress as she could reach on the run. Zilpha was ahead of her, in the room, and took over the chore immediately, silently, until the stiff black dress fell away almost as if it had a life of its own.

The calico by contrast felt cool and lightweight, and she took a deep breath of utter enjoyment and wondered why she was still wearing mourning in the dead heat of summer in a place where no one would ever see her and no one could care less.

"Sunbonnet," she directed, and Zilpha pulled that out of her closet with the sure hand that knew exactly where every article of clothing was to be located, even if it would never be worn again.

Cassandra jammed it on her head and turned for the door.

"You take someone wif you."

She heard the voice and stopped short. Zilpha—*chiding* her? She turned and Zilpha stared at her, stone-faced, emotionless.

But she had spoken. She, who had not said one personal word to her mistress in eight years, opened her mouth again and the words really did come forth: "You take someone wif you. You done heard right. Dat Daggett just waitin' to get somethin' 'gainst Miz Taggart.

86

Ojim done seed him watchin'. You hear, you take some-one wif you."

She didn't hesitate. "I will."

"You get dat lazy Leola, hear?"

"I hear you."

"Don' matter none they's a hundred workers round and about you. You do whut I say."

"I will."

She felt it then, something she had not experienced since Jesse's death — a subtle threat that knifed its way through her complacency like a fish through water. She was shaken by it and profoundly moved by Zilpha's warning.

Leola, however, was nowhere to be found; the slow moving Elsie was the only maid not engaged in some task or another who could be removed from the house on an instant's notice, and Cassandra dragged the bewildered servant after her out the door to join Ojim in the cart.

"What I be doin' heah?" Elsie mumbled as the cart rumbled down into the fields at a pace that made it seem as though Ojim were racing demons as well as time.

When he brought the cart to a halt, he jumped out and motioned to Cassandra and Elsie. "Come."

"Me, too?" Elsie demanded in disbelief. "I got to pick cotton? I don' do dat kind work, Miz Taggart; it ain't fittin for me to go in de field like dis."

"Hush!" Cassandra felt herself losing patience quickly — too quickly — and she knew exactly why: Zilpha had disrupted her dream and she was deeply disturbed. "You just come with us, you hear? You don't have to work, you just have to be here."

"I don' wanta be heah."

"Stubborn girl, you be where your mistress tells you," Cassandra snapped, and Elsie fell silent.

Cassandra turned to Ojim. "All right. Now . . ."

"Come, Miz Taggart, I show what we got to do now. I know just what we got to do."

She followed him into the fields, trailed by the unwilling Elsie, and for the next hour, he tagged the best plants, the strongest, most topheavy plants, and he showed her the clean, healthy bolls that would yield the seed to increase and improve the succeeding year's crop.

"Den by de end o' dis week, maybe sooner, we gonna come pick dese heads off de stalk and we gin down dese bolls and we gonna weigh the seeds and make sure we got de strain pure as pure for de next seedin'. Dis is how it look, and when we done wif de ginnin', you gonna come look-see down de gin house, Miz Taggart, so you know just what's what."

And she saw, and she knew from his tutelage already, which was a healthy stalk and which would die, and how to spot blight and the damage of rust which turned the leaves of the plant brownish-black and caused premature loss of the boll. She knew there was a threat of cotton caterpillars and that the common defense against them was to import turkeys to roam the fields.

And she knew, too, that the work had not even begun, that there were costly dangers inherent in the processing of the crop and that she could lose everything through the carelessness of her workers or through the vituperative nature of Mr. Daggett, who might omit a step in the processing or switch the order in which things were done, or through carelessness, neglect to fully gin the cotton and cause it to become stained and yellowed. And that was besides the dangers posed by nature. Too much rain, too little hoeing, frost, a storm that could wash away precious topsoil; the boll could open too early or never open at all.

But Mr. Daggett was not going to defeat her. She would watch him every step of the way, even if she had to spend the rest of the picking season in the gin house. She would make sure nothing stained her cotton and nothing got in the way of a successful baling and sale in Savannah, and she would haul it to the flatboat and steer the damned thing there herself if necessary.

Nothing would stop her—not Daggett, not Jesse's will, not the redoubtable Mr. Greve.

She would be the one and only lady planter of Riveland, because that was the only choice she had.

And when she strode up the steps to the veranda after Ojim let her out, she felt her power and the awesome responsibility she held in her hands.

It was getting to her; she felt it. Riveland was beginning to creep into her soul and wind its tentacles around her ambition, and that was dangerous. So dangerous.

She was amused at the way Elsie flew out of sight the moment they entered the vestibule.

Zilpha appeared out of nowhere, and stared at her with just the faintest expression of approval. "Yo' wish, Miz Taggart?"

She didn't even know. "Oh—some hot water in my room. I would like to wash."

"Yes'm." Zilpha disappeared as mysteriously as she had come, and Cassandra wearily climbed the steps with echoing regrets surfacing in her mind like swimmers going down for the third time. If only Jesse had . . . if Mother could have . . . I wish I hadn't . . .

She shook away the mood as she entered the bedroom, hers and Jesse's room that they had shared and which she now occupied almost like a penance.

She heard the doorbell faintly below, and she made a disgusted sound. Mr. Greve, undoubtedly. She hadn't seen him for a week, maybe two, and she didn't want to see him now, either, but she had no choice.

She opened the door just as Zilpha was about to knock.

"I know. Mr. Greve is here."

"No, ma'am. It ain't Mr. Greve."

"Who is it then?"

"Don' know, ma'am."

She looked at Zilpha's impassive face. Useless to try to

89

get any more information. "I'll go see."

"Yes'm."

She walked slowly to the landing and down the first ten steps until she came in sight of the door.

He was standing in the doorframe. Sully had not allowed him to come in, but he had not chased him out. He might have been scared to death of the stranger. The man was a mountain; she had never seen anyone so tall in her life.

He was a man-mountain, dressed in rough breeches, boots and a cotton shirt, and he carried a jacket of some sort; he looked as wild as a mountain cat with his long hair and scruffy beard and his all-consuming blue eyes, so light and startling against his brown face.

He was an Indian, he had to be, or a mountain man and he had just lost his way, or he was a barbarian pure and simple and he had come to kill Jesse and he didn't know Jesse was dead.

She took another step downward, and the stair-step creaked.

He heard it; he wheeled toward her instantly, with a mountain cat's precision, and looked directly up the stairs.

She knew he couldn't see her — not yet — but somehow he knew she was there.

"Who are you?"

She thought her voice was strong, full of authority. It might have quaked, just a little.

"Ma'am?"

His tone was respectful; she couldn't tell a thing from that one word.

And the only thing she knew was, she was alone in the house and there wasn't a servant capable of coming to her rescue if this man-mountain proved to be a menace.

"Who are you?" she demanded again, steeling herself to take the next step down, and the next.

"Ma'am, I'm looking for Mrs. Jesse Taggart."

She drew in a tight, deep breath. His voice was like honey—thick, rich, liquid. Educated. Now where would a man-mountain get an education, she wondered distractedly.

She stepped down another step and now she was in his sight. "I am Mrs. Jesse Taggart," she said imperiously. "Who are you?"

He smiled at her conspiratorily. "Why, I'm Coltrane Taggart, ma'am, Jesse's son, and I've come home to stay."

Chapter Seven

*No, you're not! I made you up. You don't exist. You
don't even look the way I pictured you. I'm dreaming.
Go away!*

She said none of that; her hands gripped the banister
to keep her from falling forward in her astonishment. She
heard the words she really said, but she felt as if she were
listening to someone else from far away.

"Excuse me. There is no one in this family named Coltrane Taggart," and she almost choked on the name; this
could not be happening. "I would appreciate it if you
would leave."

But the man-mountain did not turn and go away. With
willfully bad manners, he edged himself into the vestibule, his head cocked slightly as though he were listening
intently — and looking.

"Well, ma'am, I can't do that."

"Of course you can do that. This is a mean and vicious
trick, and I promise you I won't listen to any explanations. Please just leave." She turned her back to him,
damning the fates that there was no one in the house who
could throw him out. Trane Taggart was a figment of *her*
imagination and he had no right to barge into her house
making false claims and scaring her half to death by the
sheer size and rusticity of him.

"Ma'am . . ." He moved closer still to the staircase; she
heard his step and she whirled before he could get an-

other inch farther.

"Are you still *here?*" She didn't know how she could remain so calm. On the other hand, she didn't quite know what else to do, short of trying to toss him out herself.

He smiled gently at the insolent question and looked down at himself, and then back up at her, noting her tightly clenched hands on the banister, and the tautness of her slender body. "I reckon I *am* still here, and I'm still Coltrane Taggart, ma'am, and I sure hope you come to grips with that real soon."

"I have no idea who you are," she snapped, sliding down another step. Maybe, she thought desperately, if she got a little closer to him, she wouldn't feel so intimidated by him.

But he was smiling again, that disarming smile of pure enchanted enjoyment, and she didn't know what to make of it. And she knew what he saw: calico and curls and the militant light in her eyes which didn't scare him at all, obviously, and she didn't know what he found so enjoyable.

"I'm Jesse Taggart's son by his first wife," he said, his voice liquid now with concern over how he sounded to her.

"No, you're not," she contradicted instantly. *No, you're not; you're someone I invented and you don't belong here because you don't exist, and there is nothing you can say to make me believe you. And anyway, I'm dreaming this, I HAVE to be.* "My husband had no children by his first marriage. Good afternoon, sir."

"Jesse Taggart disowned his son," he went on, almost as if he hadn't heard her, and his story was so similar to the one she had contrived that she was speechless. "The boy ran away when he was real young—real young—and he never did come back, and Jesse Taggart had a streak of real cussedness in him, ma'am, as I expect you know, and he treated the boy like he was dead."

"There was no boy," she ground out in pure fear. How did he know *her* story? *How did he know?* "He had no children. There *is* no Coltrane Taggart, and I want you to leave."

"Ma'am, I appreciate your plain speaking, but I am home to stay and we'll straighten this out somehow."

"We will not straighten anything out. My husband is dead. There is nothing to straighten out. He never had a son. He had no children. *None*." But her emphatic surety did not budge him and she sought something, anything to scare him into believing she could not be duped by him. "Nor did my servants know you."

"Of course not, ma'am. I never saw them before in my life, either."

His easy admission floored her. "Just leave. I can't waste any more time debating the issue."

"He must have brought in a whole new retinue of servants and workers when he married you, ma'am. I told you he was a mean cuss," he mused, ignoring her. "It would have been just like him. Damn, I wish I had gotten to see him before he died."

"So do I," she muttered, coming down another step. A man-mountain, she thought dispiritedly. It didn't make any difference how close she got: big was big and rough was rough and he was both, and decidedly scruffy up close.

His light, bright eyes immediately noted her distress. In fact, he had noted everything about her, from her blazing green eyes to her steely posture, to the taut grip of her hands on the banister, and he felt enormous sympathy for her. On the other hand, she was nothing like the woman he would have expected Jesse to marry.

Jesse liked women who could be bullied and tromped all over. Jesse never would have chosen a woman of spirit, nor would he have married a woman of great beauty unless she were remiss in another area.

He would have bet money that Jesse would have sought

out another woman of the quality and submissiveness of Coltrane Taggart's mother, and the moment he had heard about Jesse's so-called baby bride, he had been sure he could just ride on up to Riveland and establish himself.

He had anticipated dealing with a young, inexperienced, and naive girl, someone he could just ride all over and get his way, just like Jesse. He hadn't really believed that Jesse would *never* talk about his son.

"I was going to make it up with him," he added, almost as an afterthought.

She stiffened. *No, you weren't; you couldn't. That was MY story. You couldn't know that. You're a vicious impostor.*

It was so close, so similar; who could have done this, who could do this to her?

Who knew—except Mr. James Greve?

Lord . . . oh, it made sense, it made so much sense! She felt a wash of relief flood her body and mind. Of course it was Greve—he had hated the idea of Jesse's son, he hated the letters; he had thought she never noticed his expression every time she produced one of them. Hadn't she sensed his reluctance, and hadn't she felt he was after something else—something other than his explicit administration of Jesse's estate?

And didn't Mr. James Greve believe that Coltrane Taggart was real? Of course he would hire some actor to portray him—to what end, she could not guess: maybe to throw her into a panic. He had almost succeeded, too.

The tension eased out of her. She could deal with the man-mountain now. Mr. Greve was behind this, and how clever he had been. He had terrorized her right in her own home, and his plot was positively devious. After all, she had never met Trane Taggart, either. Who was to say what he looked like or when he might have suddenly taken it into his head to pay a visit to Riveland, despite all his protests that he never wanted to return there again?

Diabolical.

She felt so calm. But what did she say to him now? *I'm sorry you missed him.* It was a good act; he had exactly the right tone in his voice: I was going to make it up with him. Lovely.

She came further down the stairs. "He never talked about a son. I am truly sorry you didn't get to see him before he died, just for that reason. But of course you can substantiate your identity?"

His head lifted slightly, warily, the mountain cat now detecting a scent; something had changed mightily in the several minutes they had been talking—he felt it at once. Everything about her had changed from outright fear to a subtle confidence.

"No, ma'am, I can't," he said cheerfully.

"I didn't expect you could," she murmured. "We'll just have to disbelieve each other, I'm afraid. I certainly can't let you in my house merely on your say-so that you are my husband's son. And you must understand that since I never heard of a son prior to today, I can't in good conscience welcome you into my home. Now—you go on back to Mr. James Greve, and you tell him everything I said."

He really admired her gumption. She was right down at the bottom of the staircase now, looking right up at him with that blazing assurance, and her words totally bewildered him.

"Excuse me, ma'am?"

She even appreciated his very realistic confusion. "You tell Mr. Greve what I said: you're very good, but you didn't fool me, you hear?"

He felt a flash of anger. "I wasn't trying to fool you, ma'am. It's just as I said. I came home to see my father, and I'm damned sorry it's too late."

She smiled. "That's good. That's very good. Where did Mr. Greve find you?"

Now her smugness was getting to him. Maybe Jesse

96

was right: there was something to be said for females who knew their place. "I'm just going to plant myself here until you listen to me."

"That's fine," she said complacently. "Mr. Greve should be around in a day or two . . . maybe a week . . . and then we'll have it out. You just stay there. But mind you let Sully close the door at night. You'll have to decide if you want to stay inside or out."

"Now wait a minute . . ."

"*You* wait a minute, you barbarian. You can't come barging into my home, pretending to be someone you're not, and . . ."

"Who's pretending, damn it? You won't even listen to a word I'm saying!"

"You can't prove it, and I don't know anything about it, and you just get out of my house."

"I'm not moving."

"Fine. You can be my human totem pole. But you cannot be my husband's son."

She glared at him. He glowered at her.

And into the raging silence walked Mr. James Greve.

"What is all the shouting? I could hear you down the drive, for heaven's sake. And who is this man?"

Cassandra wheeled on him angrily. "What do you mean, who is this person? You know perfectly well who—"

She stopped short at the sight of his face, his bland, open, curious expression as he surveyed the height of the stranger as if he had never seen him before, and the slippery stranger took instant advantage of her momentary hesitation. He moved like a mountain cat, getting between her and Mr. Greve with the ease of a knife sliding through butter, his hand extended, the words right on his lips before she could say another word.

"I'm Coltrane Taggart, sir."

Her eyes never left Mr. Greve's face and his response irritated her; if he knew the man-mountain, he was a better actor than all of them put together. He grasped the stranger's hand in a hearty grip, saying in a smug, just-between-us-men tone of voice that rankled her mightily, "I was wondering when you would get all-fired weary of all her endless questions and letters, and come to see to matters yourself."

But he hadn't been wondering at all; he was damned flabbergasted by this turn of events, and the rustic appearance of Jesse Taggart's son. "I'm James Greve, Jesse Taggart's lawyer and the administrator of his estate. But Mrs. Taggart has written you all about that." He turned to Cassandra and went on, "I told you that you shouldn't be bothering him about every little nit and nay that goes on around here."

"Mr. Taggart assured me it was no bother," Cassandra said coldly, deliberately ignoring the man-mountain, who looked very amused. "Mr. Taggart was *quite* sure that he would not be paying a visit to Georgia anytime soon, and indicated he was happy to help with *any* little problems. I cant imagine why this man showed up here."

She looked at him defiantly, daring him to answer.

Mr. Greve stepped into the question directly. "He wanted to see things for himself, obviously. I will be happy to sit down with him and . . ."

"Excuse me," Cassandra interrupted, her voice still dripping ice. "I believe that Mr. Taggart has no jurisdiction over what I do, nor has this gentleman proved to my satisfaction that he *is* Coltrane Taggart. Now, Mr. Greve, if we have business . . ."

"This is rude," Mr. Greve said chidingly, a little put out because he wanted very much to talk with Coltrane Taggart; he needed every bit of information from this man, including the family history that Jesse Taggart had not thought to tell him — anything that would help him prick a little loophole in the will. And he didn't need Miz Taggart's obdurate nature interfering once again.

"Who else *could* he be?" he demanded, a shade belligerently.

"He has no credentials," Cassandra said, holding the man-mountain's bland, cool blue gaze.

"Where are you staying, sir?" Mr. Greve asked.

"What does that prove?"

"I took a room at the Riversgate," the man-mountain said, his voice laced with amusement.

"Well, there. The Riversgate wouldn't rent to someone who was not a gentleman."

"I stand corrected," Cassandra said drily. "The stranger is a gentleman. We still don't know if he is Coltrane Taggart."

"Test him," Mr. Greve said.

"Excuse me?"

"Test him, the way you did in your letters," Mr. Greve amplified. "Coltrane Taggart would surely know things about the house and grounds that you do but that an impostor wouldn't."

"I —" Her voice stuck in her throat. Test him . . . oh, Lord. Test him on what, when she knew nothing about his life at Riveland except what she had invented for her letters . . .

"I'm agreeable, ma'am," the man-mountain said, easing himself into the conversation for the first time.

Slippery, she thought again, and her heart started to pound. If he were the actor she thought he was, he would have come prepared to answer some questions. A man-mountain just didn't barge into a plantation like Riveland and expect people to accept him for who he said he was. He was smarter than that.

His lips twitched underneath the disreputable-looking brush of mustache and beard. "Ma'am?"

"Mr. Taggart answered all my questions in his letters. I really don't see the point of interrogating this pretender, Mr. Greve. He can't be Mr. Taggart, because Mr. Taggart is in Baltimore."

"So I was," the man-mountain agreed smoothly, "but it

99

happened I had some business down Charleston way, and I figured I was probably close enough to pay you a visit."

"Did you, now?" Cassandra murmured. "How kind of you to send word ahead, sir."

"Wasn't time for that, ma'am. Caught a steamboat heading downriver to pick up a load of cotton and figured I'd go while the going was good."

"How opportune," she agreed with alacrity.

"I'm mighty impressed by my welcome back to Riveland," he added for good measure, and she knew he was still laughing at her. She didn't know what else he knew, except that she was in a bind because of Mr. Greve's request and he was very willing to help her out and secure his identification.

Well, she wasn't going to hide behind pretty words and flowery phrases. He and Greve had to have cooked this up between them, and she was going to make sure they both got burned for coming too close to the fire.

"No one has welcomed you back to Riveland, sir," she said edgily.

"Well, ma'am, I must tell you—just riding up that old driveway one more time, I felt a real sense of homecoming."

"The flora, the fauna and the stablehands embraced you?" she interpolated caustically.

"Something like that, ma'am, except of course there are all new people here, and the servants and workers I grew up with were obviously sold before Jesse went seeking a new wife."

"This is true," Mr. Greve put in. "Mr. Daggett mentioned that very fact to me just the other day."

Cassandra's blazing green gaze smote him before he could say another word. "We will discuss another time the advisability of your taking up Riveland's business with my overseer," she said cuttingly. "Meantime, I wish that this stranger would remove himself so I may go on about my business." She turned away from both of them,

100

toward the staircase, hoping—praying—that they both would just go away before she had to deal with Mr. Greve's request that she test the man-mountain.

"I expect Mrs. Taggart and Jesse shared the same room as he and the first Mrs. Taggart," the man-mountain said, his voice confidential and carrying, at the same time that she put one foot up on the riser. "Biggest room on the second floor—center of the house—the one that opens out onto the balcony. Jesse used to like to go out and sit there in the early evening and kind of survey all that was his, isn't that right, Mrs. Taggart?"

She stepped up to the next riser, and then turned around to face him. "Mr. Taggart did no such thing during our marriage, sir." No, he kept the curtains closed and the lights down low, and he had kept her intimidated beyond all reason with his demands for a son.

And she had given him one finally, and this buckskin barbarian was not *he;* it was some kind of plot, and she was not going to let either him or Mr. Greve outwit her.

Besides, there could be a dozen ways that this silky stranger could have learned about the layout of Riveland. For all she knew, Mr. Greve could have gone skulking around Riveland without her knowledge. Sully wasn't authorized to deny him whatever he might have asked; Sully would have known only that he had visited Missus Taggart, and that would have made him someone to obey.

"We did not share the center room," she added politely. "That was given over to my mother while she was alive, so your assumptions prove nothing, sir."

She hated the light in his eye; it meant he was up to the challenge and he would not let her set one more foot up the steps.

Well, she was up to his challenge, whoever he was. If Coltrane Taggart weren't a figment of her imagination, she really would have been tempted to believe him; he was a wonderful actor.

She squared her shoulders. "Jesse Taggart was a mean-spirited man who never talked about his first wife, nor about his son. There is nothing in this house to suggest he ever had either, if it comes to that, so your vast knowledge of where things *were* sir, is meaningless to *me*."

That set him back a step. But he recovered.

"Nevertheless, ma'am, it does make you my step-mama," he told her kindly, as if this were the one thing she had been waiting to hear.

"It doesn't make me your step-anything," she growled at him, "except one step away from having you thrown out." She had never experienced such frustration; how did one get rid of a man-mountain without having him carried away bodily? "You haven't proved you are Coltrane Taggart to my satisfaction. *He* is in Baltimore and *you* are trespassing."

"I don't believe he is," Mr. Greve said suddenly.

"I don't believe *you*," she retorted.

"Miz Taggart . . ."

"Mr. Greve—"

"You can't send away Mr. Taggart's son."

She felt like biting him. "Mr. Taggart would never pop up on my doorstep like this. You saw his last letter. He wouldn't leave his family—"

"No, ma'am, I surely wouldn't," the man-mountain assured her, "except that—"

"I don't want to hear it . . ."

"—the chance came along and I knew it was almost seeding time at Riveland and . . . and since Jesse had always done that and this was your first time . . ."

He was so damned clever, she wanted to choke him. He was making it all up as he went along, pulling the clues out of the conversation and the air. Every plantation along the little Midway was putting up seed; it was such a good guess, it was disquieting.

"Well, you see," Mr. Greve said.

". . . I thought I'd come and see to helping you myself," the man-mountain finished, with that air of talking

102

to a recalcitrant child.

"I'm much obliged you upped and just left your family," Cassandra said, unyielding to the last inch. That explanation hardly sat squarely with her, and he sensed it.

"Oh, no—no, ma'am. I didn't just up and leave them. I was on business in Charleston, as I told you. Of course I made sure they were adequately taken care of." He smiled at her benignly, his light, bright gaze taking in every nuance of expression on her lovely face. Her skepticism was palpable and her unwavering green gaze was distracting. "I could never have rested easy if I thought any harm could come to my . . . dear wife and my sweet children."

"Oh yes—the children," she murmured. "Are there a lot of them, Mr. . . . . Taggart?"

He noted her use of the name. "A whole houseful, ma'am," he returned promptly, his senses immediately alert. "You'll be amazed when you meet them," he added, buying a moment's extra time.

But how many? How many? Damn her, what number had she conceived in her mind and what had she told that ass Greve, who was looking at him expectantly. He was operating on pure gut feeling, or he might have been amused at the thoroughness of her inventing of him. But he had to pass this test, and there was just one second where he caught a glimmer in her eye that told him more than words or emotion: she had concocted the most outrageous and viable number she could think of, and she dared him to come up with the number.

What number, what number? How many children would keep the estimable fictional Mr. Taggart *very* busy?

"Three boys," he said carefully, and went on, "th-ree girls—" Yes! Able guess, by the merest twist of her lips, and what else, what *else?* "—and perhaps more good news likely soon," he added triumphantly, embroidering still further, successfully, by the look on her face.

You damned quick-witted, lying rogue! This is MY cre-

103

ation, MY Coltrane Taggart! Don't you dare usurp him.
She clenched her fists in the folds of her dress, unable to deny it, because she couldn't remember whether or not she had told Greve, or whether it had been mentioned in one of her letters.

"Well, there you are," Mr. Greve said.

"I find myself nowhere," she said, forcefully keeping her temper. "I find it very hard to believe that Mr. Taggart would conscionably leave home, preparing to do business, and not take one piece of identification with him."

The perceptive witch. "It was stolen, ma'am."

"Oh truly, how convenient. Before or after you came to Georgia?" she asked sweetly, dangerously.

"It was a very disreputable steamer," he retorted.

"So it's possible that any day now some other *gentleman* might turn up on my doorstep claiming to be Mr. Coltrane Taggart, is that right?"

She had him there. "Anything is possible, ma'am. But he wouldn't know much about Riveland. And he surely wouldn't be claiming you as just his stepmomma," he added, his light, bright gaze swooping over her from head to foot in the most insinuating way possible.

The arrogant bastard. "Neither are you," she shot back. "You have no claims whatsoever, Mr. Whoever You Are, so you might just as well go back wherever you came from." She turned to Greve. "I want this man out of here."

He shrugged.

And the man-mountain intervened again. "Coltrane Taggart has *no* claims on his daddy's estate?"

Finally! She had him. "Mr. Taggart was fully informed of all the provisions of his father's will," she told him, trying to keep the gloating note out of her voice. Let the impostor wrestle with that, she thought triumphantly; let him give up in disgrace and get out of her house. It looked unlikely that there was any other way to remove him other than to prove that he was lying. How nice he had handed her the opportunity on a silver salver.

He stopped himself from answering back by sheer force of will. *Fully informed of all the provisions of his father's will . . . ALL the provisions*—what kind of provisions? He needed every ounce of deductive reasoning for this one. *All the provisions . . .* Which meant what? The baby bride inherited? And her fictional Coltrane Taggart, limp-wristed weakling that he was, had accepted *that?*

She was waiting for him to say something, and there was that look in her eye again, as if she could almost follow his thought processes. It was damned unnerving to have a woman look at a man like that, especially if she were as beautiful as Jesse's baby bride. And had the snap of the whip in her voice, and steel in her ribcage, and more determination than ten men to defeat him.

He admired that, he truly did. She wasn't a baby, and she was hardly a bride now, and there was something in her combative stance that spoke of her treatment at Jesse's hands; it was the thing in her that made her so hellbent on vanquishing him.

On some level, he wished he could let her succeed; she was a worthy opponent, and she had him on the question of the provisions of Jesse's will. He just had to think his way out of this obstacle—and fast.

"Maybe I had second thoughts," he said slowly, his lightning gaze still riveted on her face. "Maybe I came to see for myself . . ." No, that wasn't the tack. "Maybe I'm . . . maybe I'm thinking about . . ." *Hell,* about *what?* ". . . about an investigation." Damn—a horseshoe in the air— going nowhere—

But she reacted. Again, the faintest movement of her mouth, a thinning, an anger quickly hidden, and her composure regained. A thought to be pursued. Furiously, he assessed what that word could mean to her. A court might hear testimony about their marriage, and Jesse's state of mind when he died. They would dredge up the old stories about Jesse and his son and make a lot out of that — probably enough so that it made sense that Jesse had disinherited his only son, especially if he thought he were going to conceive a whole new brood of sons.

What would an investigation find?

Something to do with the will, something to do with Jesse's son. Something to do with Jesse — what could scare her so?

How Jesse died?

She wished he wouldn't look at her so closely. She didn't have the luxury of allowing herself a single untoward thought, lest it be revealed in her expression, and she felt terrified now and couldn't let a minute of it show. Investigation. God, this man-monster was turning her world upside down in the space of thirty minutes. He was quick, intuitive, and there was something on his mind that had nothing to do with Coltrane Taggart.

She couldn't let him walk out the door if he were threatening an investigation. She felt that close to murder; if Mr. Greve hadn't been standing right in the hallway, she would have devised a way. *Investigation.* Her heart pounded painfully. They would find her guilty of murder and she would truly have nowhere to go; she would be jailed for the rest of her life. Amazing how Jesse had taken care of even that possibility in his hellish will.

She had to be strong, she could not back down an inch, or this man-mountain would *sit* on her, and she would never find out who he was or his purpose in pretending he was a man who did not exist.

"There is nothing to investigate," she said firmly, "as you would well know — if you were Mr. Taggart, which you are not. There is nothing more to discuss."

So strong, he thought admiringly. But he couldn't be diverted by that. He needed to figure out why the lily-livered Coltrane Taggart of her dreams wouldn't have

106

questioned a will that cut him out directly. *Why?* Because a man didn't write letters about things of such a monumental nature, damn it.

"Perhaps it was something that was not to be discussed in a letter, Mrs. Taggart," he said silkily.

She started. He had an answer for everything, didn't he, and it just proved how slippery he was, and how dangerous.

And maybe she, in her innocence, had given him all the clues he needed to piece it together so he could intimidate her.

She didn't know. Maybe she would never know, but if the man-mountain walked out her door this afternoon, she would live in torment until he made good his threat. And she would live in terror if she had to acknowledge him as Coltrane Taggart when they both knew Coltrane Taggart did not exist.

And now she had to tread very, very carefully. The man was daunting, both in his appearance and his lethal words, and she still did not know if he and Mr. Greve were in league with each other.

She knew nothing except her feeling of foreboding that everything was about to come crashing down on her head.

"There is nothing that cannot be discussed in a letter," she said finally, matching his tone. "Mr. Taggart and I are in complete accord about *everything*."

"And so we are," he agreed neatly. "But it would be unseemly of a son not to request an explanation of every facet of his father's last year; surely you agree that that is fair and proper."

"Mr. Taggart assured me . . ." she began heatedly, and then stopped.

She was letting down her guard, letting him smell her fear. Oh, the mountain cat in him inhaled the scent as if it were perfume. He fed on it; he watched her with those lancing, bright eyes that were so disquieting.

107

"Apparently it was of no consequence to Mr. Taggart," she began again, her voice calmer, in control. "He had made his fortune by the sea and wanted no part of his father's legacies. It is hardly my place to inquire into the details."

His fortune, eh? Coltrane Taggart a wealthy man! It was amusing. In reality, Taggart was a man who had lived for far too long by the seat of his pants, a man who had to see the down side of thirty years before he realized it. Some men never had second chances. But he aimed to take his. He just didn't know how to coerce this golden witch into letting him grab for the golden ring after Jesse had tossed it to her.

"But still—a man would want to see evidence of his father's denial of him, don't you think, Mrs. Taggart?"

"I don't think," she snapped, out of patience with him and her overriding fear. "I think you have overstayed your welcome, and you are not entitled to any further explanations, since Mr. Taggart has all the facts at his disposal in Baltimore." Oh Lord, she had cast the stone. She couldn't bear it anymore. She wanted him out, in spite of his threats. "I bid you—"

"Now, Miz Taggart." Mr. Greve at last, showing some mettle—or, she hoped, about to implicate himself somehow. She waited expectantly, her heart thumping so loudly she was sure both he and the stranger could hear it.

"I think you cannot know whether this man is Coltrane Taggart—"

"Nor can you," she retorted.

"And," he continued, ignoring her, "we need to delve into this a good deal more carefully than just standing in the doorway and bandying words."

"*We* don't."

"I believe he is Mr. Taggart."

"*I* don't."

"I believe he is entitled to the answers to his questions."

108

"Then you answer them."

"Miz Taggart," he said patiently, "I think we should meet again in the morning after a good night's sleep."

"Good. Go away." She felt near to tears. The man-mountain would leave and immediately in the morning contact a judge and that would be the end of it. All of it. She hated Riveland, but she did not want to languish in jail. Oh, damn it. She took a hard, deep breath to pull back on her frustrated emotions. She had to get a grip on herself. She had to find out who this man was; she had to protect herself.

"We'd be wasting a lot of time if we went back to town," the man-mountain said. "Two hours back, two hours here . . ."

"Oh?" She felt a wallop of relief: *he* wanted to stay and he was giving her a way out. And she wanted him right where she could keep her eye on him, but she couldn't betray that to him. She couldn't just leap on his veiled suggestion. "I see. You walk into my house claiming you are someone you're not, and then you expect me to offer hospitality while you tyrannize me with accusations and threats?"

"That's about it, ma'am," he agreed cheerfully. "Besides that, I gave up my room at the Riversgate."

"Because you probably couldn't pay for it," she retorted.

"Unkind, ma'am."

"Then that presupposes you were sure of your welcome."

"I expected to be reunited with my daddy," he said softly, edging into the lie. "And I got me a new step-momma instead."

"You got you nothing," Cassandra said tartly, "except a room for the night. It would tarnish Riveland's reputation for hospitality if I sent you back to Carthage at this hour."

"I wasn't aware Riveland had . . ." Mr. Greve began.

109

"It doesn't," Cassandra said succinctly, and then turned and called loudly: "Zilpha!"

She appeared instantly, as if she had been waiting beyond a door somewhere close by. "Ma'am?"

"These gentlemen will be staying the night. Please ready two rooms and inform the cook and ask Sully to decant a bottle of wine and some whiskey for the gentlemen. They will also want to wash, and perhaps we can find a fresh shirt for each of them among Mr. Taggart's belongings . . . if you gentlemen don't mind?"

"Oh no," Mr. Greve protested. "No need."

"Much obliged," the man-mountain said simultaneously.

"I will see you at dinner then, Mr. Greve and . . . what *shall* I call you?"

"Oh, Trane will do just fine, ma'am. All my *friends* call me Trane."

Chapter Eight

The man-mountain had unmitigated gall.

All my friends call me Trane . . .

She couldn't get over it. So there was no question: she would have to sneak into Mr. Impostor Taggart's room and search his belongings for some clue to his identity.

She had planned it all out during dinner when Mr. Greve obligingly relieved her of the burden of having to carry the conversation.

It was, in some ways, very simple. She had to somehow immobilize the mountain who moved like a cat, or else he would devour her. Two short pieces of rope would do it, easy to obtain from Ojim after she courteously dispatched her guests to the library to take brandy.

She had put Mr. Greve at the far end of the hall, and with no little malice, she had given "all my friends call me Trane" the central room that he had so movingly described as having been Jesse's and his first wife's.

It was very plain to see how he had devised that little bit of business. All the windows of that room, and the balcony, were the first thing one saw coming up the drive. So easy to concoct a little story like that: the floor was the bedroom floor; therefore the center windows must be a bedroom.

Her mother had loved that room too, loved the view. Wanted to be exactly where she could see company coming. She had expected it. But company never came, and she could never understand it.

Cassandra shook away the memory. The most important thing now was to catch the pretender in his lies to be sure he had no claim whatsoever on Riveland—or her.

. . . they say . . .

Another disquieting little voice, dredged up from memory or imagination, assaulted her, and she shook that away, too, before it gave words to the thought that hovered tantalizingly around her consciousness.

She twirled the two pieces of rope around her fingers as she paced edgily around the room. You had to take your enemy before he could take you, she thought, girding herself. And you didn't fool around with a mountain lion who was as quick as a crack of lightning. You got him in restraints before you even got near the cage.

So be it.

She had prepared herself as well: she had changed back into the lifeless calico dress that gave her such freedom of movement, and she had put on a pair of soft slippers.

It was almost time . . .

She opened the door and peeked out. Silence. But there was a finger of light just beneath the stranger's door.

She closed her door and leaned against it. She wouldn't even have to work in the dark, she thought, once she had bound up his hands. She could have a light. She could stand over him and gloat when she found the thing she sought: proof of his duplicity. And then he could not investigate anything. He would just have to go away.

Two deep resonant bongs tolled the time, and now when she slipped into the hallway, she saw that everywhere it was dark and everything was quiet.

There was a matte stillness all over the house, all over her. She felt calm and confident. Righteous.

She moved down the hallway to his room and gently tested the knob. It turned readily in her hand, and she paused a moment to check that she had both pieces of rope. The darkness enveloped her, and she opened the door and slipped into his room.

Here now was the scent of *him* — rustic, unreal, outside anything she had ever known. For the first time she faltered. His sleeping presence was a living thing in that room.

. . . all my friends . . .

The sheer audacity of that statement propelled her forward. She put out her hand to feel for the cool marble surface of the dresser right on the wall by the door. From there, she edged into the room and around its perimeter, groping as she went along, seeking an article of clothing, his bag — anything.

Too dark. Her searching hand touched the pine bedframe too soon and she recoiled.

She sank to her knees and felt around on the floor — there, his boots, mud-encrusted, molded to the shape of his long legs. Her hand slid up the elongated shaft, probing for a cut in the leather, some place of concealment, but there was nothing.

She groped around some more near the washstand where Zilpha had provided towels and a bar of soap, and then turned back and crawled around the bed.

No clothing anywhere on the floor. Nothing but the boots. And no bag.

Now, near the fireplace — her hand came in contact with the tufted chair beside it and the rough feel of cowhide — well-used cowhide, soft, pliable to the touch: his jacket.

She pulled it down and ransacked his pockets. A knife. A flint. Silver. A comb. So little, and no papers. She felt as though this dearth of belongings were mocking her.

She folded the jacket and placed it back as best she could and moved forward again, her hand groping. It was eerie, crawling around like an animal in the dark. All her senses were alert, everything keenly focused on her quest, her stomach knotting as each foray yielded nothing.

113

She groped for a piece of furniture and got to her feet. He had to be wearing his trousers. She would have to go after his hands, and she hadn't, in her heart of hearts, wanted to grapple with that.

Nevertheless, the die was cast and she edged over to the bed; biting her lips, she stretched out her hand to get some sense of where he lay.

Oh God, his leg . . . He was too close, and she might have known it. She stifled a sound as her hand came in contact with the rough fabric of his trousers and the heavy weight of his leg. He was sleeping on his side, his back to her—his arms folded across his chest, his legs angled upward, the cover thrown carelessly over the foot of the bed.

Oh Lord . . . no telling when or if he would turn . . . and if she grabbed for his hand she would awaken him, and *then* where would she be?

He moved—the bedsprings depressed and she heard the shift of his body settling in a new position.

Her heartbeat drummed in her ears as she tentatively reached out to ascertain the new placement of his body and touched bare skin, and she flinched.

But this was no time to be a coward. A body at rest was not the same as a beast in a body; this was not Jesse, this was a man of inordinate guile who had to be neutralized before he convinced anyone he was Trane Taggart, a figment of *her* imagination.

Her hand skimmed his torso. He was lying belly up now, almost as if he were inviting her to explore his body, one arm dangling down off the edge of the mattress.

How perfect.

She took a deep shuddering breath and pulled one piece of rope down from around her neck where she had worn it, looped it, and slid the loop over his wrist and pulled it tight.

* * *

It was the last thing in the world he expected as he waited tensely to see what she would do next. He felt his arm being jerked upward and then just suspended there.

Hell-damn-fire.

Jesse's baby bride had some damned gumption, tackling him in the dark in bed like this. But he had been cornered in worse situations. All a man had to do was keep his sense of humor.

All a man had to do was just let her carry out her little scheme and turn the whole thing backward on her. A man didn't need two good hands for that.

He waited in the silence and he heard her, finally, and felt her presence on the other side of the bed, felt her surprisingly strong hands grasp his other arm, loop something rough around his wrist, felt her pull and then lift his right arm to immobilize it as well.

Well, well . . .

He heard the scrape of a flint, and then the dull glow of the kerosene lamp limned her body as she turned to face him.

And then he saw exactly what he thought she had done: she had bound both of his arms at the wrists and tied them to the bedposts, and she was standing over him enjoying the sight, damn her.

For one fulminating moment, he felt like a fly caught in the web of a damned black widow spider. And she was going to crawl all over him and take pieces of him, nip by nip, and she looked as if she was going to enjoy every moment of it.

On the other hand, he might enjoy every moment of it, too. A man could never tell where he might find the opportunity to savor something unusual.

"I hate to see my guests in a bind, Mr. Impossible," she said sweetly, setting the lamp down on the dresser. "But we really like to make everyone feel comfortable and secure."

"Much obliged, ma'am," he growled. "I couldn't feel

more attached to Riveland if I lived here myself."

She smiled graciously, still rather astonished that she had seemingly caught him so completely by surprise. She rather lied the idea of him trussed up and squirming. It made him less overpowering, a mere mortal man with a particularly hairy chest.

"Try to show some restraint, sir. You haven't proved your identity yet."

"My dear Mrs. Taggart, I don't intend to confine my remarks to the mundane. It becomes obvious why you are here."

"Indeed—it was necessary to control you in order for me to search your room—and now *you*."

"I'm captivated by the thought," he murmured, and she stiffened warily at the glint in his eye.

It was time to make the next bold move, and even with all her courage, she still had to find enough brazenness within her to reach over his body and unfasten his pants so she could whip them off.

With him watching.

Especially with him watching.

And those eyes—those glimmering, light, bright eyes . . .

She kept her own eyes resolutely on the task at hand: the nerveless fingers of her left hand inserted themselves into the waistband of his trousers to lift it closer for better access to the buttons—

The heat of his bare skin scorched the knuckles of her hand and she felt like thrusting an elbow into his nose. Her fingers made short work of the button closure and she darted around to the foot of the bed, grasped the ends of the legs and pulled hard.

He grunted as she ripped his pants from his body and held them up triumphantly.

He smiled his crooked smile. "Search away, black widow," he invited mockingly, as an interesting new complication presented itself even as he watched.

116

There was something very enticing about being held in thrall by a woman who was determined to undress him.

He watched her fascinatedly to see what she would do next.

Her eyes were riveted on his groin and his irrepressible manhood and its unmistakable bulge.

Her lips thinned. She knew all about the untamed parts of a man's body, and his was no different from Jesse's. She just happened to have had the foresight to keep the rest of his body in check, and so she felt no threat from his stiffening masculinity. She was rather pleased with herself, actually, and her compressed lips turned into a pleased little smile as she began rifling through the pockets of his pants in a most businesslike manner.

He had to be prescient: there was absolutely nothing in his pockets, front or back. She threw the pants aside in disgust and threw a long, speaking look in his direction.

"*I* have nothing to hide, black widow," he murmured, his voice laced with amusement again.

Time to match him, wit for wit, word for word. He didn't scare her. He couldn't do anything while he was tethered to the bedpost. She was willing to take her chances. She could be as impudent as he. She really was enjoying the vision of her nemesis in subjugation.

"I want to see for myself," she said audaciously, coming around again to the side of the bed. "Buttons are such a nuisance," she added apologetically, as she reached for the waistband of his thick cotton drawers. "It really gives a woman an appreciation of how men feel when they are confronted with them."

"It really can be irritating to work around—*obstructions*," he agreed silkily.

She shot him a pained look. "But not too *hard*," she muttered, as she made short work of the row of buttons, her fingers brushing tormentingly against his manhood without her giving any sign that anything at all was unusual.

117

She went around again to the foot of the bed. "It's entirely possible you somehow bound your papers against your body in a least likely place," she told him, frowning as she pulled on the legs of his drawers and the conspicuous protrusion in the most likely place surged into view.

He was hiding nothing beneath his clothes except a mass of wiry hair that furred his chest and grew in an inviting line downward toward his genitals and then fanned out all over his long, long legs.

There was only one thing to see, and that was his beautifully made body and his towering male member thrusting so masterfully upward.

She looked him up and down as if she were standing some distance away. She knew everything she did not want to know about what men did to women and how it was accomplished. Jesse had been a rutting pig—nothing more, nothing less—never interested in the delicacy and intricacies of her sex or his own.

And she could envision very well what a mountain of this size could do to her in the dark if she had not gotten the best of him. Here was the proof standing proud and tall, a conqueror at the ready and no willing victim.

It was a curious thing, all thick, hard, rounded flesh that somehow elongated itself into an angle of possession from which there was no escape.

And if his hands had been free, she would have had to run for her life by now. He would have had her, had he caught her skulking around his bedroom like that. He would have vanquished her and made her pay the price.

She came around once again to the side of the bed, and bent over him.

She was the conqueror this time, and he could do nothing but lie still, lashed to the bed, leashed to her will.

She paced around the bed, looking at him from all angles, trying to make some sense of his nudity and the complete essence of him distilled into that one centered

118

part of his body.

It wasn't a weapon, a symbol of brute force as she remembered it. It was only skin, only flesh, thick and hot, tactile and mysterious, inflexibly *male,* inexorably *there.*

She didn't know quite how she felt being confronted by the most purely masculine part of him, but she was aware suddenly of his avid gaze.

"Never had a woman wanted me so bad she'd tie me up to have me," he murmured, just a little discomfitted by her dispassionate perusal of him.

"They just must not have known how to get a leg up on you," she retorted softly, and the look in his eyes deepened.

The thought was gorgeous, but he couldn't tell what she would do next, or even if she would do anything. He knew what he wanted her to do, but that was pure wishful thinking. There was something about the black widow that seemed curiously untouched.

She had him and she didn't know quite what she wanted to do with him. The most irksome thing was that she had really come looking for something that would identify him, and now she was confronted by the very thing that confirmed his voracious maleness.

The situation aroused him, and he didn't know if it were because she had been Jesse's wife or because her air of innocence touched him. If he had his hands, she would not now be on her feet. He clamped down on the thought as she moved again; this was no time to alienate her. His ferocious manhood couldn't stand it.

The atmosphere in the room changed to one of unalloyed latent sensuality.

"Touch me, Cassandra," he whispered; he had to try.

Her head snapped up almost involuntarily. *"You're* touched, Mr. Impostor. I'd rather bury you. I think I *will* bury you," she added vengefully, because she did not know what else to do, and she hated his smug surety; she had him helpless, and yet she was still more impotent

119

than he. She wished she hadn't started with him at all. She wished—Her agitated hand came in contact with the cover on the footboard, and she grasped at it and threw it onto his body. It drifted downward softly to cover his belly gently.

"You've barely concealed the evidence," he taunted her.

"I'll make sure I cover it up completely," she hissed, coming around again to the bedside and grasping the edge of the blanket to yank it upward.

"I'd like to cover you," he growled, watching her carefully, waiting for the moment she was right by his side, and then he thrust himself upward and shot his right leg outward to circle her body and tumble her onto his blanket-shrouded torso.

His body twisted agonizingly to the right to give him the leverage to wrap his long, strong legs around her like a vise; the rigid length of him was like an iron bar between them, and she was disturbingly aware of its fulsome power and her helplessness.

She still had her hands; she pushed at him and pulled, and she pummeled his naked legs and thighs in a frantic fury.

"Now who is trapped in the web?" he muttered, constricting his legs more tightly around her waist and twisting them both to the left so that she had to lie on top of him, her punishing fists braced against his chest and pushing with all her might.

"Let me *go*," she ground out, thrusting her body upward again, so that she was straining against his legs—and his increasing frustration at his shackled arms.

"Then we'll sleep the night trapped in each other's web, black widow. I'm looking forward to it."

She pushed away again. *Sleep* with him! The silence lengthened interminably while she grappled with that. What would she be willing to do, after all, to get out of that room? She would not sleep with him. And he couldn't possibly—without the use of his hands.

What could he mean? What could he *want?*

"What *is* your price," she whispered finally. She was too tired now, and he seemed to have inexhaustible strength. The pressure of his legs around her had not abated, nor had he begged for mercy. His manhood was like an iron rod digging into her stomach, and her one overriding desire was to get away from him and his enveloping sex as fast as she could; otherwise it would become permanently imprinted on her body.

She wasn't sure it hadn't happened already.

He smiled tightly at her capitulation. He felt a whole storehouse of conflicting emotions about her. But first and foremost, he wanted her and he could see the thought of it scared her to death.

But a man had to begin somewhere, he thought. He would not be leaving Riveland any too soon. There was always time on his side. Time to begin, time to pursue, a time to embrace—

"Kiss me," he commanded, and she reared back, shocked.

"Never."

He smiled that odd crooked smile. She was too beautiful, too tantalizing. He *needed* that kiss. "My price, black widow."

"Your pride, you mean," she said belligerently.

"Value it how you will; that is what I want."

"You'll have to prize it from me."

"Oh no, my lady—willingly; I would never force you."

She laughed derisively. "No, you would never use force."

He tugged at his bonds. "Neither, apparently, would you. And yet here we are and the choices are plain: you pay the price or we sleep together for what is left of the night."

Or what was left of her nerves. She wriggled against him uncomfortably, well aware she was only making matters worse.

121

He sensed her capitulation. "Come, kiss me."

"How can I even find your lips in that bush of hair?" she demanded querulously.

"You'll find them," he assured her. "Come closer."

Her expression was positively tormented as she lowered her head, her eyes tightly closed, hoping against hope to swipe his mouth and be done with it.

But the strength and will of the man were something she hadn't reckoned with. He lifted his head to meet hers, and slanted his mouth across her with the utmost precision. She couldn't get away. His lips touched hers, seeking at first, and then probing with all the repressed hunger of a man who had been tried beyond his endurance.

And she knew nothing of those kinds of kisses; she knew Jesse's thick, rough kisses that bored deeply into her mouth, taking, sucking, overpowering, demanding only, possessing and leaving her bereft.

She didn't know how to respond to him, and her kiss was tentative, remote, and she was humiliated beyond all reason that this stranger should know this secret about her.

And it *was* a secret; for eight long, unimaginable years, Jesse Taggart had used her without a trace of tenderness and with no love whatsoever, and now she could not even keep up that pretense.

"Don't pull away," he whispered, torn by her innocence and his need to taste the womanliness of her.

"Don't do this to me."

"Kiss me again, Cassandra."

"I *can't*." She was so agitated she never heard his use of her name.

"One more time. One more sweet time, Cassandra, and I'll let you go."

She groaned deep in her throat, and bent her head forward once again.

Yes, it was better this time. Her mouth sought his

122

quickly to get it over with, but he wouldn't let her, not this time. Now he knew—his playful tongue entered her, seeking the sweet honey of her mouth.

This time, she had some idea of what she must do. Hesitantly, she gave him her tongue, and he took her, and this time she felt the pangs, like little well-aimed darts, assaulting her deep in some centered part of her in response to his heated kiss, and the uninhibited pulsation of his masculinity tight against her belly.

Slowly, his legs unwound from around her, and the moment she felt it, she pulled away from him so abruptly she almost fell off the bed.

And now she had to look at him again, and it was the hardest thing she ever had to do.

His eyes were guarded now, his body taut, waiting on her. "Untie me."

"I'll send Sully."

"*You* will untie me before you leave this room."

"What guarantees do I have?" she demanded cautiously.

"I won't follow you."

She nodded, swallowing hard. How had she come to *this?* She kept her eyes averted as she unknotted the rope and pulled it from around the bedposts. His arms dropped to his sides almost as if they had no motive power whatsoever.

She quelled her urge to touch them, to touch him.

He lifted himself onto his elbows, the long spare line of his naked body as elegant as a statue against the cover on the bed. "Good night, black widow," he said mockingly, and she knew she had gained nothing.

But neither had he.

And everything had been meaningless and part of some game she did not understand.

She could never run fast enough to elude him.

She closed the door behind her emphatically.

And listened outside.

And heard nothing.

It took a while before he could pull himself up to a sitting position so he could swing his legs over the edge of the mattress.

Damn, his arms were burning with the tension of being held aloft for the better part of an hour, and some other parts of him were throbbing with the tension of being held forcibly away . . . but that was another story.

He reached beside the bed for his boots.

He was absolutely sure she hadn't found it, but he had to make sure: it was the one thing he had made provision for, but nevertheless, a man had to be cautious where a black widow was concerned.

He held up the left boot and turned it upside down and steadied it between his knees so that the heel was upright. He gave it a quick little twist, and it turned on its hidden hinge.

He inserted his fingers to feel for the strongbox receipt, and he smiled in satisfaction as he came in contact with it, folded four times over and buried deep within the hollow heel of his battered, tattered boot.

Chapter Nine

She could not shake the sensation of his mouth on hers, his rock-hard body compressed against hers so tightly.

Black widow . . . black widow, oh yes. She dressed in severe black the following morning. She wanted no mistake about who was in charge and who still was the intruder. This nonsense about Trane Taggart had gone on long enough—dangerously long. He and Mr. Greve had been very clever about it; she marveled that they had almost convinced her that they had never met each other.

But she knew differently, and it was time to end all that and get on with the work of Riveland so that she could run her life the way she wanted it.

And if she wanted to do that, she thought, as she made her way downstairs, she was going to have to pretend the previous night had never happened.

He was alone in the dining room, a half-filled coffee cup by his side, finishing the remains of a rather bountiful breakfast. He was just lifting the cup once again when she entered the room, and he looked up at her with those light, bright eyes and she knew instantly he was not going to pretend nothing had happened, and she thought she just might die.

"Morning, ma'am. Join me. There's plenty here."

Like he owned the place, she thought resentfully, seating herself. Well, she couldn't just fold under every time the mountain spoke to her—she would never get rid of him.

Elsie sidled into the room. "Whut kin I get you, Missus?"

"Coffee will be fine," she said briskly "And fresh biscuits. Obviously Mr."—Oops—and she still hadn't called him by any name yet—"our guests were early risers."

"Yes, ma'am." Elsie didn't understand any of that. She heard "coffee" and "biscuits" and she knew just what to do. She returned within minutes with a hot pot, a fresh cup and a cloth-covered basket of steaming biscuits on a tray.

Cassandra poured the coffee and made an elaborate ritual of taking a fragrant, hot biscuit and buttering it. "Is Mr. Greve still asleep?" she asked casually, before taking a small manageable bite so she wouldn't have to speak to him further.

"Well, ma'am, he's gone."

She almost spit out the piece she was chewing. "I beg your pardon?"

"He's gone. Left at sunup."

Left before he had to give up the answers to my questions, she thought balefully. "He didn't even have the courtesy to tell me," she muttered, swallowing a long, hot mouthful of coffee. Too hot. She almost choked.

"No, ma'am. He probably thought you'd be sound asleep."

She sent him a searing look. "As I was."

"I was sure you were, ma'am." He took the pot and refilled his cup.

"And he just left *you* here."

"Thought you wouldn't mind—"

"I *mind* . . ."

"—too much."

"And you don't feel you've overstayed your welcome?"

He smiled crookedly. "I don't hardly feel I've been welcomed at all, ma'am."

"Just like the prodigal son," she said nastily, biting hard

126

into her biscuit the way she wanted to bite into him. Daylight did not make the situation better. He exuded power and surety, and she dearly wanted to defeat him.

"Exactly."

"Except that *you* are a prodigal and prodigious liar."

"Unkind, ma'am. What I am is Coltrane Taggart, and I'm damned if I know why you're having such a hard time believing it."

"We've been through all that, sir. I know who Coltrane Taggart is and where he is, and he's not here and you are not him," she said flatly.

He smiled that odd little smile again. "But what if I am?"

She pretended to consider the possibility. He really was something; he had an answer for everything, and if she really wanted to be charitable, she supposed she might thank him for keeping her mind off other things.

She shrugged. "You can't prove it."

"Nor can you," he said stringently, and her green gaze flashed to his instantly.

"And perhaps," she added airily, "you wouldn't have to, if Mr. Taggart had not contacted me several months prior to this. Too bad. Your scheme is just not going to work."

"There is no scheme," he said testily.

"You and Mr. Greve have been very convincing, I must say," she went on, as if he had not spoken. She bit into a second biscuit to allow her words to resonate in the turbulent silence.

He was definitely running out of that affable patience with her. Her skin tingled as he sipped his coffee and watched her like a predator over the rim of his cup. His expression told her he was not going to allow her to get away with anything, not even negating last night.

"I have to agree, ma'am," he said finally. "Mr. Greve had much to say that convinced me that you have a lot to lose here if Trane Taggart appeared out of nowhere. Too bad," he echoed, matching her tone, *"your* scheme is not going to work."

She dropped her cup, and driblets of coffee spattered all over the tablecloth, all over her. "What do you mean, Mr. Greve had much to say?"

He smiled again, and took his leisurely time reaching for a biscuit in the same infuriating way that she had done. "I mean, he wasn't averse to going over the conditions of the will once again with the man he believes to be Jesse Taggart's . . . issue."

She froze.

And then very slowly she lifted her coffee cup. If she were drinking, she didn't have to speak, and she would have a moment, maybe two, to consider how to fight Mr. Greve's betrayal of her express wishes. Damn the man—he had no loyalty at all if he were tattling her private business to a pure stranger— even if he believed him to be Trane Taggart.

She had to calm down, she had to combat Greve's treachery . . . but how? *How?* It had to be a conspiracy; it was the only answer.

And what did she have in her arsenal to use against it? Words—stupid, unenforceable words. And yet, there was no denying: the timing was suspicious. She had to hint at it. No, she had to say it outright, just to throw him off balance.

"*I* find it a little too coincidental that my husband's heretofore unheard of 'issue" conveniently appears on the heels of his father's death in order to contest a clause in the will that might remand everything over to *him,*" she said acidly. "And I find it a little too convenient that his own father's lawyer is the one volunteering this hitherto undisclosed information to the man who can make the most use of it, and who has the least proof that he is who he says he is. Now, don't you find that just a little *too* . . . advantageous, Mr. Charlatan Taggart?"

His fist slammed down on the table. "I'll tell you what I find just a little too convenient, black widow: the fact you say you never heard of Jesse Taggart's son. A saving grace in *your* favor, wouldn't you say? If you never heard of the

128

man, he can't exist, is that right? And when he turns up on your doorstep, you can deny him altogether. But strangely enough, stepmother of mine, you claim to have been corresponding with him since just after my father's death, and I find *that* specious as hell."

She could almost cave in against that heat. She couldn't let down her guard now. She clapped her hands loudly instead. "Bravo, bravo—perfect indignation, Mr. Impostor. Nicely done."

"I'm not *nearly* done, my dear Mrs. Taggart—not by a long shot. I swear I'm not leaving here until you acknowledge my identity *or* I decide to investigate Jesse Taggart's death."

She clamped down on that cold frisson of fear that his words sent spiraling through her, and raised herself slowly out of her chair. Now she must meet his threat, all sails flying in the wind. "Fine with me, stranger. You just stay put here where I can keep my eye on you. You're dangerous, sir, running around the county claiming to be Jesse's son. I'd rather institutionalize you because you're mad, but maybe you'll come to your senses before you do anything really out of line, and meantime I can counteract anything you might take it into your head to do. Yes, sir, that suits me fine. Just fine."

She was almost nose to nose with him, and her anger was palpable, fed by that dread word: investigation. She would do almost anything to prevent an investigation, even let a deranged stranger stay on Riveland.

After all, Mr. Greve would be a frequent visitor—the traitor—and Mr. Daggett was not too far away, nor Ojim. She would be perfectly fine, and he could try to convince her he was Trane Taggart, and then maybe, eventually, he would realize it was fruitless and he would just go away.

Short-lived hope. She looked into his eyes—his implacable light blue eyes which were hard with purpose now. He was her enemy—and she was his, and this challenge was nothing less than a duel over who had the right to own the persona of Mr. Coltrane Taggart.

She watched him, he watched her.

She couldn't fathom what he expected would happen if he stayed for any length of time on Riveland.

"Dat man am lookin' aroun' way too hard," Zilpha said one afternoon a day or two later.

Her head jerked up. "What do you mean?"

"He takin' notice of ever'thing now, Missus. He gonna start lookin' fo' dat Coltrane birthright, and he gonna find it—if dey is one."

"There isn't," Cassandra said firmly.

"He pretty sure, Missus."

"He is *not* Coltrane Taggart."

"He got de day fo' lookin' while you is busy wif Daggett or you is in de office," Zilpha pointed out stolidly. "Ain't no one gonna welcome a man who be like Mr. Jesse after all dat."

"No . . . ." Cassandra said thoughtfully. But she knew there was nothing in the house. She had gone over the rooms again and again years ago when she had come to Riveland as a bride, looking for some clue about his first wife, something that would tell her what she was doing wrong and what the other woman had presumably, prior to her death, done right.

But there wasn't even a hint of the presence of another woman in the whole of the house. Jesse had wiped her out as thoroughly as Cassandra had claimed he had obliterated her fictional Trane Taggart.

There was just nothing for the impostor to find.

"He checkin' out all de doors, Miz Taggart. He lookin' hard for some place dat ol' Mr. Taggart could've lef' somethin' fo' him," Zilpha said.

"*What* doors?"

"Dey's a whole floor up and over yo' head, Missus."

"I know that." But she hadn't discovered it until she had been hiding from Jesse one day, and she had opened a small, unobtrusive door at the end of the corridor on the bedroom floor. She had thought it was a closet and she would be safe, but it was the entrance to a steep, narrow, winding staircase, and when she climbed it, she found still another door at the top—heavy, forbidding, locked.

"I done watched dat man and den I gone to see whut he doin' up dem steps, Missus. I wouldn' be surprised if dey was ghosts up dem steps."

Cassandra looked at her thoughtfully. "The door is still locked?"

"Only dem ghosts kin get through *dat* door, Missus," Zilpha said emphatically.

"I think I'll go look at it."

She took a lamp. She remembered the space as being dank and stuffy, and dark. She remembered not having worn a wide hoop skirt the first time she climbed those steps.

Once again she donned the calico, so useful in tight situations, and she and Zilpha climbed the narrow staircase to the top and she touched the thick wood of the door.

There was a thick, black rectangular metal plate over the keyhole, and she ran her fingers over that, absolutely sure that Mr. Call-Me-Trane was already looking for the key. Where would Jesse have hidden such a thing, anyway?

She wished she were a ghost so that she could just haunt him and scare him away.

. . . haunt him—

She fingered the lock plate again.

If she could get in . . .

If she could lure him up there—

The lock plate was bolted into the wood. Something that was bolted *in* could be taken out, she thought, and *he* couldn't risk doing something so overt. A chisel—an axe—they would make an inordinate amount of noise. But she could do it, and she could make sure he knew she was doing it.

"Call Ojim," she directed Zilpha. "Tell him to bring an axe, a crowbar—a prise—anything that might get off this lock box."

"Missus . . ."

"Do it!"

Jesse was not a sentimental man. The storage room, illuminated by one dusty oriel window, held a collection of long-out-of-use furniture, and not too much of that, either. A chair. A table. A bed frame. Moldy curtains, the brocade in musty threads, a motheaten Chinese carpet. No desk, no boxes, no dressers, no hiding places that she could immediately see.

She held the lamp high and the shadowy corners jumped out at her. The floor creaked. The room was small, but there was a plank door embedded on a far wall. There wasn't a trunk or cabinet, there were no paintings or lithographs of any kind. It was as if she were looking at someone else's left-over life, someone who perhaps had owned the house before Jesse Taggart. If he had had memories, he had not stored them here.

She pushed against the plank door and it opened readily. This entrance led to still another attic, perpendicular to the first, at the end of which was a small, square, eight-paned window.

And it, too, was empty, except for a plain pine table at the very end.

She stepped over the sill with great care and entered the second attic. The closed-in atmosphere was stultifying, the dust almost choking her.

She examined the table. It was a plain, scrubbed-top table, a kitchen table perhaps, and it had no drawers, and there was nothing underneath it, nothing attached to the underside. It was as utilitarian as a piece of furniture could be, and it gave her no clue to Jesse or anything else.

But it was a wonderful place to put a guttering candle to illuminate a ghost. . . .

She ran out of the storage room, past the splintered door, to find Zilpha. "Get me as much mosquito netting

132

as you can find."

"Yes, ma'am."

"And you find that man and you tell him the door is open up there and I've been searching around and you don't know if I found anything."

Zilpha frowned. "How I'm gonna do dat?"

"Wait till you see him upstairs. Maybe he'll ask."

"He don't ask no one nothin', Missus."

"Then you tell him."

"And whut you gonna do?"

She smiled grimly. "I'm going to *haunt* him."

Of course she couldn't be precisely sure when or if he would come up to the attic, but surely his curiosity would get the better of him sometime. He was probably a subtle man: he wouldn't race right up there, but she couldn't take that chance. She was looking toward spending at least a week in the deadly matte air of that attic.

"I done tol' him," Zilpha said the next afternoon.

"And just how?" she wondered.

"He was lookin', and I was comin' by wif some laundry I just happen to be carryin', and I says, 'Missus done open de attic door, sir,' and he say, 'Oh, dat what all de noise was 'bout,' and I say, 'Yes, sir,' and now he know, Miz Taggart."

"That's perfect," Cassandra said. "Now, you have to help me hang that mosquito netting over that little attic door, and then I have to make a clean place to keep those draperies when I'm not using them up there. We have to make sure he doesn't do his exploring during the day, Zilpha. You or Ojim have to haunt the bedroom floor and make sure he is forced to go up there by night."

"Yes, ma'am."

"I will, too."

"Yes, ma'am."

She watched him. And he watched her.

There was something disquieting about returning to this childhood home as a man. He found it a little spooky to wander the hallways and peek into rooms and places the descriptions of which he had carried in his head for years, unchanging, unremitting. He found it the same, and not the same, and it was all the more eerie for having been the province of another woman and still to see it so clearly the same and well-remembered. He felt as if the spirit of Jesse's first wife permeated the place; he could be fourteen again, and she could be waiting down the hall, the two of them conspirators against the wrath of Jesse Taggart.

The sensibility of her pervaded the bedroom floor of the house, the place most unchanged through the years, except for the bedroom that had belonged to the boy-man, Trane. That had been dismantled piece by piece, and he had a dark vision of Jesse in the kitchen square behind the house, burning every last piece of furniture in vengeance. And the shade of that boy's mother gazing helplessly out the window, unable to bear it, incapable of fending off the violence of a man who operated by nothing more than his whim of the moment.

He hadn't been able to shake the feeling since the moment he walked up the steps to the bedroom floor; he expected to see Marigrace at the door of the bedroom she shared with Jesse.

He had been astounded to find a locked attic door; it gave him hope that perhaps she had found some haven, some sanctuary from the toil of being Jesse's wife. It gave him faith that perhaps she had left something there for the boy-man who had run from the nullifying atmosphere of Riveland to a place that held more promise and no regrets.

He circled that attic like a general planning an assault. But every time he approached it, Cassandra wandered out of her bedroom. Every time he put out his hand to turn the knob of the door to the stairs, Zilpha happened by on some errand or the other. Every time he set foot on the

134

first step, Ojim appeared, ostensibly to take care of some household duty.

He began to think the damned household was haunting him, and he would have to take a leaf out of the black widow's book—he would sneak up there at night, and he would, by damn, find what he was looking for.

He waited a day . . . two, feeling possessed by the wraith of the anguished Marigrace, and the mystery of the locked door.

He wandered out to the fields to escape the oppressiveness of his feelings about the past, and he found great dissatisfaction there, too, in Daggett's handling of the work crews. It was almost time for the third hoe-down, time to turn the fields, and rake between the cornstalks and plant the peas, and—he knew the table of events like the back of his hand.

He knew Jesse's wife spent a good deal of time in the office and that she went out in the fields as well, with Ojim and Elsie in tow. And he knew she also supervised the work of the house, and when he was looking hard, *really* looking, he saw the changes from the Riveland of memory, the Riveland which had been governed in a hard atmosphere of repression, by the whip and the foul word.

But Jesse's possession had been just that: full proprietorship of his animate objects, who were there to do his bidding—even his wife. The only holdover now from Jesse's regime was the heavy-handed Daggett, who wielded his crop and his whip with equal fervor.

He was in the field the second day when Daggett exhibited his usually covert frenzy of impatience with his workers—women, this time—who seemed not to be sowing seeds fast enough to suit him. His curses filled the air, his arm moved in a thrashing motion easily visible from a distance.

"Do that again, you bastard, and I'll throw you off the place."

Daggett whirled to face the implacable stranger. "Who the hell are you?"

135

"Your nemesis, you son of a bitch."

"Go to hell."

"We'll see who gets there first, mister; I'm watching you, and *I'm* not leaving soon."

"Hell—you're just the lily-lady-bitch's manservant, and you ain't got nothing over me, you shit."

"I'm Trane Taggart, you bastard, and I got my daddy's mean streak in me—and it's a mile wide. You better watch where you walk, Daggett, and mind how you talk. I'm watching you."

Daggett looked him up and down with a sneer on his lips. "Oh yeah? I heard about you from that pantywaist lawyer, mister, but I'll tell you somethin': I rode with Jesse Taggart for eight years and I ain't never heard of no son. And you don't look like him, neither. You don't scare me, mister, and I ain't takin' no orders from some buckskin hayseed. I ain't takin' orders from no one, mister, and you can go tell that lily-handed lady-bitch up the big house. Daggett ain't takin' no shit from no one. . . ."

And he wheeled on his horse and raced off down the track before the stranger could haul him up on the whys and wherefores of his rights as Jesse's son. There wasn't no son—he would have bet his riding crop on it. A man didn't ride side-by for eight years and never talk about his son. It wasn't natural. There was nothing about the stranger that was natural, from his height right down to his authority over the fields of Riveland.

The bastard was making it all up, and Daggett didn't give a damn why; he was already trying to think of a way to use the situation to his own advantage.

He watched Daggett's receding figure with mixed emotions. The funny thing about it was that he felt perfectly at home acting the part of Trane Taggart as an adult. What a laugh Jesse would have had, seeing him riding the fields of Riveland as if he really was the son and heir, as if he'd come back to stay.

The nasty little faraway figure could have been Jesse, could have been the whole damned specter of his past.

Or his future.

He felt as if he owned the place. He felt as though he might still.

There was no telling what was up in that attic, even if Mr. Jesse's wife had already searched it.

Maybe he would take *his* turn tonight.

He watched her.

She watched him.

Across the table and over the candlelight that separated them at the dinner table, under the fans wielded by Elsie and Leola, they ate dinner in a searing silence.

Something about him was different this second night, but she wasn't sure that it wasn't her own skewed thoughts altering her perceptions. She couldn't look at him without remembering his mouth, his body, his nakedness, his *blackmail.*

She couldn't forget her first feeling of triumph at having brought him flat on his back; she couldn't forget his knowledgeable kisses and her tearing innocence of them.

It was easier *not* to look at him, but she was sure that he would interpret that as fear, and she wasn't afraid of him now. She was going to win this battle of wits, and he was going to leave Riveland—and *soon.*

The problem was, he looked too comfortable across the table from her; he was wearing a fresh white shirt, courtesy of Jesse's belongings, and it fit him well—too well. Over it, he had had the courtesy to put his well-worn leather jacket to give at least the appearance of formality, and he wore a string tie as well, which, she supposed, was better than nothing.

And—he had shaved.

Oh Lordy, he had shaved, just hacked off that bushy, scratchy beard and mustache—and her face went hot as she remembered the feel of it against her own smooth

137

skin.

"Ma'am?" His voice came at her softly, liquid with humor now, as he perceived that she apprehended the difference in him.

"Excuse me?" Time to become the lady of the manor, the black widow.

"You were saying something?"

"Oh no, I have nothing to say to *you*," she returned, her voice just a little sharp. She would not let him back her into a corner, not again.

"I'd be obliged if you would call me by my given name."

"I would be happy to, if you would only tell me what it is."

"Well, I have, ma'am."

"I still don't believe you, stranger."

"I sure believe in you—Cassandra."

"Oh no—you don't have permission to call me by *my* given name."

He smiled that crooked little smile and raised one eyebrow. "Stop me."

She stood up abruptly. "I intend to."

"I like your spirit, ma'am." Among other things, he thought admiringly; she was all in black again and the severity of it only illuminated the sweetness of her face and her steely slenderness that was now impressed on his body forever.

"That is as intangible as your claim, stranger."

"A spirited defense, Cassandra, but your threats are as insubstantial as my birthright."

"Your 'birthright' is nonexistent, stranger. You won't ever find enough proof to convince me," she retorted, pushing her chair back with a kick of her right foot. "There is no point in talking anymore."

"No, ma'am. We don't have to *talk*," he agreed softly, and she felt that awful wave of heat inch up to her cheeks. She had to stop this man; he was too smooth, too insinuating, too accessible. And since he was all those things, he couldn't possibly be Jesse's son, because Jesse was none of them, and she had invented Trane Taggart to begin with.

She gripped the edge of the table in frustration. *"You* are here on sufferance only, stranger—"

"Believe me, ma'am, I'm suffering," he interpolated, just to get her rattled.

"Not more than *I,* I assure you," she snapped. "You are a madman and I won't allow you to run around pretending to be my husband's son—"

"—when everyone knows *he* is in Baltimore, safely far away," he finished for her, with that odd little smile. "Well, the solution is right at hand, ma'am: you just send off a letter to Trane Taggart in Baltimore and invite *him* to come visit Riveland . . . along with all his proper papers, of course."

She gritted her teeth. "We have been through this already; Mr. Taggart has been invited and declines to leave his business and family," *and you stay out of my story and my invention and my life!*

"He is a very giving man. I am not so giving, nor *for-*giving, Cassandra."

"But I am not taking from you, sir. You are *mis-*taking from me, and *I* am not a *for*bearing person, stranger. This won't go on much longer, in spite of your surety and my lawyer's absence."

"Don't issue challenges to me, Cassandra. You know I'm up to them."

"You're just a man, stranger; a man can be gotten 'up' to anything," she shot back unthinkingly, and then stopped short, angry at herself that he had goaded her into even the merest reference to what had happened two nights before.

He smiled again and she wanted to slap that quirky, knowing smile from his lips. "I'd uphold that notion, ma'am," he murmured appreciatively, but she didn't appreciate the comment at all.

"Good night, sir," she said emphatically.

"Don't think you have the upper hand, ma'am."

She took a deep breath as she pushed her chair back under the table. He was a rogue and he had a smart mouth, but so did she.

"But the upshot is you still haven't proved anything," she said roundly, "and I can't wait to see you get your comeuppance." And she turned on her heel and walked away, delighted she had gotten the last word, and aware he still had more to say.

But she couldn't spend time bandying words with him. She had already spent one long, fulminating night in that dusty attic waiting for him to appear, and she intended to be there tonight as well.

She couldn't let herself wonder if it were a useless gambit; he *had* to be curious, she was banking on it. It was obvious he would never find anything relating to Trane Taggart anywhere in the house, but surely it was possible he might find something indicating that Jesse had never had children with his first wife, and he surely couldn't afford to let anyone else get to it first. He would come to the attic, she was sure of it.

Once again, deep in the night, she moved out into the hallway and through the door at the far end of the hallway, carefully holding her ingeniously devised costume around her as she climbed the narrow staircase, entered the storeroom and made her way into the attic.

There was a candlestick on the table, and a pillow on the floor, and she sank onto that in a heap of mosquito netting from which Zilpha had fashioned her garment. It was like a monk's robe, with a long, shapeless body and two long, winged sleeves that covered her arms and hands, and there was a hood which she would pull over her face to blur her features. When she finally heard him come, she would light the candle, and the flickering glow of the flame and the gauziness of the netting would turn her into a ghost to be reckoned with.

If he came—

If she didn't fall asleep. Outwitting him took so much of her energy; she felt peculiarly tired tonight, and she

140

thought it was as much emotional as physical. He was taunting her, playing with her, and he had no fear of anything she tried to intimidate him with, and that scared her.

The mountain without fear. He hunkered and hulked and took everything in his stride, and she was scared he might defeat her somehow.

She heard something. A shuffle. A creak. A firm step. Another. Her heart pounded, her hands grew cold, nerveless.

Closer. On the landing now, outside the splintered door.

She snatched up the flint and lit the candle with shaking hands, and set it on the floor. And then she pulled the hood over her head and, her heart racing, she waited.

The thought of the attic loomed over him like some bothersome mosquito. If the spider lady had been desperate enough to break into it, she probably thought there was something to find up there. Maybe she had even found it. Maybe she hadn't. Whatever was there, he needed to find it, even if it were the merest trace of a refuge that might have given Marigrace some pleasure.

Of course Jesse had been a cunning old dog. He wouldn't have just set Trane Taggart's birth papers on some table, locked a door and waited for someone to chop it down thirty-four years later.

And the old bastard *had* locked it. And the spider lady hadn't given it a thought until her undercover servants had told her he had been inspecting it. A damned bad break for him.

Nevertheless, he couldn't leave a single stone unturned, and he had found a fertile field in Cassandra Taggart. The randy old bastard, taking a child as his second wife and using her so badly. He had a lot to pay back that old shit. A damned lot. Nothing was going to stop him, either, not lawyers or wills or the enticing Cassandra. And he knew now just how to divert *her* from his purpose.

Too bad he couldn't bed down in her room and search

the attic at the same time.

He paused on the topmost step and held his lamp up to look at Ojim's handiwork with the axe. He had hacked the damned thing to smithereens.

My lady must have been *very* anxious to get into the attic.

He pushed open the splintered door just as a light flared from somewhere beyond him in the darkness. What the hell —

He doused his own light, set it down and edged into the nimbus-illuminated darkness.

He was in a room, not very large, not very crowded with furniture or objects. He felt a tinge of exasperation as he could just make out a table and a bed frame leaning up against the wall opposite where the glow of light emanated.

Damned old Jesse had no familial feeling at all. Hell . . . He kicked sharply into a chair directly in front of him, and pushed it out of his way impatiently. What the hell was beyond that door?

The light wavered, diffused one moment, bright the next, and he saw that it radiated from still another door along the wall where he lurked.

Well now . . .

He inched closer until he was just at the edge of the doorframe. The light flickered and blazed, and he squinted to see beyond the shadows and the pinpoint of the flame.

There was something there —

Hell!

Some . . . *thing* —

Amorphous, eerie, undulating in and out of the shadows with unnerving regularity . . .

Jesus . . .

For one moment, he froze, feeling an all-encompassing sense of something unnatural — and a *presence*. For one indelible moment he thought: Marigrace . . .

And then the light went out and he was left in the darkness with his pummeling heart and pounding thoughts.

Godalmighty — she had been as real as real to him since he had set foot in the house . . . and here she was, her spirit — adrift, seeking asylum, never to find rest . . . not after Jesse, not ever . . .

No, that was fanciful, crazy even; he had to get a grip on himself, but the darkness didn't help, or the sense of that unearthly presence just at the moment when he had been thinking about Jesse and family . . . how perfect —

He was not *that* gullible.

He leaned back against the doorframe wall.

Someone thought he was.

That thought popped into his head concurrently with the next one: someone was still in that room beyond the doorframe.

He took a deep breath.

It was *not* a ghost.

And it would have to come out sometime.

It was just a matter of waiting the thing out.

But it had to believe that he had turned tail and run, and that sat hard with him, especially given his first reaction.

Stealthily but pointedly, he inched his way back to the door of the storeroom, groped for his lamp, knocked it lightly against the wall so that the presence would hear and approximate where he was, set that down again, stepped onto the landing noisily and sat down gingerly to remove his boots.

Everything was too damned hard in the dark, he thought moodily, setting them down on the step below where he sat. He was damned sure he would trip over them on his way back down the stairs, but no matter: he was going to root out the ghost, and damn the consequences.

He shut the door noisily behind him as he crept back into the storage room and felt for the wall.

Now . . . He jackknifed up to his feet and slowly moved toward the doorframe just as the light flicked out-

143

ward again.

He went rigid against the wall. *Damnation!*

He heard movement and he drew in a sizzling breath. Damned hard *not* to believe in wafting spirits with all that going on, but he had the element of surprise on his side. The thing in the next attic was *not* subhuman, he was sure of it. But it was damned unnatural how the thing moved with barely any sound.

He was a patient man; he had waited a long time for a lot of things, but in some respects, he could not wait to see who was wearing the draperies beyond the door.

But he had an inkling.

He heard the soughing sound of fabric tearing as something reassuringly substantive blocked the light momentarily. And then it was gone, and it was time for him to move.

He stepped into the light and leaned against the doorframe.

She sensed his presence and dropped her gauzy curtain and whirled.

Damn! Caught in the act . . .

She lunged at him, hoping to catch him off balance and thrust him backward.

He caught her, grasping her forearms and immobilizing her hands.

"What a tangled web you weave, spider lady," he murmured, pulling her closer.

"What a rude guest *you* are," she said snippily. "It's rather ungracious of you to repay my hospitality by sneaking around my attic."

"As if you didn't have a clue I would come."

"Who knows what a madman will take it into his head to do?" She shrugged, trying to wrench her arms out of his tight grip.

"And the black widow is always ready to prey upon a convenient victim."

"Or a willing one," she hissed. "This is absurd. *Let me go.*"

"You're absurd if you thought this hocus-pocus would scare me away."

She stopped struggling. "You had a moment."

"Your imagination, spider lady."

"Oh yes, you had a moment," she repeated knowingly. "You thought of someone."

"Only *you,* black widow. Who else made sense?"

"Someone you thought of," she said again because she could see that her sense of that discomfitted him greatly; she wished she had an equally strong sense of who the person was, but there was, after all, only so much a ghost could fathom by instinct.

"I thought of *you,*" he said, and the words hung suddenly in the air between them. She became aware of the grasp of his hands on her arms, and the closeness of the atmosphere, the closeness of him, and the fact that they were isolated from the rest of the house, in a small, hot, confined space where his words had a wealth of meanings she did not want to hear.

"All right," she said "You caught me."

"Yes indeed, black widow; your prey trapped *you* and now you have to pay the price — again."

She stiffened. "I know your price."

"Good. That saves a lot of talking."

"I won't pay it.

"Don't expend your energy denying me, Cassandra. I promise you, I will demand satisfaction and I will get it."

"But we won't sleep together tonight," she said tauntingly.

"You won't get out of here tonight," he said pointedly.

"I'll scream the house down," she threatened.

He looked at her consideringly for a moment. "I don't think you will."

She opened her mouth; she *had* to, and he clamped one hand over it instantly. "Don't fight me, Cassandra. Kiss me."

"Mrmph," she growled through his heavy palm, while her freed hand pounded the fingers that grasped her other hand.

"You are just determined to do violence to me, aren't you?" he whispered. "But you can't get away from me, black widow. I'll always surround you. Watch me do it now . . ."

He removed his hand from her mouth and slowly slid it upward into her tangled gold curls, and his trailing touch sent a spiral of feeling in a long curlicue down toward her toes.

Next to him, in spite of her feisty defiance, she felt like a doll he could manipulate any which way he chose. She felt his arm slide hard around her waist, she felt his words, "Fight me now, Cassandra," and the challenge drain out of her body as his lips touched hers and those aching little darts zinged a path to places and feelings unknown.

"You want my kisses," he murmured. "Put your arms around me, Cassandra." He used her name as if he were rolling it around in his mouth, savoring it, tasting it. She slipped her arms around him and his free hand cupped her cheek. "Kiss me now, Cassandra."

She wanted to protest, she really did, but the clean, firm line of his mouth was just near hers, and now that the awful scratchy beard was gone, she wanted . . . she knew exactly what she wanted.

She wanted to *practice*.

She must be insane; this man had no sensual hold on her whatsoever, except his mesmerizing kisses. And in the dark, where memories were forgotten and made anew, she saw no harm in kissing him as the price for having tried to trick him.

She wasn't done with him yet. A man who was engrossed in a kiss would be less likely to be involved in other matters.

She lifted her mouth to his, and her lips grazed his lower lip.

"Willingly, Cassandra."

She covered his mouth, feeling the soft pressure of his

mouth against her pliant lips. She licked his lips to tease him; she did all the things that he, with his insatiable demands, had taught her two nights before, and he responded instantly, eagerly, deepening the kiss, overruling her, demanding her, taking her the moment she hesitated.

This was so very different, she thought, her heart racing in panic. This was real. This was a man who *wanted* the woman he held in his arms, a man who had intended to inflict a teasing punishment that had escalated into something much more, a man whose stiffening manhood and lush kisses were meant to be a prelude to the ultimate, and unimaginable, coupling with him.

Never!

Her panic turned to sheer terror.

Who was to stop him in this candle-dark out-of-the-way attic?

Her heated body warred with her outright fear. He had unerringly found the thing to use against her, the point at which she was weakest, most needy.

His kisses overpowered her, gentled her, demanded she respond to him. She felt herself responding to him, and she clamped down on her unruly nature as hard as she could.

She pulled away from him, and was stricken to see that she was breathless.

"Cassandra . . ." He breathed her name with such *need,* she didn't know how to fight him.

But he was a man, still. A man did what he was permitted to do; sometimes he took, most times he had the weapons with which to make a woman capitulate, and she could tell she was fair on the way to giving in to him herself.

This had to stop.

"I need a moment," she whispered. She needed an hour. No, she needed to get out of that attic as fast as possible.

She had nothing at hand.

No, she still wore the mosquito net robe, but she wished heartily she had had the forethought to hold on to the

147

curtain; she could have slapped it over his head, pushed him and run the moment he appeared in the door.

Maybe she still could.

She lifted her face to his, kissed him lightly, and whispered, "Can't I get out of this awful scratchy netting?"

He couldn't see her face clearly; the candlelight flickered from the floor behind her. He heard the sultriness in her voice, he felt the raging need in himself, and he loosened his arms around her just enough . . . a little more, so that she could pull at the sleeves and slide the thing over her head, and . . .

Damn her! . . . Over his head, all gauze and fuzz, and he felt her push him and he stumbled backward into the storeroom and crashed into something. The light went out, and her footsteps, careful and quick, receded from the storeroom and down the steps before he could even get his bearings.

He picked himself up slowly, tearing the netting away from his face like spider webs out of his hair. How apt.

He crawled to the door of the storeroom, feeling for his lamp. His hand hit the glass sharply and it crashed down the stairs.

The black widow's trap, he thought wearily, getting to his feet; who was the unsuspecting victim?

He was beginning to believe it was he.

Chapter Ten

She watched him. He watched her.

She had to get him out of her house before things got messier than they already were.

"Where are you going?"

"I thought I'd ride out," he evaded her question.

"I'd like that, if you promise to keep going."

"I'd like to oblige, ma'am, but you know I'm here to stay."

"I know you're here so I can keep my eye on you."

"Yes, ma'am," he said meekly, as he cinched his saddle with a practiced ease she had not been hitherto aware of. The stranger knew horses.

She watched him ease his mount out of the stable yard, and canter down the drive, and veer out toward the river.

Why the river?

She found out later. Daggett stormed into her office, thrusting his riding crop an inch away from her nose.

"You tell your lily-bellied house servant to keep his damn gut out of my business."

"Mr. Daggett," she said gently. "How nice to see you. Which house servant is that?"

"That piece of lint that calls himself Jesse's son."

Her eyebrows rose.

"The fields are *mine,* Miz Taggart; he ain't got no call tellin' me what to do."

"*Did* he do that?"

"Interferin' with my handlin' of the wimmen . . . You tell 'im, Miz Taggart; he ain't nosin' around in *my* fields."

She almost felt sympathy for him, but she knew him, she knew too well his "handling."

"What did he nose out, Mr. Daggett?"

"What he had no business gettin' into: them wimmen is lazy in the sun, ma'am, and you know it. You gotta move 'em if you want that work gettin' done. You can't let them fill their no-account heads with excuses they're gonna visit on any damn body comes out to the field and shows a little sympathy—if you get my meaning, ma'am."

"I get it," she said drily.

And then Zilpha: "Dat man am ever'where, Missus. Ain't nuthin' misses dat man's eyes. He lookin' fo' de proof, he lookin' fo' to take over, he lookin' all over."

"Where?" Cassandra demanded sharply.

"Just ever'where, Missus. You got to watch dat man."

"So do you," Cassandra advised her strongly.

"I do fo' you, Missus."

"I appreciate that."

Everywhere . . . looking to take over—how could Zilpha voice her very own fears so precisely?

A hand-delivered letter arrived from Mr. Greve and she opened it eagerly. He had gone back to Atlanta, to wind up some business there that he had left to tend to her affairs. He was sure that she would carry on capably and that Mr. Taggart would prove his identity and his worth to her by the time he returned.

She crumpled the letter and tossed it in the fireplace. "Coward," she whispered fiercely. He was hiding; he was probably at the Rivergate Hotel at this very moment, but he would never open his door to her.

Then again, he had probably been very happy to relinquish the reins to the forceful Trane Taggart, who seemed so very willing to take them in hand.

She would kill first.

And surely she had not exhausted the possibilities for convincing him to leave without instigating an investigation into Jesse's death.

She had to think.

He was already out in the fields, trying to overset Daggett's authority. He hadn't tried anything in the house, except to make love to her, and that was incidental to everything else, and something she just wasn't going to dwell on.

Maybe it was time for another letter from *her* Mr. Taggart, the generous creature who had willingly given her his time and advice, and never once contested her inheritance.

Wonderful, wise, fatherly man; I couldn't have made up a better mentor than you, and I wish that stranger had had the sense to keep his nose out of it.

How ought the story to end?

They were all still treating her invention as if he were real. If he were real, she thought, there might be someone in and around Carthage who remembered him.

What an interesting idea.

Of course, he had been gone a long time, and some of the plantations on the Midway had changed hands over the years, and of course Jesse had not been very sociable with her, so there was no reason to believe it was different with his first wife. It was probable the community of Carthage knew of Trane Taggart, but maybe it hadn't seen much of him at all when he was growing up.

Maybe Jesse contained him too much right here on Riveland, and it was one of the reasons he had run away and to this day never wanted to come back.

Lord, she had a fertile mind for a story.

Well, someone would have to know him, if the tantalizing idea shimmering around the edge of her mind were to materialize.

Who . . . who—who?

There had been a family . . . could she remember the name now? It had been eight years; they, the husband and wife, had come to welcome her to Carthage and had retreated quickly under Jesse's disapproving eye. They had been neighbors, they were probably still farming cotton on the Midway, neighbors, never seen, hardly known.

Trane Taggart might have known them. Maybe, when Jesse's hard nature got too oppressive, the boy Trane had sneaked downriver to visit the kindly couple who had no children.

Ooh, nice touch. They had had no children, and that was why she remembered him so fondly.

She would be about sixty now. Maybe he had died. Or had leased out the plantation. Yes, better. Leased it out. Good. So strangers were farming it, people who didn't know Trane Taggart and couldn't care less.

Except this old lady, who had heard—in a roundabout way—that Trane had come back to Riveland.

Good.

And she wanted to see him.

Better.

And she would confront the stranger, and she would say, in her cackling voice: *You are not Trane Taggart.*

Perfect.

Her name was . . . her name was Mary Whitwood . . . Yes, that sounded familiar. A gray-haired lady. She could manage that. She had saved all of her mother's clothing and accoutrements, had packed them away in some far off corner where Jesse had been sure not to look.

And hadn't he been happy when her mother died?

And because Raylene had betrayed her, she had not mourned her.

She wouldn't dwell on that, either. The past was unreachable, unchangeable; it was to be lived with, borne like a cross, a rosary of sins counted off in odd moments when memory rose from the dead.

Or when someone chose to unearth it.

Her mother had worn gray, black, dark blue, matronly colors, newly made for the wealthy matron-mother of Riveland. And all starkly dated. No matter. There was something there she could use to impersonate the aging Mary Whitwood: there a shawl, here a cap. A box of powder, as she thought she remembered, when Raylene had

152

taken to cosmetic subterfuge to try to appear younger in order to attract Jesse. Henna, to hide her graying hair. Rouge. A cane, when she became infirm and Jesse had abandoned her.

She stifled the rage she felt welling within her. The thing she understood was that Jesse would have gone after Raylene or anyone else, and there was never anything she could do to stop him.

It had never been her fault, but it had taken her several years after Raylene's death to realize that, several years of torturous self-blame, subjugation, and finally denial. She had grown, but still, the rage was there and she never knew if it were against Jesse or against herself for having been party to it.

Well, she could now fit her mother's clothes and that would have some value — if this ruse worked.

She spent several days perfecting her disguise: the long, dour dress, the powder-grayed hair, the henna-washed skin with color sunk into the lines that already etched her face. A small pillow on her back, below her neck, to give her the posture of age. Glasses to conceal her bright eyes. Lacy gloves to hide the fact her hands were not bent with arthritis. A veiled hat to distance the pretender still further from the illusion.

And finally, the voice, the "Mary"-voice: high-pitched, cracked, faintly querulous.

She looked in the mirror and she didn't know herself. It was an image of how she might look in forty years. It was inconceivable.

She enlisted Ojim's aid, and one morning, he drove her, in the carriage, down toward the river where he could connect with the road and she could easily change into her costume and then proceed to enter Riveland down at the long winding drive.

She didn't think she had been even that far away from Riveland in years, and she wondered why, after Jesse's death, the first thing she hadn't done was go right into Carthage and celebrate.

153

It was a nondescript vehicle; all the servants knew it, but it hadn't been used in years. Jesse had gone horseback, and she hadn't gone at all. The only troubling prospect was Ojim's presence, and she solved that by leaving the carriage a fair way down the drive and having Ojim turn it around so that he would not be facing the house.

Five minutes later, she was up on the veranda, briskly knocking at the door.

"Yes, ma'am?" Sully, ever so polite, bowing her in.

"Where's that Trane Taggart that's come back to town as sudden as rain?" Cassandra demanded in her high-pitched "Mary"-voice.

"Pardon, ma'am. I call Zilpha. You wait."

Dear Sully—always correct . . .

Zilpha marched in suspiciously. "Ma'am?"

"I'm Mary Whitwood," Cassandra told her brusquely, still in her "Mary"-voice. She was bent over slightly from the thrust of the pillow on her back; she had to look up at Zilpha like a turtle out of her shell, and she was finding it onerous at the very best.

"You is from downriver," Zilpha said, identifying her to her own satisfaction. Now she had her connected, she could elicit other business. "Missus ain't available right now. Whut kin I do fo' you?"

"I want to see that rascal Trane; I heard he came back, and I recollect how he was like a son to me."

"Yes, ma'am, he here."

"Bring him to me," she directed imperiously.

"Yes, ma'am," Zilpha said with a straight face, and Cassandra wondered if she recognized her mistress at all. She imagined Zilpha stalking the stranger, catching up with him finally to tell him Mrs. Mary Whitwood awaited his pleasure in the reception hall, and how she was most anxious to see him.

After a short while, he came, with Zilpha just behind him, and she was furious with herself that she had not planned for the fact she would have to look up to him.

"Who are you?" she demanded peevishly.

154

"I'm Trane Taggart, ma'am," he answered easily. "Surely you remember?"

She hunched herself over still more, and then cocked her head and slanted a look upward at him through the concealing veil. "You ain't Trane Taggart. He wasn't that tall."

"No, he wasn't," the pretender agreed smoothly. "I wasn't but a boy when I left Riveland, ma'am."

"Sad day, sad day," she lamented in her high-pitched voice. "Who are you, anyway?"

"I'm Trane Taggart, ma'am; I did tell you."

He wasn't losing his patience with her yet. "Why don't we sit down and talk a little?"

"I can't stay. You ain't Trane. You ain't the boy I know."

"I promise you, ma'am, I am." He looked at her closely and she turned her head away and rocked her body in the way of older people. "I remember the things you remember."

"No, there ain't nothing you remember. You ain't Trane Taggart."

"Don't you remember the time Jesse chased me all the way down to Whitwood and Robert hid me in a bale of cotton and sent me down the river?"

She shook her head emphatically. "No, that never happened. Trane didn't do things like that. He came to help Robert when Jesse could spare him. He was like a son to me." She let her voice waver on that note, feeling a gush of frustration at his facile ability to invent a story for himself that Mary would supposedly know.

"Oh, and then there was the time I climbed up that hill of corn to help Reuben with the husking and Jesse climbed up right to the top to get my hide. You remember that, Mary?" His voice was just as rich and creamy as satin and Cassandra couldn't tell what was the truth and what was the lie.

"No, that *didn't* happen, young man, and I don't know why you're making up such scurrilous stories about Trane

Taggart," she scolded him sharply. "I can't stay to waste no more time, mister. I don't know who you are, except you're cruel and unkind to an old lady." She got up abruptly and almost knocked the pillow from its precarious perch on her back, and then she turned to look back at him. "You *ain't* Trane Taggart."

She marched to the front door where Zilpha stood, her mouth slightly agape. "You tell your mistress: Mary Whitwood came and that disrespectful man ain't Trane Taggart."

"I tell her," Zilpha said.

"You just disremember," the pretender said.

"Or maybe you do," she retorted as Zilpha opened the door. "Good day."

Zilpha closed the door behind her and she slowly walked down the drive to the carriage. She wanted to run, damn his eyes — he was slippery as a piece of silk . . . and he could tell almost as good a story as she, the wily mountain lion. He knew when to pounce — he knew when to play with his prey.

He could take one swipe at her lady spider and she would never spin another tale. She shuddered as she climbed into the carriage and pulled off her hat and reached for the pillow to ease her numbed back.

Well, there were corners and ceilings she hadn't yet explored. She wasn't done with Mr. Call-Me-Trane yet.

But she had the feeling he wasn't done with her, either.

He watched her. He had the grim feeling he couldn't let her out of his sight, or there was no telling what — or who — she would get up to: an apparition one moment, a feisty old lady the next . . . *damned fine job, Cassandra,* he saluted her silently over dinner, *but I would know that mouth anywhere — now.*

He wanted to know that mouth again; there wasn't a veil or cosmetic or voice that could disguise it from him ever again.

"I hear Mrs. Mary Whitwood visited today," Cassandra said casually at dinner, going on the attack immediately. "Zilpha tells me she didn't know you at all. I believe that proves my point, stranger."

"The old lady's eyesight is failing," he said calmly. "She saw Trane Taggart last twenty years ago. How could she know him today?"

"Instinct," Cassandra retorted.

"She didn't remember incidents that are vivid in my mind as if they had happened yesterday," he went on slyly. "Maybe Mrs. Whitwood is the impostor."

Her fork paused in mid-air. "Maybe *you* are too clever by half, stranger, but the fact remains that you don't have a paper or a proof of who you are, while I have a dozen or so enormously descriptive letters from Trane Taggart in Baltimore which prove he is who he says he is."

There! Let him stew on that.

"You mean the far-removed Trane Taggart, who doesn't take *issue* at all with his step-mother's portion or the circumstances of the death of his father. Yes, I believe we've heard a great deal about *that* Trane Taggart." He picked up a forkful of food he did not feel like eating. "Of course the fact remains that he isn't here, and I am," he added, scrupulously echoing her tone, "and Mrs. Whitwood's visit proves nothing, either."

She felt like gnawing on the table. The man was impossible, an immovable mountain just determined to plant himself on Riveland and stay.

It had been — what — almost a week since he had arrived and Greve had abandoned her, and she felt as if it had been a year.

"Nothing proves anything," she said snidely. "How convenient for you."

"And Trane Taggart languishes in Baltimore, unwilling to show his face in the cotton fields. How convenient for you."

"Sure, for then you couldn't be he, could you?" she snapped.

157

Or he snapped, because he suddenly thumped down one large hand on the table, pushed himself away and got up and left her.

Good, she thought, he was getting sick and tired of hearing about the exemplary fictional Trane Taggart. On the other hand, she couldn't let him out of her sight for a moment.

She threw down her napkin and ran out into the hallway, but there was no telling which way he had gone.

Wait—there was a light under the library door.

She darted across the hallway, intending to listen outside the door to get a fix on what he was doing. Jesse's desk was in there, and a cabinet but she had gone through those. She hadn't, however, looked through every book in case there were some papers hidden that Jesse hadn't meant for her to see.

She stood by the doorframe, her hand poised to turn the doorknob and thrust open the door.

A moment—two—no sound from within—she twisted the knob and pushed in the door at the very moment a shot rang out and ricocheted off something very solid. Too solid.

"Trane!" she screamed, throwing herself on the floor.

Another shot, vicious, deliberate. His voice from deep within the room, etched with anger and pain: *"What the hell do you think you're doing?"*

She didn't even have time to assess what he meant. Instantly the room was flooded with servants and light, and she raised herself up slowly. He was sitting next to her, holding his arm, and around him, Sully, Zilpha and Leola were looking down, Sully holding a lamp and Zilpha tearing strips right off her petticoat.

"Clever lady spider," he muttered scathingly, wrapping the clean white cotton strip around his arm. "You called out the one thing that would get my damned attention and totally disarm me. I tell you, Cassandra, you do have a way with words. Grab that end, lady, and *pull.*"

She pulled, he winced, and Zilpha knelt down to tie off

the ends, but still his blood soaked right through the bandage.

She was shaking, and she hardly comprehended his words, but something sank in—something that meant he was accusing her . . . of what, she didn't know. . . . *the one thing . . . disarm me . . .*

She had called his name.

She had called him Trane. . . .

"Oh lady, you are a piece of work," he said acidly, as he watched her carefully unwind the makeshift bandage. "You were standing right by the door, right in the direction the shots came from."

"I did not shoot you," she said, keeping her voice neutral and her eyes solely on the messy wound as she swabbed it with whiskey, the closest thing to hand as she waited for Zilpha to prepare the lead extract and oil-soaked lint poultice she would apply to his arm.

"Your aim stinks; the bullet lodged in the bookcase somewhere," he added nastily. "Damn. Take it *easy*."

"You don't even know if I can handle a gun," she snapped, probing gently at the edge of the wound; the bullet had swiped him right in his upper arm, leaving a painful gash. She felt his whole body knot up as she blotted away the blood.

"I would lay money on it, black widow," he said with such surety that her hand started to shake. How could he know?

She didn't answer him. "Here's Zilpha," she said, keeping the tremor out of her voice with some effort.

Zilpha carried a tray, across which was laid a fresh cotton cloth with which she would bind the poultice to his arm, and she proceeded to do that as Cassandra cleaned away the last of the blood.

"I want to find that bullet tonight," he said, gritting his teeth as the soaked lint touched the raw edges of the wound.

159

"You have to rest," Cassandra said automatically, taking over the bandaging from Zilpha's hands.

"I don't have to do one damn thing, Cassandra, except find that bullet. And I'm going to get to it before the spider lady pulls it into her web."

"You can't . . ."

"I *can*. You're a ruthless woman, Mrs. Jesse Taggart. You tied me up, you tried to scare me off, you . . ." He stopped short and looked into her intent face, so close to his as she knotted off the bandage. She had no idea he knew she had played the grumpy Mrs. Mary Whitwood. "There's no telling what else you would do," he went on, a little less stringently. She was too close, close enough for him to scare *her* a little. "You're capable of using a gun, Cassandra. You're a damned efficient lady when you set your mind to something."

"Nonsense," she said briskly. "Yes, I want you gone, but I would never stoop to shooting you."

"Somehow that does not reassure me."

She was beginning to feel a pulse of anger. "Well, fine, you search for the bullet and break your damned head while you're at it, and perhaps you can blame that on me, too."

He smiled that elusive little smile. "Well, ma'am, I'll tell you—just to spite you, I'm going to do no such thing."

"That's not funny."

"No, ma'am," he agreed instantly.

"I wish you would leave," she added fretfully. "You're not getting anywhere and it's obvious your scheme isn't working, so . . . I won't hold a grudge, I promise you."

He smiled again. "Oh but, ma'am, I can't do that. I really think I've made some progress."

Her head snapped up then. "Perhaps you have. You've made yourself damned comfortable here for a stranger who has no claim on me."

"I didn't mean that, ma'am," he said gently. She was close, so close he could read every nuance in her expressive, faintly exasperated green gaze, so close he could have

160

run his fingers through the molten gold of her hair, close enough so he could have cupped her chin and kissed her firm flexible lips without moving six inches from where he sat.

The air grew hot with promise—and her resistance. He wanted that kiss; she wanted to escape him. It was too much: she was an assassin and a lover all in one breath.

"What *did* you mean?" she demanded sharply.

"I just meant that you finally called me by my rightful name."

Had she?

"It was the heat of the moment," she defended herself. "You don't shout 'hey you' when bullets are flying."

"And certainly not if you are holding the gun."

"I won't listen to this. I just won't let you out of my sight, that's all, and we'll end this . . . this pretense before Mr. Greve returns."

"We'll be sleeping together then," he interpreted with every show of smug male satisfaction that he knew would get her hackles up.

She wished she had a gun in hand right then. Maybe she was capable of shooting him. She could have done it, just aimed the barrel straight on into that cocksure male smile of his and let it go.

"I prefer to let sleeping dogs lie, stranger."

"I have a penchant for sleeping bitches myself," he retorted, feeling both amused and exasperated by her. "I'm not letting you five inches out of my sight tonight, lady."

"Don't be stupid—you have to rest that arm, and you surely can't do that comfortably on the floor."

'I thought you'd be gloating to have me at your feet."

"I'd rather have you at my mercy."

"A man does need a whomping heap of forbearance when dealing with a spider lady," he agreed easily. "I can bunk out on the desk, Cassandra. A nice solid surface to support my arm . . . an excellent idea, actually—"

She wheeled away from his reasonable voice and his unreasonable demand, torn between not wanting to spend

161

the night anywhere near him, and her need to keep him directly in her sight.

Or she could just give up and go to her own bed. After all, what havoc could he wreak after midnight since he had already prowled the attic, searched the library, interfered in the fields . . . He obviously thought he owned the damned place.

"I'll come to bed with *you*," he proposed.

"Oh *no*." The words just shot out of her mouth. "No. You go your way; I'll go mine."

"You're not going anywhere I can't see you, lady."

Inflexible now, and he had her backed into a corner. She couldn't trust him worth a damn, either. "Fine with me. Just fine. That way, we'll at least know where the other stands."

"Or lays."

"Or *lies*," she shot back.

He threw up his hands. "You got me."

"I would dearly love to 'get' you," she said grittily.

"I know I'm getting *to* you, black widow."

"I'll get around that," she vowed. "Yes, I will. You're here on sufferance, stranger."

"Oh no, get it straight, Cassandra. I'm here because I'm Jesse's son, and I've threatened you with an investigation into Jesse's death—and for some reason, that scares the life out of you."

Chapter Eleven

Well—that was plain speaking.

He was too damned perceptive for his own good. She wished she had shot him; it would have ended all this confrontation and argument.

"You're crazy," she said.

"Let's go to bed," he said, and she had no choice but to precede him up the steps and down the hallway to his room.

"One bed, Cassandra."

"I don't suppose you'll let me tie you up again," she ventured hopefully.

"I'd prefer to deactivate your busy little hands."

"How about I call Sully to tie us both up and then we'll know for sure who is doing what to whom?"

"I think you're losing your senses, spider lady. Things are not that bad. Sit down."

"Someone shot you."

"You shot me."

"I won't listen to this."

"I admire a lady with spunk."

"You're a skunk; who cares what you admire."

"Call me Trane, Cassandra."

"I'll call you 'Strain'—you are stretching my nerves and my patience to the limit."

"You have to call me something."

"Stranger does the job nicely."

163

"We won't be strangers after tonight."

"I daresay after tonight you will seem stranger to me than before."

He shook his head disgustedly and sat down gingerly on the bed. "You sure do like to hone your tongue on a man, lady."

"Excuse me, but it isn't as if you haven't whet your own words on the grindstone of pure greed."

"Jesse would have laughed his fool head off to see this," he muttered, easing himself back against the pine posted headboard.

In her turn, she walked edgily to the other side of the bed and touched the coverlet. There was nowhere else to sit in the room; it was either the bed, or she would have to stand. Gingerly, she sank onto the edge of the mattress, as far away from his large body as humanly possible.

"Jesse never laughed," she said pointedly.

"Oh hell, he would have just loved this, the rotten bastard."

No, Jesse hadn't loved anything applicable to children. He wouldn't have found any humor in the notion that some strange man-mountain had caused an uproar by claiming to be the son he couldn't have, and the creation she made up to compensate for it.

On the other hand, she had a story to explain that, too, and she resented him poking his fiction into hers. "Trane Taggart would not have come back. Jesse wiped him away as completely as if he had never existed."

"He did, and he did a damned good job of it, didn't he, lady?"

She smiled tightly. "So he told me in his letters."

He frowned. "It isn't so far from the truth."

"Right, because it sounds good when you pluck the clues out of the air," she said nastily. "You've been doing a positively admirable song and dance here. You're *very* good."

"So are you, lady."

Her mouth set. They were going around in circles. Now she was a would-be murderess—and he had not stopped being an impostor. She could watch him struggle with his arm and trying to sleep, or she could just get out of the room altogether.

She stood up abruptly. "I'm going back to my room."

He shot off the bed. "Oh no, you're not."

"We're getting nowhere."

"I like to think we've gotten somewhere, Cassandra. *Sit down.*" He loomed over her and she sat back down tentatively on the edge of the bed. He loomed over her like some great primitive statue, the pain etched on his face as he inadvertently maneuvered his arm at some awkward angle.

He edged back to the foot of the bed and sat down heavily on the mattress. "Not a minute out of my sight, Cassandra."

She shook her head hopelessly. "Fine. I know how to make *you* disappear." She closed her eyes.

And she listened.

He was quiet, too damned quiet. He moved like a cat. She had no sense of him in that room, not even that he was still seated on the bed with her.

And then she felt something at her wrists, and her eyes shot open.

"Caught in your own web, spider lady."

He was sitting right back on the edge of the bed, looking like a cat who had lapped up a huge bowl of cream, and her wrists were secured to the bedposts as lightly as a feather. She hadn't felt a thing.

But she felt something now. She characterized it as murderous rage, and he looked amused as she twisted her body and thrust her legs out toward him viciously.

"Oh, it's a fearsome thing to see an enraged black

165

widow," he commented, shifting his body out of the way of her flailing legs. "But it is nice to know that occasionally she can be impeded. A man likes to feel he has control sometime."

"You have *nothing,* stranger," she spat at him.

"Oh no, Cassandra, I do have you. And I don't think I would be remiss if I demanded of you what you took from me the last time."

"I won't even ask what that was; I think it will be quite amusing to watch you struggle with taking off my pants."

"Ah yes, that too," he murmured. "I really wish this arm felt well enough to do the thing justice, but I promise you, Cassandra, I will do my best."

She refused to react to that. What could he do, after all? She wore endless petticoats and underthings under her dress, and it would take him an hour to unfasten everything else, and he would have to undo her arms in order to get it all off. She was safe. There wasn't much he *could* do.

She must have slept because it was coming near dawn.

He was still smiling, that odd little smile, and she wondered at her reaction to it. Sometimes it was downright infuriating, just like now, and she wished she could just smack it off his face.

The worst thing she could do was pull and push and get him more determined.

She could just lie still like a rag doll and let him do his worst.

She didn't like that alternative either.

He leaned over and began removing her kid boots, and she recoiled.

"Oh now, spider lady, what's good for the spider must be good for the prey . . ." Her boots went on the floor in a thumping heap.

"It takes a lot of spirit to trap a man in his own bed,"

166

he went on, sliding off her serviceable cotton stockings. "Of course, a man tends to wear a lot less to bed to begin with—"

He reached for her drawers, at the expense of the pain in his arm. He flexed, and they slipped off easily from her body and he tossed them on the heap of her shoes and boots.

"It sure would be a lot more convenient if a woman only wore trousers to bed . . ." he mused, as he reached for her skirt, and lifted it up to get at her petticoats. "Thank goodness you don't wear those hoops around the house, Cassandra; I'd hate to think—a man could cut himself to ribbons on the damned thing."

"I like the thought," she said through clenched teeth.

"I was sure you would."

And she didn't like the thought of him having a full view of her nakedness and that she could do absolutely nothing about it. She wasn't going to give him the satisfaction of protesting, but she had to do something. This was a whole other matter from the reason she had tied him up in his room when she was searching for something specific. This was purely ornery.

"You don't look happy, Cassandra."

"I'm enjoying this immensely."

"So did I," he said lightly. "But I'll tell you, black widow, there's a price to pay for everything."

"I'm finding that out," she ground out.

"But are you prepared to pay?"

"Are you?"

"I believe I'm paying my head off right now, Cassandra." His eyes grazed her naked lower torso. "I believe you could pay and never count the cost."

"What is your price—this time?"

His light, bright gaze skimmed upward to meet hers. "One precious kiss, Cassandra."

"*Nothing* else?" She couldn't quite believe him. He

167

had her right in a position where he could do anything he wanted. She was beginning to wonder about him, about what was really on his mind, and who he really was and how she had even allowed him to take advantage of her this long.

"Say yes, Cassandra."

She licked her lips. She knew his kisses; this wasn't a fleeting thing he was demanding. It was her whole-hearted participation. It was her soul. And if she kissed him—*if*, how could it not lead to something else with her body right there for his taking?

"You remember my kisses, Cassandra. Say yes."

She remembered, she remembered what he had taught her about honeyed kisses and the seeking heat of a man's mouth. Oh yes.

"And then you'll let me go?" she temporized.

"I'll arrange to let you go," he agreed. "All for one sweet taste of you."

"And nothing more?"

"Not now, Cassandra."

And what did that mean?

"All right." Surely she was a Christian martyr going to her certain death . . .

He knelt on the bed beside her and eased himself down until he lay next to her. And then slowly, he maneuvered himself over her and onto her, and his arms at either side of her head.

"Hello, Cassandra."

"Get it over with."

"A tempting invitation, black widow. More tempting just to keep your mouth shut than to listen to your alluring words."

"I have no words to describe *you*."

"No, your mouth will do it for you, Cassandra. Don't turn away; I *will* have you."

And she couldn't, she couldn't turn away from the

warmth of him; there was something about being immobilized that made her feel everything just that more intensely. His kiss was raw with a kind of need that was inexplicable to her. He wanted her, every last sensation of her. He probed her, he plunged into her, he felt the shape of her with his avid tongue.

She felt the shape of him, engorged and demanding at the naked triangle of her femininity. She felt her body gush with heated response, she felt herself answering his kisses firmly and surely, giving and taking, demanding from him almost mindlessly as if some other part of her were answering that sensual need in him.

She wanted to capture him as he had captured her.

She twisted wildly to free her legs so that she could envelop him, trap him. She lifted herself and wound herself around him and hooked her ankles together and she still was not strong enough to contain him.

"Oh, a spider lady's legs — she does know what to do with them," he murmured against her mouth.

But he was so much stronger than she. She could hold onto him but she could never trap him, and that was the way of a man and a woman.

Now she knew what sensual hunger was, and what it was for a man to desire her, to entice her and then not to take her.

But that would come, she could see it in his eyes.

"Such kisses, Cassandra . . ."

But maybe not. He would never be sure, and she would never give in.

She couldn't hold him with that primitive strength with which he had enfolded her.

Her legs ached, and her mouth felt swollen and raw and she would not let him go.

"Tenacious spider lady," he whispered. "Soon you will hold me with your legs and arms and all of your body."

"No . . ." Her protestation sounded so weak with her

voice thick with the taste of him.

"Oh yes . . ." he promised, shifting for one last naked taste of her. "You know now."

She knew nothing. Nothing, except that he would not take her now and she did not understand at all.

He eased his aching body off her, and looked down at her. Daylight arched through the windows, and she looked absolutely luscious on the bed with her bare, tempting body and swollen lips. He could have spent the day just kissing her until she came to him of her own unendurable desire.

But he wanted her whole, all of her, surrounding him, demanding him, inviting him.

"If I stay another minute, spider lady . . ."

"Stay," she whispered.

He was stronger than she, then, in her nascent discovery of her power.

"I'll get Zilpha."

"Trane . . ."

"You can be coerced to say my name, black widow," he said as he opened the door. "I'll remember that."

And then Zilpha came running into the room. "Missus!"

"Don't say a word," Cassandra growled fiercely.

"I didn't see nuthin', Missus," she swore as she cut Cassandra's hands free. "Ain't nuthin' happened here you don't want no one to know."

She found Ojim lurking outside the door. "What is it?"

"We takin' de corn today, Miz Taggart."

"I'm coming."

"So am I." His voice behind her startled her.

"No need," she said airily. "Rest yourself, stranger. I trust you found the bed was comfortable."

170

"I find the thought of you running around alone here damned uncomfortable."

She shrugged. "I haven't thought about you at all. Fine, come along. We'll be down in fifteen minutes." She turned to him. "Fifteen?" He looked revitalized; he didn't look nearly as drained as a man should who had stayed awake the whole night.

Now how was that, she wondered interestedly. How did a man who had been dead on his feet a moment before rise up looking fresh and raring to go?

"Ojim stays here, between us," he ordered without even asking. "You report if one of us leaves our room and goes someplace else."

Ojim looked beseechingly at Cassandra.

She sent him a vexed look. He had no right demanding anything of Ojim. "Our guest is understandably nervous, Ojim. There's no telling who might be hiding in the attic who might want to shoot him."

Ojim understood none of that. "You say I stay, Missus?"

"Stay, Ojim."

They were out five minutes later, waiting for Ojim to bring round the gig.

"I'm going to continue to impress you with my ungentlemanly ways: I'm getting in first so I don't have to rest my injured arm against the carriage side."

"Fine, I wouldn't turn my back on you now for all the cotton on Riveland."

She watched him climb in, noting that he was careful to keep his eye firmly on her hands, and she followed, amused, and ordered Ojim to proceed as soon as she closed the door behind her.

The gig lurched forward and down the familiar track.

"Things were less parsed out when I left," he said musingly as the gig rumbled down one road and then another that criss-crossed the fields in a well-ordered grid. "Didn't used to rotate the fields with regularity, and Jesse was just experimenting with whether he wanted to grow long or short staple cotton."

"I guess he decided," she said shortly. "Of course all of this detail is meaningless to me because I wasn't here and Jesse never talked about it. I thought I made that clear."

"Lady, nothing is clear where you're concerned," he said feelingly. "I don't believe a word of it anyway."

"*You* don't have to," she snapped. "I have to believe you—"

She never finished: the gig bounced into the air and slammed down at an angle, throwing her sideways and halfway out the door, which had popped open. The horse, spooked, strained into a gallop, dragging the wheelless gig behind him, turning and twisting on and off the track.

"*Ojim!*" he roared, pulling at Cassandra's body with his one good arm.

He could feel Ojim straining at the reins, pulling, pulling as the horse veered sideways and then back onto the track again. He felt the strain in his own arm as he got Cassandra back into the carriage and onto the floor. He could only hold on and pray Ojim could get control of the lead horse, but the thing wanted to run wild and he wouldn't heed restraint.

The gig dragged along another hundred feet and then suddenly fell forward as Ojim uncoupled the horse to let him run, and toppled out of his seat.

And then there was silence.

Cassandra took a tentative step, leaning on Zilpha's arm, and nodded her head. "That's fine. I'm whole."

"No, you ain't. You hurt, and you got to rest, Missus."

172

"I can't afford to, you know that. Where is our guest?"

"He walkin' de floor, Missus, like he waitin' fo' a baby."

He should be worried, she thought grimly, lowering herself down onto her bed with the utmost care. There were still portions of her that ached to the touch, and there was a part of her that was absolutely sure she knew how the wheel on that gig had come so conveniently loose.

"Dey is dumpin' de corn outside de kitchen square, don't you worry none 'bout dat," Zilpha went on. "Ojim see to ever'thing just how you wishes, Miz Taggart. You not to worry 'bout nothin'."

"I'm not worried. I'm bruised, and I'm not happy."

"Yes, ma'am. I bring you somethin' to eat."

"I'm going downstairs, Zilpha. I can't stay in bed. I'm fine, I promise you."

"You got pain, Missus. Better you stay in bed."

"I've got one pain I have to take care of, that's for sure," she agreed tartly. "You just give me your arm and get me downstairs."

"Yes, ma'am." Zilpha held out her arm, and Cassandra got slowly to her feet and leaned against her.

She negotiated the hallway slowly but with little trouble. The stairs were harder, since she had to bend her knees; they stopped at every step, and she held on tightly to the banister as well.

Ojim was waiting there, his arm bandaged, his expression gloomy. "Don' know how dat happen, ma'am," he began, and she brushed him away.

"I have an idea, and it's not your fault, Ojim. You just make sure that corn gets into the cribs this week, please."

"Yes, ma'am."

"And now . . . " she said the words out loud, taking a

deep breath before she slowly shuffled her way into the library. She expected to find *him* there, and she did, but he had not been expecting her to come downstairs. He was up on the library ladder, balancing himself with his injured arm, running his free hand over the walls and books in increments of several feet at a time as he could reach them.

Walking the floor, ha! she thought sardonically. He was climbing the walls, and it had nothing to do with what happened to her. He hadn't expected to see her at all tonight, or he wouldn't be up on that ladder.

"Your concern touches me," she said from the doorway.

He froze. *Hell and damnation.*

"You didn't find the bullet," she went on artlessly as he began his difficult descent. "Oh please, don't go to any trouble on my account, when you've put yourself to so much trouble already."

"What the hell does that mean?"

"I mean, wheels don't fall off of carriages of their own volition. I mean I think someone tampered with my gig, and furthermore, I think that someone was you, that's what I mean. And since you were so anxious to sit on the far side, I think it's obvious that someone was you," she added for good measure as the expression on his face turned stony. "You had good reason, stranger, and frankly, I don't know you from Adam, and you are abusing my hospitality criminally. It's time you left before any more 'accidents' happen."

"Now ain't that a pretty speech, ma'am," he drawled, keeping a tight rein on his temper. "You shoot me, I try to kill you. It sounds like a story someone made up, doesn't it? And we know who the storyteller is around here."

"We surely do, stranger. Any man who walks into a house claiming to be someone he's not, and has no pa-

174

pers to prove it, is the biggest damn storyteller I ever met."

"Yeah, and I'm still here, lady, so that means something I've said has merit—"

"Your threats are meaningless to me," she ground out. "Do all the damned investigating you want, stranger. Just pack up and get out now."

"I'm going to turn the investigation a new way, black widow; I want to know why you're kissing me with the one hand and gunning for me with the other. I'm *not* leaving."

"I'll have you thrown out."

"By whom? Daggett? Greve—if he ever shows his face around here again? Ojim? One of your field bucks?"

"I'll call in the sheriff, stranger, and I'll make the biggest stink you ever heard this side of the Little Midway. You tampered with that wheel and I'll prove it."

"You can't prove a damn thing."

"Neither can you, but I can prove you are not Trane Taggart."

"You'll have a damned hard time explaining what I'm doing on Riveland, lady."

Oh Lord . . .

"Get out of this room. My house is closed to you, stranger, except for the guest room and the dining room."

"You won't stop me."

"I'll give it a damned good try," she vowed.

"So will I," he shot back, and stamped out of the room.

She limped after him to be sure he either went upstairs or into the dining room, and then she went to find Zilpha. "Tell Ojim I need three men in the house to watch our guest."

"You gonna track dat man?"

"We're going to try. We need three *smart* men, maybe

175

two boys so we don't arouse suspicion."

"I tell 'im."

"I'll just . . . I'll just go back to bed now, Zilpha."

"I take you."

"You make sure they watch him, you hear?"

"I do dat."

Ojim recruited two bright boys and one strong hand who was working as a carpenter and sent them up to the big house the next morning.

When he came out of his room, he didn't even notice the worker fixing the banister railing. When he came outside, he never saw two boys playing and chasing after newly purchased chickens which had somehow wandered onto the front lawn.

When he went to the stables to choose a horse, he was gently turned away by Ojim.

When he tried to get into the library, he found the door locked, and from the outside, the curtains closed against his prying eyes.

Cassandra meant what she had said.

"Now where you off to?" Zilpha asked gently as he impatiently pushed his way out onto the veranda. "We got to change yo bandage. Missus remind me to tell you. Come along now, mister."

He couldn't object without seeming churlish; he felt like a child following her down the hallway to the ell of the kitchen where she seemingly had everything prepared.

"Where is your mistress?"

"She restin'." Zilpha's magical fingers went to work, unwinding the bandage, gently lifting the poultice. "Dis healin' nicely. We change poultice, bandage up again one mo' time, and all gonna be well wif you, mister."

Was it real, her concern, or just a waylaying tactic? Even after his arm was securely bandaged, he had to wonder. Even after she kindly offered to bring him a tray in his room so he wouldn't have to sit alone in the dining room, he wasn't sure the offer was more to keep him confined than concern for his comfort.

He felt frustrated by the constraints. He couldn't search, he did not any longer have the freedom of the house, and now he had to watch every move *he* made as well as every move she made, and that was tearing on his nerves.

He walked out of his room and there was a slave girl polishing the woodwork. He went into the fields, and those two playful boys were chasing each other all up and down the track to the cotton fields. He took a walk past the garden, and there was Zilpha directing Elsie or Leola to plant something, or hoe, or weed—he never could tell which.

He slipped into the morning room, where there was a desk and a cabinet as yet unsearched, and Ojim ambled by on an errand for "Missus," and waited patiently for him to abandon the place. He corraled himself in his room, and Zilpha knocked on the door to see if he were all right.

The black widow had her housefolk trained, he thought grimly as he spent another futile day trying to put himself into Jesse Taggart's mind to figure out where he would have left a clue to his first marriage.

He wandered into the formal parlor where the furniture was rigorously arranged to discourage guests from overextending their welcome. Everything was opulent, of the finest material and workmanship in this room and this room only. It was Jesse again, putting up a front to put across an effect. Maybe he had done it when he married Cassandra, just to please her, but surely she had discovered quickly that his taste was upcountry, worn and proud.

In this room, two stiff sofas vied for attention by the fireplace. Centered between them was an incongruous

177

parlor table which was the height of a dining table, so that if a guest sat on the sofa, he would be seated lower than the table.

There were side chairs scattered around, annexed to small tea tables, and a bookcase serpentine-front desk between the two front windows.

The bookcase was empty, its casement doors locked.

He felt the familiar sense of futility as he ran his one good hand over the woodwork, looking for some kind of indentation, or a hiding place for a key.

The slant top of the desk folded down on its supports readily, but there was nothing to discover there, either.

It was as if some elf had preceded him and discovered every secret. Maybe the elf was Cassandra. Maybe he was playing a fool's game to even challenge her. He wasn't going to gain much. Jesse had left his only son high and dry, and that had been exactly what he expected—no more, no less.

He looked around him furtively to see if Ojim were skulking around, and then he lifted the first pair of pulls of the lower drawer and slid it open.

From behind the bi-fold doors of the parlor, Cassandra watched him with unalloyed interest.

The man was damned clever, she had to say that for him. He didn't give up easily. He had to know that every nook and cranny of the house had been gone over—first by Raylene, truth to tell, and then by her, as her curiosity about Jesse grew along with her maturity and her infertility.

She still had no inkling what he wanted on Riveland, but she knew that Zilpha and Ojim had frustrated his search for it with great tact and dispatch, and now it was her turn to take up the vigil.

It was so easy to spy on him since Zilpha kept up the

178

story that "Missus is restin'," and he couldn't contest it because she kept the door locked.

She watched him from behind the brocade curtains of the dining room as he explored the underside of the table, trying to find papers or a packet taped there with adhesive.

She watched him from the root cellar door as he poked and prodded everything in the kitchen, from the pots to the drying spices, to see if something could be concealed there.

She followed him out to the stables and hid behind a stack of baled hay as he approached old Isaac about saddling up a horse. She saw him look up at the hayloft and she felt a clutch of terror at her heart.

"This where Mr. Jesse died?" he asked casually as Isaac turned away from him.

"I wouldn't know dat, sir. I wasn't nowhere here." He paused a moment. "I don't find no horses free fo' ridin', sir. I apologize fo' such lack."

She saw the pure frustration gather into a murderous expression on his face and vanish almost immediately as he stamped out of the stable.

She was pushing him, and she knew it. She wondered how far she could go.

The July heat exacerbated everyone's temper.

"Time fo' shuckin' de corn," Ojim announced. "Soon time fo' to bring in de cotton."

"Jesse used to pass around a jug."

She knew the voice. "I'm impressed by your incessant details, stranger, but he never did that when I married him."

"Might be good incentive to start. Daggett will only whip your men."

"That's my lookout, my problem."

179

"I'm the only one looking out, Cassandra."

"No, you're the only one making trouble."

It was too hot to argue. Even he seemed weary and indifferent.

"I wish you would just leave."

"Oh, I don't believe you want that at all, spider lady."

They sat on the veranda, lethargic in the sultry heat.

"Let me help," he said impulsively.

"No."

"You know Daggett will undermine you and ruin a hundred good bales if he isn't watched."

"I know."

"And Trane Taggart of Baltimore is nowhere around."

"I haven't written him," she said stiffly.

"And he was such a loyal correspondent."

"This is none of your business."

"I am Trane Taggart."

"You are a nuisance," she said edgily, her first instinct to run quelled by his off-handed reference to *her* Trane Taggart. She had to play this one through; she must never allow him to trick her into revealing that *her* Trane Taggart wasn't real. She was angry at herself that she hadn't prepared for this contingency, either. It almost seemed as though when Mr. Greve took himself out of town, he took the need for the letters with him.

She did not have to justify the letters to the stranger. *He* was telling the lie. *He* had to justify himself to *her.*

She went very still, very attentive, waiting for him to pursue the notion.

But maybe it was even too hot to wrangle about that. He was equally quiet, struck by something that hadn't occurred to him before. He had been approaching the whole question of Trane's identity from the wrong direction.

And now he had a new tack and he knew just what to look for; it was so simple, he wondered why he hadn't thought of it before.

No matter. A man picked up his challenges whenever they presented themselves, and never looked back. A man surely didn't waste regrets on his own stupidity.

A man made his opportunities, too. They couldn't watch him every hour of every day; the next morning he did not appear for breakfast, and over the course of the following hour, as he listened at his door, he heard footsteps, he heard Zilpha, he heard Cassandra.

"De mister ain't come out de room yet, Miz Taggart."

"Or else he's come out and no one saw him."

"No, no, Rufus done kep' his eye on de door; he ain't come out yet."

"He climbed out the window, then."

"No, no, Amos, he watchin' de windows. Ain't no one come."

"Get Eli up here quickly. I want to know when our guest emerges."

"Yes, ma'am."

He had what — five minutes — ? He opened the door a crack. The hallway was empty, and he slipped out of his room and edged his way carefully down the hall to Cassandra's room.

He opened the door slowly; he had no way of knowing she hadn't retreated to her room. He was gambling she hadn't.

The super-stillness felt almost ominous. But the room was empty.

Cassandra's room.

He hadn't seen this room before, and he closed the door gently behind him and leaned against it to give himself a moment to get a sense of the place that she had inhabited with Jesse Taggart.

It was as plain as a room could get. Every piece of

furniture was unadorned pine, from the dressers to the washstands and the bedstead.

There was no joy in this room. The floors were wide plank, covered by a utilitarian braided rug. The bed jutted out onto it from the center of the room, covered by a worn, limp quilt. There were two dressers and one commode and one washstand placed almost haphazardly along whichever wall they fit.

The only piece of furniture that reflected anything of Cassandra was the desk by the window. It was almost overpoweringly ornate in contrast to the rest of the room. It looked like a table; its single paneled pedestal base was turned toward the wall so that what he saw first were the two thick turned, reeded legs that belonged on a dining room table rather than a desk. A small gallery surrounded three sides. Behind it, back to the front windows, was a small side chair with carved rails and a needlepoint seat.

Here Cassandra sat and . . . wrote letters to someone named Trane Taggart who had settled himself neatly and nicely far away in Baltimore.

He was too damned tall for the chair, but he sat in it anyway, and pushed it away from the desk so he could look at the drawers in the pedestal.

Every one of them had a molded pull and a rosette keyhole surround. Each one was locked except the center drawer and he pulled this one out and surveyed its contents, which were pretty much what he expected: paper, inkstand, pens, a pen wiper.

An account book, shoved way in the back of the deep center drawer . . . blank except for a list of a half dozen or so dates—

Like a code.

Recent dates? He couldn't tell, the year wasn't appended to them. But the months dated from late March—

He closed the book thoughtfully and placed it carefully back where he had found it. The dates ended in early June; there was no entry for July.

Half dozen or so dates, he mused, as he checked every corner of the room for a place that could conceal all six plus feet of him. Not much choice there; he certainly could not use the closet. She was probably in and out of it twice a day or more. His bones didn't align well with delicate black silk dresses and caged steel hoops.

Six or seven dates from late March, he thought, as he knelt to look under the bed.

The bed had been made to accommodate Jesse. It sat a little higher on its frame, its side rails were a little longer, and he could just slide underneath it without having to scrunch his body up too tightly.

From that position, with his head up against the headboard feet, he could see a nice angle of the desk against the window.

That was fine. He got back out from under the bed and set a pillow on the side chair—which wasn't half as pretty as Cassandra—and squeezed himself under the bed again.

Yes—he could just see the pillow, and that was fine. Cassandra wasn't the only one who could keep a vigil to trap a lie.

He was wagering he had scared her very badly when he had mentioned her not having received a letter from Taggart since Greve had gone. He was betting one was going to turn up real soon, and he was going to be under the bed, watching Cassandra compose it.

She wasn't at all bothered by the stranger's reference to the letters—not a bit.

She sat at her desk with the account book in hand,

183

ruminating over the dates that signified when she supposedly received them. There had not been one since Greve abandoned her business for his. But so what? He was the only one who mattered in terms of her producing the letters.

On the other hand, Mr. "Call-Me-Trane" had heard her refer to them so often that maybe it did look suspicious that there hadn't been one for almost a month.

She couldn't let that alarm her, she *couldn't*. The man had found nothing relevant to his case, and she did not need to prove *hers*. *He* was the trespasser. He was the one making threats.

But still . . .

She took a deep, uneven breath. The situation was getting more and more precarious: the damned mountain seamed to be settling in to stay.

She felt trapped by him and the intensity of him. Nothing she had tried with him worked, and she was running out of ideas.

Maybe the thing to do was to present a new letter from Trane Taggart. He would be hard put to deny it — or *he* — existed.

Oh, but he was doing such a good job of it.

Maybe now it was far away enough from Jesse's death so that an investigation wouldn't prove anything.

She sighed. There was always the question of a conspiracy between him and Mr. Greve; it was still the only thing that made sense. And it was also a very good reason why Mr. Greve absented himself so fortuitously.

She wondered if she could, based on that, wrest control of Jesse's executorship out of Mr. Greve's hands. She wondered if any court would even listen to the trail of events since his death.

It all sounded like a comedic play.

She stared at the paper in front of her on the desk. She couldn't think of a thing to write that would explain why Baltimore Trane had not kept up his correspondence with her.

She thrust herself out of the chair and paced the room impatiently. She was letting "Call Me Trane" get to her, and if she did that, she was going to make a huge mistake long before Mr. Greve returned to the scene.

Nevertheless, she would be prudent to have a letter or two ready for presentation, especially since the fields were in the midst of the sixth hoe-down, and harvesting would begin in the early weeks of August.

She hoped "Call Me Trane" would be gone by then.

Probably not.

He hadn't done too much harm yet, except exasperate the life out of her.

And demand your kisses—and make you feel things you don't want to know about . . .

But that was another story, the one she resolutely put an ending to before it even had a beginning, let alone a middle or a life.

A letter from *her* Trane . . .

She took a deep breath.

He had been away. That made the most sense. And he had been a little concerned because he knew—of course—that the harvest was imminent, and he had . . . he had what—

Hoped to reach her in time to . . .

No—wanted to let her know that he was back home . . .

Yes—with his wife and beloved family . . . all *six* of them, she thought venomously, three *boys,* three *girls* . . .

The man couldn't kiss her like that if he had a wife back wherever it was he came from. She wished he would go back there—

She stopped short.

She had a feeling something was not right.

185

Yet everything looked the same, and she had Eli comfortably posted outside the stranger's room so that he couldn't come skulking up on her while she was preparing to reincarnate Trane Taggart. But still, she had the sense of something not in symmetry, and she didn't know if it were within herself, her bedroom, or just the whole situation in general.

All those children . . . He had picked it up right out of the air, and he had kissed her like that anyway—

The man was a liar *and* a cheat.

Dear Cassandra,
   My deepest regrets that I have not communicated with you sooner.

Good. She wrote that down experimentally as she leaned over the table-leg side of her desk.

   Urgent business called me away at the very moment I knew you would need my counsel.

No. At the very moment he was preparing to write to her, knowing the harvest was imminent. Better.

That was good, that was fine. He'd been away, he hoped she hadn't had any serious problems and that she had coped well, as he was sure he had. He was now back home with his loved ones and would she be so . . . kind as to . . . assure him that all was well and that the harvest was proceeding as she wished. Sincerely, etc.

That would do, for the first draft. She folded the letter and tucked it away in the upper drawer of the pedestal and locked it emphatically.

He made the faintest hiss with the intake of his breath as she slammed the drawer shut. Well, he had watched her, he had seen it. She had been writing something, and he would assume it was a letter.

She was ready for bed now; he could hear her footsteps rustling around the room, the closet door opening, closing. A drawer opening. The splash of water from the washstand basin.

He carefully rolled over onto his left side. He could just see her eyelet-trimmed drawers and her stockinged feet, and if he moved an inch or two more, he could see her whole body, the upper torso bare from the waist up, with her blue-ribboned camisole draped over her hips while she washed.

She turned to the light which emanated from the lamp on her desk, and the shadows caressed the curves and hollows of her beautiful breasts, emphasizing the taut, dusky nipple and the soft underside just made for the palm of a man's hand.

He ached to hold her, to feel the texture of her skin, to taste it, to be the one to incite her desire.

But he was looking at innocence: those breasts had never felt the needful caress of a man who wanted her. That body had never been held by a man who wanted to explore her passion and arouse her desire. She had never been loved by a man who wanted to possess her totally and claim her soul.

Jesse had crushed it all out of her.

And he wanted to resurrect it so badly . . .

Her drawers fell to the floor and her long, slender legs walked to the bed. He heard it creak as she sat down; he saw one leg lift off the floor and come down again completely bare, and then the other. He saw her white cotton stockings drop to the floor as she stood up again and walked to the dresser across the room where she came fully into his vision, naked, desirable, and completely unaware of it.

He drew in his breath again as she opened a lower

drawer and bent over to remove a fresh nightgown.

She slipped it over her head slowly and inch by inch it grazed her body as it slid downward to her feet, long-sleeved, proper, of the finest lawn, almost transparent, as it hugged a curve here, draped over the lushness of her buttocks there, rested delicately on the lusciously taut tips of her breasts.

She took the silver-backed brush from her dresser set and began briskly working her hair. The motion of her arm thrust her chest forward; her breasts trembled as her hands braided her hair for her evening's rest.

A moment later, she was back at the bed, climbing in, wriggling around to get comfortable before she thought to snuff the light. She rolled over onto the other side of the bed and off, doused the light and climbed back in.

It was going to be a long night, he thought, winding his arms around the back of his head to cradle it.

A very long night . . .

And yet—she lay awake, perturbed by something she couldn't define, aware of some different atmosphere, unable to put a name to it.

Secure in the fact she knew it couldn't be the stranger. *He* was sound sleep in the room down the hall.

Chapter Twelve

He stole a horse the next morning.

It wasn't that easy, either. He awoke with a start in the early hours of the morning when he heard the bedroom door close, and he had a fine long moment of panic while he considered whether Cassandra had risen and gone or Zilpha had just delivered a tray.

Either way, he could not waste much more time in Cassandra's room; he waited for some clue that she still was in bed, but there was no movement at all above him.

Finally, he grasped onto the tightly woven rope support under the mattress and pushed himself out from under the bed.

She wasn't there.

Her scent was there, pervading the place, invading his senses.

He inched open the door.

Damn, Eli was still in place, implacably in front of his bedroom door, just waiting for him to step foot out so he could sic his mistress on him.

She sure wanted his tail.

He catwalked over to the window, and leaned over the desk chair to look out. Yep, Ojim, at sunup, working that garden as if his life depended on it.

Cassandra had him covered.

But there were two other windows in her bedroom,

since it was a corner room. Jumping out wasn't a bad idea. If he wanted to break his neck.

He couldn't use a sheet either—Cassandra would know, sure as the sun, he had been spying on her.

Hell.

He opened the window tentatively, slowly, and leaned out. The best he could do was a trellis of roses that climbed up that side of the house.

He went out feet first, reaching for the latticed wood structure that was fragile at best, and might not even support his size or weight come to that, and he found it, hooking onto one rung of it with his boot heels and hanging out the window by sheer effort.

One hand then—reaching for the trellis—God, if the thing broke . . .

But parsimonious Jesse—he wouldn't build a thing that could break easily—except a marriage—he liked a thing to be done once and never done again.

The trellis held as he edged his upper body tightly against it, and the climbing rose vine prickled his skin, even through his shirt and his pants.

Cautiously he climbed downward to make no noise, diving off the last half of the structure and into the bushes below as he heard footsteps and voices.

It was done. Ojim strode by on his way somewhere, and he held his breath until he was out of sight. Then he crawled through the bushes to the back of the house, to the kitchen ell and then beyond, all on his knees, until he was hidden from the house by the square of outbuildings surrounding the back garden, and then he got to his feet and raced toward the stables.

It was barely sunrise by then, but he knew Daggett was already rousing the slaves for the next day's work, and he was sure Isaac was already abroad.

He didn't need above a minute—maybe two—to liberate one or the other of the horses from its stall.

He heard Isaac's footsteps shuffling in.

He led his mount by its mane through the back maze of the barn and out into the sky-blue morning.

Another moment, he was up on bareback and galloping out into the fields.

"He ain't moved, Miz Taggart."

It was noon. It was impossible.

She bit her lip. Maybe something had happened to him. Maybe he was unconscious. Maybe—

She knocked on the door loudly.

No answer. She turned the knob and swung it in savagely.

The room was empty, the bed not slept in.

Maybe he had outwitted her again.

She stormed down the stairs. "Where is our guest, Ojim?"

"I ain't seen 'im, ma'am. He ain't been down this way or he have to pass me."

"Zilpha—"

"Ain't been nowhere near de kitchen, ma'am. Can't figure how de man can just be gone like dat."

She drew in her breath harshly. She didn't know, either. She couldn't figure a lot of things.

She ran back up to his room and made a quick, cursory search. He had not been in that room last night.

Damn, the man was dangerous.

Slippery. A mountain cat prowling her house in spite of her precautions.

She didn't like the feeling she had about that at all. She slowly walked down the hallway to her room, dreading to open the door, apprehensive of what she would find.

She paused at the door and forced her reluctant fingers to grasp the knob and turn. She held back for a long moment, and then she resolutely pushed her way in.

The bed was unmade. Her underclothing lay where she had dropped it the previous night. Her nightgown was still draped across the blanket rest on the footboard.

She moved farther into the room.

. . . And the window was open. Wide open.

Wide enough for a man to fit through—or a mountain cat.

He had been in her room last night—but *where?*

She whirled, and threw open the closet door; that wasn't big or deep enough to hide a man-mountain. Where else . . .

Oh God—she had been writing that letter last night and he had been in the room . . .

. . . behind a curtain? Not hardly. Under the bed . . .

Under the bed—she fell on her knees and crawled to the bed. There was room. She went under, compressing her body so that she could squeeze beneath the side rails. Roomy under there for her, but she wasn't tall. On the other hand, a mountain would have to ball himself up in order to avoid detection; why not? From this vantage point, he could have seen everything.

Everything.

She felt a hot wave suffuse her whole body

. . . everything—

"ELI!"

He had seen her writing the letter.

He had seen . . . he had seen—her . . . undressing.

She could hardly contain her fury. He had seen . . .

"ZILPHA!"

. . . And he probably planned to . . .

She breathed deeply, trying to control her fury.

He probably planned to come back again—tonight maybe—to catch her in the act.

The act of what?

She looked up at the underpinning of the mattress—thick, stout rope wound and tied to cradle the mattress. She wanted to wind that rope around that man's neck and *pull*. . . .

Not even Jesse . . . had ever watched her—

Her body grew hot, her breath suffocated. She rolled on her stomach and wriggled out from under the bed.

"ELI!"

She knew it was her voice, but it just didn't sound like her. Nothing would ever sound like her again.

She went to the window; there was no air to cool her burning cheeks. He had either jumped, or he had climbed down the trellis. She hoped he had jumped. She hoped he was lying in the bushes with a broken neck.

"Missus?" Eli's gentle voice behind her.

She turned to face him, not knowing why she had called him or what she wanted him to do.

She didn't know where the stranger was, and she didn't know if any plan she made would even work.

But she had to do *something*. She rubbed her hand across her eyes wearily. It was too much. She had to think.

He would undoubtedly come back tonight because he wanted to watch her write the final draft of her letter from Trane Taggart. He would not give up his successful hiding place; he had no other options besides.

Nor would it be enough for her to scare him out from under the bed. She could not eke any satisfaction out of that, not at all.

She wanted violence, she wanted the bed to fall right on his head. She wanted . . .

But why not?

She moved quickly over to the side rail. "Eli, come help me lift this mattress."

He came to her side and pulled up the mattress for her while she tested the rope support. But it wasn't only

193

the support that held the thing together. There were four iron latches at each corner.

She stared at them a moment and then at Eli, and then she knew exactly what she wanted to do.

"Mr. Daggett fo' to see you, Missus."

But Daggett wasn't waiting for announcements or explanations. He pushed his way into the small parlor where she was sitting and staring out the window, waiting with vindictive anticipation for the night to come.

"HE FIRED ME!"

"I beg your pardon?"

"The sonovabitchin' manservant of yours fired me, and I don't take that from no one, Miz Taggart. He goddamned *fired* me!"

"He had no right to do that," she said as calmly as she could, and even she felt Daggett's wrath. The mountain cat prowled, and he mowed down everything in his path, silently, subtly, and he disappeared before anyone could take a gun to him.

"He ain't stayin'. Jesse's secret spawn ain't pullin' no rank on me."

"I didn't fire you," Cassandra said. "I want you on. I can't pull in the harvest alone."

"Get the damn bastard to do it, ma'am. I'm gone."

"Mr. Daggett—"

"I ain't listenin'; I don't hear nothin'. You never backed me up. You never gave me the fields. You can just go and pick them yourself."

He stormed out, and she felt as if she had been hit by a tornado that had lifted her up, shaken her around and thrown her back down to earth again.

He had fired Daggett . . .

What do you do now? He made the decision for you. Do you write to Taggart-Baltimore and ask if it were

194

My dear Mrs. Taggart—
He was perfectly right, of course. One doesn't maltreat one's slaves . . .

One didn't coddle them either—
She couldn't get over the nerve of him, the uncombat-
able sheer gall of him to walk in her house, claim he
was Trane Taggart, and then take over her slaves and her
cotton fields.

Oh, but the day was young yet. Daggett might be
gone, but the man-mountain still had her to deal with,
and if she didn't find him this afternoon, she would
surely come to grips with him tonight.

She had never looked forward to anything so eagerly
in her life.

She kept her servants on guard and highly visible,
with the instructions that they were to turn a blind eye if
they saw him near or in the house.

"He ain't comin' back," Zilpha predicted. "He be
scared whut you gonna say."

"What can *I* do to *him?*" she said, forcing herself to
be calm. "He's hardly afraid of me."

"Dat man ain't got no honor."

"We don't know what that man has except audacity."

"Wasn't no fights in de fields today just 'cause dat
Daggett ain't aroun'."

"I suppose that's good news."

"Dey don' know whut it mean."

"I don't, either."

"You hopin' dat man comin' 'round tonight."

"Not with explanations," she said wryly. She didn't
know what to think, either. Daggett had disappeared

and not even Ojim could search him out, and for all she knew, her men were running wild in the fields instead of hauling corn and cotton.

And she didn't want to find out.

"No, he ain't de 'splainin' type," Zilpha said sagely. "He a taker. He see whut he want and he go after it, and it don' matter nohow 'bout how he come to get it. He after takin' sumpin' from Riveland, but I'm thinkin' he don' know whut it is."

"He is a pretender, and I'm going to prove it, and I'm going to get him off Riveland and then maybe we'll have some peace."

But what was peace?

Was it having a home and a means by which to obtain income? Was it knowing she wouldn't have to worry about anything again in her life so long as she followed the rules laid down in Jesse's will? Was it having children—was it finding love?

Or had peace come the day Jesse had pitched backward over the hayloft and fallen to his death?

She had aged so much since then, and she had grown not at all.

Jesse never could have expected a man claiming to be Trane Taggart, a son of his, would walk through his door and totally take over.

Neither had she.

She waited. There was something about the waiting that was almost luxurious, as if she were anticipating a lover.

She wanted to do nothing else but savor the fact that he would find his way to her because there was something he wanted. He was a clever man, this "Call Me Trane" impostor. He had only to catch her with the letters and he proved that her Trane was the false one, and he was real.

It was like a chess game: she was the queen and he

was the upstart knight in pursuit.

She checked the room. All was in readiness. The lamp was not yet lit. She had put out the paper and her pens, and made sure that otherwise the desk drawers were locked. Leola had made the bed as she did every day, and had tended to her nemesis's room just as if he had spent the night there.

But she knew he was looking for the one good moment he could sneak into her room.

He had fired Daggett . . .

Really, the whole episode kept her fulminating during her dinner, which she pointedly ate in the dining room. She went back to the small parlor afterward and let Elsie serve her a glass of lemonade. It was really too hot. And too upsetting.

Of course there was also the question of undressing. If she were to convince him that she knew nothing of his presence in her room, she could not just get into bed clothed. She would have to undress again.

She bit her lip. She didn't know if she could do that.

But on the other hand, everything had to be exactly as it had been the night before; otherwise he might get suspicious.

What was her nakedness, after all? She had seen *his*, and it hadn't seemed to embarrass him one bit.

It had discomfitted her mightily, but she wasn't going to think about that; she would never let it happen again. She had never even dealt with that with Jesse; Jesse was hard, sudden, quick in the dark, and she never knew what it had been about.

No matter. She would undress in front of the stranger solely to exact her revenge, and she would love doing it. He would never have her and he would never have a piece of Riveland, and by morning, he would be gone.

"Come upstairs with me," she whispered to Zilpha, and the two ascended the stairs at precisely ten o'clock.

At her door, Cassandra motioned for Zilpha to go on down the hallway and wait.

Then she turned the doorknob and pushed in her door, stopped, turned around and called out: "Oh, Zilpha—wait a moment . . ." and darted back into the hallway.

"All right now," she whispered, "go back downstairs the back way and go to sleep."

"Whut you doin'?"

"I need to approach my room from a distance. Now just go. Everything will be fine."

"I don' like it."

"Don't worry. Go now . . ."

Zilpha threw her a speaking glance and left her.

She turned back to her room and slowly walked toward the threshold. She saw only darkness under the bed.

What if he weren't there?

He had to have come. He knew she was writing the letter, he would want it—it would give him something to use against her and it wouldn't require him giving up any secrets.

He had to be there.

She inched closer to the open door, flattening herself against the opposite wall to get a better view.

Wait!

There . . . the faintest outline of a foot desperately pulling backward to avoid the light.

Her heartbeat accelerated. Her mind flew forward in time, pacing through all the things she would have to do before she lay down on the bed. *All* the things . . .

She licked her lips and entered the room, heading directly for her desk to light the kerosene lamp, and then to the far wall to turn up the gaslit sconce.

She felt it then—the same sense of presence she had noticed the night before. Damn him, he had been here

198

then, right by her feet, right under the bed. She wanted to bend down and kick him, but instead she walked back to the desk and seated herself.

She still needed a moment to compose her thoughts. She was still going to write a letter, but not the one he supposed, and she was going to fold it up and put it in her desk drawer, and she was going to make sure he saw exactly where he could find the key.

Then she was going to undress and she was going to do it slowly and tantalizingly and she was going to make him wish he had never tangled with *her*.

And then she would have her revenge.

Dear Mr. Greve, she wrote,
Things have gotten totally out of hand here. I require your presence as soon as may be convenient and I trust that will be *soon*.
　　Yours sincerely, etc.

That was fine. Now she needed to rework it, play with it a little to waste time . . .

Dear Mr. Greve,
You are a charlatan and a conspirator and I'm taking you to court to regain control over my life.

Not likely.

Dear Mr. Greve,
The only person who knew anything about Trane Taggart, besides me, was you. The evidence is conclusive: you and he are in a conspiracy to swindle me. I rest my case.

She was getting fanciful now, pushing time back so she would not have to take the final step to lock away the letter and begin undressing.

She snapped out the drawer impatiently; on top of her growing pile of Trane letters lay the one she had written the previous night. She took the Greve letter, folded it, and placed it on top of that one.

Too bad she couldn't tell how much he could see of the desk from under the bed. She dearly wanted to hide the Trane letters just in case something went wrong.

Nothing would go wrong.

She wasn't going to make it easy for him to find the key.

Unless he popped out from under the bed right now and wrested it away from her. But he wasn't going to do that; he was a mountain cat, sleek, quiet, ever so cunning. He would wait, he would pounce, he would play.

She moved out from behind her desk and over to her closet.

It was time.

She slowly unbuttoned the tiny jet buttons that marched down the front of her plain black silk dress. He couldn't see that. She didn't think.

She hated black, she hated mourning Jesse. She eased her arms out of the sleeves while she unhooked the skirt from behind, and the steel hoop that supported it.

Boned and caged—a woman's lot, and not even a mountain cat could penetrate the tenuous steel braces that surrounded her. She unhooked the petticoat support and pushed down hard on it to gain enough purchase to step out of it.

It stood there, another presence in the room, as filled out as if her shadow wore it, her petticoat and skirt still appended to it.

It was a dastardly thing and she hated it, but far worse, she hated the boned corset she was required to wear with all of her mourning dresses. She unhooked that and tossed it in the closet so that she was only

200

clothed in her camisole and drawers, her stockings and boots.

Just like last night.

She chewed on her lower lip. She couldn't imagine deliberately flaunting herself in front of a man.

. . . maybe she could . . .

Hadn't Jesse always said temptation was all around him? Hadn't he believed a man couldn't help himself because woman was so vile and seductive?

She wondered if she were vile and seductive as she stood cowering by her closet door.

What did it mean to be vile and seductive—that you would undress yourself in front of a man and revel in the fact he watched you and wanted you?

Something deep inside her reared up and heaved over at the thought. The end result had to be the same: that dark quick penetration that left you gasping and feeling used.

But he would never get that far. She would kill him first.

He had seen everything there was to see the previous night. It would be like repeating a performance she had not known she had given.

Still she hovered.

What had he thought?

What did it matter?

It was almost as if he weren't there, except that she knew he was. And she knew what he wanted, and it wasn't her.

Anyone would look if he couldn't help it.

If she just ignored it, pretended that it was last night and that she hadn't known—

Whatever she did, it would be deliberate and conscious, and that was the thing that held her back.

She had never done anything like that in her life.

She felt so tense, she thought she would scream. But

if she did not walk over to that washstand, she would never set things in motion.

She moved, one foot in front of the other, straight line, right for the washstand, already topped with the freshly filled ewer and bowl and clean towels.

Last night—what had she done? She had removed her boots before she had gone to the washstand. She wished she had remembered that.

She braced her right leg against the commode near the washstand and removed her boot, appalled by the fact that her drawers split open so widely at the opening when she raised her leg.

She kicked her boot across the room and stood looking at the offending commode because she had no choice but to remove her left boot the same way, thereby exposing herself to his prying eyes.

She would do it quickly, but even quickly could not prevent the thin cotton from stretching tightly against her buttocks as she leaned forward; nor could her bent arms hide her nakedness.

She kicked that boot across the room and it hit the closet door and fell with a satisfying thunk, as she watched, hands on her hips, wondering what to do next.

She had to wash, and if she remembered right, she had removed everything else, by degrees; first the camisole . . . she pulled delicately at the ribbon and it came apart in her hand. She pulled the neckline away from her chest and eased her arms out of the straps, still covering her breasts with the body of the garment.

But that wouldn't do. She had been fully and completely bared to his gaze and she must do the same this night in order not to arouse his suspicions.

But she had no doubt she would be arousing something else.

She let the bodice drop over her hips almost resignedly.

He isn't looking, he isn't there . . . I'm going crazy, knowing he's there and undressing in front him anyway . . . this isn't worth it—

She picked up the pitcher and poured some water into the basin and took a washcloth and dipped it in the water. *There—almost done. Stockings next—I think—and drawers . . . Oh Lord . . . I can't even perch on the edge of the bed to do this—damn, I should have planned this better—stockings, now underdrawers . . .*

She left her undergarments where they lay and padded back to the washstand completely naked.

What does he think, what does he see?

How could she help wondering? She knew what she saw, as she worked the soapy washcloth up and down her legs and thighs. She saw a short blond woman with a discontented mouth and a bosom that was wholly out of proportion with her body. She saw long legs and a short waist and she wished she could have reinvented her body the way she had invented Jesse's son.

Next—the nightgown from the lower drawer of the dresser.

Finally; it slipped cool and light down her body, obscuring her nakedness, emphasizing her thrusting breasts and taut nipples, the curve of her hips.

She took her brush and beat at her hair.

Almost done, almost done.

The lamp now—in bare feet, she padded back across the room to snuff out the kerosene lamp and turn down the gaslight.

The moment was almost at hand. She was so nervous; if anything went wrong, she would just bolt for the door and lock it behind her.

She needed to get back on the other side of the room . . . she hadn't thought—damn, and the lights were out: more evidence of her spontaneous planning.

She crossed her fingers, and felt her way around the

bed, and very slowly and carefully she climbed onto the mattress.

Below, on the floor, he lay rigid, every muscle tense, his manhood stiff as a poker, his mind blasted with images of her naked innocence.

The mattress depressed above him and there was a blissful moment of silence.

And then the whole bed collapsed around his head.

Chapter Thirteen

Son of a bitch.

The footboard and side rails clattered to the floor and her weight and the mattress settled neatly right on top of him.

She was trying to kill him—it was the only explanation. If the shock didn't get him, he would suffocate—but not before he got her first.

He wrenched his head to the side to get the smell of the mattress out of his nose, and then, experimentally, he moved.

All in one piece. So far, so good.

He inched his body to his left . . . that still worked, and her weight shifted slightly so that she was not directly on him. That was good, because if she didn't run *now*, he was going to dump her on the floor and jump her.

Maybe not. He wasn't sure all of *him* still worked, but he was damned sure the spider lady had caught him again, and he didn't damn like it one bit.

He moved again.

She was not moving, but then again, maybe that was another trap, designed to see whether he were in a viable position to come after her.

He was planning to be in a very viable position in the next minute.

He waited.

She remained motionless. Maybe she thought she had

killed him. No, injured him badly. Maybe she was waiting to see, to gloat.

He was getting mad.

He shifted again, and this time, he felt her move.

He heaved up his side of the mattress and lunged at
her—and grabbed her bare foot with his left hand.

"Let me go, damn it!"

He pulled himself out from under the mattress, still
grasping her foot, and hauled her toward him.

She clutched at the edge of the mattress, and pushed at
him with her free foot. He grabbed for it, and got her
heel in his face. "Damn you!"

"Let me go!"

"You're crazy."

"I hate you!"

He snatched at her flailing foot and felt the full weight
of it strike his shoulder. "You hellcat . . ."

"No more dainty spider?" she taunted, lifting her body
like a bowstring to evade his reach.

"You're a goddamned menace."

Her foot came at him again, and he marveled he had
the strength to make another grab for it. He caught her
ankle on the downswing, and with one mighty wrench of
his arms, he yanked her toward him and catapulted himself on top of her.

It was the only way; only the full force of his body
could contain her, but he had a hell of a time making her
realize that. She was all writhing arms and legs beneath
him, arousing him with her unintentionally erotic movements.

But he was big and he was overpowering and it finally
got through to her that he was not going to let her go.

He was so heavy on her, so hard against her, that she
didn't know quite what to do. She had sprung another
trap and he had caught her—again.

"You trying to kill me, lady?" he asked finally.

"I think so," she muttered, refusing to look at him.

"I know what you're up to."

"I know what *you're* up to," she countered daringly. Or was that foolhardily?

It was dark, after all, and she couldn't see his face, nor could he perceive the abject fear in hers. The blackness enfolded them like a comforter; no one could see, no one could hear. They were alone in some isolated world compounded only of the softness of the mattress, the hardness of his body against hers, his desire and her resistance.

The heat of him melted all barriers; she felt as bare as if she were naked; she could feel every inch of him nestled tightly against her, and she heard the rasp of his breath as he fought to contain his anger and his rising excitement.

"You're dangerous," he growled. "You don't know what you're doing."

"I only know what you're doing, and you tell me who is dangerous: a man who walks into my house, pretends to be someone he isn't, fires my overseer and takes over my cotton fields? Or a woman alone who is protecting her legacy and her livelihood? You're a barbarian, nothing less, and I'll do anything to get rid of you."

"I'm Trane Taggart, lady, and I wish to damn hell you would get it through your head."

"It's meaningless; you have no business here."

"I came to see my daddy. I didn't know he had passed away."

"It's funny, Trane Taggart said the very same thing in his first letter from Baltimore." *And it's MY story, mountain, and you can't have it.*

He grew very still. His arms moved, upward, to surround her head.

He settled his body more heavily on hers in the palpitating silence. He wanted her to feel the undeniable solidity of him, the *reality* of him; he wanted to get into her head and remove the Trane Taggart of her imagination

and replace it with the actuality of *him*. He wanted . . .
he *wanted—*

The silence grew with what he wanted, erect with possibilities, alive with antagonism.

"There is no Trane Taggart in Baltimore," he said slowly through gritted teeth.

"There is no Trane Taggart in this house," she shot back—oh God, she was going crazy; the mountain was going to crush it into her, force her to yield in all ways. It was pure stupidity to oppose him. It was easier to acquiesce—but she couldn't give it up, she *couldn't*. It was *hers*, all of it, he couldn't take it away just by his say-so. Trane Taggart was *her* fabrication, *her* necessity . . .

. . . they say . . .

WHAT WAS THAT?

She shook her head violently from side to side, trying to dislodge something that swirled tantalizingly around the edges of her fraught memory. No, it was nothing, she remembered nothing.

"He is in your bed, black widow."

"He is in Baltimore, stranger."

"Your lie," he said calmly. He hadn't moved. He just lay on her, surrounding her, overpowering her, waiting, waiting—the mountain cat and his prey.

"Yours." She had to attack; a cornered animal fought, didn't it?

"You wrote the letters."

"He wrote to me."

"Everyone thought he was dead."

Oh yes—but how could *he* know that?

. . . they say . . .

"So he told me," she said insolently.

"No one knows that but me," he contradicted, and his voice had a dangerous edge to it. "You wrote the letters."

She felt his hands come closer, touching her head, his fingers threading through her hair, and her heart dropped in pure animal terror.

"I know the letters, black widow."

"No." Oh God, the dark, the dark . . .

"I picked the lock on your desk drawer."

"No—"

"You wrote the letters. There is no Trane Taggart in Baltimore—"

. . . they say . . .

"No! Yes! . . ." She was shaking all over—he broke into the drawer so subtly and carefully that she had not noticed? He had read the letters? Her body reacted wildly, bucking upward in denial. *No . . . NO!*

"There is no Trane Taggart—*do you hear me?* I made him up. *He doesn't exist!* I made him up the way you and Greve made him up so you could just walk in here and steal Riveland away from me. *He is not real! He doesn't exist"*

She felt as if she was falling, going down into a deep black hole, annihilated forever; his fingers stroked her hair, her only connection to some kind of reality.

And his voice, calm now, assertive.

"He exists."

"No . . ."

"I am he."

. . . they say . . .

"Say it," he commanded.

"No . . ."

"I am Trane Taggart—"

"I don't believe you," she exploded, reaching for the last ounce of resistance within her. What did it matter he had read the letters? What did anything *she* had done matter? *He* was the interloper. *He* was the liar. *He* was the fraud.

"It doesn't matter what you believe, black widow. Just say it."

"That won't make it so. *I* made the man up, name and all . . ."

. . . they say he had . . .

"Maybe you didn't," he said, and there was an odd note in his voice.

"No proof, stranger. No locks I can pick, no evidence you are, none that you aren't. But I invented him, and I know." She was picking up steam now. She had almost let him intimidate her. She had almost backed down and given it to him. "And you know it, too," she added for good measure, feeling the vibration from his body at her renewed antagonism on the point. She would never let herself be coerced again; he had almost done it, she had almost done it to herself.

"I know who I am., Cassandra. And *you* know it."

"I know you and Mr. Greve cooked this whole thing up between you."

"God, get that out of your head—I never saw the man before the day I arrived." He was feeling futile now; she had outwitted him. She had admitted her complicity and denied it in the same breath. Trane Taggart was never going to see the light of day at Riveland.

On the other hand, she couldn't physically fight him. She was there, beneath him where he wanted her, and she would never ever move until he decreed it. His mind ran riot with images of her as he dueled with her about Trane Taggart. He loved her feistiness and her refusal to back down to him. And he hated the fact she would not concede.

He hated her fear and the unthinkable reality that Jesse had had her before anyone else. He wanted to wipe that away, to give her another memory for another time—and that was the strangest thing of all: it was becoming more important than anything else.

He almost didn't care what happened to Trane Taggart. Jesse's death, long before he came back, made everything seem immaterial except what Jesse had done to Cassandra.

Or what he himself was doing to her. And wanted to do to her.

210

"That's *your* story," she said insolently.

"No, no, spider lady; you wouldn't have fought me so hard if you didn't believe it."

"I want you out of here." How puny it sounded while the mountain was crushing her into a furrow of her featherbed.

He began stroking her hair again. What fine, thick hair she had; the curl wound around his fingers as tightly as a bedspring. He wished he could see her face, her eyes. She was too calm beneath the hard temptation of his body. She was too centered; she had gone from almost totally hysterical to intensely rational, and a man didn't trust that in anyone, especially a woman.

And a man especially didn't trust a black widow when he knew in the dark she was still spinning webs.

"I'm going nowhere, Cassandra. You need me."

"I need the devil about as much as I need you," she snapped.

"The devil can't bring in your harvest, spider lady. I can."

Oh Lord . . . she hadn't quite forgotten about Daggett—yes, she had . . .

"We'll call a truce, Cassandra."

"I don't bargain with the devil."

Wrong challenge. His body shifted against her again, pouring heat out against her, making her aware of his rigidly held-in-check passion. She sensed his face near her, she could hear his breathing, and then his voice came at her in the dark, a mere whisper; "Then you can go to the devil *with* me," and his mouth closed over hers before she could protest.

Soft, angry kisses, his teeth nipping at her lips almost hurting, his tongue salving the bites, seeking her, insistent, demanding . . . she didn't know kisses like these, and he had kissed her before—but not like this. These were the kisses of a man who wanted the sensual life of the woman he held in his arms. This was a man demand-

211

ing everything: her desire, her soul, her complete capitulation, and she didn't know it was hers to give. She didn't know how to give, she didn't know if she wanted to give . . .

He sought the sweet honey of her tongue, he found it, he sucked it, he held her tight and close as he caressed her, and she drowned in the succulence of his possession.

The darts assaulted her, sweet little piercing sensations that attacked her very vitals; her body moved with them, she couldn't help herself, the sweetness was almost unbearable—unknowable because she had never experienced such a thing before, delicious and frightening in the intensity of what she felt, what she wanted—she wanted *more*.

How could he do this to her, her demon, her savior—she didn't know which; she couldn't think—she could only *feel*.

His mouth lifted from hers, just a fraction. "We'll call a truce, Cassandra."

"A truce of what—the truth?"

"What *is* the truth now?" he murmured, delving into her mouth again.

"I don't know," she whispered, but maybe she knew . . .

"*I* know," he said, his voice a breath away from her mouth. Oh, he knew just when she moved, when she licked her lips, when she opened her mouth to speak, to deny what he knew or if he knew—his mouth devoured her words, played havoc with her sensibilities, taught her a whole new language. Whatever he knew, he knew *this*, and she was willing to concede almost anything to him to remain in the lush sensual world of his kisses.

"*My* truth," he whispered, punctuating the succeeding words with soft wet little kisses. "I . . . am . . . Trane . . . Taggart . . ."

"I—"

"*Say* it."

She swallowed hard, accepting his kisses, denying his reality.

His lips hovered a whisper above hers. "Say it, Cassandra."

Her mutinous lips denied it, but he knew how to punish her. He swooped down on her, he invaded her mouth, he was ruthless in his possession of her tongue; he aroused her so ferociously, she could only open her mouth and invite him to take her.

He refused to yield to her provocation.

"It doesn't matter now," he whispered. "Say my name, Cassandra."

And then she knew—the moment she gave him his name, he would fill her again and never let her go.

"Say it."

She felt his fingers moving, stroking, finding her cheeks, her mouth.

"Say it."

She felt them settle on her lips where his mouth had just kissed her, she felt them stroking her, inciting her, demanding it from her as intensely as his kisses demanded everything else.

"Say it, Cassandra."

. . . *they say he had* . . .

But then, who was to say?

His fingers delved in her mouth, lovers, waiting to feel each nuance of her lips as they moved, and that was almost more frighteningly sensual than anything.

"Cassandra . . ." The breath of her name on his lips, waiting for her invitation, heis to give, hers to say.

"Yes—" she sighed, trying it out, "oh yes—*Trane*."

His fingers moved with her lips and then his mouth crushed hers and his voice, a rasp against her lips: "*Again—*"

"Yes, Trane," she breathed, and opened her mouth again and this time, this time he came to her, this time he enveloped her in the lush wet sensuality of his mouth and

213

hot hard heat of his body, and this time, she could not separate the one from the other.

And the blackness. She knew a different blackness now, a hot, closed, luscious world, bodies rocking and rocketing together, imprinted on each other, made for each other, where the dark penetration became the means to a sweet surcease.

She had never, ever wanted it, the dark penetration, but she wanted it now, driven by his voluptuous kisses, by her shattering response, by her wanton body that felt it so deeply, so insistently, that nothing less would do. It was outside of her, had nothing to do with her. It just *was*.

He knew. He knew he knew he knew he knew—he lifted her, his hands possessed her, everywhere, everywhere; he stripped off the fragile nightgown that impeded his hands, he explored every inch of her in the dark, the fertile dark; his hands memorized her, lifted her, contained her; his fingers surrounded her, stroked her, massaged her taut nipples, the lush curve of her buttocks, delved deeply into her wet satiny fold, spread her legs and teased her, cupped her there, caressed her there, listened to her rapturous moans as she felt him there, as she demanded him there.

This was unlike anything she knew with Jesse.

She felt him nudge her, and then he took her hand. "Feel me," he commanded, his voice husky, and he guided her hand downward to the thrusting rigidity of his naked sex and closed her fingers around it.

She understood this. It was flesh—hot, demanding, powered by his thoughts, his needs—his kindness. Touching it in the deep dark aroused her still more because she knew what it was and what would happen and now she was ready for it.

But she had never known this—his hands touching her, preparing her, spreading her legs apart gently, pushing gently—entering with the softness of an exploratory kiss, and slowly, exquisitely filling her with the hard virile length of him, pausing once, twice, so she could feel every massive inch.

Her body convulsed, spangling little sensations radiating out from the center of her where he lay within, all thick and hard and deep. He thrust once, and the heat shattered, spiraling through her body; he thrust again and the sensation went spinning out of control, so intense she ripped her mouth away from his and screamed and began to cry.

In the dark . . . "Oh, Trane," she moaned, the tears streaming down her face; how did she tell him she wanted to feel that naked sensation all over again?

Her tears wet his mouth, his chin, his tongue—he licked them away, he kissed her lips, he sought her tongue, he drowned in her innocent response that no man had ever taken from her before.

He moved, and he moved—"Hold on," he growled, because he was an animal elemental, strong, powerful in nature, mating in rapture and in lust; he could not get enough of her, she begged for ever more of him. And he gave it to her, thrusting and twisting within her as deep and as hard as he could, where he was, the connection was spellbinding, so intense, so all-encompassing, that when the feeling came again for her, he felt as if it had broken all over him as well.

Oh but no. Her shuddering groans did not wipe out the reality of his hard need; it was still there, throbbing, pulsating, driving him to completion. She was done and she wanted more, the mere sensation of all his manhood driving into her, racing to possession, culminating in a gut-wrenching torrent of seed deep, deep within her, in the fertile darkness of her velvet core.

He slept. She did not.

In the aftermath, she wondered how it had come to this: that she had accepted him as Trane Taggart, and she had allowed him to do to her what only Jesse had ever done.

How Jesse had abused her.

How extraordinary the actuality was.

And wasn't she well and fairly caught now? She did need him, she would have to acknowledge he was Trane Taggart, and she would have to exist from now on with only the memory of this night. It hardly seemed fair.

She wanted more. She knew it instantly; her body reacted fully and thoroughly even as she thought about it, squirming suggestively against his quiescent manhood.

She felt it move, just a bit, and she felt excitement unfurl within her at the thought of it. Again? Tonight? Oh Lord . . . again—She rubbed against him once more, and his robust manhood surged deliciously against her naked skin.

Yes. She reached for him, taking him without hesitation, exploring him, feeling him until he was a thrusting tower of granite in her hands.

Yes. He came wide awake, all of him, she sensed it, and he let her play with him, never moving, never reacting, pretending to be at rest to give her the time, the freedom to handle him as much as she desired.

She couldn't get enough of touching him. His maleness was a living thing that sounded an answering chord deep within her in a place not to be spoken of or plumbed anywhere but in the hot, dark depths of the night with him.

And she wanted that, now, again; her body felt billowy and open to him, her arousal blasted through her, leaving her shaking with an intense need that only his possession of her would slake.

"Trane . . ." She whispered his name, she begged for him in her affirmation of him; how did she beg for his potent manhood to take her in that shuddering waiting moment of pure primitive need? She closed both hands around him in mute supplication. "Trane—"

Oh, the possibilities of the dark: the dark was hands and mouths and naked skin, it was feeling and touching, incitement, rapture—opulent feelings aroused, explored, caressed, kissed . . .

Her mouth—he was not done with her mouth; her breasts—he had barely evoked the sensations she could experience in her hard-tipped nipples; her whole body, open to him, inviting him: she was backed up against him, her buttocks writhing against the taut root of his manhood, his fingers encircling the taut peaks of her breasts. He had not entered her, not yet, and she reached down between her legs to hold him with her hands, both of them, playing with the hard ridged tip of him, stroking it, sliding her fingers all over it, feeling the rounded shape of it, teasing it, squeezing it, feeling a wash of pleasure so fierce, she almost exploded with it.

His hands skimmed downward to the lush fold of her velvet cleft, inserting themselves there to explore her provocative heat. She moved against him as his fingers began a rhythmic possession of her and he thrust against her, lightly, meaningfully.

"Like this," he whispered into her ear, "like that . . ."

"Oh yes . . ." she sighed, because it was just as good.

"Hold me tighter," he rasped, as his manhood drove urgently against her gripping fingers, and he played with the undulating pulse of her wanton sex.

Oh yes—she strained against his questing fingers, bearing down on them, writhing her body in a primitive rhythm he matched with his own stroking thrusts.

Oh yes—once more, once more again, again, again, *again*—yes, yes, now . . . now . . . she groaned as his torrid caresses broke into an incandescent shimmer of radiant silver—all over her body, all over, all . . . over—

. . . and he exploded into her hand with a racking release that matched her own.

In the morning he was gone.

She hadn't dreamed it; she was naked in her bed, her fingers sticky with the residue of him and her nightgown in shreds beside her.

The bed was a mess; she could hardly remember that she had intended to exact some kind of revenge on him.

No matter—Ojim would rig it up again before this evening.

She stretched luxuriously, feeling an unaccustomed sense of well-being, and a strange thought struck her: *a man could make a living with that kind of talent.*

She pushed the idea away. A man didn't just ply his way up and down the river looking for recent widows whose husbands hadn't treated them well.

But he was so good at it.

Look at how he had turned things around with her.

How many other identities might he have?

Oh, nonsense—making something utterly impossible out of a momentous night of discovery—

Yes, but—she couldn't let herself drown in it—or he would take over. And he could. He was capable of it. And she was capable of falling apart every time he touched her. Look at how she had allowed him to punish her for not bending to his will about his name. Look at how she had begged for his kisses, begged for his loving.

He was more dangerous to her than ever now, and if she allowed herself to sink into that morass of memory and luxuriate there, she would be handing control over to him because of the very thing she denied: his ability with a woman in bed.

Dear Lord—she jumped suddenly. Less than twelve hours ago, she had been nervous and nervy about revealing herself to him while he watched her.

She didn't know how much more there was left to reveal: a man had eyes in the dark, a woman swooned in his arms with her eyes shut.

Damn it.

She padded to the closet and yanked out a silk wrapper and tied it around her shimmering body defiantly.

He was a damned sorcerer.

. . . the very devil . . .

And she had gone to hell and back with him—

Just as he had said . . .

"Good morning, Zilpha. Is our guest awake and about yet?"

"He in de field, Missus. Why you ask?"

"I was wondering," she said airily, but her offhandedness did not fool Zilpha one bit.

"I send Elsie," she said, her face impassive, but she knew—even she knew, and Cassandra was immediately aware of it—something had changed.

Damn again.

The stranger was a damned magician.

She didn't know whether Zilpha had sent Ojim for him or whether he appeared because it was time for breakfast, but ten minutes later, she looked up to see him standing in the doorway, dripping with sweat, his light, bright eyes fixed on her intently.

She could hardly look at him. She buttered a piece of bread instead.

"Good morning, Trane," she said finally.

"Ma'am—"

And Zilpha behind him, overhearing her greeting: *"Whut* you said?"

"I said good morning. Do sit down, Tranc. I assume you have not had breakfast yet." Her mind worked furiously, trying to decide how much to say, how much to leave out, whether to acknowledge the sensual tension between them or to act like the lady of the manor, as if it had never happened.

Impossible.

Nor did she owe Zilpha any explanations, either. However, Zilpha had spied for her, informed for her, taken her side, shown her loyalty . . . Zilpha was a slave, for heaven's sake . . .

"I've decided to acknowledge our guest as Jesse's son, Zilpha. Please bring another cup for his coffee."

Zilpha's dark eyes flashed, her head bowed. "Yes, ma'am."

He applauded her silently as Zilpha exited the room.

"You're hired, Trane," she said carefully, lifting her cup to her lips to give her a moment to study him. His presence now was a whole other matter. How he looked, what he said—it had been another man in that bed with her last night. That mouth . . . those hands . . .

He wasn't the mountain anymore, he wasn't a cat. He had an identity and she had given it to him, and now he had a purpose, and she had bestowed that as well. No matter he had blackmailed her into it.

There were ways of controlling him, she was sure of it. The only thing that interested her at this moment was how he appeared to her this morning.

He didn't look like the man who had made love to her last night.

He looked like Trane Taggart, the man who had come back home to claim his birthright. It was as if the two stories had merged and become one the way she and he had the night before.

"I'm obliged, ma'am. I didn't think you'd forget."

"No," she said slowly, "I didn't forget." She didn't need to say more; her eyes said it, and he responded. He was mesmerizing, with his sweat-soaked shirt clinging to his arms and chest and that bright, knowing gaze settling just on her lips, reminding her, goading her and then sweeping downward as if he could see her body through her clothes the way he had "seen" her naked the previous night.

It was unnerving, that prescient look; it made her want to drop everything and beg him all over again. Her limbs

220

felt boneless. She licked her lips. She knew she was falling into the honey of that memory she desperately needed to guard against.

She knew he was remembering her resistance and her capitulation in his hands. She didn't know how she was going to resist his presence one door down the hallway.

"I think you should occupy the overseer's house," she said suddenly as the thought swung into her head from nowhere.

"Ma'am?" Now he looked a little disconcerted.

Good.

"I think you should live in the overseer's house," she repeated, each word precise and unmistakable.

"It's a pig house," he growled, not at all pleased with this turn of events. "A pig couldn't live there."

"Ojim or Eli will clean it out and Zilpha will make sure you have everything you require."

He thought about it a moment. "Everything?" he asked silkily, that light in his eyes again.

She lowered her avid gaze. "Certainly more privacy," she said softly because she had to let him know that he must do what she wanted now and she would reward him. That was the way it would be, it *had* to be.

"A man does like his privacy," he agreed as Zilpha returned with fresh coffee, plates and cups and an assortment of breakfast delicacies.

"Ask Ojim and Eli to see to cleaning Mr. Daggett's quarters, please. Mr. Taggart will be occupying the house from now on. Zilpha . . ." she said warningly. "You're to supply Mr. Taggart with whatever he wants."

She turned to him. "Just tell Zilpha what you need."

"I need you."

"I'm not a requirement," she said a trifle stiffly because she didn't quite know how to react to that. No, some part of her did. *What you need—I need you* . . . she looked at her hands, the hands that had grasped the living heat of him with such ferocity last night, and she could not

221

believe she was the same woman and he was the same man.

She was not the same woman.

She wanted him, right there, right then.

She got up from the table, and looked down at him. "Trane."

"Cassandra."

"I'll see you later."

"I'm counting on it."

She closed her eyes and shuddered. She was counting on it too.

The overseer's house was a brick cottage, two rooms deep, one on either side of a small staircase that led up into a loft. One room had been intended as a parlor and kitchen, the other as a bedroom.

But that had been assuming an overseer had any civilizing influences governing him, Trane thought in disgust as he kicked his way over the trash on the floor into the house.

He looked around dourly. There was potential here. It wasn't any better or any worse than a lot of places he had lived in his life, and he would take whatever Cassandra offered and make it work for him.

. . . what Cassandra offered . . .

A tigress—a gorgeous, wanton tigress whom he was going to tame and possess within an inch of her life . . . Godalmighty, who could have known? And after Jesse, too.

Ojim followed him into the room. "Dis be fo' hogs. We need whole day cleanin' and antiseptin', Mr. Trane."

"Do it, then," he ordered. He couldn't possibly allow Cassandra here before the work was done. And he didn't know how he could stay away from her one night. One day.

One hour.

"Yes, Mr. Trane."

"Do it today."

"Yes, Mr. Trane."

The corn was cut, ready for shucking, piled high in the square of buildings around the kitchen. He had a work crew ready to tackle that at sundown, and a half dozen jugs of something potent to keep them going. He rubbed his face. Cotton wasn't ready yet, but the top bolls were heavy with promise. Any day now, any day; it was surprising to him how much he remembered of what he had been told.

Old Jesse hadn't been any kind of a teacher, and his only son had resisted every attempt to be taught, and still, something stuck. Something fermented, in all those years, into a usable brew, and it astonished even him.

It would be all right. Trane Taggart was going to see it through.

The air was heavy, hot, sultry, the day was far too long, and she had far too much time to herself.

The summer was the worst. In the early years, she used to watch their neighbors, belongings piled high, steamboating up the Little Midway to climates more amenable to the summer heat. Only Jesse refused to go, and she had learned to bear the oppressive heat—but this—this was something tangibly different.

This was her first summer without Jesse, the first harvest without Jesse. The first time she had been on her own, ever.

The first time there was a magnetic lure down to the fields.

It was the heat—it made her thoughts spiral around the weight of her clothes and how much nicer it would be if she could just remove them. And the heat made her think of the dark, and the close, hot intimacy of her nakedness and his. And the heat suffused her body every time she

223

thought of the luxurious sensation of being possessed in the hot, straining darkness, and the allure of it in naked daylight.

"We got two men and five wimmen down in dat Daggett's house, Missus," Zilpha told her. "He were one dirty man. And I don' see dat man he gonna be no better."

Zilpha's voice wrenched her from her reverie and brought her straight back to reality. "I had no choice."

"No, ma'am, dat not so; he done made it so you ain't got no choice."

She felt a tremor at Zilpha's words. Zilpha was right— he had made it so by the simple expedient of getting rid of Daggett.

Oh Lord . . . her jumbled instincts might not be so far-fetched after all.

"And he ain't no Trane Taggart, neither," Zilpha added for good measure. "Mr. Jesse's real son, did he have one, wouldn't sleep in no overseer's house."

Cassandra closed her eyes. "He couldn't stay here."

"He was doin' it."

"Not for much longer."

"He could of done, if he was Mr. Jesse's son."

"Zilpha—"

"Don' matter none he a man and you a woman. You his stepmomma and he entitle' to be in his daddy's house. It ain't right, Missus, you go callin' him Mr. Jesse's son."

"I don't know that he isn't," she said wearily.

"And I knows he ain't," Zilpha said with finality, leaving the room.

She sighed. The intricacies of what was due family members had never concerned her; she could not let Zilpha's disapproval sway her. Whoever he was, he belonged in the overseer's house, and Trane Taggart was just as good a name for him as any.

Two men and five women tackling the job of cleaning that house—she didn't have too many more working around the big house herself. Elsie, Leola, Sarah, Josie

224

. . . Mr. Daggett must have been a pure out-and-out animal.

No matter—she must make Trane comfortable until the cotton crop was harvested, ginned and baled off to Savannah, and she was utterly determined about that.

The rest was a gift she never expected, and had to use wisely and with caution.

But she didn't feel cautious, she wanted to be reckless. She wanted suddenly everything *now.* The waiting seemed interminable, and there was nothing to say that she would see Trane Taggart any time else today. How would she stand the waiting and the wanting?

She couldn't imagine, but she could not conceive of what yesterday had been like, in the time before she understood the nature of her own passion.

She sat on the veranda in the late afternoon, watching nothing and everything, secure in the idea that Trane was taking care of everything, and her slaves were taking care of him.

She heard a hum and then what sounded like a chant, and she got up slowly and walked around to the back of the house where the corn was laid by in a huge mountain beside the smokehouse.

One man had climbed to the top and was shouting out the chant, and a dozen others sat around the heap below, and another dozen children, handing off the ears of corn as each was shucked, and still another handful of women and girls raking off the leaves and piling them into baskets and then into a waiting wagon.

"Where can we go?" It was Trane, at her elbow, surveying the scene with satisfaction.

Her body gushed with anticipation. "Not in the house, not tonight."

He kept his eyes on the workers. "I need you now."

His powerful scent assaulted her senses. She licked her trembling lips.

The sun was slowly starting to sink westward. The at-

225

mosphere surrounding the shucking was almost like an event: everyone's attention was riveted on the caller and the workers. She wouldn't be missed—he could join her almost instantly. But in the house, not where Zilpha could find them.

"My office," she murmured under the sound of the chanting.

"Five minutes."

She turned away from him and sauntered up into the house and darted through the rooms and out the front door. She would have to take the long way around, but then, so would he.

There was no one around when she approached it, a small frame building on the edge of the fields. The one window within faced east, to give her the morning light. There wasn't much furniture, either—Jesse's double-pedestal desk, a spool-turned armchair that she had added for her own comfort since it was upholstered, a table by the window where she spread out the account books, and next to that, along the perpendicular wall, a bookcase secretary where she stored the record books.

There was a worn carpet on the floor, which she kicked in her haste to enter the place unnoticed, and she closed the door carefully behind her, her heart pounding with anticipation.

Hadn't she dressed carefully today? No hoops, no corsets, no impediments. No hope as the day progressed. How wise of him to be circumspect. How the waiting had intensified everything. *Everything*.

She waited breathlessly by the door, trembling with impatience.

The door opened just a crack, and he slipped in, his hands already unfastening his trousers to release his rampant manhood. She melted into his arms, and into his luscious kiss, and he turned her toward the wall and thrust his engorged sex tightly against her yearning body.

"Oh, I waited for this," she whispered, between his

greedy kisses.

"I wanted your kisses," he murmured, avidly devouring her lips, her tongue, drinking the soft nectar of her inner lips.

"Don't stop; I needed your kiss all day."

"I wanted to hold you and feel you," he whispered, distracted for a long moment by the curve of her lower lip as he sank his teeth into its lush fullness.

"I feel *you*," she sighed, writhing her body against his towering manhood.

"Kiss me, Cassandra . . ."

She opened her mouth to him, to his hot possession of her, to the wet, sucking, greedy kisses she had craved all day. Her hands roamed his body, feeling his sticky, sweaty shirt, the contour of the muscles beneath the fabric, inhaling the scent of a man who had worked the fields and come racing to her with uncontrollable desire for her kisses and more.

She moaned deep in her throat as he deepened each long, wet kiss.

"This is unbearable," she whispered.

"Tell me . . ."

"Don't make me beg."

"Don't make *me* beg, Cassandra."

She felt him lifting her skirt and the long hard lunge of his maleness against her legs, between her legs, probing for her, demanding her.

". . . Ahh . . . Trane . . ." She licked her lips and he caught her tongue with his teeth and nipped it lightly.

"Tell me more, Cassandra . . ." he whispered urgently. *"Tell me—"*

"Oh yes . . ." He found her, his lusty length parted her, he bent his knees ever so slightly and thrust upward, and he slipped easily within. "Ohhhh—"

His mouth covered hers again and they rocked back and forth, and he began his pumping drive to possess her, his hips undulating against her, plunging and thrusting,

227

and all she could do was wrap herself around him and give herself up to the lustrous sensations within her.

Oh, and his torrid kisses, and the sense of him taking her, the excitement of where they were and what they were doing, the whole galvanic sensation of his ravening need for her and her unquenchable desire for him fused in a tumultuous rocketing release, and they sank simultaneously to the floor.

She was almost insensate with explosive feeling. He held her, for as long as she would let him, but even as her excitement waned, she knew she had to get back in control.

She pulled herself upright, and smoothed out her skirts. He helped her up without a word, and she turned her back to him, and went behind her desk.

Then she turned to face him and she said, "You can go now."

Chapter Fourteen

So he was her houseman, just as Daggett had implied. The irony of it didn't escape him, nor the humor. The black widow was not going to let Trane Taggart step an inch out of line.

She thought she had him trapped, but he himself was not sure who was in thrall to whom. But he was going to find out. The night was still young, and his blood still ran hot for her.

The night was sultry, dark with promise. Ojim had built a bonfire back of the house where shucking went on and on into the wee hours. It was a celebration now, with drink, and food, and the working chant back and forth, back and forth, the children loading the ears into baskets and onto the wagon to be taken to the corn house for storage. There would be corn for sale and corn for the table, feed for the stables, and leftovers for those able.

And later, they would tend to their own garden patches and Ojim would come around to harvest the blades, but that was not for weeks yet, before the next harvest of corn, and the taking in of the first blow of cotton.

Cassandra looked out on the scene from her small parlor window and felt again that secure sense that everything was proceeding properly, and she knew it was because Daggett was gone and Trane had taken over.

And in no small measure, her surety was aligned with her own feeling of assurance in giving herself to him.

What a marvelous thing it was, the connection between them, and the elusive, stunning culmination that was the ultimate expression of it.

It wasn't love, she thought, watching the rhythmic pull and rend of the arms of her workers. It was something apart from that, some ineffable discovery that was linked solely to the possibilities within her that Jesse had not chosen to discover. He had never been that kind of man, and this man, this Trane Taggart, was as different from him as night from day.

She could love him, for exposing her soul and defining her pleasure. But if she allowed herself that selfishness, she would want more, she knew she would want more, and confining limits of Jesse's will negated more. She would have to tell him there could be no marriage, there could be no children, nor could there be a life away from Riveland.

If he were Trane Taggart—

. . . they say . . .

The damning little phrase was like a buzzing fly; she wished she could swat it away.

On the other hand, the man most certainly was an opportunist. He was using her, and she had in truth put him in his rightful place, and she would use him the same way for as long as it took to pack her bales and send them downriver.

The mistress did not consort with the overseer.

But the mistress felt the secret thrill of knowing that she had and she would, and it was the most gratifying thing she had ever done.

"Ojim never done fixed yo' bed, Miz Taggart; he too busy wif dat man's fixin's."

Well, she knew what Zilpha thought, but that didn't matter.

"Have Leola move my things into Mr. Taggart's room until he does, and change the bedding, too."

"I ain't never gonna call him no Mr. Taggart," Zilpha muttered.

230

"*You* don't have to call him at all," Cassandra said tartly. "We'll have Ojim work on my room tomorrow."

"*Yes,* ma'am. He gonna be busy tomorrow."

"Well then—Eli will do it. Or—or no one will do it and I'll just stay in the big room."

"Yes, ma'am."

Exasperating Zilpha; who would have thought eight years ago that Jesse's death would effect such a change in everyone. And now that Daggett was gone, there was a different atmosphere altogether.

Daggett wouldn't have made a party out of the corn shucking.

Trane had done that, and he had started laying the field into assigned tasks for when the cotton would be picked, and he had been intensely efficient in the past day or two since he had gone into the fields.

He loved the land. Whoever he was, however much he protested, he loved the land.

She made her way upstairs finally, grateful that the carousing and noise was at the back of the house, and the big bedroom faced front.

There was one sconce lit in the hallway, and she had forgotten to take a lamp, and the bedroom was dark. No matter, she knew her way around it by heart. Leola would have laid her nightgown at the foot of the bed, and she could just drop her clothes and leave them where they lay.

She removed her dress and petticoat, and groped for the nightgown. It wasn't there. Bemused, she thought of going into her room and getting the lamp, but it didn't seem worth the trouble.

She sat down on the bed and removed her boots and stockings. No one but Zilpha would know she had slept in her undergarments, and that was as good as no one knowing.

She climbed into bed—and up against the rock-hard presence of a mountain.

"Trane . . ." she breathed.

231

"Come kiss me, Cassandra."

"Oh yes . . ." She reached for him willingly, aroused instantly by the thought he had been lying in bed, naked by the feel of him, and just waiting for her, passionately erect and yearning for her touch, her kisses.

He wound himself around her, crushing her against his naked body, enfolding her utterly. "You wear too damn many clothes," he muttered thickly.

"Tear them off," she whispered provokingly.

He ripped off her camisole with one tight, compressed jerk of his arm as her fingers caressed his bulging muscle. But her underdrawers he slid off her body, caressing and feeling every inch of her lower torso with great attention to the curvy hollows and secret places that only he knew.

"Tell me to go now," he growled, as his fingers tantalized the tempting fold of her seductive sex.

"Ah . . . I want . . . you . . . to come closer," she groaned in between his lush, possessive kisses. He came deep within her, his fingers exploring her sweet heat with expert thoroughness.

She held him tightly, her hands moving precisely up and down his arm as he caressed her, and across his belly and up his chest, fingering the crisp hair all over him, marveling at his size and his strength and how he tempered it into sensual caresses that made her feel as if she was floating on a thick sweet cloud of pure voluptuousness.

She never wanted it to end, his kisses, his deep sensual probing of her, his nakedness hot and pulsating beside her, rigid with wanting her, potent, powerful, lusty.

"I want you *now*," he rasped, as her hips began a primitive dance, enticing his fingers, inviting him.

"Oh yes, Trane . . . I want you deep inside me . . ." She sighed as his fingers slipped from her moist, intimate heat.

"This way . . ."

She felt him move—everything was feel and touch and hands and mouths touching, guiding, caressing—he sat up, his back against the headboard, his legs angled out, his rock hard length towering upward, and she moaned as he guided her to her knees, to his possessive kisses, to straddling him and lowering herself so that he entered her hot velvet at her command.

When she understood how it would be, she braced her hands against the headboard, reveling in the feel of his hands cupping her buttocks and guiding her slowly and surely downward so she would feel every inch of him sliding ever so slowly deep within her welcoming fold.

"Oh, I love this," she groaned as she encompassed more and more of him. His hands squeezed her buttocks, caressing them, exciting her; his mouth claimed one luscious breast as she worked downward into his hot, hard possession of her, and he sucked the tempting point of her rock-hard nipple greedily until she felt almost ready to explode again.

"Oooh . . . Trane, tell me what to do," she moaned as his hands grasped her hips now.

"Move for me, Cassandra; show me how much you love it."

She drew in her breath in a long hiss and licked her lips. She moved; it was like a dance, it was like riding him. She undulated around and over him and downward and upward, and every way she could think of, riding him, teasing him, demanding him. She felt slippery, wet, totally his, totally hers, possessed by that same insensate desire to erupt with feelings and desires that were both new to her and old as if she could have known them in some other life.

She owned him tonight; she could not see him in the roaring darkness. She could only touch him, kiss him, feel the ineluctable fusion with him and share the final glittering white-hot spending of passion that consumed them both.

"We dolin' out de stores today," Zilpha said, handing

233

Cassandra the key to the storehouse. "We done let a mountain o' work slip by, Missus. I done took care o' replenishin' de candles: got dat ol' Sarah workin' over dat, and dat lazy Leola down de dairy workin' over de butter churn, and we gonna get fresh butter soonest."

"I would have done the candles," Cassandra said.

"You is busy," Zilpha said pointedly.

"I need to order stores anyway," Cassandra said, ignoring that. She calculated quickly: it was mid-July now, but the time had gone so quickly she was hardly aware of it. Her mind was solely on the next time she could see Trane. She lived from moment to moment in a high fever of expectation. She could not get enough of him, he wanted her endlessly and she wanted him, too. The house and her usual responsibilities were the last thing on her mind. She only waited for the moment when Trane would approach her sometime during the day — almost every day.

"I'm ready for you," he would say, and she would sneak a covert glance at his loins and the proof of his desire.

"The office."

"Hurry."

She would fly to the office, he might be there ahead of her, she might arrive before he did, he would slide into the cool, dark recess of the room and the lush, inviting recesses of her mouth, and he would take her, over the desk from behind her, holding her naked buttocks, driving her with long, hard, lusty strokes until she came in a wrenching convulsion of pleasure.

"My house — tonight."

She tingled with anticipation. It was hard to slip out of the big house and get down to the field. But she did it. She knew how to avoid Zilpha now, so that they could have a voluptuous hour of sensual exploration.

Sometimes he waited in his bed, naked, tight and taut with desire for her. Sometimes he met her at the door and tore off her clothes, and took her on the floor. Once she waited for him, demanding his sweat-soaked work-hard-

234

ened body fitted against her and deep within her the moment he came from the fields.

It was hot, so sultry hot. She was so aware of her body; she had eliminated undergarments: she wore calico dresses now, and she looked like a servant, but she didn't care. She was ready for him, any time, any place, as he was ready for her.

"The hayloft . . ."

Oh yes, the dark, cool hayloft in dead of day, where they could be alone and concealed, and they could strip each other's clothes off and play with each other in enthralling secret.

"I need to talk to you."

Hot and hard from the fields he came to her one burning afternoon.

"We'll talk in the small parlor," she said coolly for Zilpha's benefit, and then she could close the door and lock it, and play mistress of the manor who would make him beg for her favors.

"Oh so cool and touch-me-not today," he whispered, as his hard-muscled arms surrounded her shoulders and trapped her arms. He was bulging with desire for her; she felt him against the light cotton of her dress and her hands snaked around behind her to work his massive maleness free.

She arched herself against him as she gripped him and played with him, pulling him against her, writhing against him, subtly lifting her dress inch by inch so she could feel his nakedness against her naked buttocks, and ultimately, between her legs as she straddled him, and bore down on his long, hard shaft.

She loved feeling him this way, just between her legs, potent and powerful, like granite, not penetrating, just nestled where she could feel his rock-hard length, and his long, caressing fingers unbuttoning the front of her dress, seeking her pebble-hard nipples.

She thrust her breasts into his hands and lifted her lips

235

for his rapacious kisses. "We don't have much time," she whispered. "Hurry . . . kiss me . . . feel me —"

"I have you," he groaned, his fingers surrounding each taut nipple and constricting gently.

Shimmering gold flowed through her veins.

"Ohhh — again . . ."

He flexed his fingers and held her nipples lightly within his grasp, and the luminous sensation slithered ever downward until it settled between her legs in a paroxysm of exquisite pleasure.

"Dear Lord, what was *that?*" she whimpered as her body climaxed in one last, wrenching spasm.

He didn't answer — he couldn't answer; she felt his hips pumping from behind her, reacting instinctively to the sensation of her splendor; he needed her now, and she knew it, and she lifted her dress and guided him unerringly within her for the last drenching moment of his release.

She loved their coupling, and his relentless virility.

She didn't like the word "love." Hadn't she vowed never to love anyone? Hadn't she thought love was a story in a book, and the dark penetration was a thing to be endured and not thought about in the light of day.

And now there was this: her sensual secret. Her hot need. Her greedy enveloping of everything Trane Taggart offered her.

How far away she had come from being Jesse's wife.

And how much she did not care what would happen next.

One hot early morning, he came to the office.

"I couldn't get you out of my mind."

"I'm here."

Oh, and she was, and it didn't matter when he came or how or what he wanted. She wanted it, too.

"Get on the desk."

She drew the shade over the one window, and locked the

door, a precaution so early in the morning, and she sat herself on the desk expectantly, her eyes riveted on his naked ramrod manhood.

"Come to me," she invited him, lifting her dress. "*I* need you."

His light, bright eyes followed the hem of her dress as she raised it above her hips and tied it behind her waist.

"I think about you all the time," she whispered, "I'm getting nothing done, nothing. I just want your kisses, I just want —"

He came to her then, sliding his arms around her, inserting himself gently into her, exploding in a racking release before the first stroke. "God . . ." he hissed, wrapping his arms tightly around her shoulders. "Oh God —"

"Trane —"

He smiled his odd crooked smile. "We'll try again, my lady. Come sit on my lap, Cassandra."

He cradled her against him in the upholstered chair, and he kissed her lightly, lovingly, and his hands . . . his hands were all over her, all over. "Spread your legs for me," he whispered, and she allowed his fingers between her legs to enter and possess her that way, to find the voluptuous little sweet spot that sent her instantly over the edge of her passion.

"Cotton is ready fo' pickin'! Cotton is ready fo' pickin'!"

It was Ojim's jubilant cry, and it was nearing the end of July and the seductive heat had not diminished, not in the air, not in her body.

Zilpha had her canning strawberries. "Dem' bushes is burstin' and you is burstin' and I don' know whut's goin' on, Missus, but we got work to do."

Zilpha was right. She couldn't let her feelings for Trane Taggart, or whatever his name was, overwhelm everything else.

In the two weeks past, she had had the eerie sensation of

feeling joined with him, married to him, the two of them running Riveland as it was meant to be run, with a future to look forward to and children somewhere in mind.

How stupid of her.

But he was so perfect here, and she was so perfect with him, within him. They worked, they gratified their senses, and they slept to see the following day. They weren't talking, but she almost believed they didn't need to talk; their bodies spoke for them, pleasuring and worshipping each other in the fullest sense of carnal knowledge.

In some senses she felt she knew all she needed to know about him. When he was centered within her, she was full and complete and nothing more was needed—ever.

"De cotton, de cotton!"

Trane had gone out before the first call. He had determined the bolls were showing and ready, and Ojim was lining up the baskets and Isaac was pulling the first cart out of the barn into the fields.

The work now had really begun.

Everyone picked. Everyone.

She wouldn't see Trane, she knew it, for days maybe, and she wondered how she was going to bear it.

Everyone took a basket and a sheet and everyone picked and emptied the baskets into the sheets and the sheets into the carts which took the bolls to the cotton house to dry.

And this was only the first pick.

Everyone knew what to do. Everyone worked in the dry, steaming, vicious sun, even Trane, up on his mount one moment, down and urging the next, calling for water here, a fresh sheet there. Eli drove the supply wagon and everyone had a fair turn at the water, a practice so different from Daggett's that the workers didn't know what to make of it and could barely feel gratitude for it.

No matter. Everyone worked, everyone had a task, and the cotton poured into the cotton house at twenty to fifty pounds per man per workday as the week progressed.

In the kitchen, Leola stirred the heavy iron pots while

238

Zilpha and Cassandra picked and sorted fruit. In the house, the small cadre of servants caught up on laundry, dusted and swept, and picked cucumbers from the garden and prepared a brine.

There was ironing to be done, carpets to be rolled up and taken out to be beaten, floors to be cleaned, the copper pots to be scoured.

There were a hundred small chores to be done on a timetable of seasonal need, and Cassandra felt as though she could dispense with all of them, but the reality was, the work must be supervised and done, just as always.

They put up a batch of strawberries, she and Zilpha, and potatoes and corn. They cut endless pounds of cucumbers and chopped carrots, broccoli, cauliflower, tomatoes, all vegetables added to her kitchen garden at the last when they began the planting. They made catsup from tomatoes, pickles from the cucumbers, plucked cabbage for an evening's dinner.

She almost had no time to think. Everything centered around the crop, the picking of the cotton and there just was no time for anything else.

But the thing that felt so good to her was the knowledge that Trane was in the fields and the cotton was coming in.

It was so hot in that third week in July that she dispensed with her nightgown altogether and brought Elsie up at night occasionally to fan her until she fell asleep. Trane was not going to come; he was exhausted, living in the fields as the bolls opened to white in the amazing heat, and the workers had to pick as fast as possible.

They were working together, she and he; he *was* Trane Taggart, he was Jesse's son, he loved the land, and he had come back in spite of Jesse, in spite of everything . . .

. . . *they say* . . .

In the raging heat of the fourth week, as July merged into August, and hundreds of pounds of cotton was carted to the cotton house, she went to the fields in the little gig that had been long repaired, and she watched the workers, and she watched Trane, and she yearned for a life which was not possible for her.

She could not allow herself to love him.

When the cotton was baled . . .

She wouldn't think about it—

In the deep, dark night sometime in early August he came to her. Elsie had gone and with her, the relief of the fan that was like a hot, puffy wind, settling nowhere, cooling the ceiling maybe, but not her. She lay awake in her bed, thinking about *things*.

She had never really talked to him. She felt a rushing urge to know everything about him, everything; the way she knew his body she needed to know his mind. But there was no time for that, as the cotton bolls kept opening in successive rows, successive plants.

There was no time for anything, and she felt as if time were her enemy, racing with the production of the cotton, and that time would win and she would lose.

But she didn't even know what that meant. She tossed and turned over that question for a long time, and finally she gave up, got up, put on a lightweight wrapper and went downstairs.

Sconces burned in the hallway, the wicks lowered to emit just enough light for her to see where she was going. The house was asleep, vigilant Zilpha nowhere around to take her to task.

She opened the door, hoping for the semblance of a breeze, and the stultifying heat forced her back inside.

It was so quiet.

"I'm here."

She jumped. "Trane—"

He appeared from behind the staircase. "Come." He held out his hand.

"Where?"

"With me now."

She gave him her hand and he led her to the back of the house, to the small parlor. "I didn't think—"

240

"Don't think." He closed the door gently and locked it. "Come."

In the dark again: his arms were so strong around her, she ached for his kiss. He untied her robe and let it fall to the floor. "You were waiting for me."

"Maybe I was."

"I've been dreaming of you."

She wound herself around him. "Tell me."

"Dreaming of all the things I want to do to you."

"Do them."

"God, I've missed you."

"I know . . . I know . . ." Careful, careful — she loved this too much, she wanted him too much.

"Lie down."

"Oh yes—"

She groped for her robe, and spread it beneath her and lay down, trembling with anticipation.

She heard him shucking his clothes, and beyond that, a metallic sound. She felt him sink down onto the floor next to her, she felt something warm and slick touch her skin.

"What are you doing?"

"What I want to do."

She knew what it was: the keen scent of strawberry filled the room as he spread the contents of one jar on her body, over her breasts, down her belly, sticky-sweet with promise, on her lips where he could suck the sugar from her lips and tongue; on his fingers where she could suck between his avid kisses, everywhere she could want it.

Oh, and he was hers, and she was his, and his mouth began that delicious exploration of her strawberry-tipped breasts, sucking the sweetness avidly, until she felt the whole of her life was centered right on those two turgid points of her body.

But there was more: his tongue swiped the gelantinous preserves from her midriff, from her belly, from the thatch of hair that crowned her femininity, seeking her in the density of the fruit . . .

241

Oh there, oh *there* . . . he knew where *there* was; his tongue unerringly found that sweet, sweet spot, all there for her, demanding her response, commanding everything from her shimmering body. She bore down on him, her hips writhing, her hands in his hair, flexing, pulling, guiding him to bring her to the final shattering culmination.

It was endless, it was endless, she felt as if she could not stop and he wouldn't release her until every last bit of feeling drained out of her.

"Oh yes," she groaned, "oh no," and she pushed him away violently as the sensation eddied into ripples that broke over her body in small, shaking chills.

He came onto her instantly, poised above her until she lifted herself to receive him totally and fully. Now, now, now . . . this woman, this unknown, incredible woman, his woman—he thought it, he felt it . . . no one would have this woman but him. He didn't know how, he didn't know when, but he knew she was his forever and always and he would find the way to set aside the lies and the truth that had brought him here and bridge the reality between the two.

Fate had brought him here, and Jesse's legacy, and he meant to use them both to seal his fate and his future with this woman alone.

This woman, this woman, this—pumping, relentless, ferocious response to this one passionate, innocent, beautiful, desirable *woman*—he collapsed on top of her, spent, replete, content with wanting her, starting to love her.

Chapter Fifteen

Mr. Greve returned in mid-August, in the midst of the picking and the first stages of preparing the cotton for market.

Everywhere he looked there was movement, from the big house down to the fields, and he felt a precious contentment that everything seemed to be going well.

"Miz Taggart," he greeted her.

"Mr. Greve," she said, extending her hand.

"You look well," he said, but he thought she looked better than that. She looked . . . she looked intense, alive. Less defeated.

"Thank you. You look like a coward to me, Mr. Greve."

He hadn't expected a direct attack, but he supposed he hadn't yet come to grips with the fact that Miz Taggart was a forthright and sometimes surprising woman.

"Now, Miz Taggart—"

"Let's talk about it out of the heat, please. Zilpha! Bring us some lemonade on the veranda—unless you would prefer something stronger, Mr. Greve?"

He waved the suggestion away. "Lemonade will do fine."

He sat himself heavily on one of the wicker chairs deep in the shade of the porch overhang. There was no breeze; there was just sun, shade and unceasing activity. "This is very pleasant, Miz Taggart."

"We can hardly stand to be inside, Mr. Greve. This is

one of the hottest summers I ever can remember. Ah, here is Zilpha."

And there was a tray with tall glasses beaded with water in the heat, and just the faintest sense, as he picked one up, that the water had come from a deep cistern that had cooled it enough to be palatable. And it was: cool, refreshing, tart. Like Miz Taggart.

"I see you've come to terms with Trane Taggart," he said as he set aside his glass.

She was staring out to the side of the house and the track that led to the field and the river. "What? Oh yes. Yes."

"I knew you would," he said smugly.

The statement didn't register with her, not at first.

And then—*"What?!"*

"I said I knew you would come to terms with him."

She turned to face him, a speculative look on her face. "How, how could you know that?"

"He's Jesse's son, and you found out he was telling the truth, just as I did."

She felt as if something had gone out of kilter. Mr. Greve had believed in her paper Trane Taggart, had accepted him unconditionally until the stranger appeared . . . she didn't understand; Trane Taggart was an erotic game that she and the stranger played with each other, and Mr. Greve knew nothing about that.

"I—" But how to explain it? She chose plain speaking, as always. "I thought it was a conspiracy between the two of you to deprive me of Riveland."

He had the grace to be silent a moment; her supposition in fact honed too close to the amorphous plan he had conceived from the moment Jesse Taggart walked in his door and outlined the provisions of his will.

The fact of Coltrane Taggart had been an unwelcome shock to him, and, he was still recovering from it. He, too, had hoped to prove that Trane Taggart was a fraud, and he had come up with something worse: the truth.

"I'm honored by your honesty," he said at length, "but

unhappy you could believe such a thing of me."

"I don't know you any better than I know *him*." She motioned behind her, keeping her steady green gaze pinned to his face. She was caught right in the crush again. She couldn't admit she had invented Trane Taggart, and she could not deny the man who had lived for more than a month on Riveland wasn't he.

. . . they say . . .

It was like a ringing in her ears. And Mr. Greve knew just how to take his time and string her out until she felt like screaming.

"I checked," he said finally.

I checked . . . you stupid girl . . . I checked . . .

. . . they say . . .

. . . they say he had a son . . .

. . . ran away . . . disowned him after . . .

Raylene's voice so many years before—oh God, it had been real, all of it had been real . . .

She swallowed hard, clenching her fists to control her shaking body. "You—checked, you said?"

. . . never know he existed . . .

. . . and he came back—

"My dear Miz Taggart—a small community like Carthage . . . well, sure, there have been many changes, but there are old-timers who remember Jesse and his first wife, Marigrace. They say . . ."

. . . they say . . . they say . . . they say . . .

". . . Jesse kept so tightly to himself no one knows when Marigrace died or how. They say the boy ran off when he was fourteen or so and no one's ever heard from him since, and when Jesse brought you back to Riveland, that's when they knew that Marigrace was gone and the boy had never come back.

"But here's the odd thing, Miz Taggart . . ."

"Yes?" she whispered.

"They say he was headed Texas way. They say after a while everyone gave him up for dead. Nothing about Baltimore, or a family . . ."

245

"No . . ."

"Jesse was a hard man."

"He was."

"And he never told you a word of this?"

"No." Her lips felt stiff, her body hollow. Her mother had known, had told a rebellious fifteen-year-old girl something about it who couldn't have cared less, and then she forgot it—except that in the deepest recesses of her mind, she remembered it, and she made it her own.

He was real.

His family . . . the six children waiting while he toiled in the fields of Riveland—how *did* she explain that?

And how did it sit with him that Jesse had wiped him off the face of the earth and he inherited nothing?

And had he been so attentive to her out of desire—or because he wanted to ultimately disarm her so he could fight for his birthright?

. . . dat man . . . he gonna start lookin' fo' dat Coltrane birthright and he gonna find it—

Zilpha had been right—and *he* had known it all along.

She sent word to him that Greve was back and his company was requested at dinner.

He dressed, as much as one could in the heat: jacket was required, of course, and a fresh white shirt, again courtesy of Jesse's belongings, the string tie . . . no concessions from him. Every detail of the dinners in Jesse's house was etched in his brain.

"Mr. Greve."

"Mr. Taggart."

"Cassandra."

She was dressed in flowered muslin tonight, trimmed in green velvet that matched her eyes. Dressed for Greve, he wondered, with a shot of jealousy gripping his vitals.

Dinner was simple: chicken, corn bread, roasted ears of corn, tomatoes, cauliflower, broccoli stewed in butter, creamed corn, roasted potatoes—a man could hardly eat so much in the enervating heat.

"We're sorting through the first pick, Cassandra, and we've set a crew to the whipping machine—that's where we refine the cotton another step to take away impurities and such that we missed sorting it," he explained to Greve, who, for one moment, was very grateful he hadn't had the task of seeing to these precise gradations of production.

"We won't gin until later on when the weather comes cooler and the whole pick is in," Cassandra added. "So we don't send it downriver before the end of summer."

"Well, my dear Mr. Taggart, it seems *you* haven't forgotten anything of the work of Riveland."

"No," he said easily, "it all came back to me like I just left yesterday."

"And yet it has been—what—fifteen, twenty years?" Cassandra asked, and he shot her a curious look. She had never asked a question like that, in the whole two months he had been here, barring their sparring over the story of his life.

"Twenty years, Cassandra, as you well know," he said, attentive and wary now all at once. There was something different about her tonight. She was still bright and radiant, but she was almost too much of those things, and he didn't like it because it wasn't on account of Greve.

"And Texas, of course," she added, still in that high, bright voice.

"There was Texas," he agreed cautiously.

"And Baltimore . . . and your wife and children," she pounced.

Uh oh. "Of course," he said glibly, "but you do remember that when we decided I would stay through the harvest, I sent a message to my dear *wife,* and she ultimately declined to join me here because it was too much of a chore to pack up the family for such a short time."

"Yes, yes, I do remember now you reminded me," she said hastily.

Trane turned to Greve. "I have a partner in Baltimore— my wife's *brother,* as it happens, and when I'm away, he sees to the business and makes sure my *dear* wife and children want for nothing."

"How fortunate you are," Mr. Greve murmured, dabbing at his lips, avoiding his eyes, and Trane knew instantly what had happened: Greve had found out the fiction was real and now Cassandra knew it for true as well.

Now he knew what to look for, he could read it in her eyes. Her gaze skittered past him every time he tried to catch her eyes; her movements were edgy, tempered with a kind of hesitancy as if she couldn't believe it, but something had convinced her, and it wasn't Greve.

He couldn't convince a man of anything, but he had left Trane here alone with her before he knew the truth, and he had come back here hurriedly after it had proved out.

He wondered what that meant. But above all, he wondered what it meant to him that Cassandra could not deny him any longer.

"Texas to Baltimore . . . " Mr. Greve mused, eying the robust amber color of his cognac in the lamplight. "Ummm . . . Jesse liked his cognac, obviously. It appears to me he was a close man with a dollar."

"He was," Trane said shortly.

"Texas to Baltimore . . . landlocked to land ho. It must have been an interesting twenty years," Mr. Greve said, raising his glass to Trane and sipping appreciatively.

"It was," Trane said without elaboration, and sipped from his snifter. Jesse wouldn't have liked it that Trane had eased his way back into Riveland and was savoring his stock. The old bastard wouldn't have liked it at all.

"And six children . . ."

"There's Coltrane, Junior, James, named after Jesse since I don't hold grudges—begging your pardon, Cassandra—and David, after my wife's father. Then of course there is my dear wife, Lavinia—"

Cassandra choked.

"—after whom we named our first daughter; and I can't forget . . . Mary, and finally there is . . . baby Phoebe."

"You must miss them," Greve said.

"They are my life," Trane said with a straight face.

"In Baltimore."

"Even as we speak, Mr. Greve. Now you mustn't worry about my family. They are used to my travels. Of course this situation is slightly different, but you can imagine that my dear wife . . . Lavinia is most anxious for me to render all the assistance I can to poor Cassandra, since this is the first time she is bringing in the pick by herself."

"Poor Cassandra is most obliged," she said caustically.

"And most obliged to Mr. Greve for his trouble on my behalf. I would like to invite you to stay the night, Mr. Greve"—she just avoided Trane's hard look altogether—"since it is such an arduous trip back to Carthage."

"I'm obliged, Miz Taggart."

"The same room, Mr. Greve. I believe Zilpha has already seen to everything."

She hadn't, of course, but Cassandra would attend to that; she perceived Trane's obvious displeasure at her spur-of-the-moment invitation, but she needed the buffer of Mr. Greve in the house or she might fall to pieces altogether.

She needed time to think.

She did not need Trane Taggart and his mesmerizing mouth and hands in her bed this night.

Dear God, he was *real*—

She didn't think she *knew* it yet.

She didn't know what to do. She didn't know if she should do anything.

Yes, she did—she had to stay away from him.

How could she do that?

Trane Taggart was real; everything she had invented about him was real, including his wife and children—since he had claimed them.

249

Oh Lord, she didn't know how, she truly didn't know how she was going to cope with this, and the memories of all they had done together. He could not have come back to Riveland solely to help her bring in a difficult harvest of cotton. There was another story, the one he hadn't told, the one he had written when he ran away to Texas, and the one that had compelled him to come back to Riveland alone and forgotten twenty years later.

The possibilities scared her. The word "investigation" which she thought had been tamped down away in the heat of her battle to prove him an impostor suddenly loomed large and frighteningly as the most obvious possibility.

He had come to make amends with his father and to claim his inheritance, and if he were Jesse's son, it meant that Jesse was not the barren one, and Jesse's son would not want to see Riveland in the hands of a woman who could not reproduce to pass on his inheritance.

He meant to fight her for it. There was no other explanation that made sense; he had seduced her to discredit her and he had weapons now to use against her, and she had never felt so frantic in her whole life.

If he took Riveland from her, he would give her nothing; he would send her away and *he* would make his home here, raise his family here. He would never choose a naive woman who was barren.

God, how stupid she was, how gullible, how desperate. She could never go near him again.

But how could she reasonably deny him after all these weeks of . . .

Her body went cold at the thought of everything she had done. She was as wanton as a woman of the streets — worse, because she knew she would not have to pay the ultimate price. But — it was her word against his . . .

She felt utterly trapped, as if she had been put in a cotton press and the screw was being turned over her slowly, surely, inevitably . . .

No, she had to think.

This thing was not an avalanche coming down on her head to bury her. Not yet, anyway. The question of Jesse's fertility could be dealt with later; she just could not cope with it now. The main point was that he had claimed to be Trane Taggart, and he *was*. Greve had said—hadn't he?— that he had discussed with him certain provisions of Jesse's will. It was all cut and dried. He had only threatened her with an investigation into Jesse's death because he wanted to stay on Riveland, and she had not believed him.

That was the story so far.

And he had not been a loving son to Jesse, so how could he come roaring back to Riveland demanding some kind of fair share of *her* inheritance?

There . . . that made some sense.

The only real question was, why had he come back at all?

He didn't look like a man who would be eager to mend fences. He looked like a man who was stubborn and determined, and who would have clashed with Jesse all over again the moment he stepped foot on Riveland.

The "why" of it tortured her, and two things became obvious: she could not act any differently toward him, and she must find out why he had come back to Riveland.

And then she could figure out what to do.

But there was nothing to do; everything remained the same. He was out in the fields before sunup, and she and Zilpha were assigning tasks after breakfast, and Mr. Greve came downstairs ravenous for breakfast.

She joined him at the table, although she had already eaten.

"My compliments as always, Miz Taggart."

"Thank you." She felt as if she had three dozen questions to ask him and she didn't know where to begin. There was nowhere to begin, because he had fully believed that reprehensible story she had concocted about the mythical Trane Taggart.

"So things are running well here," he said after a while,

251

having downed a generous portion of ham and eggs, biscuits and gravy and fried potatoes.

"So it seems," she temporized. "Of course, neither of us has thought beyond the point of getting the cotton downriver to Savannah. I assume Mr. Taggart intends to return home and take up his business once more, and I must then find a new overseer."

"Well, yes—of course. I was surprised you had let go Mr. Daggett, but that was your decision to make."

"With Mr. Taggart's advice," she amended, lest he think she had acted out of pure feminine contrariness. Surely all the contingencies of the will still stood, even if Mr. Taggart were now on the scene instead of behind the scene.

"I never thought otherwise," Mr. Greve said, taking a second cup of coffee.

"And he, of course, would be the 'issue' in that curious clause in the will, would he not?" she ventured, uncertain as to how to proceed—not sure she even wanted to know.

"Oh, indeed. But there's no question. He could contest, of course, but . . . he's been away for twenty years. That is a fact. And Mr. Taggart Senior was in sound mind to disperse his estate to whomever he chose. So that settles all questions, and clears up all the mysteries."

"I'm so glad," she said. But still . . . what if Trane Taggart began asking questions? What if he weren't satisfied with her explanations?

No—she wouldn't think about that. "What happens from here on then?" she asked him.

"Well, it's my job to administer Jesse's estate; it's just that Mr. Taggart's appearance on the scene has make it a great deal easier. I can see, by the way, that it would have been a grievous error for me to have forced myself on you in an advisory capacity, Miz Taggart. There is a great deal more to all this than I ever envisioned."

It was an apology, and she nodded and made a dismissing motion with her hand. Still, the words had come so easily to his mouth, almost as if he had rehearsed this little speech upstairs. It cost him so little; he was still in charge, and she still must answer to him, and he knew it.

"In any event, I will continue to conduct business at the Riversgate. You need only be aware that the Carthage-Midway Bank is prepared to honor your drafts and pay all bills come due from your factor as soon as the cotton is delivered to . . . now let see, what was it? . . . Vecsey's in Savannah."

"That's fine. But what may I draw on for my own expenses? We will need certain stores before the bales are sent down, and material, because it is almost time to think about winter clothing for my slaves, and I do not make my own cotton material as some wives do. Let me think: the usual things—flour, coffee, molasses, sugar. Wool—we do knit our own stockings, however, but still . . . oil, of course, wine—we must always be hospitable—and you see how the list grows the longer I sit here."

"Of course. Let me calculate . . ."

She jumped in again: "I must warn you that I do intend to take a trip as well, Mr. Greve, and there must be money for that expense as well."

He stiffened slightly. "And where do you propose to travel?"

"No farther than White Sulphur Springs, sir. You understand, I have not been off Riveland since practically the day I arrived."

"I didn't know."

"Or perhaps I didn't tell you when we were wrangling about this provision."

"All right, I'll arrange things, Miz Taggart. Your husband seemed always to have a reliable surplus year to year, which I must add was very unusual."

"Yes, but he went nowhere and did nothing and spent not a penny on Riveland that wasn't necessary to increase or purify the production of the cotton."

"Perhaps he was wise."

"Or perhaps he missed a lot in his single-mindedness." Including his wife, she thought, what he had missed with *her.*

253

"Very well, Miz Taggart. I certainly won't beg the point. I'll send you notice of the exact amount you will have at your disposal and how you may get access to it."

"Thank you, Mr. Greve."

"Of course, I will want to speak to Taggart before I leave."

She stiffened. "I don't know quite where he is, Mr. Greve. There are hundreds of acres in cultivation and they are working twelve hours a day on whichever one—on any given day—will yield the most pick."

"Surely you can send someone to find him."

She held his gaze mutinously for a moment and then shrugged. This was not worth a battle of wills between them. She had the manpower to waste searching the fields for Trane Taggart, and he obviously intended to flex her power.

"Yes, I believe Eli is free to do that."

She summoned him and he went off reluctantly. Mr. Greve went on, "You need only notify me when you wish to leave Riveland. I will make it my personal duty to check here to make sure all things are in good stead in your absence."

"I'm obliged," she murmured, her resolve crinkling against his patronizing tone. She almost never wanted to leave Riveland at all if it meant his presence on the place, but that was foolhardy. He obviously did not mean to obstruct her plans, and that was important.

They waited fifteen minutes, a half hour before Trane came stamping into the dining room, an uncomfortable half hour because she had nothing more to say to him that wouldn't lead to questions she would prefer not to raise.

"Ah, Taggart. I just need to ascertain that you plan to be here through the harvest."

Trane looked at her, his light, bright eyes raking over her as if he could see beyond the small pale oval of her face, and into her heart, her mind.

"Those are my plans," he said finally, and it seemed to Cassandra that he had phrased that assurance in a very

254

temporizing way, as if there were a mitigating "but" attached that he didn't want even to say.

"Well, that's fine then." Mr. Greve turned to Cassandra. "You are perfectly in compliance, and I'm satisfied."

Trane's eyes narrowed as he swung his gaze from Cassandra to Mr. Greve and back again. "Compliance"—what the devil did that mean? He really had to give it a long moment's thought, and then—Jesse's will. Greve had gone over the provisions with him before he disappeared—something about her not leaving Riveland, ever, and forfeiture to Jesse's brother Jackman, and some other nonsense about her not marrying, and getting an advisor . . .

Oh yes, and the business of 'issue' as well. Oh yes, now it came back to him.

"I'm much obliged *you're* satisfied," he said, with not a little venom. "We finished now? I got a crop to bring in."

Greve raised his hands. "Just making sure all was by the letter, Mr. Taggart."

Cassandra sent him a long, challenging look. "You can go now."

"Oh no, ma'am, I'll just stay around until Mr. Greve is safely away—by the letter, that is. Wouldn't want anything to spoil my . . . um . . . stepmomma's day."

Oh damn, now she would have to be alone with him—and look at that Greve, looking thunderstruck that he claimed that relationship with her, when he hadn't mentioned it for at least a month. It set her hackles up immediately. That drawl was too kindly, too knowing, too mountain cat.

His carriage had been brought around, probably at Zilpha's presumptuous and accurate request, and Greve took his leave with much ceremony.

They stood on the veranda steps, watching until he was out of sight and even after, until enough time had elapsed so that he had negotiated the drive and had to be on the main road to Carthage.

"The man's a bore; I don't know what the hell Jesse was

thinking of," Trane said disgustedly.

"None of us knows," Cassandra said stonily.

"Busy lady. Make time for me today."

She felt a violent impulse of resistance. But everything had to seem normal. She took a deep breath. "When?"

"I don't know. I don't know how close we can move to the house by sundown. And I don't know if I can wait till then."

She licked her lips. "Come . . ." Come where? There wasn't a foot of the house that wasn't being washed, scrubbed, waxed or utilized by one servant or another. "Come to the attic," she whispered finally, a little flicker of excitement stirring deep within her. She couldn't contain it. Her whole mind shifted to that enveloping anticipation. Her body twinged with desire at the thought of secretly meeting him again.

The attic was perfect. No one had gone up in the attic since Ojim had broken into it; no one would think to look for them there, and she, in the interim, could sneak up some pillows and quilts for their comfort; she could rig up a curtain over the telltale window; she could make sure it was as safe a rendezvous as possible.

Her heart pounded wildly as she watched him ride away.

Just one more time, one more meeting; she would be careful, she would let none of her fears betray her to him. She would enjoy the moment, she would.

She could not give him up—not yet, not yet.

Chapter Sixteen

Five days passed, burdened with work and the unrelenting steamy heat of early August, and she pounded restlessly through the days, her whole heart and mind focused on him, her body demanding his caress, and Mr. Greve's visit receding into the background like a bad dream.

It was as if it hadn't happened.

But she felt edgy anyway, and she knew why. She just didn't want to dwell on what it really meant; she only wanted to think about that afternoon in the attic when she had deliberately planned to come up in advance of him, and found him waiting for her instead.

There was something magical about it, the way he had just seemed to appear there in spite of all her careful preparation; everything about that afternoon had been irresistible, from the first touch of his hands to his insatiable kisses.

Here words were superfluous. Here, the tight, close air of the attic added to the sultry, thick atmosphere of excitement, and he laid her down on the table which he had spread with the quilt and she pulled up her skirt in a haze of aching desire, and he came to her, all primitively, elementally male.

She caressed him, she watched him; bracing herself on her elbows, she could see exactly and precisely everything that he did with her.

His torrid manhood claimed her, sliding deep within her

wanton heat, centered in her, center to her world. She loved watching his ultimate virile possession of her, the movement of his hips as he thrust deeply into her, and she could see every long, lunging stroke. She loved his hands cupping her buttocks and guiding her against him, lifting her to give her purchase to undulate with him and against him.

Her eyes, full of the secrets of Eve, her mouth, her suggestive movements as he held her tight against his loins, taunted him, teased him, incited him to longer, stronger surges deeper inside her, driving her passion harder and harder, greedy for every nuance of expression on her face, every evidence that she loved what he was doing to her.

Her eyes were riveted on the lusty fusion of their bodies, her hips bearing down on his massive length, using him, demanding him, writhing against him in pure erotic pleasure, an elusive smile on her lips that teased and tormented him almost past his endurance.

But she couldn't win. She knew it even before she admitted it. His prowess was too much for her; she wanted to give in to him and to her clamoring body.

Another moment, and another still . . . she felt the vibration, the rippling, twisting sensation of her body going tumultuously out of control, spiraling into a fathomless gush of climactic release that wouldn't end, that couldn't end . . . that he fell into wildly, willingly, mindlessly.

It was too much — and not enough.

He pulled her down next to him on the pillows on the floor. "Oh God, I could keep you here forever," he whispered, holding her tightly against him and winding his fingers through her hair. "I want more, and I'm drained to the dregs, lady. You've got me topsy-turvy for you and I can't go one hour without thinking about it."

"I know," she murmured. "Me, too."

"I can't even guess how it could end for us."

"Ask your wife and six children in Baltimore," she said lightly.

"I *can't* ask you, Cassandra."

Her skin tingled. "Is that good or bad, Trane?"

"I could kill Jesse for doing that to you."

"So you know the terms of the will."

"I told you Greve had outlined the whole of it to me before he conveniently disappeared."

"Did he?" she murmured. And back in the dark days when she had believed him to be an impostor, had he used that against her? Did she remember that right?

Should she be squirming with desire in his arms at this very moment?

"We'll deal with it—somehow," he swore, gently stroking her riotous curls. She loved when he did that, and it calmed her—just a little.

"But what happens when you must leave?" she asked after a while.

"I hadn't thought about it."

"But you must have—friends, family, some kind of life wherever you came from?"

"Greve had the right of it, Cassandra. I went to Texas and I came from Texas, and I don't know if I'm going back to Texas anytime soon. Baltimore sounds like a fine and prosperous city, but I'm not heading back there, either, so I expect my mythical wife to be writing you some pretty scathing letters. I just don't see her cottoning too well to a stepmomma who looks like you, who kisses like you . . . who arouses me like you do—"

"Oh God, Trane—"

"I know. I know. How could you give me a *wife?* We have to talk about that—not now, not now . . ."

"We will, I promise." Well, she meant it, then.

"I have to go."

"Yes." But nothing mattered but that he was leaving her.

"I'll try to see you in the morning, before we start. I'll be in the office. Come to me there, Cassandra."

"I will."

How could she help it? She wanted all of him that she

259

could possibly savor before it had to end.

And it had to.

Quiveringly awake, she waited for him in her office right by the door in the early hours of the morning. The door opened just a crack, and his voice breathed: "Cassandra."

"Hurry," she whispered, and he slipped into the darkness with her once more, his mouth instantly claiming hers.

"We don't have much time," he said huskily. "Sit on the chair."

"Why?" She felt a thrill of erotic sensation. It didn't even matter why.

"I know what I want to do."

It was barely dawn, the light was dim, the furniture hulking shapes in shadow. She sat in her chair, and he knelt before her, a supplicant before his goddess; he lifted the skirt of her dress, and he lifted her legs up so that he could bury his head between them and make love to her with the most carnal kiss of all.

He had done it before, but never like this, with her body slanted to his mouth and his body at precisely the right height and angle to savor her feminine secrets in the most ravishingly intimate way possible.

She angled her legs to open herself to him in shameless invitation to explore her as deeply and thoroughly as he wished.

It generated a wholly different kind of feeling, a delicious swell that mounded upward and upward lightly, tensely, unbearably, penetratingly into one long, soft shudder of culmination.

"I will take you in the fields with me today," he whispered, as she undressed him and rained soft kisses all over his throbbing member, and loved it and stroked it, and took his explosive release into her hands.

And she remembered that above all, five days later, when the thought of what he meant by mentioning Jesse's will at all tormented her deep in the night.

". . . *I can't ask you* . . ."

He knew all of that, and it made all of his protestations of desire specious, and she couldn't bear that. Nor had she yet confessed to her own duplicity, and the fact he had made reference to it put her directly on her guard.

She just couldn't let his sensual sorcery get in the way of the reality; he had had a purpose in coming back, and she had had a purpose in inventing her version of him.

And those two things could not be compatible.

She had to find out his purpose; she had to learn more than just that he came from Texas. She had to discover where in Texas, and what circumstance there had compelled him to come back to Georgia.

Yes, they had to talk. But more than that, she had to get him to talk, and it was on his mind the following Sunday night when he joined her on the veranda in the late hours of a scorching August evening.

"I had forgotten how hellish the summer is when you're bringing in a crop," he said idly, folding himself down onto the top step beside where she sat in a rocker fanning herself.

The opening was there and she forged into it. "You're telling me that Georgia is worse than *Texas?*"

"Hell, I don't know; we were about ten miles from the coast—maybe twenty. It didn't seem that much hotter, but I swear I can't remember now. I feel like I'd never been gone."

. . . *miles from the coast* . . . She knew nothing of Texas geography. The coast could be a thousand miles long—or a hundred.

"Except for Jesse," she added carefully.

"Oh yeah, lady, it's a damn sight better without ol' Jesse around, that's for sure. I'm bettin' you feel that way, too."

"Jesse was a hard man."

"Don't have to tell me."

"He wanted what he wanted and he made sure he got it."

"That was Jesse." He was silent for a long moment, almost as if he were debating whether to ask the question on his mind. But the darkness had been his friend, where all things were possible, and he stared out into the blackness and said, "What did he want with you?"

There was only one answer for that. "Sons."

"He had one."

Her heart fell. "But you see—it was like you didn't exist."

"How long after did you marry him?"

"I don't know, Trane. I was sixteen, and my mother arranged it. I didn't know anything about . . . about your mother, except that Jesse had been married a long time before, and I knew nothing about you." *No, I thought I knew nothing about you, but how do I explain that?*

"You *thought* you knew nothing about me," he qualified.

"Yes."

"And so when Jesse died, and put all those damned impossible provisions in his will, you just kind of 'made up' a son for Jesse out of his first marriage, one that had the right name and even some of the right story."

"But he had no son that I was aware of—after we were married."

"That just doesn't sit square with me, Cassandra."

"No, I know. I believe my mother did tell me about a son months before she accepted Jesse's proposal. I think she checked up on Jesse and she heard about that and she told me, and I was fighting so hard not to marry him, I just don't think it registered, not anywhere that I consciously remembered it, anyway. Do you see? It just came up from nowhere, the idea of it, and the name and why nobody knew about him—you . . ."

"I have to think on that a little. It's so crazy—"

"No more crazy than you're going off to Texas and never coming back for twenty years. My God, you were—what?

Ten? Twelve?"

"Fourteen, thank you, and at least I had a damn fool idea where I was going."

"Somewhere ten miles off the coast of Texas?" she said in disbelief.

"Oh no, ma'am. I was headed to Galveston—I knew exactly where I was going."

And I didn't, she thought. They had been of like ages, too, when he left and she arrived so many years apart. But she didn't know what it proved, except that he hadn't started out on some aimless journey and wound up somewhere in Texas. Galveston. A place to begin. A place to end.

If she didn't end here.

"How *did* Jesse die?" he asked abruptly.

"He fell out of the hayloft in the barn," she said quickly, bluntly, before she could mire the half-truth in a mud of words that might raise more questions than she could answer.

"Just like that."

"He was up on a rickety ladder," she added carefully, her heart pounding—this time with the fear of words and his perception of what she was saying and what she did not say. "He lost his balance. He hit his head on the fall down."

"And knifed himself in the bargain," he added dourly.

So he knew . . .

"That's how I found him," she said through stiff lips. It wasn't far past the truth. Somehow she had shimmied down the damn support of the loft, pretended to have entered and run to call Ojim immediately. Everyone had believed it: she had gone looking for him, she told them—the reverse of the fact that he had come looking for her with murder on his mind.

"And he had this will, with this lawyer . . ." Trane shook his head.

"Mr. Greve made a very good case for my naming *him-*

self my advisor."

Of course he saw the picture instantly. But even so — He rubbed his eyes wearily. "That's the damnedest story I ever heard, Jesse's damned will and you making up stories about a son you think isn't real . . ."

"Any damneder than the son walking in the front door a month after his father dies, after twenty years?"

"I don't know, lady. I have to think about which story sounds least likely."

"I don't think mine will win," she said.

"No," he said. "Jesse fixed it so no one could win."

Everything sounded so farfetched now, she felt as if she were living in a different story, one that someone else had made up.

She was beginning to feel the pressure of events: her erotic idyll could not continue much longer under his astute questioning and the improbable chain of events that resulted in her marrying Jesse, Jesse's death, and Trane's arrival, both in fiction and fact.

She felt trapped, with Jesse on one side and Trane on the other. Riveland was a prison from which she could not escape. She had no mobility and all her nerve seemed embedded in her voracious femininity.

She needed a plan; she needed a way to escape. She had nothing practical, except her ravenous sensuality and some small ability to carry on a business. She could use a gun . . . maybe. She didn't know if she remembered how to use it; it seemed so far in the past that she had planned to defend herself against Jesse with one.

She was a bundle of useful skills, she thought mordantly. She had never even gone into Carthage by herself; Jesse had had everything delivered by boat, right up the Little Midway River.

She had never learned to ride; she had never learned . . . No, that wasn't true; she had learned all the know-how to

264

run a house and take care of a cadre of slaves. That was what Jesse had needed, and that was what she had become. Everything, except mother to a son.

Stepmomma . . .

Dear heaven, how did she defend herself against Jesse's son?

The answer was—she didn't. She couldn't.

No, she didn't want to.

What she wanted to do, peripherally, was be able to save herself when the time arrived.

If she could ride a horse, she had decided, she would have more mobility than if she depended on a driver and a carriage. *In other words, you could make an escape more efficiently if you needed to.*

The thought sounded so bizarre, even in her own mind. Escape from what? Something that was already a punishment?

Nevertheless, she routed out Isaac and demanded he teach her the rudiments of staying in a saddle.

"Missus don' need fo' to know how to do dis," he protested. "Ain't got no huntin' here, ain't got no reason fo' goin' in de fields now Mr. Trane done come. Ain't fittin' fo' de Missus to be ridin' when she kin be *took*."

"Saddle the horse," she said implacably, ignoring his arguments.

And she stayed on. She could not have said she was comfortable, those first several mornings, but she stayed on as Isaac first walked her around the pen so she could get the feel of the movement of her mount.

Around the fourth time out, he flicked the horse into an easy canter—but that took her several days to master, along with her attendant aching body.

By then, Trane had come around to watch her progress in the early hours before he called his work gangs out in the field.

265

"You don't ever sleep," she said.

"Neither do you."

There had been no more talk of Jesse's death or his inopportune arrival. There had been work and more work, and her small progress riding, and the chores of the moment. She thought he had been staying away from her, that he could not believe what she had told him and he was just going to keep to himself until the cotton was picked down and they put it through the gin and moted it and baled it for shipping. And there were weeks to go until that final step.

Weeks.

He watched her wrestle with the sidesaddle and the motion of the horse, uncomfortable because her natural instinct was to lean into the gait with her whole body—correctly, of course, most unladylike, and much more practical.

"Saddle her up my gear," he told Isaac one morning.

"Dat ain't fittin', Mr. Trane."

"No one will ever know, except us."

"I don' like it, Mr. Trane."

"You don't have to," Trane said, walking the horse into the arena where she waited. "You'll ride him Texas-style today, Cassandra. It's going to change your life."

And he liked watching that, her long, strong legs gripping the belly of the beast with the fervor and passion with which she gripped him and rode him. It was an erotic thing to see a woman in motion with an animal, rocking with it, leaning into it, embracing it.

It was arousing as hell.

"Come to me tonight, Cassandra," he whispered, as she cooled down her mount and brushed him down just the way Isaac had shown her.

She was exhilarated from the ride and from the knowledge that Trane had been watching her, intently. "Are you sure?"

"Oh, ma'am—I'm very sure about *that*."

266

But the days were so long now, it was hard to sneak away before near bedtime.

She was a shadow on the pathways, clothed in black, a shawl over her head and shoulders and swathed around her face. She entered the thankfully dark doorway and shed her shawl in the dimly lit parlor.

"Trane?"

"Come."

She entered the bedroom slowly; he was there, lying in bed, his arms behind his head, waiting for her, thinking of her. There was the merest glimmer of light from the kerosene lamp on his plain pine dresser, and it illuminated his towering need for her.

She loved the fact that just thinking about *them* aroused him so fully and undeniably.

"Stay still," she cautioned him. "I'm going to undress you."

"Without tying me up, I hope."

"I didn't know what I was missing," she whispered teasingly, as she reached for his boots and removed them one by one, tossing each of them over her shoulder into the dim recesses of the doorway and beyond.

His pants next, with the loveliest few moments of playing with unfastening them and feeling his erection elongating beneath her very hands, and then they too were gone, over her shoulder, out the door. Socks and drawers next, in one swoop so that he was fully and tormentingly naked from the waist down.

"Enough," he growled, levering himself off the bed and reaching for her. "I can't stand it . . ." His fingers caught the collar of her dress and, pulling downward with one muscular yank he stripped her dress from her body.

She was naked beneath, and he breathed, "Oh yes," and gently turned her and pushed her, facedown, onto the bed, and came and lay over her, tightly fitting himself against her so that she could feel every elongated, throbbing inch of him.

267

From this position, he could whisper enticing things in her ear and straddle her legs to thrust his granite manhood against her lusciously curved bottom. From this position, she could feel the length, the heat, the hardness of him in a totally new way: her senses were all feel and touch; she could not see, she could only appreciate the raw power of his maleness as he covered her nakedness totally.

"I watched you riding," he whispered.

"I know."

"I loved watching that horse between your legs."

"Did you? I love something else," she murmured suggestively, wriggling slightly under his weight to force her body tighter against his tenuously thrusting member, "between my legs. . . ."

"Don't I know you do," he groaned, shifting his body an inch or two — he couldn't bear to leave her — and sliding his hand under her belly to lift her to her knees. "Don't I just know it. . . ." His potent sex nudged at her, seeking her seductive promise, finding it, and the ease of penetrating her in this intimate reverse way was utterly breathtaking.

He plunged himself into her, backing her up so that her buttocks fit tightly against his hips, and he let her feel him that way, deeply joined to her, connected by one primitive, elemental power; his hands splayed over her buttocks, feeling the cushiony softness, the roundness, the nakedness of her open to the nakedness of him.

And then she writhed against him brazenly, and he felt a roar of pure male possessiveness deep within him, and he answered her taunting, teasing challenge with a forceful statement of his claim.

He surged into her, ferociously thrusting, taking, feeling —

. . . *I love something else* . . .

A man could drown in a woman with words like that. He was drowning, her body a turbulent sea of lust beneath him, all motion, motion, motion, undulating, shimmying, wriggling and writhing in her own savage dance of demand.

His malehood, her femininity—naked, primeval, wanton; he would tie her up to keep her with him always. . . .

He felt it then, the constriction of her body, the long soughing "oh" in rhythm with each shuddering, violent eruption of pleasure, deep, too deep to know, to comprehend the sense of his relentlessly pumping maleness driving her to this mindless, sobbing pleasure—

And he felt it then—his shooting star of white-hot release, spurting with a violence that emptied every ounce of him deep, deep within her—too deep to comprehend her gorgeous hot, velvet sex driving him into this mindless, shuddering pleasure.

She slept with him.

She truly hadn't meant to; she had been going to make love with him and then pick herself up and go back to the house. She woke up curled into the curve of his body just as the first gray dawn light showed through the window.

She slipped out of his arms and tiptoed around the room retrieving her dress—what was left of it—her shoes, her shawl . . . No, that was in the parlor. She slid the dress over her head and fastened the one or two buttons that remained, and stepped into her shoes and then bent to pick up his socks, his underdrawers, his pants.

In the hallway, just outside the bedroom door, she found his boots, one by the staircase, the other lying just by the parlor . . . and something next to it. Something white right by the heel. She picked it up curiously, and froze at the faint sound of movement from the bedroom.

She didn't have time to look at it; she thrust it into her shoe and picked up the boot . . . odd—the heel was askew, as though it had been knocked off its pinning when it landed on the floor.

She listened for a moment before she moved it. It moved. It swung on some kind of a hinge, and as she repositioned it, she felt it snap back into place. The sound was inordinately loud in the dim lamp-lit doorway of the parlor.

Should she chance it? He could wake up any moment once he became aware she was not in the bed. She twisted the heel tentatively, and it swung away from the body of the boot. She bit her lip and probed inside the heel. It was hollow; the whole thing had been hollowed out so something could be concealed—the paper she had tucked into her shoe.

She snapped the heel back to its normal configuration and picked up the second boot with shaking hands. There was something on that piece of paper that Trane Taggart was trying to hide. She wished she could just open it and read it and confront him with it, but now she had to get away before he discovered the thing was missing.

She placed both boots just inside the bedroom door, and on shaking cat-feet, she grabbed her shawl from the parlor sofa; wrapping it around her, she slipped out the door and ran all the way back to the house.

She expected he would follow her in thirty seconds. She was so scared. A man did not fix up a boot heel like that unless he truly had something to hide.

And then there was Zilpha, right at the front door the minute she came darting around the far corner of the house.

"Where you been?"

"I took an early morning walk." She was shocked she even had the composure to answer coherently. The paper burned her skin. She had to get somewhere she could look at it in private.

"You sleepwalkin'," Zilpha said tartly.

"I need to change my dress. I'll be back downstairs in ten minutes," she said, ignoring that, and she brushed by Zilpha and dashed up the stairs into her room, and locked the door.

Now it was light. Now . . . She threw herself into her desk chair and kicked off her shoe. The paper flew into the air and landed on her bed; she grabbed it and opened it, a flimsy little piece of paper, folded in fourths, compressed to an almost minuscule proportion.

It was a receipt, written on the Carthage-Midway Bank — Jesse's bank — no — *her* bank. She read it in an instant. She didn't understand it. It was a four-line receipt with the date, the ornately printed: *In Consideration* and *Number* and *Name* filled in meticulously, and a name signed at the bottom.

She read it twice.

June 15, 1859
Carthage-Midway Bank
In consideration of: ten dollars
Receipts box number 321 to
Name: Mr. Cole Trager 5 months to be redeemed on presentation of bearer

Hidden in his boot.

She sat down slowly on the bed. All the clues were here. She had only to make sense of them.

His name was Cole Trager — *not* Trane Taggart.

She didn't feel any small triumph that she had been vindicated. The story had hardly begun.

He had been in Carthage beginning in June — and when had he arrived at Riveland? A few days after that?

He went to the trouble of renting a strongbox at the bank.

For *five* months. Not one. Not a week, a day. Five *months*.

Cole Trager.

Similar, certainly. But not the same. Not nearly the same.

A man with a secret, just as she had suspected, except

271

there was another layer added to the complexity of it: he wasn't Trane Taggart, and he had no right to anything of Jesse's at all — ever.

And he wasn't Trane Taggart, the issue of Jesse's impotent loins, either, and the relief she felt about that seemed like something peripheral to the question of her inability to conceive; but somewhere deep in her mind, she was very aware of it. It meant that there was hope; there was always hope, in spite of the facts, in spite of the proof.

Mr. Cole Trager of Texas . . . somewhere near Galveston.

Just picked up and came to Riveland for reasons that she couldn't possibly conceive. Maybe one that made a little sense: he had known someone from Carthage, someone who knew all about Jesse, and he was an opportunist and a swindler, and he had come to take advantage of Jesse's poor widow.

She liked that story as well as any other.

But the idea that his artful lovemaking was part of some grander scheme made her body burn with betrayal.

He had not ever expected she would find out about him. It was pure bad luck for him that she had tossed his boot onto the floor. But now she had it — his lie, his deceit, his perfidy.

The rest didn't matter. She could never add the cost of discovering her submerged sensuality; she had already paid the price and enjoyed it. His corruption was now part and parcel of it and she could never let him touch her again.

She needed a plan. She had to get rid of him, and bringing in the crop now was secondary to that; she had a vision of him forcing her to hand everything over to him — anything could happen with a man who had lied so blatantly and calmly, a Judas in her cloister.

She felt frantic again.

272

She had to hide the thing. What if he found out? What if she hadn't replaced the heel exactly, and he noticed it?

Where in the whole of Riveland could she conceal a flimsy piece of paper like that? A hundred places came to mind, but she knew, she was sure that, if Cole Trager ever discovered it was missing, he would tear Riveland apart to find it.

He would tear *her* apart to find it.

Chapter Seventeen

She knew exactly where to hide the incriminating piece of paper.

"Zilpha! Have Isaac bring around the carriage. I'm going into Carthage."

"You whut?"

"I'm going into Carthage," she said firmly.

"Whut you gonna do dere?" Zilpha demanded suspiciously.

"I'm going to . . . I'm going to — get some supplies."

"We don' need nothin', Missus."

"Oh yes we do, Zilpha. We talked about it: the wool, the coffee, the flour . . ."

"We just send word downriver like always, Missus. Ain't no problem 'bout dat."

"I'm going to Carthage," she said again, exasperated because her trip was such an unusual thing that everyone would know about it — and talk about it — including the erstwhile Trane Taggart.

She supposed she could just steal a horse from the stable and ride off at dawn, but it seemed ridiculous: she was the mistress of the house, and no one should question what she wanted to do or why.

"I never went when Mr. Taggart was alive, and yes, that *was* his express wish. But he's not here now, and I am, and it is time I went to town by myself."

"I come," Zilpha said. "You cain't go by yo'self alone,

274

Missus. It ain't right."

"Isaac will be with me, and I will be fine," she said, but she wasn't sure about that. Who in her right mind didn't know the way to town or where to find the bank? Eight years, and she had allowed Jesse to prevent her from doing anything a wife would do normally, even if her husband were absent carousing in Atlanta, or wherever Jesse went to spend his energy and his seed.

That surely wasn't worth dredging up on top of everything else.

She had dressed for it, too, and she felt strange in her formal black silk, boned and corseted and hooped to a fare-thee-well. She had the shawl wrapped around her, and a little hat and veil tilted over her blonde curls, and gloves, and just all the folderols she had never bothered with around Riveland, and she felt like a mechanical doll. Someone would wind her up soon and point her in the right direction and off she would go.

"The carriage, Zilpha. And Isaac will drive, just as he did for Mr. Jesse."

"I don' like it," Zilpha grumbled, but she went off to summon Isaac, and Cassandra paced edgily around the front parlor after she left.

She needed to avoid seeing Trane Taggart today. God, how could she call him Trane now? She didn't want to see him, but things never worked out: he might come roaring up the drive any minute, or he might be in the fields past sundown. He was a hard worker, she granted him that, but his nefarious plan had to have included investing himself in Riveland. And now everything he had done took on a suspicious cast, and she would go crazy if she thought about it another moment.

"Isaac say he come in a little while. He busy wif Mr. Trane's business."

Cassandra frowned. If she made a lot of noise over Isaac obeying her before Trane, she would make things seem odder than they already were. On the other hand, if she had to wait, she might just explode out of nervousness

275

into sheer hysteria.

"I will wait on the veranda," she said calmly. "He must finish what he is doing and attend to me; you tell him, Zilpha."

"Yes, ma'am," she said, eying Cassandra balefully. Oh, Missus was strange today, and she didn't want to know what she was about, picking up and going off to town suddenly like that, when she had never done the like before. "I tell him."

Of course she didn't think that Trane might be with him when Zilpha delivered her unconditional message, but it was her bad luck that he was, and as Isaac brought the carriage around, Trane followed behind, leading his own horse, consumed with curiosity.

And there she sat, pure black widow, and if he could find the temptress under all those pounds of black dress, he would be damned. It was as if she had caged herself up and put a 'don't touch' sign right on her forehead, which was covered now with a drift of black illusion veiling.

"Morning, Cassandra."

She started. "Good morning—Trane . . ." Oh, Lord . . . right there, she almost tripped all over his name. Her knees felt weak; surely he could read everything in her face. She sought frantically for something to say.

"Did you sleep well?"

Wrong thing, stupid reference . . . He could just pick it up and gallop away with it.

"Did *you?*"

That was pointed. Was there some underlying meaning to it? Did he know? Were his avid eyes raking her body because he was *looking?*

How could she answer that?

"It was very *hot* where I slept, Mr. Taggart. I felt today I could use a change."

"Isaac tells me you've never gone to town since you came here."

"No, I never have. So I'm going today."

He couldn't fight with that one. She was the boss, and

he had no call questioning what she wanted to do or where she wanted to go, but it seemed downright sudden to him.

He kept watching her and she kept fidgeting. Finally Isaac opened the door of the carriage for her and she walked slowly down the steps of the veranda to face Trane, furiously trying to think of something to say that would enlist his sympathy and allay his suspicions.

"Maybe you've never been a prisoner, Trane, and maybe you don't think that being immured on a big, beautiful plantation like this could be like being in a cell. But I promise you, Jesse Taggart made life hell here, and I'm only just beginning to pick up the pieces. Everything is in my hands now, and you know that, and I'm taking just small, small steps to make sure it remains that way."

"Yes, *ma'am,*" he said, helping her climb into the carriage. "God, I'd like to go with you."

Her skin tingled at the vibrant tone in his voice. She looked around the luxurious closed-in carriage with its thick-tufted seats, and she thought of all the possibilities; and she knew for this moment that everything was the same for him.

Her relief was almost palpable, and the fates were kind as well: she was saved from having to answer as Isaac flicked his whip and the carriage moved forward with a precipitous lurch.

Her banker was Mr. Ward and he wasn't really sure he quite understood what the beautiful Mrs. Taggart wanted.

When she arrived, she had asked to see the gentleman in charge, and she had introduced herself and talked about her husband, whom of course they all had known. He had expressed his sympathy at her loss and assured her that Mr. Greve was seeing to matters in a most expeditious way and she need not have any concerns on that score.

She in turn had requested the details of renting a strongbox. He told her it was quite an easy matter and if there were no other way he could help her, he would just direct

277

her to a clerk who would take care of it.

She, however, wanted his personal attention. She asked for an envelope, which he gave her, and she sat in a corner for a long moment, inserting something into it and sealing it, and then thinking about what to write on the back.

When she handed it to him, he saw she had inscribed her name and the word "will."

"That will go in the strongbox, if you please, Mr. Ward," she said — really sweetly, he thought, except that she wanted to *see* the actual box.

He summoned his clerk, who brought in a box so that she could examine it and how it sealed, and then she nodded and placed the envelope inside, and the clerk wrote the receipt.

"Now," she went on, "I should like to rent still another box, if I may, Mr. Ward."

Now he was baffled, but he sent for the clerk to bring another box, and she requested another envelope, and in this one she inserted the receipt to the first box, sealed it, signed her name, and put that in the second box.

She bit her lip as the clerk wrote out the second receipt. She really didn't know if even that were enough of a precaution to take once Trane discovered the missing receipt. It would have to do. Mr. Ward was looking at her as if he thought her more than a trifle eccentric. Or a trifle too saucy for someone who was a relatively new widow.

"Is there anything else, Mrs. Taggart?"

And he was also a shade too obsequious, but she supposed that was due to Jesse's standing within the business community in terms of his bank account — the full sum of which Mr. Greve had yet to apprise her.

He had, however, said she could draw upon it.

Perhaps she should test her ability to do that.

This was all so oppressively new to her, and she supposed there were women who had no fears about approaching their husbands' bankers and asking for money that was rightfully theirs.

She was scared to death to do it, but she was not going

to ask Mr. Greve, and she was not going to show Mr. Ward anything except that she expected he would comply with her request.

"I believe there is, Mr. Ward. I will need to write a draft for expenses while I am in town today."

"Oh, but generally, Mrs. Taggart, Vecsey's would take care of anything you wished to have sent to Riveland and submit the bill to us. Or at least, when your husband was alive . . ." His voice trailed off and he lifted his wire glasses from his nose fitfully. Women didn't know a thing about how their husbands ran businesses; he knew that from experience. Mrs. Taggart was too new to understand that. She merely wanted some pin money, to flex her newly minted degree of freedom. He had heard that Jesse's long-gone son had come back to Riveland, and he had been in no small measure relieved. He couldn't see the widow managing to send the crop to market by herself, or with inadequate management.

By far the best person to administer a man's holdings was a man's son, he thought. "Well, just tell me what you want, Mrs. Taggart; I'm sure there will be no problem."

She perceived it all — his hesitancy, his patronizing look, his reluctant decision.

It was *her* money, *her* legacy. She stiffened her resolve; this man was not going to demean her just because she was a widow. "No, I shouldn't think so," she said haughtily. But how much *did* she want? How much was the most outrageous amount she could demand? She had no idea. When he was alive, Jesse had dealt in hundreds of thousands of dollars worth of marketable cotton of varying grades, depending on the crop. A hundred dollars seemed too little to request in light of that knowledge, and a thousand perhaps a little too much, given this was her first foray into town — of which he was very well aware, due to Mr. Greve and his penchant for telling people things they didn't need to know.

"How much will you require, Mrs. Taggart?"

"Five hundred dollars will be sufficient," she said

grandly.

He didn't blink. He once again summoned the clerk, who brought a checking draft into the office, and he told her how to fill it out.

She signed her name with a flourish and handed it back to him. The clerk took it, and Mr. Ward bade her to make herself comfortable for ten minutes or so while they counted the money from the safe.

And there it was: within moments, a pile of bills in her hand, in an envelope tucked safely in her reticule, and Mr. Ward bowing her out of his office as if she were some *grande dame*—which she also disliked, but then was not the time to tell him. He was a rather ridiculous little man, barely as tall as she and finely dressed as his customers expected of him, and extremely conscious of who possessed the wealth in and around Carthage and who did not.

Mrs. Taggart was wealthy, and his attitude toward her, no matter how pernicious, conveyed that to her very nicely and in a way she could use for future reference.

She thanked him, she shook his hand politely, and when he retreated inside the gold leaf decorated doors of the bank, she turned toward the street and felt another one of those moments of pure panic.

Carthage was a vital little town, full of movement and purpose. People were going everywhere; she had never seen so many people in one place since before she came from Atlanta. She couldn't envision where they all could be going or what they could be doing. She felt as if she had stepped out of a fairy-tale book and into a place that had no basis in reality for her.

She was sure it had been a vastly smaller place when she had arrived as a bride with Jesse. But now, besides the bank and the Riversgate Hotel and numerous other small boardinghouses, there were also a cotton exchange, several mercantile stores specializing in different ranges of merchandise for different customers: there was a store for farm implements, and still another for houseware items.

There were several dressmaking establishments, a warehouse — one in town and one down by the Little Midway — there was a library, and a building occupied solely by offices of one businessman or another — cotton factors, lawyers, a doctor.

She was dazed by the lot of it, and she hadn't even perceived the whole yet. Her immediate need was to see Mr. Greve, and so she instructed Isaac to drive to the Riversgate.

"Cain' do dat, Missus. You cain' go in dat place nohow by yo'se'f."

"I can. Mr. Greve is my lawyer, Isaac," *and not my lover,* she thought acidly. It was just impossible to be a woman and go about your business in a town where there were a hundred prying eyes walking down the street at every moment.

"I must see Mr. Greve," she repeated, and Isaac climbed wearily up onto his perch and she climbed defiantly into the carriage, and he set it in motion to travel the several hundred feet to the front door of the Riversgate.

"I fetch de mister," Isaac told her, and she dared not argue with him. He was back in a moment. "He ain't dere. We goin' home now, Missus?"

She really had no more business to transact, but she had been desperate to give Greve the receipt to the second strongbox. However, she was beginning to rethink that. He believed in Trane Taggart, and he thought little Mrs. Jesse would stay safely home on the fertile acres of Riveland and never come into town, and she was just willing to wager that Mr. Ward had already sent a messenger to find Greve to tell him of her unconscionable demand for her own money.

Everyone was an enemy, she thought. She could trust only herself and her own powers of deduction, instinct and intuition.

And so be it. "We need to order those stores, Isaac. Find out where, please. I promise I won't try to hunt up Mr. Greve myself. In fact, I've changed my mind about seeing him at all."

"Yes, ma'am," he said, but she could read the thought behind his eyes: *Good.*

No, Greve was not her friend, she thought. He was a man in control of thousands and thousands of dollars in land and crops and he hadn't yet let it go to his head. But that didn't mean the thought wasn't there. He had too much control and she had too little, but nowhere in Jesse's legacy did it specify she did not have use of whatever funds she required whenever she wanted them.

She foresaw a fight over that as well, and having to bargain with him as to how much money she could withdraw at any given time. Damn Jesse. Damn him for tying her up like this and complicating things endlessly with power-hungry bankers and lawyers and sons who turned out not to be sons. . . .

And what *was* she going to do about Cole Trager?

She almost wished she weren't the legatee. Or that she could die and come back as her own legatee and just break Jesse's will altogether.

She didn't want to die. . . .

. . . Greve had executed a very simple will for her in which she had left everything to her unreasonably long-absent sister who never wanted to come back to Georgia again. . . .

. . . Ungrateful Linnea not to have written to her after Raylene's death . . .

. . . always supposing she had even gotten the letter . . .

. . . She had just gone off with Mr. Wiltshire and all his money and hadn't had a thought for Raylene or her. . . .

She was being damned generous to turn Riveland over to the feckless Linnea. . . .

Of course if she died, there was no telling if anyone would even be able to *locate* Linnea, and then what?

. . . Therefore, it made incontrovertible sense that she ought to take some pains to be sure her legacy went where she wanted it to. . . .

Which was to *her,* without conditions, provisions, stipulations, specifications, restrictions or limitations.

What a gorgeous idea. Because then she would not need Mr. Greve; she would not need Mr. Taggart/Trager. She would need no one, and she would be within her legal right to dispense with all of them, everyone.

Was she crazy? How could she do that?

She could do that; she knew she could. It was just a matter of planning, hair dye, skin color and some rouge. Raise her voice, affect an accent . . . She didn't know anything about accents, but that was a minor point. She would need different clothes, she would need . . . a foolproof death, some papers to prove who she was (not like that ridiculous Cole Trager, except that now, of course, she knew exactly why he had none); oh, oh — her mind raced ahead, leaping from detail to detail. It just required planning, a week at the most. She could purchase everything she required today. She fingered the money in her reticule. She had the means, she had the imagination, and she might yet break the chains that bound her.

Isaac appeared in the window. "We goin' to Lovell Mercantile, Missus."

"Thank you, Isaac," she said dreamily as he mounted the perch and the carriage lurched forward again. Yes, perfect; just the place to purchase flour, coffee, molasses, henna, rouge, and bolts of georgette silk just like what Linnea would have worn had she ever shown her face in Georgia again.

Of course Linnea couldn't know about her, Cassandra's, bequest. Linnea would just have to show up at the front door on a "visit" to her beloved sister.

That would take care of itself. The thing that wouldn't take care of itself was the outrage of Mr. Greve who did not waste a minute driving to Riveland to chastise her.

"Five *hundred* dollars, Miz Taggart. You really should have had Mr. Ward consult me," he said, trying to contain his anger, his rage, his unnameable emotion that she would go behind his back and appropriate what was rightfully hers.

"Five hundred, Mr. Greve," she confirmed tightly. She had to stand up to him now. It was her money, no matter what was in his mind about how she should have access to it or how she should or should not spend it; he didn't scare her, with his blustering tantrum.

"You should have at least . . ."

"No, I shouldn't, Mr. Greve. *You* should have notified me, as you said you would, about what I might draw on, and that is all you should have to say in the matter. This is *my* money, not yours."

That was a blind swing at his pretensions, and she saw immediately that she had hit the mark: he thought of everything concerning Jesse's legacy as *his,* from the cotton crop right down to the money reposing in the safe at the bank.

"A woman does not concern herself about money matters," he said stiffly. "It is perfectly plain to me this is why Mr. Taggart left those discretionary matters in *my* hands and required that you have an advisor."

"There is nothing in the will that mandates I must ask you for permission to use my own money, Mr. Greve. This bequest is restrictive enough without your amending clauses to suit your own purposes. I can read, Mr. Greve; I know exactly what I am entitled to and what I am *not.*"

That stopped him for a moment. "Your point is taken, Miz Taggart, but I cannot agree with it. You certainly *must* provide me with some accounting of how the money was spent."

Her hackles rose. "I certainly must *not,* Mr. Greve. It is *my* money."

"It is the estate's money. And it is money to cushion crop failure and below-value market and many other contingencies you would know nothing about."

"Truly I wouldn't, Mr. Greve. My account books must be a passel of lies I cooked up to keep my husband from finding out that we really were destitute," she shot back

284

angrily. "I think you are overstepping yourself, Mr. Greve, and that I may have good reason to bring a court action to bear on this. I will not tolerate being treated like a child and made to account for what I do in my own home with my own money. I trust that is clear."

"It is a rare court, Miz Taggart, who would find in favor of a woman running a man's estate into the ground."

"It is a rare court that would be presented with proof that the reason it stands today is because the man's wife paid off his excesses and kept things running, Mr. Greve. You know nothing about it, *nothing*. You would do well to fight for the discretionary power that you *are* entitled to by the terms of the will.

"I have not contested one single condition imposed upon me by my husband. I will not have you impose artificial conditions over and above those. Is *that* clear, Mr. Greve?"

"You cannot fritter away your husband's hard-earned money."

She did not know how to shut him up. He would never concede this point, not if she argued for a year with him, or presented him with her account books, or even with some conciliating detail of how she intended to use the money.

Her anger boiled over. Here was yet another cause for finding a way to relinquish her bequest back into her own hands. Then she wouldn't have to worry about Mr. Greve, or mysterious long-lost brothers she had never heard of, or sons who didn't exist, and "issue" who wouldn't investigate Jesse's death. It made so much sense to her, she wondered she hadn't thought of doing it before.

"Mr. Greve," she said slowly, clamping down hard on her indignation, "we cannot agree on this. I would never 'fritter' away my husband's estate, nor would I maltreat the legacy he left me. I had thought it was very plain to you on your various visits to Riveland that I am capable of running the business of the plantation, and more than that, capable of learning that which I do not yet know. Your

285

assumption that I am a thoughtless fribble is insulting to me—and to my husband, who made no specification as to how I may use the money, in which case I think you may safely infer that *he* thought I was capable of managing it *and* controlling my impulses."

He was silent a long time under this righteous lashing, and she thought at last she had gotten through to him, that he wouldn't beg the point anymore. But no. "If I may say so, Miz Taggart, you, to my knowledge, have never had any money in hand."

She bit her lip in vexation. "This is true, Mr. Greve. But that thought obviously did not trouble Mr. Taggart, since he did not make a provision dealing with it, and he went to a great deal of trouble to mandate those other restrictive conditions to my inheritance. I feel strongly that if he felt I were not capable of handling the money, Mr. Greve, he would have added a lengthy"—and punishing—"proviso to that effect. I trust when you think about it, you will agree with me, Mr. Greve."

"I cannot conclude that yet, Miz Taggart," he pushed on stolidly.

"And we have been arguing the point for two hours or more, Mr. Greve, and good manners forbades me from sending you out the door at this juncture. Please stay the night and take all the time you need to think about it."

"You are so kind," he murmured, but he didn't think she was kind at all. He thought she was flexing power that she did not have and he wanted to quash her immediately. Yet every argument she put forth was sound and unemotional and went right to the heart of the matter, just as if she had been a man face to face with him contesting her rights rather than a frighteningly clear-thinking woman who reasoned like a man.

He exhausted her, her mind and her body, and she felt as if she needed at least a week to recover from that onslaught—and it wasn't even over yet. He just wasn't going to concede the point, and he would argue it with her for years, perhaps.

So now she had the money and the incriminating little piece of paper that said she owned a strongbox at the Carthage-Midway bank, and she didn't know where to put either.

But she did know that she had been right not to confide in Mr. Greve, and she felt so thankful he had not been there when Isaac sought him out. Everything from now on was her decision, her battle, her victory — because in the end, she was going to win.

Greve's presence complicated matters, as it always did. Trane moved around the periphery of the dinner table as he followed Cassandra and Greve into the library for the post-dinner cognac that seemed to be a little ritual with every one of Greve's visits nowadays.

And she was looking too radiant tonight, too animated, and he wasn't sure it didn't have as much to do with her unexpected trip into Carthage as it did Greve's equally unexpected visit.

Whatever it was, it was interfering with his intense desire to have her alone with him tonight, and he didn't like it one bit; nor was he happy that Greve was to spend the night — again.

"Doesn't that man have a life of his own?" he demanded in an undertone as she came to refill his snifter with just a jot more of that luscious amber liquid.

"No, he thinks Riveland is his life," she said caustically, and she hoped he heard her. But no, he was too busy appraising the luminous leather volumes lining the shelves of the room, books that had never been opened except in secret by the ever-curious and intelligent Cassandra.

"How can I see you tonight?"

Oh Lord . . . In the middle of her nightmare with Greve, she had not for one moment remembered the dazzling coupling with him the night before.

"I don't think you can," she said, tingeing her voice with too much sincerity, thankful, in her heart, that Greve's presence gave her an excuse to avoid him. And perhaps that had been why she had extended the invitation.

"Cassandra . . ."

"How can I?"

"Find a way."

"Trane, he is . . ." But she couldn't tell him: Trane the Impostor Trager had no right to know her business — or Jesse's. "He is not finished with his business with me. I can't take the chance: he might want to continue the discussion after you leave."

"I can't take the chance he might want to start something."

"As if I would let that pompous bore say anything to me that didn't have to do with Riveland or the estate. Please, Trane, I'm annoyed enough with him as it is."

"Well you should be, lady. He is an ass, and a man who was handed too much power over too much of your life."

"I know it," she said, her gaze turning speculative as Greve turned to join them again.

"A wonderful library, Miz Taggart."

"I'm so glad you appreciate it. I have had a wonderful time with it myself."

"I see," he said, and he really thought he did. A bookish woman — it explained everything. She wouldn't give up, either, he saw that now; she would argue the point right down to the ground and never give an inch, nor would she concede to a more knowledgeable authority.

He could see he was not going to be leaving Riveland any time too soon.

"That ol' man has just ensconced himself in that library and he's having a high old time making his points, isn't he?"

"I don't have much choice about that, Trane. He's the executor, and the only thing I have on my side is the fact there is one thing that Jesse didn't specifically spell out instructions about. And he can't cope with the fact that I

288

understand that."

"Get him out of here, Cassandra. I'm aching for you."

"I'm doing the best I can, Trane." Well, her half-hearted best: she didn't want him gone, not yet. She wanted him in the house, a buffer between Trane's raging needs and her own to which she could not allow herself to succumb.

She wanted him there just as long as *she* needed him to be there, and she was working frantically to arrange things so she could set her plan into motion.

"He's a leech."

And what are you, Mr. Trane call me Cole Trager Taggart?

"Another day, no more," she promised, and she wondered at the ease with which the lies came tripping off of her tongue. She did not want Mr. Greve to go back to Carthage at all, because she did not want to be alone ever again with the man who called himself Trane Taggart.

She had to work quickly; only one element of her plan had not fallen into place, and that one was the hardest part of all. Everything else was at the ready, arranged within this three-day respite of Mr. Greve's extended visit.

She couldn't stretch things out much longer, and she couldn't put Trane off more than another day.

She rather marveled at the mechanisms of her body: the ravenous hunger she had felt for him had dissipated completely and something piercingly vindictive had taken its place. It was a marvel of protectiveness, as if somewhere deep inside herself her body moved to surround her with a way to negate all that he had come to mean to her.

She felt grateful that she did not have to deal with the complication of her restless desire. It was gone, as completely as if someone had snuffed it out.

. . . snuffed it out—

"Mr. Greve?"

"Miz Taggart."

"You are not going to come around to my point of view, Mr. Greve; I think that has become quite obvious."

She was seated behind the desk in the library, her hands

289

folded in front of her, her hair a golden halo around her head, a faint smile on her lips that just dented one corner of her mouth.

He seated himself opposite her. "I think we are at an impasse, yes, Miz Taggart." He took off his glasses and began to examine them in the flickering sconce light, and she followed his motions with her gaze, and noted how the flame flickered sometimes just a little too close to the brocade curtains by the window.

"Well, what *is* to be done?"

"I have a suggestion which would in some measure pacify me and still leave you with some degree of discretion over the money you withdrew."

"And what is that, Mr. Greve?" That flame was bothering her mightily. A small flame like that could start a conflagration that would destroy everything. Unless of course preventive measures were taken.

Or someone caught it in time.

She *knew* there was a reason she had invited Mr. Greve to stay. She barely heard his solution as the last point of her plan meshed neatly into the rest. "I beg your pardon, Mr. Greve?"

"I'm sorry, was I not clear? I am suggesting that you return half of the money to Mr. Taggart's account, and keep the rest for pin money."

Pin money! *Pin* money! As if she were some wayward schoolgirl who needed trinkets and trifles and he were some indulgent father doling out the wherewithal for her to purchase them!

She stood up abruptly. "Mr. Greve, this really has gone far enough. I will not return the money I withdrew, and I reserve the right to spend it as I see fit. There's no point to discussing this or trying to bargain about it. We will just have to agree to disagree about it. But I will tell you: if I find any obstruction on behalf of Mr. Ward to my withdrawing future funds from *my* account at the bank, I will take steps to see whether you can be removed as the executor of Jesse's estate."

290

He settled his glasses back on his nose, and got up slowly. "With great difficulty, Miz Taggart, let me assure you on that point. Any court would certainly concur with my determination to conserve as much as possible of cash on hand."

"Indeed, Mr. Greve, your efforts are most appreciated — when they are not misdirected. I bid you good evening, sir."

"Miz Taggart." He lumbered to the library door, turned, seemed about to say something and thought the better of it. Her mind wasn't even on him, or the money. She was staring out the library window into the darkness, and at the last, she wasn't even aware that he had gone.

He was just getting ready for bed, having spent some time reading and thinking, when he smelled the pungent odor of smoke.

Not in his room. He thrust himself into his pants and ran out into the hallway, aware suddenly of the hubbub outside and in as Zilpha came racing up the staircase with Ojim close behind.

"Stay back, Mr. Greve," Ojim shouted.

"But —"

Ojim threw open the door of Cassandra's room.

The place was in flames, the curtains, the bed . . . "*Water!*" he screamed, and pulled off his shirt to start beating at the fire.

Eli came rushing through the scattering house servants with the first bucket of water, throwing it blindly into the room.

"You fool," Zilpha shouted. "Get some sense. Get dat line, get dat water. You — Leola — you find dat hip bath; we got to fill dis room wif water, you hear? You hear?" Her voice was totally panicked, her hands pushing, pulling, tearing off her skirt so she too could beat at the flames as the line formed and the next buckets of water were passed up the steps in a frantic chain.

291

"Dis ain't doin' no one no good nohow," Zilpha panted. "Where dat Mr. Trane? He ain't gonna let dis house burn down, no he ain't . . . oh no he ain't . . . no . . ." Her voice trailed off in a sob as her skirt caught and she had to throw it on the burning bed.

"WHERE'S CASSANDRA?" Trane's voice boomed all over the house as he dashed upstairs, two steps at a time, and thrust himself into the knot of water bearers.

"We don't know," Greve said faintly. No one had even thought about Cassandra. She couldn't be in there, she couldn't; the flames were starting to eat away at the connecting wall —

"Damn it — get every damn blanket you can possibly find, all the water, every hand — Eli — *everyone* — anything you can find to smother this — I don't care if we pull up all the rugs or curtains. *Get going!"*

He whirled toward the room. He could see what the others could not: the fire had blazed up the curtains and out to the bed and now on the wall. The rug was smoldering, and the desk. The bed was gone, but there was still a chance — still —

But *Cassandra* —

He pulled a bucket and a quilt out of Isaac's hand and launched himself into the room.

Chapter Eighteen

"You son of a bitch—you could have gotten to her sooner."

"Mr. Taggart—" No, he had better not try to reason with a man who was grief-stricken. Taggart wouldn't listen to a word he had to say, not one word.

Trane sat in the library, his hand gripped around what remained of Cassandra Taggart: a ring, some charred hair, burned fragments of bones, a piece of dress—and he was inconsolable. For a week now, Mr. Greve had tried to speak to him and he would not be spoken to. He wanted to blame him, Greve, for not having perceived sooner that Cassandra was in trouble. Well—

They had smothered the flames; the man had been heroic, beating away like a madman. . . . He couldn't think about it. He couldn't even watch, and the end result was the same: Cassandra was presumed dead in the flames, and now he had the disquieting task of administering the will that she had had the foresight to prepare.

Of course on the other hand, he didn't need even to reveal to anyone that Cassandra had a will. He would just go to see Mr. Ward very quietly and perhaps together they could apply to probate to appoint *him* residual legatee, since Cassandra had violated none of the conditions, nor had her husband specified an heir in case of her premature death.

Well, that was best left for sometime in the future.

Ojim and Eli were preparing a grave for Cassandra's remains, although what they would put in it, he couldn't guess. There was only so much salvaged bones and ash; he didn't know how anyone could tell what was Cassandra and what was the pillow sham.

He knew that was heartless of him, but he couldn't help feeling as though fate had taken a hand so that he could play out part of his dream.

Trane Taggart hardly mattered in the scheme of things: he didn't have a claim, not after twenty years, and if he disputed it, Mr. Greve was willing to take him before a court as well.

The thing that worried him was the fact that the money had probably burned up in the bedroom as well. Five hundred dollars . . .

He shook his head. What he could have done with five hundred dollars—It would have lasted him years, living comfortably and elegantly. It had probably been swept up in the ashes that Zilpha and Ojim had lovingly preserved to inter in the grave next to Jesse Taggart's on the hill.

"She never even screamed," he said dolefully. "The thing was ablaze before anyone got to her. Really, Mr. Taggart, I promise you—"

"Yes, yes. What happens now?" Trane demanded impatiently.

He hadn't thought. It had been more than a week since the fire, and every effort within the house was directed toward salvaging the ashes and preparing for Cassandra's funeral. The work crew was half-heartedly picking the river end of the field, and the women were harvesting potatoes and the second crop of corn. But there was no life in the place, and he was sure the pick was behind schedule, even if the first batch of cotton had already gone to gin.

"I think we wait to do anything until the crop has gone downriver; don't you agree?"

Trane blew out a long breath.

He supposed he agreed. He would agree to anything.

He would get the damn cotton baled and out and then he might just be allowed to mourn.

Oh God—Cassandra . . .

"Of course, you will continue to run things here until . . ."

". . . until? . . ."

"Until the crop is in," Mr. Greve finished triumphantly. No use overplaying his hand with this man: he looked like a poker player, and he wasn't so devastated that he wouldn't try to protect his own interests along with Cassandra's.

No, Mr. Greve was going to play a lone hand—and he held all the aces before he even started.

The pain just would not go away.

Trane went up to her room every day, almost as if he thought he would wake up from some awful dream and really find her there.

But all he found was charred furniture and sodden bedclothes, ashes and futility.

He could not believe it. She had been in his arms one minute, gone the next. How did loving a woman sneak up on you so fast that you felt like life was over with her untimely death?

And how did the damn fire start anyway?

He could think of a dozen explanations, ranging from carelessness to someone wanting outright revenge, and he knew at least one man who qualified on that score.

He even went looking for him, scouring the saloons of Carthage and the towns beyond, looking for the swaggering Daggett, drowning his conscience in a cheap bottle of whiskey.

He found him too, and he would have killed him, if some saner heads had not prevailed; and now Daggett was after his hide too. Daggett didn't forget. Daggett hadn't found work after Riveland, and he knew just who the yellow-bellied usurper was, and he was coming to get

295

him, and the hell with the death of the lily-handed mistress bitch—who cared? Who goddamn cared?

He felt like that himself, Trane did, and he could have drowned himself in all the cognac in Jesse's excellent cellar, but none of it would ease the pain of losing Cassandra, not during, not after, when he would really have to cope with it.

He had never experienced anything like this in his life; nothing could ease the pain.

He went into the fields, he worked himself to exhaustion, he returned to the bed in which he had made love to Cassandra. . . .

Cassandra the witch; Cassandra the spider lady; Cassandra, his lover . . . Cassandra no more.

There was a mercifully brief ceremony a week later. Greve had contacted a minister, though Jesse had never been affiliated with any church in town, and both he and Greve and Mr. Ward the banker and the entire household of slaves and field workers attended the burial.

"You know, I only met her once," Mr. Ward said to Trane, pumping his hand enthusiastically, "but she was quite an amazing woman, your . . . your—"

"*Step*mother," Trane supplied, wincing inwardly at having to put up this pretense to some pompous stranger.

"Yes, stepmother. I'm so sorry, Mr. Taggart. Excuse me now, won't you?"

He nodded, and watched Mr. Ward promptly slip his arm into Mr. Greve's and the two of them walk off together.

Two peas in a pod, he thought, and both of them after only one thing: Cassandra's peace of mind, even in death.

The work went on. It was nearing the end of August— hot, utterly steaming.

Greve came and stayed at the house for a week, and

left when no one paid attention to him, not even the servants. They had work to do, too; Zilpha made sure it got done, and she had no time to waste on the likes of Mr. Greve.

Trane had a crew moting the first stand of cotton that had been picked. They were close to baling their first three hundred pounds, and he was damned looking forward to seeing the end of it.

It was the one good thing about the job: there was an end, even if, the following spring, they had to begin all over again.

He began to wonder, as he woke his work crews early, and set out their tasks, what the disposition of Cassandra's estate would be. Greve was taking a damned long time about it, he thought. Someone should know—that bluejay banker. *Him,* as next of kin . . .

Next of kin—shit . . .

God . . .

Or did Greve think that he, Trane, might be scared off from asking about it because of his past history with Jesse? The man was a fool.

"I'm going to town," Trane told Zilpha, who had been very attentive and solicitous after Cassandra's death, insisting he stay in the big house, and take over the central bedroom, and let her do for him how she used to do for the missus.

He had agreed, both to annoy Greve and to get out of the close, sated atmosphere of the place where he had shared that last shattering union with Cassandra.

But being in the house only magnified the sense of everything he had shared with her on a sensual level. He violently regretted they had not talked.

There were a thousand and one questions he had to ask her—and there was no one to answer; a thousand and one things he wanted to know, and they were all buried with her, ashes in his mouth.

He hardly knew whether to stay or go: it was easier to stay.

So he went to town instead, and bearded Mr. Greve in the lion's den of the bar of the Riversgate Hotel.

It was perfectly obvious this was the place to conduct business. Deals were being transacted right before his very eyes with the nod of a head, the crook of a finger.

Greve saw him first, and went to meet him and draw him away from the noise of the crowd.

"Have a drink, Taggart. Do you good. Nothing like that stuff out of your daddy's basement: this will go right to your gut and knock you flat. You look like you could use one."

"Set 'em up," Trane said, motioning to the bartender.

"What's on your mind?" Greve asked casually, downing his whiskey in one swallow.

"Don't rightly know, Mr. Greve. Things've slowed down to a walk. Got my people working like a machine just bringing in the crop, just like Cassandra would have wanted."

"Glad to hear it, Taggart, very glad to hear it."

"Now what troubles me, Mr. Greve, is what comes next."

Greve stiffened perceptibly. "What do you mean?"

"Well, I mean that Riveland can't rightly run itself on the heels of its mistress's death. There has to be some provision for who carries on—like Cassandra's will, perhaps."

"I—"

"Can't imagine my stepmomma, who was so precise about things, wouldn't have made sure things were going to be taken care of in event of her death."

"Well, you see . . ."

"Seems to me," Trane interrupted, "that if she didn't plan so far ahead as to make a choice about it, seems to me that her next of kin would most likely be awarded control of her estate. Wouldn't you think, Mr. Greve?"

"I—I'm not sure just quite what the law provides on that subject," Greve said firmly. "I think you have a point, though." He hadn't spent hours hanging around

298

the Riversgate and not learned how to handle a fractious client. The rules were simple: agree with him, follow up, derail him as fast as possible.

But he had to make the decision instantly. Would it be easier to tussle in court with Trane Taggart, who had some filial rights, or would he be more-successful with the unknown Linnea Wiltshire, long-gone-away sister of Cassandra who might never show up to claim her inheritance?

Would it be easier to manipulate Mr. Ward — or a missing heir?

The answer was simple.

"It seems to me Cassandra did make some designation in case of her death; I swear, I wasn't thinking about it, Taggart. It was right after we came to terms on several matters pertaining to Mr. Taggart's restrictions. You can understand it went straight out of my head."

"Oh yeah, I can sure understand that," Trane said with a touch of irony that he was sure was lost in the quagmire of Mr. Greve's earnest assurances of his good faith. "Why don't we just check it out right now, Mr. Greve? You know I'd rest a damn sight more easy if I was sure that my stepmomma had done the right thing."

He didn't think it was coincidental that Mr. Greve could not lay his hands immediately on a piece of paper that Cassandra had purportedly signed six months before.

It was just the way the man had always operated that made him edgy, and he saw it as his clear duty to protect Cassandra's legacy.

"But of course at some point you will be planning to return to Baltimore, and your family," Mr. Greve pointed out, wishing heartily that he had planned to be on a steamboat out of Carthage that very week.

Damn. Baltimore. His loving wife and six children . . . he had sure let Cassandra railroad him into that one.

And now he was stuck with it.

"Well, I'm thinking hard on having dear Lavinia pack up the family and come stay on Riveland until this is settled," he said blandly, looking Greve flat out in the eye, daring him to deny he had the right.

Greve had the grace to look away. "Well, we must take things as they come, Mr. Taggart. I certainly will come straight to you when I unearth Cassandra's disposition."

"You do that," Trane said coolly, but he was raging inside. He had no satisfaction from Greve whatsoever, not even the knowledge that her will was readily available and could give him some clue as to what she had wanted done.

But at least she had made one. God, what a smart lady, what a loss, what a goddamned . . . *hell* . . .

A man could break his back in the fields, crying and not looking where he was goddamned going. A man worked three dozen slaves, he couldn't hide his emotions, not for long; he didn't know if it were better or worse that he publicly grieved. There was just no way to stop, and too much damned work to get done. Fields had been too damned productive this damn year—Jesse would have laughed his fool head off at the whole son-of-a-bitch scenario.

But the bastard had to have had a sense of humor to have chosen that lily-livered weasel Greve for his lawyer. Give a man like that power and he goes berserk, wants it all, just like Cassandra said—thinks of it all as being his own and doesn't want anyone else to touch it. No damn wonder he was having trouble coming up with a piece of paper that would take it all away from him.

He would squeeze the man harder if he had to. Greve didn't want to deal at all with a next of kin, and especially not *him*.

It gave him *some* satisfaction, it really did, to know he had the son of a bitch on the run.

He wished Cassandra were there to see it. He wished Jesse were alive—he would kill the bastard all over again.

He wished to hell he could stop the silent tears, and the pain in his heart. . . .

"Ain't nothin' gonna bring de missus back, Mr. Trane," Zilpha said to him one morning. "You got to work de hurtin' from yo' mind and yo' body."

He laughed mirthlessly. "I thought I was doing that, Zilpha."

"No, you was lookin' while others was workin'. You got to toil. Toil take away de memory and it go back a ways till you is ready to take it out again and put it close to yo' heart. You hear, Mr. Trane?"

"I'll never be ready," he said.

"You gonna be ready sometime, Mr. Trane. You don' leave dat memory, it gonna kill you. You gotta give it space, Mr. Trane. You gotta let it die."

NO! He didn't say it; it was on his lips, but what was the point? She knew he was resisting believing it, and he knew it, and her words were meant to console him, but they only showed him he wasn't ready to give her up yet — not yet, maybe not ever.

Cassandra . . .

In his bed at night — Cassandra . . .

Was it harder in the big house, where the place was suffused with her presence? He would have been lonelier in the overseer's house. He needed to be with her, *here.* He *was* with her here. It was enough that she had sat in that chair, worked at that desk, read those books in the library, touched that decanter when she had poured him that last snifter of cognac. . . .

Sometimes it was even enough that he had had the chance to love her the way he had loved no other woman before. And sometimes it wasn't enough that he had known her for only two months — and hadn't begun to cram a lifetime of memories into that short space of time.

But there *were* memories, and that was good.

Most times, the fact that she was gone was inconceivable to him. She was merely in another room, or upstairs,

301

or in the office. . . .

Damn that Greve. . . .

It had been a week, maybe even verging on two—he didn't know, since time had no parameters for him—and still Greve had not returned with Cassandra's will.

It was time to put a scare into the bastard, he thought. It was time to get him wholly out of the picture, time he relinquished all of his estate management duties. Time to find a judge and present his case.

Time to intimidate the nit-picking bastard who was probably sitting on the porch of the Riversgate toting up the probable number of bales Riveland was going to be sending downriver any day soon, and figuring out how to siphon some of that profit off for himself.

Jesse must have goddamned paid him handsomely *and* made him promises, for him to uproot himself from some cheap little office room in Atlanta to take up residence at the not inexpensive Riversgate Hotel.

And then he had aggravated Cassandra to the point of . . . What was the use of going over the same ground? She was gone and Greve was going to be irrelevant any minute.

"Mr. Trane . . . Mr. Trane." Zilpha scurried into the room, her voice urgent. "Mr. Trane—we got a visitor."

"It's about damned time Greve got here. Send him in here, and make sure he doesn't get too comfortable."

"Ain't Mr. Greve."

"*Not* Greve? Who?"

"You come see, Mr. Trane. You got to come see."

The library, where he had taken to spending most of his time, was at the far end of the reception hallway. He followed Zilpha curiously, feeling a little frustrated that it wasn't Greve who awaited him in the entry foyer.

It was a woman, dressed in bright green, with her hair tucked up under a matching hat. He couldn't quite see her face. He couldn't quite see . . . much of her.

And then she turned as she heard their footsteps and his heart caught right in his throat.

"Hello," she said brightly.

His hope died. Not Cassandra. Very like Cassandra . . . or was she? *Who?* The hair was different—red, wavy; the body—he couldn't tell under that stylish wide hooped dress and fashionable bolero jacket. The hands—were neatly covered by matching embroidered gloves. The face . . . the eyebrows darker, thicker; the eyes, deeper but that same shade of leaf green.

The mouth—

He would know that mouth anywhere. . . .

Cassandra's but not Cassandra's.

His disappointment was like a walloping punch to his gut and his voice lashed out unnecessarily rough: "Who the hell are you?"

"I'm happy to meet you, too," she said cheekily. "I'm Linnea. Who are you, and *where* is my sister?"

He was so dumbfounded he couldn't speak.

"You're a one, coming at me like a charging bull, and now you have nothing to say?" Linnea demanded.

He couldn't move. It was Cassandra—but it wasn't. The voice was higher, inflected with a faint accent. She held her body differently, used her hands more; the tone of her voice was more facetious, its timbre light and faintly familiar. Her skin tone was different, whiter, her lips redder. She was thinner too, and there were hollows in her cheeks And that hair, two or three shades away from Cassandra's color . . .

"Who you is?" Zilpha said, her voice tinged with suspicion.

"Where's Cassandra?" the woman said again. "Tell her Linnea is here. Tell her—no, I'll tell her myself. . . ."

"Missus never said nothin' 'bout no sister," Zilpha said, moving tensely to her left to block the stranger from mounting the steps.

"Of course she did," the woman said staunchly. She

303

turned to Trane. "This is ridiculous. Who are *you?*"

"I'm Cassandra's stepson," he said neutrally. "Trane Taggart, ma'am."

"Oh . . . !" Her eyes widened at that, and then she knit her brow, trying to figure out the complications. But she didn't know anything about it, he thought. And nobody knew anything about her. "Well—where is Cassandra? No one has been polite enough to even answer *that* question."

Zilpha looked at Trane, and he got his bearings finally and said, "I think we had better invite Linnea to come in. Please—" He motioned toward the library hallway, and led her back into that room, looking at Zilpha over her shoulder all the while.

"Lovely room," she said in clipped tones as she entered. "May I sit?"

"Please."

He sat opposite her rather than across the desk. So like—so unalike. He could not merge the two pictures in his mind. It was almost as if this woman were an imitation of Cassandra, with all the right features, but all of them drawn faintly out of focus.

Except for the mouth. The mouth was Cassandra's. . . .

How did he tell her Cassandra had died?

"There was a fire here several weeks ago," he began, and immediately her lighthearted face changed. "Cassandra's room—the candles, we think, too close to the curtains—she was asleep. . . ."

"Oh my God," Linnea gasped. "Where *is* she?"

"She died," Trane said, and the words caught in his throat. "Too late to . . ."

"Oh my God . . ." Linnea rose from her chair agitatedly. "Oh my God . . . I can't believe it. . . . I came all this way. . . ." Tears streamed down her face. "Never see her again . . ." She moved to the opposite corner of the room to hide her face, and her shoulders shook as she cried unashamedly for her loss.

More than all of us did, Trane thought mordantly, as he and Zilpha looked at each other quizzically.

After a while, she turned back to them, blotting her eyes with a handkerchief she had pulled from her sleeve. "I'm so sorry. I—I had never answered her letters; I just never thought I would be taking this trip back to Georgia. God—how do I live with myself for that?" She bit her lip and turned her face away again.

"But that is not your problem, sir," she went on, when she had calmed down again. "Cassandra obviously did not speak of me, just as I hardly spoke of her. I married first, you see, and went off to England with my husband, Mr. Wiltshire, who was kind enough to leave Mother and Cassandra with a substantial stipend. Mother was angry that he did not invite them to accompany us. She thought my marriage would make things better. Only for me . . . only for me." She stopped again, her eyes spilling tears. She dabbed at them and went on:

"Cassandra wrote to me that Mother had arranged her marriage with Mr. Taggart, and then subsequently, when Mother died. I did not write back. I never expected to want to be reunited with my sister ever again. We had nothing in common, you see. But then, I didn't expect Mr. Wiltshire to . . . to die and leave me destitute. I didn't expect anything that has happened. . . ."

Her eyes overflowed again.

Trane shifted uncomfortably. "Truly, Mrs. . . . Wiltshire, is it? There is no need to justify yourself to me."

"Of course not," she said.

"You will stay, of course. Cassandra would have wanted that."

"We can't know that," Linnea said bravely.

"I know that," Trane said firmly. "Zilpha . . . the far guest room?"

"Yes, sir, Mr. Trane."

"And some dinner for the beleaguered Mrs. Wiltshire."

"I tell Elsie."

"Thank you. Now. Of course you will stay as long as

305

you like, Mrs. Wiltshire. Cassandra's estate is in limbo at present: I'm acting overseer, and the only thing we're attempting to do is get this year's crop out to market as expediently as possible. Apparently, Cassandra made up a disposition of the estate which she inherited—unconditionally, to all intents and purposes—from my father, who was her husband. I'm awaiting word on that from her lawyer. And that is all I can tell you."

"I don't even want to hear any more," Linnea said tearily. "She is buried on Riveland?"

"Next to her mother—and her husband."

"My poor Cassandra . . . ," Linnea murmured, her tears starting all over again. "I just can't believe it."

"No, ma'am."

"I will be . . . all right, Mr. Taggart."

"Yes, ma'am. I was just thinking—I'll need to remove myself back to the overseer's house."

"Not on my account."

"No, ma'am." He shook his head. He kept studying her and studying her and the differences were vast and then sometimes there weren't any at all, and he felt so off balance he didn't know what to feel.

Maybe in daylight, he thought. Maybe he could see it much more clearly when morning came.

Now here was the part where she had to be stupendously careful, she thought triumphantly as she directed Eli to set her bags on the bed so that she could unpack more easily.

She was aware of his unsettled gaze, just as she had been aware of Trane's disbelieving eyes taking her apart feature by feature as if that would prove something—or disprove it.

God, she should have been an actress, she thought. The makeover, the tears, the voice . . . it was perfect—or it would be when that fool Greve unearthed the last will and testament she had signed. She wouldn't put it past

306

him to try to cheat "Linnea" out of her rightful due. But he hadn't yet, because Trane was still in the house, and no matter how she felt about his duplicity, she was grateful he had dug in his heels at Riveland until she had returned.

Of course he would never know that.

She searched for hangers in the closet and began lifting out the gorgeously fashionable wardrobe she had managed to scrape together in her several weeks in Atlanta. Oh, it was amazing what you could do and where you could go when you had a fistful of dollars in your pocket and an unlimited imagination.

It was the performer in her; she could make up any story to suit any situation, and by invention and creativity and sheer determination, she had managed to arrive in Atlanta without anyone remarking the unsuitability of a young woman like herself traveling alone. And she had found accommodations without unduly arousing the suspicions of her landlady.

"A young thing like you—a widow!" the landlady clucked disbelievingly.

Cassandra swore it was true, and that the stationmaster at the depot had directed her with great sympathy to Mrs. Waters. "A girl has to be careful where she stays in this old city," Mrs. Waters agreed solicitously. "Now you come right here into my parlor and sit and tell me all about yourself."

She was a roly-poly woman, habitually dressed in black bombazine, which set off her pink face and graying hair, and she ran a "respectable" boardinghouse, and young Mrs. Taggart looked about as lost and respectable as a lady could be, in spite of the fact that she had journeyed upcountry all by herself. Some things could be overlooked, she felt, in light of circumstance. No one knew sweet Mrs. Taggart in Atlanta, and now she was here, Mrs. Waters would see that all the proprieties were observed.

She listened with great concern to Cassandra's tale of

307

woe about her adoring husband and the conniving relatives who had forced her away from the only home she had ever known. And she stood in complete accord with Cassandra's raw desire to pay them all back somehow for what they had done to her. After all, what could one powerless and essentially helpless young woman do against a consort of wealthy relations who wanted nothing to do with her?

Mrs. Waters expected that Cassandra Taggart would be spending a long time at her boardinghouse, but when Cassandra was insistent that she must be able to come and go as she pleased, Mrs. Waters had to reluctantly acquiesce. "But it's not right for you to be walking around the city unchaperoned, Mrs. Taggart."

"Even a widow?" Cassandra asked tartly, chafing under these social restrictions of which she had been totally unaware. Was there no place a woman was allowed some measure of freedom?

"Especially a widow," Mrs. Waters retorted. "Now look—you take my kitchen maid with you—that Lulu who serves dinner: that will make everything fine."

Well, it didn't make things fine; Mrs. Waters apparently had outlined her own role in Cassandra's story—she was going to be her guardian angel and make sure Cassandra did not make one misstep.

Cassandra took Lulu and went shopping, outfitting herself over the course of a week with ready-made, slightly tawdry dresses that fit her memory of the last visit of the disdainful Linnea.

"She buyin' everythin' she kin buy," Lulu reported religiously to Mrs. Waters, whose curiosity about her new boarder was hardly satisfied by the long talks she and Cassandra had had about Cassandra's situation. She would dearly have loved to know what wealthy and powerful family had sent poor Cassandra out on her own, against family values and mores, and in the face of public disapproval.

But then again, they had obviously softened the blow

with the one thing that could buy anybody's cooperation.

She was shocked by Cassandra's next request. "I need to hire someone to help me."

"What kind of help?" Mrs. Waters asked cautiously.

Cassandra took a deep breath. "Help in changing my appearance."

"Oh my dear, whatever for?"

Cassandra bit her lip. How far could she take her spur-of-the-moment tale of revenge, she wondered. But Mrs. Waters' greedy eyes were waiting. She was sure Mrs. Waters had exactly the information she needed.

"Because I'm going to go back, and I'm going in disguise, and I'm going to find out just how those nasty relatives of my husband cheated me. And then—and *then*—I'm going to make them *pay*."

That appealed to Mrs. Waters's vicarious sense of justice. "Exactly what do you want, Mrs. Taggart?"

She knew what she wanted: she had gotten the idea from her excursions around the city. She and Lulu had passed a theater and she had stopped short and just stared at the billboard for the longest time, transfixed by the notion that here was the answer to how to go about transforming herself into Linnea.

She smiled at Mrs. Waters. "I want to hire someone—an actress, maybe?—who can help me change my appearance so my husband's relatives won't recognize me."

Mrs. Waters had to think about it. She dearly wanted to help the sweet Mrs. Taggart, who had come from somewhere way downstate where she, Mrs. Waters, could never find out the details of whether this risky plan would work, and she hated that. On the other hand, Mrs. Taggart seemed to have a lot of money, and she wasn't averse to Mrs. Taggart spreading some of it her way. Yes, in fact, she was sure she could find someone—for a slight fee.

"You know, dear Mrs. Taggart, I am just heartbroken that you have been used so badly. And you're in luck," she said, smiling warmly and holding out her hands. "I know the very person you need."

And it worked . . . it worked—everything had worked, from the chancy business of leaving the candles so close to the bedroom curtains, to her scavenging around the smokehouse and barn for bones and horsehair and discarded offal to strew on the bed so that it would seem that the remnants of her body had indeed been consumed there. Everything had worked: she had watched from the bushes below to be sure the room had well and truly caught, and to be positively certain someone had discovered the fire before it destroyed Riveland, and only then had she made off on her adventure.

And how, with the help of Lavonna the actress with her ever-outstretched hand, she now knew how to use powders, pencils and henna, to change the contour of her face and features, her hair, and the very posture of her body to create a totally new persona; she knew how to lighten her voice and bend it into something different from her normal tone; but above all, she knew how to speak with a faintly British accent, and she was certain that it would be that accent above all that would assure her success when she finally returned to Riveland as Linnea.

She spent another week perfecting her new identity and making sure that all the details were right, and finally she felt she was just that close to leaving Atlanta to return home again . . . hours closer to being handed all that was rightfully hers and watching Mr. Greve exit from her life.

. . . And Trane.

Oh yes, Trane. Ravaged though he looked, she would send him and his secret self right back to Galveston, ten miles or so inland, right back where he came from, now that she was back on Riveland. Without hesitation. Immediately. And she would enjoy doing it, too.

She planned to enjoy *everything* from now on, just as Linnea Wiltshire always had.

The grave was so raw, it brought tears to her eyes once again, and she dabbed at them lightly with her gloved hand and a scrap of handkerchief.

She had to be careful this time: it was one of those bright, hot, muggy days, and she had been extra careful applying rouge and pencil to her face. A tear could wash away the faint blush color that stained her cheeks, or streak the pencil and light layer of ash she had applied to her eyelids to deepen and alter the shape of her eyes.

And of course daylight, clear morning light, would show everything. Just everything. And Trane was standing so close to her, his light, bright gaze raking over her features, negating the dissimilarities, searching only for what was like Cassandra.

She knelt at her mother's grave—a good excuse to lower her head. "I suppose she did what she thought was right," she murmured, touching the grown-over mound and the little cross engraved with Raylene's name that marked the grave simply and elegantly.

She was thankful she had thought of the gloves: she had a pair to match every outfit, to conceal the only other part of her body that would be visible that he might be likely to recognize. When she lifted her hands to her eyes ostensibly to wipe away her tears, she knew he was watching her carefully: he would have known Cassandra's hands. And she wasn't yet sure that he believed Linnea's face.

No matter; she extended her hand, and he grasped it and helped her up, still looking, still watching every nuance of the way she moved, the way she looked.

It was damned hard to keep up the pretense, incredibly hard to fool *him:* she really couldn't relax for a moment lest he detect something; and she couldn't back down or refuse to meet his eyes.

This was difficult, more difficult than she had thought it would be. She felt as though she must constantly attack the character of Linnea, to add those little details that would distance Linnea from Cassandra as fully and forcefully as possible.

Sometimes she thought she hadn't fooled him one little bit.

And sometimes she saw in his face that hopeless grief, and she felt so guilty she had to get out of his presence.

It was a week of waiting and watching. The first pick had gone to press and stood baled in the cotton house now, waiting for the first barges to arrive for shipment, and Trane was nowhere to be seen, for which Cassandra thanked the fates.

Zilpha was hard enough to handle, and Mr. Greve had not yet put in an appearance. That fact worried her, and she didn't know quite how she would deal with it if he wound up denying that Cassandra had even made a will.

She could make up a letter, she thought acrimoniously, but—damn it—letters had gotten her into too much trouble already. However, one of the two letters Cassandra had supposedly written Linnea *could* have mentioned something about—

And then she would look up and find Zilpha circling her like a mother cat protecting her home ground. "Yes, Zilpha?" Dear heaven—remember the accent, the lilt, the hands, the gloves, the little characteristics she had invented for Linnea.

"If you is hungry, ma'am . . ." Zilpha would begin. Or: "Can I get somethin' fo' you, ma'am?" Or: "How you is Missus's sister?" finally, when her curiosity overset her finely tuned sense of the way things were done.

She could have cried for Zilpha. She really wanted to tell her the truth. Who would it hurt, after all? And Zilpha sensed something anyway, she was sure of it.

But she told her the same story all over again. Half truths, half lies. Half wishes and dreams. When would that servile Mr. Greve come to tell her that she had inherited everything and she had only to sign the papers and he would thankfully leave for Atlanta in the morning.

More wishes, more dreams.

How risky it was to depend on Mr. Greve. Perhaps a

little nudge . . . he would not have known about letters or anything pertaining to Linnea, except the name.

A little note?

She was most anxious to hear . . . what? That Mr. Greve was ready to present her with Cassandra's will and was willing to remove himself from her life as quickly as possible. Really! Faint hope: Mr. Greve would never do anything as direct as *that*. She would wait that unctuous man out, or die in the attempt. But it was beginning to look as if she could die and come back three times at least before he would acknowledge that Cassandra had left a will.

And then, of course, Trane had removed himself to the overseer's house so she had no idea what he was doing or thinking or whether any of his suspicion of her had jelled into something more concrete.

She was feeling, at the end of the week, as though her reappearance had accomplished nothing. She had gained nothing, except that she had made Trane suffer a little, and she supposed *that* couldn't hurt him; but she was no closer to becoming autonomous than she had been when she left.

She had to take action. She wrote the note—her handwriting disguised—the day the barges arrived and Trane was busy supervising the loading of the bales.

Dear Mr. Greve:

Mr. Taggart tells me that you are the lawyer for my sister's estate. I am newly arrived at Riveland and am most anxious to know how things are to be settled. My understanding, from Cassandra, was that she had been going to attend to all business matters at the time of her husband's death.

I do hope to see you soon.

That should scare him, she thought, sealing it in an envelope.

Now what had she told Trane? Her mother had written

313

about her marriage to Jesse. She had written at her mother's death. Perhaps then she might have said in her own letter that it was scary when someone died, and she herself was planning very carefully as to how she would want things done if anything ever happened to her or Jesse.

Yes, that would cover it. Oh, she could just see Greve squirming as he read her little note.

But the lies were piling on top of lies. She wasn't sure she would be able to find her way out of the labyrinth of stories if Mr. Greve didn't settle with her soon.

He came eventually—at the end of the succeeding week. By then the second pick of cotton had been pressed and baled and stood ready to be loaded at the dock, and Trane was too busy with that to be of any help to her.

She had to meet with Mr. Greve, and after one look at his agitated expression, she knew she would have to embroider what she had written in the note.

He hadn't expected ever to see her, but she saw by the look in his eye that he knew she existed. He knew—and he hadn't intended to tell anyone? Or he was going to make up his own letters, with the faraway Linnea giving him the right in perpetuity to a part of the profit of Riveland so long as he managed it for her? And how grateful she would be?

All these scenarios rushed through her brain like the powerful cascade of a waterfall. Mr. Greve was dangerous: he was a hungry lion and Jesse Taggart had let him out of his cage.

What could *she* use to whip him back into obedience? "Mr. Greve?"

She met him at the door—no use waiting for him like a queen. Let him have to assess his reaction to her first. She knew he would be as stunned as Trane had been. More so, because he had been plotting behind Cassandra's back.

314

His shock was palpable. "Mrs. . . . Wiltshire?"

"Yes, of course," she said briskly, extending one lace-gloved hand, her accent firmly in place. And her temper.

"You are so like her."

"Well, of course I am," she said, as she led him back to the library. She wanted to be behind that desk. No nonsense here; he had been Cassandra's employee, and Jesse's, for that matter. His obligation was to them and not himself, but she could see by his hearty demeanor that it was obvious he had something to lose and something to hide. He was here to recoup as much as possible—and to find out how much Linnea Wiltshire knew.

Thank goodness Trane was out of the house.

"Did you have a good trip over from England?" he said after he had fussily settled himself into one of the leather chairs opposite the desk.

"A reasonable trip, Mr. Greve," she said calmly. *Watch the accent, Cassandra.* "Mr. Taggart, that is, my sister's . . . stepson—how odd this sounds, Mr. Greve"—*if only he knew*—"gave me to understand that my sister did indeed attend to a will after Mr. Taggart died. I trust you have some more concrete information to give me?"

He hesitated one minute. Damn—he had been hoping that the odds would be in his favor that Taggart hadn't mentioned a damned thing about it, or that Cassandra had not done some fool thing like writing to this unknown sister with all the details. Even now, with her expressionless face tilted inquiringly at him, he wasn't sure that it wasn't Cassandra sitting across the desk from him and that Linnea Wiltshire wasn't some kind of fabrication.

They looked too much alike—too damned much alike. He couldn't get away with tampering with Cassandra's disposition or denying the identity of this woman.

He would have to make a stab at gaining control from a different direction.

"Yes," he said finally. "There was a will, and it is fairly simple and straight-lined. Cassandra willed everything to you."

Look shocked, Cassandra . . .

"Oh my heaven!" She let herself register the enormity of the bequest—really, she should have been an actress. She almost felt as though she were poor Linnea, happening in on this momentous legacy. It was overwhelming. It might even be frightening, except that Linnea was as self-possessed as Cassandra had ever been. And had lived in England all those years. Yes, that was exactly the right tone to take. Shocked . . . but composed.

"It's very simple: no one knew where to locate you. And no one had any idea you were already on your way here."

"No, I didn't send word," she said, nodding. Let him have that. But not much more. She took a deep breath. "You will tell me exactly what this means."

"It is simple: the whole of Riveland, all its land, its crops, its slaves, its profit when the cotton goes to market . . . all of it."

"Stunning," she murmured. It was; it was an enormity. She had to think of that when she was reacting as Linnea must react. Linnea would never be able to comprehend the vast amount of land and money he was talking about. She would be overwhelmed. "I can't conceive."

"Of course you can't. This is why more experienced heads must prevail, now that you have most fortuitously arrived." There, that sounded fine, he thought. Not too aggressive, not too beseeching. There was a fine middle line there.

"Indeed," she agreed. "This is overpowering news. It is hard to fathom just what is involved from mere words."

"There's time . . . ," he murmured.

"Well, yes—there's time. But . . ." And how greedy should she be to take over her own estate? ". . . I would like the papers prepared as soon as possible, Mr. Greve."

"I see." He didn't see. He saw a damned avaricious English rose who couldn't even dispense with gloves in the house. How the hell was she going to take over the reins

316

of a productive plantation and *survive?* "Of course, everything is yours, Mrs. Wiltshire, but perhaps you would like to . . ."

She looked at him reproachfully. "No, Mr. Greve. I would like everything in my name as soon as possible. It is what Cassandra would have wanted."

"By all means, Mrs. Wiltshire. And then perhaps we might discuss the question of some solid management for Riveland, someone who can oversee business, while you tend to . . . well, whatever it is you want to attend to, now that you are an heiress." He smiled conspiratorially. "Another overseer, a capable lawyer—all will be as you wish, and you will be free to carry on as if you yourself had lived here all your life."

"That sounds lovely, Mr. Greve. Let us talk more when the papers are ready for signing."

"My dear Mrs. Wiltshire."

"Mr. Greve."

She closed the door behind him and kicked it violently, the way she wanted to kick *him;* but ladies never did such things.

She whirled around to find Zilpha watching her, her gaze enigmatic, and not a word on her lips.

317

Chapter Nineteen

Trane was avoiding Linnea, she was sure of it.

"He workin' dat cotton," Zilpha told her, serving her yet another lonely dinner while Elsie fanned away the flies. "He got no time for no one; he grievin' de missus."

"Is he?" she murmured. Was that good or bad? Well, he had to be present when she signed the papers, because he had to be apprised of who was now the boss.

She knew from Ojim that two barges had gone downriver to Vecsey's and that soon Riveland would have money in its account. She knew that Trane was up early, never at the house, taking meals in his cabin, and she could only conclude he did not want to look on Linnea's face, and that was all to the good.

The strain of being Linnea was intense: just the penciling and rouging every morning. And now, two weeks later, she needed to reapply the henna to her hair and eyebrows. And oh, those corseted gowns, and those hot little cotton gloves. She couldn't wait for Greve to arrive, papers in hand, to free her of all her need for machinations and lies.

She pretended to mourn Cassandra. She spent much time in her room, which was boring, mainly to escape Zilpha's eagle eye. Or she requested that Ojim drive her around the plantation fields and explain to her what was happening, which was boring. Or she sat out on the ve-

318

randa fanning herself and looking at nothing, and that was boring.

That man had better come, she thought, pacing irritably all over the first floor of the house. It was worse waiting for him now than it had been after he had read her the terms of Jesse's will. She was feeling the rage just building up all over again. She didn't know how she would contain herself.

She wanted it *over.*

Everything was conspiring against her.

Her inability to *do* anything was acting on her. But of course once she signed the papers and everything was hers, and she dismissed Mr. Greve—oh, then she would never lack for anything to do.

He came two days later, Mr. Ward in tow.

"I have sent for Mr. Taggart," she told him composedly, ushering them into the library once again and taking her seat at the desk.

Mr. Greve was not pleased at that announcement. "He has nothing to do with this."

"But he is Mr. Taggart's son; naturally he would be entitled to know that the disposition of the estate was legal and binding."

And Greve backed down. "Of course, Mrs. Wiltshire. He has been of inestimable help to you, and we must be certain that he is assured everything would be as your sister wanted it so he may return to his family as soon as possible."

"Exactly," she said staunchly. *His family*—she had forgotten about his "family." Her heart started to pound. What else had she forgotten about? Was her hiatus between arrival and confronting Mr. Greve and this final signing and sealing of her fate too long . . . had she become careless? Had she slipped somehow and had Greve noticed it? Or worse, Trane?

"Though I wasn't aware Mr. Taggart had a family," she added quickly. She could not have known that: she, in her guise as Linnea, hadn't asked, and he hadn't said.

Or *had* he? And she just didn't remember all of the lies?

"Yes, yes," Greve said impatiently, opening his briefcase. "A wife . . . six children—really, I haven't kept count. Let us get down to business, Mrs. Wiltshire. The first thing we must attend to is verification of your identity. . . ." He held up his hand. "It is true, my dear Mrs. Wiltshire, that anyone looking at you could not deny you were Mrs. Taggart's sister, but Mr. Ward and I are agreed that there must be some positive identification."

She bit her lip. Mr. Greve was a tough man, especially when he was trying to protect his own interests in Riveland and the wealth of Cassandra Taggart. But she had known that. She wasn't Trane Taggart. *She* had come prepared.

She summoned Zilpha and asked her to bring down a certain leather case that was on her dresser in her room.

Zilpha returned and handed her the case, and she opened it slowly. Here was the test of her thorough preparation to return in the role of Linnea Wiltshire.

She had thought about it long and hard, and the only thing Linnea could have in terms of identifying papers was her marriage certificate. On that, she would have put her maiden name—attested to at the time of her runaway marriage—*and* her married name. Perhaps her mother's name . . . There had been a very clever printer in Atlanta, to whom she had been recommended by the ever-knowledgeable Lavonna the actress—for a slight remuneration, of course. Yes, she had made sure that everything was in order that could possibly be requested by Mr. Greve.

"Here you are," she said, handing over each piece of paper after she scannned it. She knew each of them by heart: Linnea's marriage lines and the ticket with which she had supposedly crossed an ocean on the ship *Hullgate,* which bore her name, her address in England, her destination. Her signature.

She had even thought about that, but it had been an effort to remember, once she had ensconced herself at Riveland, that Linnea's handwriting would be graphically different from her own; and hard to remember just how she had signed the two pages which Mr. Greve and Mr. Ward were perusing with such scrupulous attention.

"Nothing further?" Mr. Greve asked, setting the two pages down on the desk.

"My dear sir, how could there be? My father lost everything. I don't think Mother quite remembered to salvage the family Bible in the rush to sell off his assets and pay his debts. And she certainly would not have given it to me. This is all there is, and it should be enough. The clerk who witnessed the marriage also witnessed to my identity at the time of my marriage. There can be no question about *that*, Mr. Greve."

Her belligerence got to him.

"Of course not, of course not. And of course the remarkable resemblance . . ."

"How kind of you to say so," she said acidly. "It has been more than eight years since I last saw my sister, Mr. Greve. You cannot want to prolong this tragedy. She obviously wanted . . . Ah, Mr. Taggart—do come in."

Mr. Greve looked up and there was Taggart in the doorway. Just like him not to have cleaned up from the fields, he thought superciliously. Never a gentleman; nothing like his father, either. He didn't know what Trane Taggart was like; he only knew he was an interfering bastard.

Trane eased himself into the room warily. "Mrs. Wiltshire . . ." Damn, she looked so like Cassandra, he couldn't keep his eyes away from her. ". . . Mr. Greve . . ."

"This is Mr. Ward."

"Mr. Ward," Trane said, settling himself in a chair just a little farther away from the desk than the two occupied by the banker and the lawyer.

Greve turned to him with an air of confidentiality.

"Mrs. Wiltshire has the entitlement, Taggart."

"Pardon?" Trane said sharply, but he didn't move; his nerves shot bolt upright, and every instinct in him came to attention.

"Mrs. Taggart's will, sir, as we were discussing. There is one, and the disposition is to Mrs. Wiltshire solely." Greve sat back with that and watched Taggart's face carefully. Damn the man, he just never gave away the show; he didn't have an inkling what he was thinking, except that he himself could — and might — contest the will. You never knew with a strange one like Taggart. He hadn't seen the place in years: feelings changed, resentments merged into political expediency. No doubt if Jesse had still been alive when he had returned to Riveland, he would have made it up with the old man.

But it was too late now. And the strong-willed Cassandra Taggart was gone, and there was only her equally unbending sister whose identity *he* could not dispute, and it looked as though that were the end of that.

"Pleased for you, ma'am," Trane said politely, watching her face intently.

She felt a flash of anger. "How could you be? Cassandra is *dead*. What good is a piece of property? How can it take her place?"

"It surely can't," Trane agreed easily, still waiting, still watching.

Damned mountain cat, she thought. She could almost see his hair standing on end, as if he sensed something but didn't know what it was. God, he knew her too well, and if she let him stay around her long enough, he would surely smoke out the truth.

She had to get rid of him.

Or she had to get rid of herself.

"Exactly what are we talking about, Mr. Greve?" she asked wearily, retrieving her papers and tucking them away before they could really examine them that much more closely.

"What you see around you, Mrs. Wiltshire: a thousand acres of cotton and farmland; four dozen slaves or more. All the buildings in and around Riveland, all the carriages, horses, conveyances, the shipping rights on the Little Midway, the account at Vecsey's, Mr. Taggart's cotton factor in Savannah—all that will be transferred to your name, as well as the bank accounts at the Carthage-Midway Bank—"

"And the strongbox," Mr. Ward put in.

Everyone froze.

Damn the man: the strongbox! She had forgotten about the strongbox. . . .

"Which cannot be opened until you institute a search for the receipt, Mrs. Wiltshire, and only if you fail to find it," he added.

"Of course," she said faintly. She couldn't bear to look at Trane. He was interested, too interested, and he had not moved a muscle. His intensity warmed the air like a simmering fire.

The strongbox . . . how stupid of her . . .

She had to get hold of herself. She was starting to act too much like Cassandra. "This is too overwhelming," she said melodramatically. "What happens next, Mr. Greve?"

"There are papers for you to sign so that everything may be put in your name," he said carefully. "And then of course you will wish to discuss what your next course of action will be with a lawyer." *With me, damn it, with me!*

She sensed his fury. She could throw him a bone and let him gnaw on it while she went and did exactly what she wanted to do. "I hope you will make yourself available, Mr. Greve."

Trane looked disgusted.

Mr. Greve's brow cleared and his anger banked down instantly to an amenable "I would be happy to."

"Then please . . . what do I have to sign?"

There were papers and papers and more papers, and her hand began to ache from holding it at the "Linnea Wilt-

323

shire" angle; sometimes she had to forcibly keep herself from signing "Cassandra Taggart," and after a while, she just didn't care.

Greve had tied the legalities of it up in a sailor's knot and dressed it up with a bow. She read every damned word because she wanted to make sure *he* could never get a foothold in her legacy again, and then she signed paper after paper, ignoring Greve's impatience with her thoroughness, shutting out Trane's interested light, bright eyes that never left her face, her gloved hands, her mouth when she spoke.

She was so aware of his washed blue gaze and the calm but alert pose of his body, which had not shifted one inch since he had come into the room and sat down. No, it was his eyes. They missed nothing.

She almost had the feeling he *knew*.

Her hand trembled as she signed the next document: Linnea Coburne Wiltshire . . . oh, the lies . . . Her gloved fingers moved almost of their own volition.

At the end, she could hardly remember what she had signed. She felt tears of exhaustion gather at the corners of her eyes.

She turned that sad face to Greve. "Oh, how I would dearly love to go away until the legalities are finalized."

She couldn't stop it—a tear drifted down her cheek.

"Well of course, Mrs. Wiltshire," Mr. Greve said quickly, thankfully. Here at last was a woman who was more vulnerable than the power-hungry Cassandra Taggart. Linnea Wiltshire knew her limits. She had tried to be strong, and now that the thing was finally settled, she could finally be herself, and avail herself of his advice and services.

"This has been such a shock to you, especially after you came all that long distance, and it must be so hard for you to walk the rooms where Cassandra lived and know you missed seeing her by mere weeks. Of course you need time away to adjust to such a tragedy."

324

"Absolutely," Mr. Ward agreed instantly.

"And I'm sure Mr. Taggart will stay on and bring in the cotton crop, so that by the time you return, everything should be in order, and you can just . . . Well, we can talk about that when the time comes."

"Exactly," Mr. Ward concurred enthusiastically.

"I'm so tired," Cassandra whispered, and the two men instantly jumped to her side. Trane stayed where he was, skeptical and watchful, and she could have throttled him.

She allowed Greve to help her up. "Thank you, Mr. Greve. Now, you gentlemen must stay to dinner. . . ."

"Mrs. Taggart always invited the gentlemen to stay the night," Trane said sardonically.

She refused to bite. "Well, yes — of course she did. That makes sense. It must be a long journey from town, is it not, Mr. Greve?"

"A fair journey," he said.

"Well, then — perhaps we can discuss where I might spend a week away from Riveland. I just don't think," she added, batting her eyelashes at Mr. Ward, "I quite comprehend the fact yet that Cassandra, my dear sister, is gone."

She patted Mr. Greve's arm. "I really will need all the help I can get."

She didn't walk the same, she didn't talk the same, or hold her head quite the same. It was the mouth — and the eyes, except the eyebrows were thicker, darker, and the eyes deeper set. The tilt of her chin — sometimes like Cassandra, sometimes not. And that high, fluty, accented voice . . . not Cassandra, and he just couldn't bear sitting across from her, in her expensive silks and satins, with those fussy little pairs of gloves that she refused to remove — some kind of skin condition, she said, when he asked — and that face that was Cassandra's and not Cassandra's . . . A man could only take so much.

But by the time he levered himself up out of that dining room chair, Linnea-who-was-not-Cassandra had been advised that White Sulphur Springs was the place to go—a mere carriage and train ride away—no more than a two-day trip, and so rewarding.

He had been patient with Greve's nonsense before, but this pet-the-little-woman attitude drove him right out of the dining room. And that Linnea Wiltshire—iron hand, velvet glove: she knew how to stroke the man to get the best from him. And she'd never get away with that with *him*.

But then, she wasn't Cassandra, and the evening's dinner made the differences all that much more palpable.

He felt crazy with grief—a man who had wanderlust in his soul and who had never needed anyone: in another time, in another life, he would have catapulted out the door so fast the minute he realized the hold a gorgeous woman like Cassandra had on him. But not this time: this time he had toppled headfirst into a swamp of sensuality that threatened now to drown him in memories. Where would there ever be another Cassandra?

Sure, he would bring in the crop: what the hell, for her—for *her*, and then Linnea-who-was-not-Cassandra could cope for herself, and he didn't give a good goddamn what happened to her. She was *not* Cassandra.

And Riveland was not his . . . never had been, never would have been. That was just a dream someone had a long time ago, and a promise he had made that he had tried to keep. It was too bad Jesse had died before the damn thing came to fruition.

And damn Cassandra for destroying a dream.

Damn her for dying.

And damn him for trying.

A man tried, he lost his soul.

He had no more soul to give: he had split it two ways and he would never be able to mend it whole again.

Not without Cassandra . . .

Not in a lifetime.

Greve took her to Atlanta and saw her to the train bound for the Springs.

Well, there it was: she had the whole, and she was going away until he filed the papers and everything was in her hands. A matter of a couple of weeks. And she would be safely away from him, and the gouging gaze of Trane Taggart who was not Trane Taggart.

She congratulated herself, as the train moved slowly forward out of the station, that she had handled Mr. Greve, she had gotten Trane to agree to stay on to finish baling this year's pick, and she had neatly escaped both of them by going off for two weeks.

Wouldn't Linnea have done that? Hadn't she taken the easy way out by marrying Mr. Wiltshire and disappearing altogether?

Of course—she knew her sister. She was so glad to welcome her back. She could just put her in the closet somewhere in White Sulphur Springs.

Except for the hair. She had to keep on applying henna to the hair; otherwise it would become two colors and she would look odd, really odd—and fast.

And she so wanted to slow down.

It was all hers—with no Mr. Greve, no Trane Taggart to complicate matters. When she returned, she would take over and dismiss them both. She would send Trane Cole Trager Taggart back to his mythical family—in front of Greve, lest he argue the family he had already acknowledged, and then she would ease out Mr. Greve and finally, she would be alone and in control.

Alone . . .

She so wanted to be alone. She never had been, except those odd times when she had gotten herself up in some guise or other and escaped Linnea, her mother, and ultimately Jesse. Hadn't that little skill stood her in good stead?

She pulled the hot cotton gloves from her fingers. Relief. She wondered if Trane-Cole had believed that little story about a skin condition.

But then, what did it matter? She didn't need to answer to him. Not after this week and signing those papers.

"Dying" was very liberating.

She would have to register as Mrs. Wiltshire, of course, in case Greve or that awful Mr. Ward wanted to get in touch with her.

Imagine him remembering the strongbox . . . and she hadn't imagined Trane's instant flare of interest —

No matter. None of it mattered. She was Linnea and everything would come to her and she would get rid of everyone and her plan had worked . . . beautifully, just perfectly.

And she was so tired. She didn't realize how tired she was, with all the emotion and all the planning, with the discovery of Trane's betrayal, with watching her room burn like that . . . Yes, there was an emotional toll, and she refused to count it, not yet — not yet.

Linnea used to take everything in stride.

She could do no less.

When you had money, you had everything at your command. She had assured Mr. Ward that she did not need an advance on her bank account in order to make this trip. She still had a good portion of the original five hundred dollars left, although she did not tell Mr. Ward this; it was so easy to let him believe that she was a genteel widow who, though she was in straitened circumstances, still had enough to gratify this whim, certainly. She didn't think that she contradicted what she had told Trane; she didn't care about anything but finding a place far away from Riveland, an anonymous room in a hundred-bed hotel that overlooked the Springs and was peopled with summer residents who habitually came to stay for a month, maybe two.

Thank heavens Mr. Greve had thought to send a wire to reserve a room. It turned out to be a cottage suite, all tucked out of the way behind the hotel, private and luxurious.

She slept a full day through, the day she arrived, and awoke refreshed the day after that, with no sense that twenty-four hours had elapsed.

She was the widow Wiltshire, and the bellboys, the busboys and the waiters were all deferential to her as she came into the dining room and among more people than she had ever seen in her life.

For one instant, she wanted to turn and run away.

The room was a mass of bodies, all seated, all talking, all looking the same, so that it seemed as if there were one body, one head, one voice.

"Mrs. Wiltshire?"

A kind voice. "Yes," she said gratefully.

"You will be one for breakfast?"

"Yes." Or was there censure in his voice?

"Your family is not with you?"

She tacked on a strained smile. "My family is to follow in a few days."

"Very good, madam," the waiter said. "Follow me."

One hurdle passed, and she didn't know quite how she had done it. She wasn't used to this. She had been crazy to come. All she wanted was some coffee and perhaps a biscuit.

He handed her into a small corner table by a window. "Madam." He gave her a menu and she chose at random: eggs, potatoes, coffee, cornbread . . . She hardly knew what she ordered. She had never seen so many quizzical eyes in her whole life.

She ate; she didn't taste the food. All those eyes . . .

"Madam has a healthy appetite," the waiter commented, taking her room number when he presented the

329

bill, and then directing her to the concierge where she might find a map—anything that would help her navigate around this place with so many people.

But getting around was a simple matter. This particular hotel, the Whitestone, was neither too large nor too small. It was just the right size to give her the anonymity she wanted and all the entertainments she might crave. Except that she didn't quite know what she wanted.

Her cottage suite was located at the far end of one of the two ells appended to the main building; each was two stories high—individual, attached apartments that one reached by traversing a covered walkway, through a beautiful enclosed garden, from the main hotel wing.

The privacy was delicious, the services provided invisible and constant. In her room, she discovered, there was a menu of things to engage her interest. She could ride, walk—in fact, she must be certain to make the promenade at certain hours, an exercise highly recommended by hotel management. She could ride, attend the nightly balls, take the waters indoors, at the pump room, or out, at the Spring. She could gamble (discreetly, of course) or she could go to the races. And she could eat, eat, eat . . . But what she could not do, she discovered to her dismay, was be an unaccompanied widowed lady of youth and means in a social circle that encompassed family, marriageable young ladies, and eligible men.

What did she know of such strictures? Or the knowing crook of an eyebrow that derided her widowhood as a falsehood to give her respectability to ply her trade?

But she didn't know. She dressed the part, she truly was shy among all those strange people, and the men fell all over themselves to accommodate her.

It was a strange experience for her. She was too old, she thought, to just now begin to flex her power over men.

The mothers didn't like it. It had taken her three days to become acclimated, and another day for the eligible bucks to find her, and still another hour before all the dis-

330

approving mommas were peering at her through their lorgnettes over their starched collars, as she walked down the promenade with all their daughters' beaux in tow.

She, however, was sublimely unaware of it. She gave each questioner her full attention, and it was as if a beam of light hit him between the eyes, and he could think of nothing else but the beautiful, elusive Mrs. Wiltshire, with her cool English accent, who might or might not be interested in him.

"But where do you stay?" one man asked.

"I have one of those little cottage suites down the long ell," she answered ingenuously, missing all of their knowing nods as they followed her down the tree-lined streets of the promenade. "Very private. Quite lovely. And the gardens. Have you seen the garden behind the hotel?"

And they would nod still more vigorously.

"And your family?" one man asked delicately.

She fanned herself; she had bought a large painted papar fan and she wielded it almost like a wedge. She could hide her face, or rap someone on the arm with it. She could smile behind it, or frown, and she most certainly could feel cooler. "Have been delayed," she said sadly. She was an actress, after all. She knew exactly the tone of voice to use, and they nodded meaningfully at each other.

"Poor thing. Of course you will let us keep you company until they arrive."

And then the elusive witch came out. "If you like," she said dismissively, as if it didn't matter one way or another; and her attitude so infuriated them, they all followed along after her to see just which one of them could ultimately command her attention.

At night, at dinner, in the ballroom, they waltzed her around, they wined her and dined her, and she would make a commitment to none of them while the jewel-encrusted mothers of the society belles hovered around the edge of the dance floor fuming at her impertinence, de-

331

bating whether to have her thrown out of the Whitestone altogether because of her unsavory reputation.

Cassandra was having fun. For the first time in her life, she was not obligated to anyone, not her mother, her sister, her husband, her advisors, her lawyer. She couldn't think of anyone who could care about what she was doing in White Sulphur Springs with all those lovely young men hovering around her.

She did not want any of them.

It seemed to her that they were very young, very callow, extremely petulant, and probably not at all capable.

And it seemed to the enraged mothers that *she* was not very young, was extremely petulant with the men, was just leading them on and never giving anyone else a chance, and above all, she was probably *too* capable.

Widow indeed, they thought, with no family and nothing to recommend her. Up from Georgia, ha! Down from Washington, most likely, looking to escape the political heat and find some new prey.

The mothers stalked her, the men pursued her, and she was like a butterfly released—finally—from its cocoon.

A week. She had been gone a week, and something of her presence still lingered.

He was sure it was that godalmighty resemblance to Cassandra that so unsettled him. And that mouth, that Cassandra-mouth, so much like hers that if he could only have the mouth, he would kiss it until she begged for mercy. If only it were Cassandra . . .

But it was insanity thinking like that. What was dead and gone would never have had a chance to flourish, and the illusion that they had both lived for those two or three weeks had dwindled into nothingness. He never would have made a place for himself at Riveland had he returned when Jesse was alive. He would have come, he would have gone. Jesse had never changed, and everything about Cassandra and everything she had ever said about him confirmed the truth of that.

There would have been nothing for him at Riveland, and the promise he had made would have been an anticlimax to his return and Jesse's response to it.

He had a feeling Jesse would have run him right off the place, and it would have made everything so futile—except that he was the only one who would ever know.

Still, those weeks with Cassandra were unforgettable, right down to his unerring feeling that he could have made a life there with her, except that, too, would have presented its own problems, apart from Jesse's restrictions.

The whole thing had gotten too complicated, but goddamn it, the resolution should not have been Cassandra's death.

If she were still alive, if he could have told her the truth, even if she had banished him from Riveland, he still would have had a chance to redeem himself, and reclaim her love.

But there was nothing to redress now—only emptiness and impotent memories.

And another day went by, picking the fields, hauling the bolls to the cotton house for drying; another day went by ginning the preceding pick and setting it out for moting while still another crew worked on whipping; he had men husking corn in the barnyard, and Eli went around over the weekend collecting the corn blades from the workers' gardens, and it was a round-robin of harvesting and working and it led nowhere . . . *nowhere*.

He had come back to the big house; Zilpha had insisted.

"Can't leave you alone nohow," she scolded him. "You ain't eatin' and you workin' yo'se'f to de bone and it ain't good."

"In spite of your own advice?" he asked her, with a trace of humor.

"You got to work; you ain't got to starve yo'se'f to

death."

She made him eat, she made him sleep. He got a crew together to clean up Cassandra's room. He wanted it restored inch by inch, with new furniture, new decorations, ready for someone's new life. He just didn't know whose.

It was nearing the end of August. It was almost the end of everything.

He sat in the library once again, with his talismans in his hand: a strand of hair, her ring, a piece of her dress.

He spread them out on the desk before him as he drank a shot of whiskey. It was whiskey now, hot and potent, the wine of oblivion. A couple of those and he could sleep at night. And Zilpha didn't chide him about it, either.

A strand of her hair, that curly springy hair that always wound itself around his fingers like a snake charmer's pet, the way she wound herself around him, all sinuous, all woman, all his.

He slammed his fist down on the desk.

He could not keep thinking of her like that. She was ashes and dust now, a distant dream interred in bedrock, forever resting . . . forever haunting him.

God, could he cry, could he forget her—ever . . .

Everywhere he turned—Cassandra. How had she in such a short time infused the whole of Riveland with the sense of herself? How had she escaped Jesse's oppression and repression and come to open herself to him? Not out of love, surely—out of curiosity, out of gratitude . . . No, not hardly, and what did it matter about intentions or ambitions or who might have been using whom?

He knew what the unspeakable end result was: he had been falling in love with her—and now she was gone.

And she had not known, and he never could tell her now.

"Mr. Trane, Mr. Trane!"

"Zilpha?" He felt blurry and kind of beside himself, as if he were watching himself from one side, as Zilpha rushed into the room.

"You got to come, Mr. Trane."

"I don't want to." No, he wanted to fall asleep right at the desk, his talismans in hand, deep into merciful forgetfulness.

"You got to come, Mr. Trane. Someone done come."

He apprehended that her voice sounded urgent. "It's too late for anyone to come, Zilpha. Who is it?"

"You got to come see, Mr. Trane."

"All right, all right." He heaved himself upward, and grabbed for his drink. A man couldn't face the night without a drink. A man couldn't begin to deal with whatever rude person "done come" without a glass of fortitude in his hand.

He didn't give a damn who it was; he would get rid of him as soon as possible.

It wasn't a *him*. His fuzzy perception picked that right out as he ambled very carefully down the hallway to the entrance foyer.

It was a woman, a shabbily dressed woman, he thought. Her back was to him, and her eyes searched the staircase that led upward from the hallway to the bedrooms as if there were someone there she particularly wanted to see.

She wore a shawl around her shoulders, and one of those curved chippy little hats tilted over one ear. Her hair, blond and streaming down her back, was the color of butter.

And then she turned, as she heard his step, and he didn't know the face at all. It was sharp, almost mean, with greenish eyes and a discontented mouth. She had been beautiful once, he thought. The bones were there, worn thin by circumstance and by life. Her body, tall and thin under the plain hooped muslin gown, looked as though it might just cave in if one more sorrow were heaped on those she obviously already bore.

He did remember his manners, fuddled as he felt.

"Ma'am? Can I help you?"

"Who are you?" she demanded, and there was something in the timbre of her voice that sounded faintly familiar to him, something about the combativeness of her. Something . . .

"Trane Taggart, ma'am. And you are . . . ?"

But he didn't need to ask. He just knew what she was going to say.

"Linnea Wiltshire, sir. Come from England, and I want to see my sister. Where is she? Where is my sister Cassandra?"

Chapter Twenty

Goddamn.

Of course he was dreaming. He was dreaming because he wanted so badly for it to be true.

And he was drunk. *"Zilpha!"*

"Yes sir, Mr. Trane?"

Zilpha appeared immediately, as if he had conjured her up out of thin air. But it *was* his dream, and that probably was where she had come from.

"This lady says she is Linnea Wiltshire."

"Yes, Mr. Trane."

So Zilpha knew.

He was more than a little drunk. "If that were true, Zilpha, that would mean . . ."

"Yes, Mr. Trane."

Because he wanted it so badly, she said the right thing. Zilpha was a treasure. This was a wonderful dream.

"And I could just . . ."

"First thing, Mr. Trane."

"Is it time to wake up yet, Zilpha?"

"No, sir. You got 'nother eight hours."

He turned back to the woman who was staring at them like she had walked straight into the local asylum.

"Who are you, really?"

"Where is Cassandra, please?" She turned to Zilpha beseechingly. "I want to see my sister. Where is she?"

"This is perfect," Trane said musingly. "She's saying all the right things, Zilpha."

"Yes, sir, Mr. Trane."

"You tell her."

"Whut I gonna tell her, Mr. Trane? It don' make no sense nohow," Zilpha said indignantly.

Really, he was loving this dream.

The woman, the other Linnea, looked tired, too tired to have him play tricks on her. He took pity, but only because it was such a wish-fulfilling dream. "Cassandra is dead," he said baldly, and as she looked ready to just fall to the floor in shock, he added, "Or rather, she is presumed dead, but she's really not dead—she came back as Linnea, only Linnea went to the Springs, and then Linnea came, so that means that it is really Cassandra at the Springs—does that make any sense? Besides," he added, pacing around her stone-still body, "you don't even look like her."

"No, I don't," she said stiffly, because she still didn't know what was real and who this lunatic was and it was easier to remain still and calm than to get excited and perhaps killed.

Better and better. How did a dream fill in all the details and make it so possible for Cassandra to still be alive? It was really amazing.

He rubbed his hand over his face. "You are Linnea Wiltshire."

"Yes, I am," she said stringently. "Who are you?"

"I'm Cassandra's stepson," he answered flippantly, and she looked shocked again. Cassandra had married into an asylum—it was the only answer.

The man was drowning in whiskey; the servant looked suspicious and ready to attack her. And this story about Cassandra being dead but not dead—she had come to the wrong place. She wanted no part of these people: they were diseased, sick. A little crazy. That huge man Cassandra's *stepson!*

"I don't believe you," she said. "I must have the

338

wrong house, the wrong family. I will leave and not trouble you again." And why not? Nothing could get worse than it was already.

"No . . . no—" Trane put out his hand to detain her. "You can't walk out of this dream. It's too good. Don't you see—if you are Linnea, then Cassandra is still alive. . . ."

He said it. And Linnea looked at him as if he had an axe in his hand and he was about to whack it over her head.

Of course she was skeptical. It did sound crazy. But it was the perfect solution: Linnea lived, and so did Cassandra.

He did not want to wake up and end this dream.

"This is Linnea," he said to Zilpha, "Cassandra's sister."

"I hear, Mr. Trane."

"What are we going to do about that?"

"I dunno, Mr. Trane. Miz Wiltshire done gone to de Springs."

"Exactly," he said reverently.

"We got to give dis Miz Wiltshire a bed fo' de night, Mr. Trane."

"Absolutely."

"You come wif me," Zilpha said to this Linnea, who was looking bewildered by this exchange. "You is in de right place, ma'am, and you is tired and you needs yo' sleep. In de mawnin' we get ever'thing straighten out. In de mawnin' Mr. Trane be able to see whut's whut, you hear? Come . . . In de mawnin', Miss . . ."

In the morning. Delightful dream. The woman didn't even protest, just allowed Zilpha to whisk her away upstairs with her shabby little trunk.

It was a good dream while it lasted, he thought as he paced his way meticulously back to the library.

For one moment he had had hope.

For one moment, Cassandra had lived again.

* * *

"Mr. Trane, Mr. Trane . . ."

He felt someone's urgent hands shaking him. Where was he? He knocked the hand away.

"*Mr. Trane—*" More insistent now, positively forceful.

"What? What? Zilpha?"

"You hear me, Mr. Trane? Dat lady done gone."

"What? What lady?"

"Dat Miz Linnea, dat other one."

"Are you joking?" he roared, jolting upright. Hell, he had fallen on the floor, from the desk chair where he had just laid down his head, just for an instant. . . ."Are you crazy? She was *real?*"

Zilpha sat back on her heels. "Dat lady done come las' night, said she was Linnea Wiltshire, de missus's sister, and I don' know whut to b'lieve, and you was b'lievin' whut you want to b'lieve, Mr. Trane. But she gone now, and we ain't gonna know whut's whut."

"Yes, we are," he growled, jackknifing himself onto his feet. "Damnation. Hell. Get me some water and a cup of coffee. *Now,* Zilpha. Jesus . . . another Linnea. Goddamn, it was a good dream."

"Wasn't no dream," Zilpha threw back at him as she scurried out the door.

Not a dream.

That stopped him full in his tracks.

Not a *dream.*

Not reality either. That woman had *claimed* to be Linnea Wiltshire.

He just wanted it to be true in the worst way.

The clock struck six. Damn—he had a crew to get out into the fields. . . . He had a head that wouldn't stop pounding, and a sense that something momentous had happened and he had missed it.

No, he thought he had dreamt it.

Eli appeared at the door, fresh clothes and underwear in hand and pulling a steaming pitcher of water on a tea table behind him.

340

"Ojim done rouse de men," he said, as he poured the water and handed a washcloth and some soap to Trane.

"Good. Tell him to start the river quadrant. I should be there in about an hour." He hoped an hour.

Hell. Damn.

She had to be walking.

Eli brought round his horse without his asking. He mounted it on a run and took off down the drive.

Damn, she must have left at sunup. Five o'clock, maybe, so she had had an hour's head start, but she couldn't get anywhere on foot.

Except he didn't know in which direction she had gone. Most likely it was toward Carthage, if she had been savvy enough to mark the way when her hired carriage delivered her.

No matter. He would find her. He *had* to find her.

"Are you crazy?"

This Linnea Wiltshire stood in the middle of the road, her arms akimbo, stamping her foot and looking, in that brief flashing instant, exactly like her sister. "You want me to go back with you to that madhouse? Are you out of your mind? Listen, whoever you are, I'm going back to that town and getting myself away from here as fast as possible. I'll . . . I'll write to my sister, and when she assures me it is safe and that she will be at the house to meet me, then I might consider coming back. And I don't care who you are . . . I'm going nowhere with *you*."

"Now, ma'am . . ."

"Don't you 'now, ma'am' me, mister. You're a drunken fool and I don't know where Cassandra is, but she's crazy to leave her affairs in the hands of someone like you. You scared the devil out of me last night, and I will *not* go back to that mausoleum with you in daylight."

"It looks better than it seems, ma'am."

341

"So do you — in daylight. That doesn't mean you're safe — or sane."

"No, ma'am. It just means we need desperately to find out that you are really Linnea Wiltshire, and I don't know how to do that in the middle of the Carthage turnpike."

"Well, I don't have any scars or marks, sir, so you can get that right out of your head."

"I never thought of it, ma'am."

"I can't bear to think what you might have thought of," she muttered.

"I thought of lifting you up on my horse and walking you back to Riveland, ma'am. It's real important that we talk — and real soon."

"I don't trust you."

"Completely understandable, ma'am."

"But — ?"

He smiled at her, that odd, crooked little smile that was perversely charming to her. She brushed her initial reaction away. This was a madman and she was miles from nowhere, and she didn't know why she should believe a word he said — except for that smile and his apologetic manner. But how could she trust that?

"Ma'am, none of it makes sense to me, either. We just have to sit down and talk."

"We could sit here," she said tartly.

"Yes, ma'am, but I do like my comfort."

"My job is not to comfort you, Mr. Taggart."

Her words, pointed and acid, caught at his heart: it was the essence of Cassandra, the very intonation, the same wicked wit. "No, ma'am," he said quietly. "Your job is to prove that you are Linnea Wiltshire, and I would much rather have this conversation back at Riveland."

She was weakening. It didn't make any sense to stand in the middle of nowhere trading words with him. It got her no closer to Cassandra, and it left her nowhere to go, either, and she desperately needed someplace to go just then. But he didn't have to know that.

"You are a lunatic," she began heatedly, and then stopped. There really wasn't any use arguing. He could just pick her up and haul her onto his horse with him and she would be back at Riveland in a trice, no matter what she wanted. And what she really wanted was to see Cassandra.

"All right," she said quietly, and he rewarded her with that same sweet, charming smile.

"I knew you'd come around, ma'am."

"Or you knew how to get around me," she retorted, and she stepped firmly into his cupped hands and allowed him to lift her onto his horse.

The thing was, the stories were so similar that they were almost interchangeable.

This Linnea had lost her husband as well, and she had come back to America with enough in her pocket for her boat ticket and to get her to Georgia. She had come to her sister as a supplicant because she was destitute, just as the other Linnea had claimed to be.

The difference was that this Linnea's husband's family had rejected her completely and utterly. They had been shocked when Jonathan returned from America with such an unsuitable bride, and their grief, when he died, was so overpowering, they had only wanted to get rid of her.

They had, after all, controlled the money, but she hadn't known that until they had arrived in London and taken up residence in the family townhouse.

Her life there had been hell, and it had been horrific after Jonathan's death, and worse later because she had no defense against the monied armor of the family. No one wanted her, no one would take her in.

The best they would do was send her back where she came from, and they prayed she would not try to take the family to court over Jonathan's portion, which was nothing at all, since his father held the pursestrings and doled out the money to him.

And that had been a shock to her. She had only wanted to leave and come back to her family.

"But there is no family," she said, as she concluded her story. "You say my sister's husband died as well, and now Cassandra is somewhere off in another state impersonating me. Truly, Mr. Taggart, that makes no sense at all."

"No, it doesn't," he said, but actually it did make a contradictory kind of sense, and it was so like Cassandra, on top of that. If she died, Linnea inherited, and Cassandra would be free of all restraints and restrictions, removed totally from Mr. Greve or any claim that Trane Taggart might have on Jesse's estate.

A Cassandra kind of solution, he thought: the spider lady spinning webs and trapping everyone within so that everything got so tangled up, no one could unravel it. Just like Cassandra.

The witch. The black widow.

She was alive . . . alive, alive —

"Dis lady Missus's sister fo' real?" Zilpha asked in disbelief.

"I think so," he said, acknowledging it finally out loud to himself.

She was alive . . . God — alive . . .

Oh, and when he got his hands on her . . .

. . . for putting them all through that . . .

"How you know?" Zilpha demanded suspiciously.

"She tells a good story. The same story, same people, same problem. It just ends a little differently." And watch her face, he thought. Sometimes it was pure Cassandra, and sometimes it was Linnea, but with that Cassandra voice, that Cassandra insolence.

But not Cassandra. Oh no, the spider lady was having a high old time somewhere in West Virginia, thinking she had wrapped everyone up in her toils.

Hell, she had. What a scheme. He was full of admiration for her inventiveness—but not much else. She hadn't given a hoot in hell who she hurt; she had only cared about getting control, getting them all out and away from her.

Darling Cassandra . . .

. . . alive—alive . . . and well and enjoying her new-found freedom to the hilt . . .

God, when he thought of that . . .

But the story wasn't over, he thought grimly—not by a long shot—not yet, not yet.

The Springs was a bustling town at the end of August; it was the last week of festivities, of fun and pleasure. There was a frenetic feeling in the air, as if everyone knew this was the last opportunity of the season and they meant to make the most of it.

The trick was to find Cassandra. Greve had known where she was going, but he wouldn't tell. It was just like the man: he wanted the secret all to himself.

Trane would not have put it past him to show up here himself; to both court Cassandra and to make a pitch for continuing as her lawyer.

Damn, the minute he thought that, he was on his way to the Springs without a thought to his wardrobe or where he might stay.

In the end it didn't much matter. There were a limited number of rooms and he took what hc could gct until he could find Cassandra.

The clothes were another matter, but there were always tailors who were willing to accommodate a man who flashed a wad of bills as thick as a horse's neck, and to make repairs and alterations on the spot for a man who hadn't the decency to bring even a suit with him.

He felt like a stuffed goose by the time he walked out of the shop later on that evening. The tailor had sewn and tied him into a stiff black formal suit and directed

345

him to the Whitestone Hotel, the site of the evening's festivities. The hotels alternated hosting the evening dances, he was told. It saved competition and bad feelings, and each in turn made its profit.

And the new enchantress of the moment was the Widow Wiltshire; wilt-she-or-won't-she, the gentlemen called her, and the bets were on to see who would be lucky enough to have her.

"Count me in," Trane said, a muscle in his cheek twitching dangerously as he left his tailor and followed his precise directions to the Whitestone Hotel.

It was an imposing four-story building, stone-white and garlanded with friezes of flowers and vinery chipped in brownstone and painted to match.

He heard the music as he entered the lobby. The first floor obviously was given over to the important things: the desk, the dining room and kitchen, the gaming room, the ballroom.

Elegantly gowned women swarmed past him and up the stairs or out to the dining room, where they were met by other women or equally well-dressed men with whom they obviously had an assignation.

There was a discreet price to pay for admission to the ballroom, and he gave that over impatiently without even looking at the amount of the bill. He was looking for Cassandra, and he did not know how he would find her in this crowd.

He circled the ballroom, watching, watching. There were tables around the perimeter where couples chatted and sipped drinks. There were corners where men and women were having what looked like critical conversations. There were dark recesses where a man could hold a woman and kiss her passionately in the heat of the moment.

But nowhere was there a woman who looked like Cassandra.

And there were many women who eyed him with great interest and not a little hope.

He never saw them.

What would Cassandra look like?

She would look like the Widow Wiltshire, with all her flashy clothes and obvious red hair. And she would have Cassandra's sassy mouth, and he would kill the first man who touched her.

Easy.

He found the bar, too—easy—and he ordered a whiskey, just a shot to warm his vitals. He would kill Greve, too, if he showed up here tonight. Texas men never backed down from that kind of fight, and he was annoyed with himself that he had let that buzzard off so easy.

Easy . . .

Everything was easy . . .

Cassandra was alive and well and bound to come to this place soon—the ever-so-reckless widow wilt-she-or-won't-she . . .

She was having a wonderful time. The men crowded around her like bees to honey. Their conversation buzzed in her ears; she heard nothing but the music and the rhythm and the sense of one of them holding her and swinging her around the dance floor.

She loved it. All the attention was overwhelming, overpowering. She didn't have to say a word; they said everything for her.

She was beautiful, they said, so delicate, so light on her feet; she dressed divinely, she was so witty, so kind. And they only wanted a small token of her favor: a kiss, a caress, her hand . . .

But oh, no, the elusive Widow wilt-she was really a tease. She had let no one near her for more than a week. No free kisses there, nor invitations for an evening's secret fondling behind closed doors in her private cottage suite.

It was enough to frustrate a man beyond his control,

those laughing eyes, those luscious lips, that *knowledgeable* air, that voluptuous body that threw itself into the dancing with an abandon that had to be equalled in her private mating dance.

One of them had to win, yet by the end of the two weeks she had been at the Springs, none of them felt any closer to finding the key to unlocking her resistance.

She was having too good a time, and she was never aware she sent them all away aching with unrequited lust.

It became a matter of a man's expertise in the art of seduction. They took bets at the Botsford Club as to who would be the first to bed her, and there wasn't much time.

So that when Trane caught his first glimpse of her as she whirled around the floor in the arms of some drooling simp, she was surrounded by a positive phalanx of slavering young bucks, three deep, moving in time to the music with her and her partner, shouting above the music, demanding her attention, demanding her smile and the promise she never would make.

He sat at a table near the dance floor; there was a gallery, raised two or three steps above it, where the eligible gentlemen could sit and conduct business among themselves or just view the dance floor for a likely partner.

And he was looking for the most likely partner, and it was taking her a damned long time to appear.

But then suddenly she was there, all in green, a soft apple green almost the color of her eyes, and he was damned if his heart didn't start thumping. As different as she looked, she was still Cassandra, and he couldn't, now he had met Linnea, understand how any of them could have been fooled for one minute.

She had counted on it, and she had so maintained her character that her hair was still the same color, and there was still the look of Linnea about her eyes. It was as if she had planned ahead, fully expecting she would see someone from home sometime during her sojourn at the Springs.

She didn't let up for a minute, he thought. That old black widow was weaving and spinning even as she floated around the dance floor, beguiling and dangerous at the same time.

And her partners knew it. He could see, without his even being able to hear the words, that little bit of desperation in the way they importuned her. He knew the feeling himself, but he didn't feel one goddamned bit of compunction for any of them.

He was just debating when would be the right time to step in and take over. And whether he should let her know her little game was up.

It would be a damned lot more fun if he didn't.

What a thought.

Why not?

She hadn't had one shred of sensibility about the consequences of her outrageous pretense.

He could pretend just as well to fall madly in love with the wicked Widow Wiltshire. She deserved it for leaving him that way and inflicting all of that pain on him. He would never forget the pain.

He felt the pain right at that moment, looking across the dance floor to see exactly in which corner her beaux had corraled her. And that fan, that flirty, dirty fan — she had become an expert with the fan — flipping it, slapping it, hiding behind it — but she could hide no more, not from him.

The time had come to balance the account, and he set down his glass slowly and deliberately, and rose to walk the tenuous tightrope across the floor straight into the spider's web.

So many men, so little time. It would soon be over,

she thought morosely, and then she would have to go straight back to Riveland and contend with *unpleasant* things like Mr. Greve and Trane, and she didn't want to think about that, not for one moment before she absolutely had to.

And here was Mr. Nelson, begging to kiss her hand. "Really, Linnea, dear, I'm perishing to touch you. Come, let me . . . don't be cold—"

"Don't be silly," Mr. Pettigrew roared. "She has the next dance with me."

"No, me." Mr. Barnard.

"Linnea . . ." A sweet voice to one side of her—Mr. Upjohn plucking at her sleeve ever so gently.

They all looked alike, they all sounded alike; she really didn't know what they all wanted of her. It was inconceivable to her even to consider that her sexual favors were in contention, and the fact that she was a widow and experienced made her a prize to be fought for and carried off like a trophy.

She had no experience of any of that, and they all were so sweet, and she just never had had such a good time in her entire life.

Of course now she appreciated all those things that Raylene had tried to drum into her head, those social niceties and all that business about how one dressed, and how one behaved, and yes, even how to flirt . . . She really wished she had heeded her mother more.

She was still feeling the effects of creating her own death. It had been a release, yes, but there was something final about it, too. She might never be able to go back; she would be Linnea Wiltshire forever, and Cassandra would be lost in time, with just one stroke of her pen, when she signed the papers on her return to Riveland.

It really was rather sad.

But she was experiencing the things that she had yearned for at Riveland: she had freedom, money, power, men at her feet. She had gone away from home

350

alone for the first time in her life. She had engineered a successful plot that enabled her to do all those things.

Except that Cassandra was ostensibly dead and she couldn't enjoy it. And she wasn't sure that she was enjoying all those men jockeying for her attention much more, either. They were petulant babies. They were mewling boys. They were playing games she did not want to join in.

She didn't know why she felt so disquieted; she only knew something was lacking, and the gay little games she played with these experienced philanderers did not fill the emptiness deep inside her.

She didn't know what would, but she knew she would know it when she saw it.

But that just made her elusiveness all that much more enticing to them. She didn't care about any of them, and it was as obvious to them tonight as an outright rejection. She didn't say that, however, and so they did think there was always hope. She loved to dance, they loved to hold her and tease her with suggestive words, and so everyone was getting something from the flirtatious hours they spent together. With luck, one of them might get richer, too, if he could just cajole the wilt-she into his bed—or hers, where the odds went still higher.

Linnea would have loved this scene, she thought wistfully, as Mr. Upjohn of the sweet voice and gentle hands deposited her as lightly as a butterfly in a chair beside the dance floor, and quickly drew another one up beside her.

"So elegant," he murmured, and how could she contradict him? He rubbed her arm gently with his fingers. "So delicious . . ."

"Mr. Upjohn," she protested.

"My dear Linnea—"

Yes, she was ever so dear to all of them, and she wanted none of them, and what she wanted she really didn't know . . . or if she did, she would never admit it.

It was too late for anything now but to carry through

her ill-conceived plan.

It was almost time to return to Riveland.

Her heart jumped at the thought.

And then Trane's voice said, "May I have this dance?"

But of course he wasn't here — she was just wishing so hard . . .

She looked up, and not only was he there, but his sheer imposing size had cleared the bucks from the chairs all around her. Or maybe he had bodily lifted them away himself.

She had to think to school the expression of joy she felt. She was Linnea. Linnea did not know him; Linnea had never kissed him, had never . . .

She thought of every forbidden thing she had ever done with him. Frantically she tried to recall every story she had told him, every lie she had invented. *Remember the accent.*

Remember you are not Cassandra.

Dear God, who was she?

Her *face!*

Was she Linnea today?

Had she ever been Cassandra?

Had he ever been Trane Taggart?

It didn't matter. In the cloying heat of the ballroom, she could see it didn't matter. He thought she was Linnea and he held out his large hand, and she smiled faintly and took it, and he led her onto the dance floor and slipped his arm around her waist, and it just didn't matter.

In the Springs at the end of a season, who you were, what you were, all the betrayals, all the lies — none of it had meaning. Only the moment was important. And the first note of the music, the first step in time, and ultimately the magic of the dance and the articulation of the man who held you in his arms and wove mysterious patterns with you around the floor.

"Mrs. Wiltshire," he murmured.

"Mr. Taggart," she answered in kind. She did not want to know why he was there, or how he had found her; she only wanted to know if he found Linnea as fascinating as he had found Cassandra, and it was not possible that he would ever tell.

He moved surely and rhythmically around the floor, and she was enchanted by the notion of this mountain of a man who moved like a cat and whose voice cracked like a whip or was smooth as honey just as he wanted it to be.

Why had he come to the Springs?

No questions. She was not Cassandra. She didn't need to know things. Better to let him tell her . . . but damn it, *when* would he tell her?

"I hope all is well at Riveland?" she said as they moved close to execute one intricate step of the dance.

"Yes, ma'am."

Drat the man.

"You look very much the gentleman, Mr. Taggart."

"Ma'am, I always was."

You always were a liar, she thought viciously.

She always was a liar, he thought irritatedly. He would have to watch her every minute. *Every* damn minute.

"Of course," she murmured soothingly. "Can't we sit and talk? I'm so anxious for news of Riveland."

I just bet you are. "Well, I came to bring you some, ma'am," he said, taking her hand and leading her off the floor and onto the gallery steps toward the table he had abandoned. The crowd was no thinner now, but the men tended, as the hour grew later, to cluster around the gallery banister, becoming that much more obnoxious and brazen as the hours wore on and they had not found a partner.

"But who is that tall, dark man?" sweet Mr. Upjohn demanded of Mr. Pettigrew, who had been elbowed out of his place by Trane's size and frown.

"A stranger, damnit, and I tell you, man, the odds go

353

down on this one; she was damned willing to go out with him, and now look at them—close as nesting lovebirds over there. I could've sworn she didn't know him from Adam, but it looks like the widow wilt-she found someone for whom she will. She was just damned waiting, and using us all in the bargain."

"I'll lay you a hundred she wasn't."

"Done, sir."

They shook hands, and slowly began edging around the crowd to the gallery to see just what they could overhear.

It was not a terribly romantic conversation.

". . . relieved to hear that the crop came in and was shipped out in good order, Mr. Taggart."

"Yes, ma'am, I did think you would like to know that."

"How kind of you to travel all this way to tell me."

"No problem, ma'am."

She felt like throttling him; she found it so hard to concentrate on being Linnea, and the fact he had lied to her, when all she could think about was the forbidden things, the things Cassandra had done, the betrayal Cassandra had felt—she who was Cassandra no more.

She could do and feel anything she wanted.

Maybe she would. "Please call me Linnea," she said softly.

"Can't do that, ma'am," he said promptly. "I'd feel mighty disrespectful of your sister."

"Please don't."

"Yes, ma'am."

Damn him.

"Well, *say* it," she demanded, and she knew she sounded petulant.

"Yes, ma'am."

She looked at him expectantly, and he could have sworn there was a whole other woman hiding deep inside her soul, someone who was not Linnea, not Cassandra—an amalgam of something she was and something she had always wanted to be.

"Linnea, ma'am."

She bit her lip in vexation. "And all is well at Riveland?"

"Just as I told you, Linnea, ma'am."

Her lips thinned as she held back a retort. "I'm so glad you came all this way to assure me things are going well, Mr. Taggart."

"Well now, ma'am, you could call me Trane."

"You're right," she said cheekily, "I could, but what would be the point?"

He didn't answer; his light, bright gaze grazed her and she knew exactly what the point was — there was something in him that responded to Linnea because of who she really was.

How on earth was *she* going to keep it all straight?

"You take my meaning, Linnea — ma'am," he drawled.

"I don't know what you're talking about."

"Sure you do."

She had totally lost control — but when? "Mr. Taggart — "

"Trane, ma'am."

The best strategy was to attack, she decided. "Why did you come here?"

He smiled that odd, crooked smile. "To see you, ma'am." He watched her emotions chase themselves all over her face.

"Why?" Ooh, dangerous ground here. She could give a thousand reasons why, herself, and they all led back to one thing: she was to all intents and purposes a wealthy widow. And she knew he was an impostor from somewhere in Texas, and it was beginning to seem more and more likely he did not have two nickels to his name. She knew *why* all right.

"You're good to look at, Linnea . . . ma'am."

His tone of voice was exactly right; her insides melted like paper set to flame.

"Mr. Taggart . . ."

He pressed it further, enjoying the discomfitted look on her face. "You have the look of your sister, ma'am, but you have warmth and character, and she had a hardness and an anger. She wasn't a *giving* woman, Linnea. . . ." He could see her teeth clench as she bit back an exclamation, and he hid a smile as he went on, "But that was pure cussedness from living with a man like my father. It had to have changed her mightily, ma'am. I felt a lot of sympathy for her."

Her mouth worked. *A hardness, an anger* . . . He hadn't yet seen hard or angry, but she was going to show him, right here, right now. Whatever it took to repay him for his unkind words about her.

"So you see me as a *giving* woman," she purred, marveling at the transparency of a man's words. Not even Mr. Upjohn had been so blatant.

"A woman who could surrender her heart . . ."

"Yes?" she whispered, her eyes wide and her expression as admiring as she could force it to be through her pique.

"To a *giving* man."

"Oh!" It was an almost involuntary exclamation, as though she hadn't expected quite that finish to his brazen pronouncement. "And are you a *giving* man, Mr. Taggart?"

"Are you interested in finding out, Mrs. Wiltshire?"

Oh, such a clever man, leaving it all up to her. But then all of those ladies' men were, and she didn't know why a mountain cat in pursuit of his golden prey should be any different.

Was she?

Whatever it took—a hard, angry woman would never count the cost; she knew exactly where her interest in finding out could lead.

"I'm interested in exploring anything of consequence to me," she said softly.

He had known she would take up his challenge. Cassandra could never resist a challenge.

356

He stood up and held out his hand once again and she took it; in the shadows, Mr. Upjohn and Mr. Pettigrew nodded knowingly to each other.

They walked, first outside in the plaza in front of the hotel where other couples paraded ostentatiously under the gaslights and around the parked carriages that looked like so many huge black birds ready to swoop the moment an occupant was ready to fly from the scene.

They were one among many who walked, and that was something that was done when a man found a woman for the evening: he was entitled to show her off, and himself.

"Where is your room?" Trane asked, and Cassandra's hackles rose.

He surely was quick about making even a hint of a suggestion to her. But, she would do whatever it took to pay him back for his hard assessment of Cassandra. She was Linnea, after all.

"I have a cottage suite," she told him, keeping her voice seductively low. "Through the garden behind the hotel. It's very private."

He smiled.

He never said anything, damn him. And that smile, that damned odd little smile: it said *I understand perfectly, ma'am,* and it never did say whether he were planning to take advantage of the situation, and she hated not knowing. She hated *him.*

They walked slowly through the garden, along the covered walkway, around once and back again, until she was right at her door. But she wasn't going to invite him in. Not the first time, and never so easily. He would have to work to get beyond her door. And work hard.

"Good night, Mrs. Wiltshire," he said coolly, deliberately.

What? But what a ploy! She had a lightning instant to think about it, and she saw it immediately. He would never take what she was not willing to give. It was up to her. Damn, it was up to her—still.

"I thought we were going to explore interesting things, Mr. Taggart," she said softly.

"Are we, ma'am?" He just loved watching her Cassandra-face assessing all the sides of what he did not say and what he meant and deciding how she should proceed. Dear God—Cassandra . . .

"You talked about being a . . . giving man."

"But I don't *take,* ma'am," he said gently.

Didn't he? But she remembered far too well the sum and substance of all the forbidden things that Cassandra and he had done in the desire of the moment. The memories were like a flood, gushing through her pores, demanding that she offer, that she take, because *she* remembered . . .

No—she was Linnea. She had none of those dreams and memories of Cassandra. If she let herself, she might go mad with longing, because the sense of yearning was like a floodgate opening.

But he couldn't be counting on that; he thought she was Linnea, and the two of them were brash impostors, linked by the destiny of Riveland.

Riveland was far away, she thought, and she had spent almost two weeks seeking something that didn't exist in the Springs. She didn't look for one moment as if she had been in mourning in all that time, and she found it curious that Trane hadn't referred to it. He surely hadn't expected to come upon her dancing and surrounded by fatuous men who wanted to make love to her.

Linnea should have been prostrate with grief, and instead she looked as though she were celebrating her great good fortune.

Wasn't it, though? And in fact it was none of Trane Taggart's business what she did at the Springs. But he was there, and he was watching her ever so carefully, and if she were a vain woman, she might have gotten the idea he had come after her with the sole intent of seducing her.

The shocking thing was . . . she wanted it. And she didn't. And she wanted to be left alone by everyone. And all these three selves were fighting hard for the upper hand, and the dissatisfied, discontented Linnea, who was every inch as much an impostor as Trane Taggart, was winning.

Cassandra could never be Cassandra again.

Trane would remain himself forever; he didn't know she knew what she knew, and he knew nothing about Cassandra's tricks and lies, and so — he must have come because he wanted to see her, as Linnea.

"Won't you give?" she asked him, with a hint of flirtatiousness in her voice. *Oh Lord, remember that accent, Cassandra!*

"What shall I give, Linnea?"

Oh, now things were turning serious.

"Tell me why you came here, Trane."

"Like I said, I came to see you, ma'am," he answered in kind, still amused by her. She had no idea he was aware of her tricks and traps. She was playing Linnea for all she was worth, and he meant to take advantage of it, just because of how much he had suffered already at her hands.

He was absolutely sure Linnea knew exactly what she was doing, every bit as much as Cassandra. He hated the hair, but it was dark: the hair didn't matter. He wanted the mouth, the body — but slowly, ever so slowly, and luxuriously, because there would never be enough time to savor what he thought he had lost.

So slowly . . .

She swallowed hard. To see her . . . "So you've seen me," she said lightly.

"Yes, ma'am, and you're recovering nicely from the tragedy."

Grrr — she should have expected that, but she felt like biting him for even mentioning it.

"Everyone is always so happy at the Springs," she said, sloughing it off with an understatement that she thought would be typical of Linnea.

"Yes, ma'am . . . and are you?"

Now: "Now that you've come, Mr. Taggart, I'm very happy."

"Pleased to hear that, ma'am." He knew he was exasperating her to the point of irritation, but it was a way to hold on to his own emotions as well. He could have taken her right then, he sensed it, but that was not what Cassandra wanted from him. She just wasn't sure which persona to present to him, and in truth, it was all one and the same. She could not be any less like Linnea than if they had been two people at the opposite ends of the country who had never met.

But it was very interesting watching her try to merge those two selves into one coherent whole.

She couldn't do it.

"This isn't very interesting," she said provokingly, with just a hint of anger in her voice. After all, he had brought the idea up; she really thought he should have followed up on it somehow, since she wanted to have her cake and eat it too. She could have him and reject him, all in the space of the number of days she intended to remain at the Springs, and when she got home, she would send him on his way, and he would have learned a good, hard lesson.

Good.

"No, ma'am," he said in that pesky too-agreeable voice that she was coming to hate.

"Well—*do* something about it," she commanded, realizing instantly how imperious and childish that sounded. Just like a rich widow who wasn't being given what she wanted on a silver platter.

"You sure, Linnea?" he asked softly.

"Yes," she said through gritted teeth. Wasn't that why he was here? Because he *wanted* to see Linnea? What did he want? Her money or her kisses? She would never know. She would just take and enjoy the one, and expose him when he demanded the other. Simple. "Unless

you were so in *love* with Cassandra you couldn't possibly be interesting at all," she added nastily.

"Oh no, ma'am; it was a pure business arrangement," he said, and he was so amused by the way she was torn between what she wanted and how she should act. "Your sister was not a *lovable* woman . . ." *(Forgive me, Cassandra . . .)* ". . . she was a practical woman. Came from being married to my father. He was a cold, hard man, Linnea. Didn't give an inch—to a son or to a wife. But she needed help and I offered, and she took it, simple as that."

Oh, she thought the steam would just pump right out of her ears. Not a lovable woman . . . *she needed help—*

She bit her lips to keep from saying something that would reveal that she was not Linnea. He was something, this mountain cat—he didn't pounce at all when he had his prey in hand; he played with her, and she didn't like the games at all, at all.

And she couldn't negate any damned thing he had said. It would be easier to shut his mouth than to shut him up.

"How generous of you," she murmured finally. "My sister must have been very appreciative."

"Yes, ma'am. She put me in the overseer's house and we never said another word about it."

Really, she felt like punching him. Not *another word about it—*

"You must have been so grateful," she said tightly.

"Oh, ma'am, it was my father's land. A son couldn't do less."

The hell he couldn't. And he had done so much more . . . including lie right through his teeth—and . . .

"A man could do *more*," she said pointedly. She had heard enough about Cassandra's shortcomings. How lucky it was that she had had the forethought to transform herself into the eminently desirable Linnea.

He loomed close to her suddenly. "A man doesn't

361

push his intentions any farther than he thinks they will go, Linnea."

"You haven't pushed anything yet," she said, with just a trace of petulance. "How far do you think you could push?"

She heard the smile in his voice again. "About as far as a kiss, Linnea."

He really was too much. But what had she expected: that he would ravish her in the garden? Or maybe she *had* wanted that. After all, in the dark, with her memories—what *wasn't* possible?

"That sounds *faintly* interesting," she said shrewishly.

"I assure you, you will be *very* interested," he murmured, taking her by the shoulders and pulling her very gently toward him.

He was so tall; she had never taken account of it, but now that she was supposed to be Linnea, everything appeared to her in a different way. She was expensively and gorgeously dressed, his hands were so gentle, he looked so tall and almost forbidding in formal black, his lips were gentle as they settled on hers, and his arms crushed her body hard against his, and he was all muscle and heat and devouring promise.

She felt one moment of hesitation before she opened her mouth to him: he had loved her as Cassandra in exactly the same way. But she couldn't have known that, she was Linnea, and she had to tamp down on those feelings of resentment that Linnea was no different to him than Cassandra.

But she had to temper her response to him, anyway. Linnea was cool, calm, bereaved, appearances to the contrary.

She couldn't let herself be *too* interested.

Just interested enough.

He was very interested, but that was the nature of men, she thought, as she returned kiss for kiss, nibble for nibble, thrust for thrust.

And the nature of woman . . .

The nature of Cassandra, he thought, as he played with her tongue, reaching beyond her pretense of reticence for the real Cassandra, the one who wanted his kisses, needed them, demanded them.

It was so hard to induce her to let go. She was determined to play Linnea to the hilt. And it was such a delicious challenge, to seduce her with the voluptuousness of her own mouth. He reveled in the taste of her, in the texture of her, in her guarded response as she grudgingly let him probe the sensitive skin of her mouth.

When he pulled away from her, she reached for him, murmuring, "More and more interesting . . ."

By then she wanted him, and she was beyond caring whether she kissed him like Cassandra or like Linnea. She didn't know which was which. She didn't care. She was enveloped by him, the feel of him, the scent, the taste . . . She had to be careful, she had to—and she couldn't remember a thing when she was consumed by him.

And then he pulled away from her, softly so that she felt the texture of his lips ease away slowly, almost regretfully, and he cupped her chin, and he whispered, "Tomorrow, Linnea."

"What?!" She was so disoriented by this reversal, that all she could do was recoil in disbelief. And she knew what that sounded like—a woman who was peeved that things were not going to get as far as she imagined.

What had she imagined?

Her perturbation was obvious, and that amused him too. Sweet, sensual Cassandra having to hold back her natural impulses—but he couldn't make demands on her, not yet. He wanted to seduce her slowly and deliciously, to make back those weeks of torment when he thought he had lost her.

"We are at the beginning," he told her, his voice soft and liquid with some emotion she did not understand. "We don't rush beginnings, Linnea. We explore them for as long as we need to."

I don't need to! she thought wildly as he moved away from her.

"Tomorrow, Linnea," he called to her as a promise.

"Don't come!" she muttered, biting her lip and searching for the key to her suite. "Don't . . ." Were there tears in her eyes? Had she wanted so much? A kiss demanded more, and a kiss was a commitment, and Trane Taggart was a man who obviously didn't honor commitments.

She let herself into her suite and shut the door with a savage swing.

In the bushes, Mr. Upjohn and Mr. Pettigrew grabbed each other, and solemnly shook hands.

Chapter Twenty-one

Tomorrow.

She awakened in a sour mood, and she wasn't sure if it was because something had happened or nothing had happened.

She had to be very careful today. She opened the curtains that blocked the morning sun through her window, and she picked up a mirror and examined herself critically in the blazing morning light.

Not good. She rubbed her hand over her face. What time was it? Seven. She had to get busy. She could see streaks of gold among the reddened curls, and all of her rouge had smeared, and her eyes looked sunken into two deep, black holes.

Tomorrow.

It could be anytime, anywhere. What was the fickle Mr.-Taggart-who-was-not-Mr.-Taggart planning to do with the grieving Linnea-Wiltshire-who-was-really-Cassandra-Taggart? Lord, it was as good as a farce. She hadn't known who she was last night—and she knew still less in the hot morning light.

Her bath first, to scrub away the remnants of the evening, and after that she would carefully apply the coloring to her hair, and sit right by the window to etch in her facial nuances so artfully that no one, let alone Trane Taggart, could tell she wasn't Linnea Wiltshire.

She wished she weren't. But how was she to know that

Trane would turn up in the Springs right out of the blue and talk such seductive talk to her? Ohhh, she couldn't wait to get back at him.

Imagine him making love to Linnea weeks after Cassandra had supposedly died. Just imagine.

She could imagine it very well. Her mouth tingled as she carefully lined her eyes with the soft pencil. Of course she wasn't supposed to know that he had made love to Cassandra. She was supposed to be flattered that he had come running after her.

Fine, she could play games. She was playing games. Her body wasn't playing games. She wanted him, and something in her felt the triumph of commanding him all over again. It was not the Linnea in her, either—he was responding to Cassandra, however deeply she thought she had buried her.

Enough. She reached for the rouge and with one careful finger, applied it to the undercurve of her cheekbone. The rapacious Lavonna from whom she had learned all these tricks had been a practical Parisian, full of joy and laughter at the thought of how prudish were American women and their oh-so-puffed-up men.

These things had been taken for granted in her milieu, and she had been well entertained watching Cassandra's clumsy fingers work with rouge, powder and pencil stick.

What a difference a month could make, she thought, as she rubbed the pink coloring into her cheeks and back toward her hairline. What an expert she had become—in *all* things.

His brisk rap on her door startled her.

"I'm not ready yet," she called to him.

"Let me in anyway."

Oh, that honeyed tone of voice, as though he were imagining whether she were still undressed, or partially dressed, or stark naked.

The thought excited her, and she played with it in her mind for one long, tantalizing moment while she put a subtle glide of color on her lips.

366

She would let him in, dressed as she was in her under-things and the frothy hooped petticoats that made it impossible for her to do much more than tend to her hair and her face. Soon, the dresser would knock on the door to help her on with her dress, but Mr. Taggart could surely stand her in good stead as a dresser.

He would dress her down instead of dress her up; he would kiss her, he would hold her. He would crunch the great steel-ribbed monster encircling her waist in his bare hands in order to touch one tender inch of her heated flesh.

She would not be like Cassandra, aching for every caress, amenable to every demand, frenzied in her abandoned desire to couple with him.

Oh no, Linnea would be cool, disdainful. She would never let him in so fast so far. In spite of last night. Contrary to Cassandra's wanton nature. She would make things as hard as possible for the capricious Mr. Taggart.

"I would just love to, Mr. Taggart," she purred, as she frantically scrambled into her dress, with its yards of flounces and finger-crippling buttons down the front.

Green watered silk again, shot with gold so that she looked as if she were walking in a halo of sunlight. The bodice was plain, leading up to a high white collar and a lace-embroidered undersleeve.

Her hair—was impossible as always. She ran a handful of honey through the tangled curl to smooth it back.

Just so. "But," she added, throwing open the door, "as you can see, I am already *dressed*."

He didn't look in the least discomposed. "Breakfast, Mrs. Wiltshire?"

She liked the fact that he didn't show his disappointment. "I would be delighted, Mr. Taggart."

But even breakfast was different. All eyes were focused on them, and then, there was something about being seated across from a strong, aggressive-looking man whose light, bright gaze wouldn't let you hide a thing. She ate differently, always aware of his eyes catching every little flick of her tongue or movement of her mouth.

She held her hands differently because she was aware of his minute scrutiny of her every motion. She met his eyes often and saw the kindling flame of desire that could not be concealed by the mundane circumstance of dining with him at breakfast.

She wanted coffee and kisses and maybe not necessarily in that order. And so did he.

What a master he was, arousing her like that so she could dwell all night on the possibilities that had not occurred. Trane Taggart . . . or whatever his real name was . . . was a man to be reckoned with. He knew an eager woman when he met one, and he knew when to ignore her protests and when to tantalize her senses, and he couldn't be doing a better job right now than if he had her alone in bed with him.

She could hardly swallow for the excitement of imagining what he was thinking, what he was feeling.

They hardly talked; did they need to talk?

No, he needed to see the sights. She had never felt so frustrated in her life. She fully expected one thing, and he dealt her something quite else.

He wanted to see the Springs and taste the water.

And taste . . . and taste—

She took him to the pump room, a quite unprepossessing building in the center of town. "This is it, Mr. Taggart."

"A glass of the waters, Mrs. Wiltshire, at the very least. I came to the Springs to taste the waters. . . . His voice trailed off as he purchased a glass and went to the pump. The water gushed up in a sudden surge and overflowed the glass.

He was good-natured about it, swallowing it in one gulp. "A man could get killed, drinking potent stuff like that," he sputtered, spitting out the last mouthful.

"I should have warned you," she said lightly, enjoying the sight of him in turmoil for a change.

"We're hardly well acquainted enough for that, Mrs. Wiltshire," he retorted, allowing the attendant to wipe him down with a towel.

"Let's do something *interesting* about it then," she suggested lightly, but it came out sounding disagreeable.

"I would love to, ma'am," he said in an undertone, as he took her arm and led her out of the building.

"You can't call me ma'am and 'love to,' " she said waspishly.

He smiled that odd, sweet smile. "We'll just see about that, Linnea. We'll just see."

The problem was, he didn't want to slip and call her Cassandra, and Linnea's name did not come easily to his lips. And "ma'am" seemed so outrageous that it was perfect. She was a "ma'am" in this guise—perfect, priggish, distant and suggestive all at the same time.

They walked the promenade in the afternoon, and all the simmering bucks couldn't keep their hands or their leering comments away from her. They took a carriage up to the Spring, which was just as uninteresting as the pump room with its foul-tasting water.

But what was more interesting was the long, slow afternoon of privacy in the carriage as they traveled back and forth from the Spring.

She was wound up like a spring, and he knew all he had to do was touch her and she would unwind completely.

He didn't touch her.

"Mr. Taggart, please tell me what there is of interest in a fusty old carriage ride up to the Springs?"

"Your good company, ma'am," he said promptly.

"It must not be terribly good company if you can't think of anything else to do but drive that damned carriage," she said haughtily. "I mean, Mr. Upjohn and Mr. Pettigrew . . .

". . . wear petticoats," Trane growled, pulling the carriage to a halt in a copse of trees just off the road and out of the sight of the casual traveler "You don't give a man a chance, do you, ma'am? You just want the whole piece of pie right now, right in your lap."

"Exactly, Mr. Taggart, and I hope it's filling."

"It's your pie, ma'am; you can devour it whole or savor it in little bites."

"How do you prefer it, Mr. Taggart?" she asked insolently.

"I like to savor it," he said huskily, as he moved just that little bit closer to her. "I like to take it little by little, slow and easy, ma'am. I like to . . ."

"Yes?" she breathed as his mouth came closer and closer to hers.

" . . . taste it thoroughly, roll it around on my tongue . . ."

". . . oh, yes . . ."

". . . every crumb . . ." His lips brushed hers.

"And then . . . ?" she whispered.

"I *eat* it," he rasped, and covered her mouth completely with his.

She groaned deep in her throat as she met his devouring kiss. She had waited for this, and how patient she had been. His questing tongue aroused her, her own need positively overwhelmed her. She felt as if she was in a private world with him where no one could see or hear, and everything that happened between them would become a delicious forbidden secret.

He held her head in his hands and delved deeply into her mouth, seeking, seeking, demanding her response, playing with her tongue, tasting the full, firm cushion of her lips with his avid tongue. "Enough yet, ma'am?" he whispered.

"This is crazy; don't call me ma'am. Don't . . ."

I won't . . . Hold still—"

He thrust into her mouth again and her whole body felt like liquid dissolving against the hard heat of him.

More . . . oh, she hadn't begged him, but he knew, he

knew.

"You wear too damned many clothes," he muttered, as he ruthlessly pulled at the bodice of her dress; she helped him, demanding his kiss as they each worked away frantically at the bulbous little buttons until she felt the light fragrant air caress the skin of her chest.

He was right, she thought excitedly. There were too many clothes, too many bones and hooks, and that awful cage that she couldn't remove without climbing down from the carriage.

And then she couldn't think; she could only wonder at the ingenuity of a man's hands that could find exactly the right place to caress and arouse, that could somehow insinuate his fingers in exactly the right place to free one tempting taut-nippled breast, and know exactly the right movement with which to stroke it to make her crazy with desire.

His hands were perfect, his mouth was perfect, and she responded with perfect abandon, giving herself to him so that he could continue forever the sumptuous feelings he aroused in her.

Her breast was the most voluptuous instrument of passion; she had never known, and yet she had known forever that if he, and only he, caressed the tight, taut nipple tip she would explode into a thousand spangling stars.

And she came so close, so close, but he was not done with his explored pursuit of pleasuring her. His mouth moved with that slow gentle *feeling* pull from her lips and settled unerringly on her tempting nipple and sucked— one hot, wet, hard pull at the sensitized peak—and thick, hot molasses just poured through her veins, from her tingling nipple right down to the center of her feminine source.

"Too many clothes," he murmured, flicking his tongue against her luscious nipple. "Too damn many . . ."

"Let's do something about it."

"I don't hardly know where to begin, Linnea." His

371

mouth closed over the stiff peak again and she moaned as the mounding feelings began building up deep inside her. It was the firm, wet pull of his lips against her breast; it was the soft laving of her rigid nipple and the pillowy sense of his lips surrounding it and just squeezing it gently; it was the deep drawing motion of his mouth as he sucked at her breast hard and hot. It was the thick streaming sensation that expanded and gushed through her whole body as she shook with spasm after spasm of pure cascading pleasure—endless, unstoppable—from that one pleasure point of her body.

It was unimaginable, and it was the most imaginable pleasure ever, never before explored, succulent in its intensity—supremely, sublimely his right and her destiny.

Gently she pushed him away as the final tendrils of feeling twisted downward and downward, and settled in that most secret sensual place, and his head lay on her breast, and they rested there for the moment, replete.

He escorted her to the Targamet Hotel that night.

"There is gaming in the back room," she informed him, tapping his arm lightly with her fan.

"It's more of a gamble leaving you out here alone, ma'am."

And he was right about that: the ravens were all ready to swoop on her the moment she walked in the door, resplendent in brown-and-gold-striped moiré. This dress bared her shoulders over a deep folded cuff of material that criss-crossed over her breast, and Trane couldn't tell if she had done it deliberately just to tease him—or them.

But they weren't serious, and he—he didn't know what he was. When he made love to her, he had Cassandra in his arms, but the voice . . . the voice pulled him in to the reality of the pretense. She would not give in, and she would carry it through.

The voice took on a fluty note as she bandied words with her assorted gentlemen friends, and flirted charmingly with her fan. He himself wasn't proof against it, either, but his one overriding feeling was that he wanted to throttle her for all the little games she was playing.

He wasn't jealous: there wasn't a man jack in the crowd worth working up a rage over. He felt instead that familiar exasperation. She didn't need to do it, and he wanted to prove to her that she needed no one but him.

There really was so little time. Greve would call her back to Riveland soon enough, and she would have to face the consequences.

But until then . . . oh, until then, she was *his* and his alone, and he meant to squeeze the most out of every moment and make it so memorable that she could never ever forget him.

Easier thought than done in this crowd, though. He could have picked each one of those puppies up and set him aside, but he figured it would be kind of a rude thing to do when they were at such a disadvantage.

But he wanted *her* and she was making it damned hard to get to her.

"Mr. Taggart," she said finally, coming around to him.

And didn't she admire the way he looked, so tall and strong and formal with his black suit and stark white shirtfront. There was something so gorgeously grim about him and his proprietary air. It made the others step back almost as if the atmosphere were too thick with his blatant maleness.

She liked that a lot. "And what is of great interest tonight, Mr. Taggart?" she asked just a little coyly when he didn't speak.

"I came to dance, ma'am. I'm hoping you will join me."

"My pleasure, Mr. Taggart," she said, holding up her arms. She loved it when he grasped her around the waist right then and there and waltzed her onto the dance floor. "And where did you learn *that?*" she murmured, settling her body closely against his.

"Where I learned everything else, ma'am—here and

there."

"What an interesting life you must have led."

"It's had its moments," he agreed, but the tone of his voice even under the music distinctly did not invite further discussion.

"Well," she said lightly, "perhaps there are new things of interest to explore."

"I'm looking forward to it, Linnea."

Oh yes, that was what she wanted to hear.

"When?" she asked tersely, her whole body seizing up with anticipation.

"Now."

She did not question where, or how. He led her, she followed; no one watched them. They were one of scores of couples seeking that little bit of privacy to talk and kiss, and perhaps something more.

They went up the stairs of the hotel, passing a dozen couples on their way up or down, and went up still another flight, and then another, until he stopped at a door.

"Here, Linnea. Now." He watched her face in the dim light of the hallway, but he knew she would never deny him — or herself.

"Open the door," she said briskly, her heart pounding wildly. *"Not* a bedroom?" She couldn't believe it. It was a room outfitted with tables and chairs, with a plush carpet beneath, and excellent lighting above. In a corner alcove were two deeply upholstered chairs presumably for onlookers who could afford not to play.

"A lot of hotel rooms in use tonight, Mrs. Wiltshire. A lot of people with the same ideas as you . . . and me. But I'm a gambling man. Are you?"

Was she? He meant — what — to take her on the floor — no, the table? Why not?

She shrugged and walked into the room ahead of him.

"There's privacy here. It's all I require."

He closed the door behind him and tossed away the key. "I beg to differ with you, ma'am. You require a lot more than that."

374

She liked the sound of that. Really, it was another woman in her body responding to him the way Cassandra had done, wanting him as she had done, for the sole sake of the experience, the connection . . . the—there was no love. There was *no love.*

"Show me," she whispered, leaning back against the table expectantly. Her dress would come off easily; she had planned for that. But she didn't know what else to do, what else to say.

The same feverish feeling gripped her that had driven her into his arms on Riveland. She wanted nothing else but his kiss and the touch of his hands, and if that led somewhere else, some other delicious place else, she was willing to follow.

She was willing. But Linnea to the hilt.

So when he came to her, and put his arms around her, she pulled back just that little bit. But he didn't kiss her. His light, bright gaze probed hers deeply, and she twisted her body slightly as she felt him unfastening the hooks behind her dress.

She licked her lips speculatively and his eyes followed every movement until his hands could push away the material from her long, strong back and get to the under-things beneath.

And he undressed her slowly, luxuriously, stopping to examine, to kiss and lick, to caress every inch of her smooth, satiny skin as he bared it to his touch.

She had made it easy—easier; she had not worn that midriff-pinching corset, and she had dispensed with the horrible steel crinoline. It was so easy for him to insert his fingers here, pull away a wisp of material there, slide it away from some other place, and completely feel her nakedness as he stripped each piece of clothing away.

When she was naked, he swept her up in his arms and carried her to one of the two upholstered chairs in the room and, cradling her tightly against him, he sat with her in his lap, his mouth seeking hers now, finally, settling deeply within her, savoring her, wanting her.

Her perfect body, Cassandra's body, invited every caress, squirming against him enticingly each time he touched her, each time his hands explored the perfect curves of her body and how exactly they fit into his hands and felt against his endlessly questing fingers.

She straddled him, kneeling on the chair, to give him the utmost freedom to caress her where he would. Her kisses grew wilder, more abandoned, as her excitement escalated.

The darkness in the room enfolded them in their private corner. She sank down onto his lap as his hands reached for her breasts, and she ground her hips against his thrusting manhood. He was so there for her, so ready, so hard and male. Her hands reached for him, pulling away at his clothing to take his nakedness into her hands with reverence and a hot desire to possess him.

She lifted herself so that she was positioned at exactly the right angle, and he nudged her, and in another luscious moment, he possessed her with all his virile power deep within her pulsating velvet sheath.

It was the most potent connection she had ever felt between them. He was totally embedded within her, pure male power contained by her, wanting her, consumed by his need for her.

His hands were everywhere, his kisses wild and wanton. She never wanted to move; this was perfect, she was full and joined and . . . perfect.

But her hips, her voluptuously moving hips could not stay still. She moved in a primitive rhythm compounded of a secret knowledge and the sensation of his fingers caressing her tight, taut nipples, and his exquisite kiss — she moved, she knew the dance, she knew the primal floodtide of desire, she knew . . .

She knew the driving wetness of her body meeting and matching the primitive thrust of his; she knew.

Her arms braced against the hard muscle of his shoulders as his hard thrusting sense of his masculinity possessed her, became the center of her world, her femininity, her life; his hands worked her hips, his mouth found the taut pleasure points of her breasts and sucked them greedily; she rode him, she rode him ferociously until she did not know what part of her was her and what was him; and she rode him hard and high until that screaming, crackling explosion of sensation that was so shatteringly intense, she thought she had died.

And then she felt him pumping deep, deep within her, his groans of pleasure a hoarse underlay to everything she was feeling and experiencing, and she collapsed in exhaustion against him.

He touched her hair, he kissed her forehead.

He almost had called her name—Cassandra . . .

They went to the races the next day. The season was winding down and many of the favorites had been shipped home already. The crowd was sparse, and it might well have been the last race of the season as well.

They didn't care. They placed their bets, and wandered through the stands while Cassandra greeted all of her gentlemen friends who were whiling away yet another day with this frivolity.

She wore flowered muslin today, with a broad-brimmed straw hat to keep out the sun, and afterward, she and Trane made their way down to the paddocks and the stables.

"I love to ride," she started to say, and then caught herself. Cassandra had learned to stay on a horse. Linnea she must make into a veritable Lady Godiva. Anyway, it *was* true she loved to ride. She just hadn't done as much as she would have liked.

"Sitting on a horse would become you, ma'am."

"I wish you would stop with 'ma'am,' " she said fretfully. How could the man make love to her like that one minute and treat her like his employer the next? Probably, she thought dolefully, because she was.

"A rich man's sport, Linnea. The only way a poor man

377

can indulge is to place his bet."

"Then you're a lot poorer today," she said spitefully.

"I'm a lot richer today, Linnea."

Oh, the tone of his voice; such meaning behind it, such depth of feeling. He had felt it too, the bonding between them.

But that wasn't what she wanted. If she felt that consuming closeness with him, she would never be able to push him out of her life. She did not want any involvement with him in her guise as Linnea. She could not let him seduce her so thoroughly and completely that she could not ultimately let him go.

But the scent of the stable was so ripe, so earthy. It assaulted her senses, her body quivered with it. If she had been with any other man but Trane Taggart . . . But it was useless to speculate about that. She would never have been at the races or in the stables with any other man but him, and she saw by the dark look he gave her, that it was affecting him too.

"You wouldn't believe a man could get so hungry in a paddock," he said humorously, his gaze settling tightly on her lips. He meant it. He wanted her, there and then, and the smoldering knowledge that the place and her presence aroused him so intensely excited her unbearably.

There were people drifting in and out of the paddock and they walked carefully to avoid meeting anyone until they came to the barn. Here it was relatively quiet and they walked around it first, before Trane opened the door and she slipped in behind him.

A kerosene lamp hung on a peg lit the interior with a dim, flickering light. They heard the gentle whickering of horses in stalls just beyond the pale light.

The scent enveloped them, elemental, fertile.

"God, I want you." His voice was hoarse, rough with emotion.

"Take me, then," she whispered.

"In the hay?"

"Wherever you want." *However you want, whatever*

you want . . . She was sending Linnea straight into the depths and beyond. She felt him lift her dress and settle her against a bale of hay, her back to him. She felt him thick and hard against her pantalette-clad buttocks, and then she felt him parting her legs, and tilting her body forward so that he could find the velvet texture of her welcoming fold.

And ever so slowly, she felt him insert himself there, pushing into her inch by long, hard inch, taking her, possessing her, deeper and still deeper until he was all tightly within her, full and thick and elementally there.

She wriggled her bottom experimentally and she felt the whole hard length of him, her sole connection to him in this exciting reverse way, and her body felt explosive with the knowledge of it.

And now he rode her and she had never been so intensely aware of the pure raw power of him deep within her, how he thrust within her with the rhythmic drive of a piston, how she met each virile thrust with a writhing movement of her buttocks that sent the shimmering tendrils of feeling twisting through her body. Oh, it was there, it was coming; all those little twisting, entwining feelings sliding all over her body, top to bottom, bottom shimmying tightly against his hips, swaying against him, provoking him, demanding from him.

He held her hips, her buttocks, he guided her movement against his, in opposition to his thrusts, in tandem with him; it was coming, it was coming.

The hard power of him driving deeply within her, the sensuous fingers of feeling, coming, fusing into pure molten gold, sliding gold, melting gold all over her, all over her body as his last torrid thrust sent her spinning over the edge and the gold poured all over her body in a torrent of purity and finality.

Once more, once more — he felt himself letting go — not yet, not yet. He felt himself go with one last driving thrust, over the edge, on the heels of her culmination, drenching her, possessing her, wanting her all over again as the eddying pleasure of his climax left him spent and hollow to the core.

"Oh my, I do believe the Widow wilt-she *did,*" Mr. Upjohn announced unhappily, peering at Cassandra as she made her way into the dining room of the Whitestone on Trane's arm.

"Well, where did that usurper come from, anyway?" Mr. Pettigrew demanded pettishly. "I just don't understand it. The man is an animal; he barely has manners, and he talks with a strange accent."

"She knew him before," Mr. Upjohn said unhappily, "just as you said."

"That still counts."

"You'll be paid," Mr. Upjohn said, his pale gaze following Cassandra and Trane around the floor as they were seated at a table across the room. "But damn, she was the sweetest thing. I can't believe she would choose that earthy heathen over a *gentleman.*"

Cassandra was feeling that herself, as she let the waiter seat her and watched Trane with avid eyes as he folded himself into the chair opposite her.

"Your gallery is taking bets," he commented as he scanned the menu.

She swallowed and tore her eyes away from him. "Oh, well, Mr. Upjohn . . . really, a most harmless little man."

"You say that with just the right disdain, Mrs. Wiltshire."

"But of course I know just how to do it, Mr. Taggart. Would *you* like to try me?"

"Haven't I?" he murmured, and she felt herself flush from her face right to her toes.

He couldn't get away with that.

"Dinner tonight, then," she said, keeping her voice light and unconcerned. "Come for me in the morning."

That got his attention. "You don't mean that."

"I'm interested in other things tonight, Mr. Taggart,

like a lengthy and pleasant dinner with you."

He almost protested, and then he caught the look in her eyes. "As you say, Mrs. Wiltshire, a pleasant dinner with a good companion can be a very interesting experience."

And they got through it — she didn't quite know how, because she was very sensitive to the tension in him, and the anger of the two gentlemen seated in the room, and she was sure if either of them knew she had planned to spend the evening alone, he would have been at her side at the instant.

But Trane . . . She had fully expected more of a protest, and she felt as if her little triumphal moment had been utterly deflated. She would be spending the evening alone now, and wondering where he was and with whom.

It would serve him right if she took herself out for the evening anyway. She had only said, after all, she didn't prefer spending it with him.

And only because he was getting too sure of himself.

"Tomorrow," she whispered, as he left her at her door, not even demanding to open the door for her, or trying to cajole his way into her rooms.

He was the most exasperating man. . . . She immediately picked herself up and went back to the dining room and presented herself to Messrs. Upjohn and Pettigrew, complaining that that nasty man had abandoned her for the evening and she was in dire need of company.

Their destination this evening was a party at the Trellis Room of the Brighton Hotel, and they were very happy to accommodate Mrs. Wiltshire, especially since it meant that Mr. Upjohn hadn't lost his bet — yet.

As she suspected, Trane was among the crowd, and she felt an unreasoning anger at seeing him there.

And he wasn't above rubbing it in. "Interested in other things, Mrs. Wiltshire? Like frolicky young puppies with no gumption to them? Swat them down and they'll lick your feet? I suppose a woman needs to wield that kind of power occasionally."

"As opposed to the kind of power you wield, Mr. Taggart?"

"I wonder what you mean by that, Mrs. Wiltshire. I wouldn't have said I have any power at all."

"That *is* strange. I would have said the weight is all on your side, Mr. Taggart."

"Sometimes, Mrs. Wiltshire, a person is sitting in the seat of power and doesn't even know it."

"And sometimes a man holds the reins too tightly and may regret it."

He threw up his hands. "I can't deny or refute that, Mrs. Wiltshire. You have me. I leave you to your gentlemen friends for the evening."

Tomorrow . . . she thought, she didn't say; she wanted to run after him as he walked away.

When she returned to her cottage suite, she found a message slipped in under the door.

It was a telegram from Mr. Greve and it was the word she had been waiting for. "All papers filed and ready for final signature. Awaiting your return home. Please advise."

Yes!

Oh no. Here was the foreseeable end to her idyll with Trane Taggart, and her ultimate revenge. She couldn't bear to think of it.

He had seduced her all over again, and she was as much in thrall to him as Linnea Wiltshire as she had been back on Riveland.

It made no sense. The man was poison, an impostor, a liar, worse than she, and she couldn't give him up.

But if she couldn't, she would lose Riveland and every plot and plan she had executed would dwindle into an irrevocable loss.

She couldn't let that go now. Everything was within her grasp. She had only to reach out and take it. A final signature, a transfer of funds and property, and it was done and she would finally be free.

She could not afford to be enslaved by the likes of Trane Taggart, and he couldn't afford her, either.

She didn't know what to do.

No, she did. She had to make arrangements for her trip back home and somehow she had to elude Trane, and she didn't know quite how she was going to do it.

Dear, busy Mr. Greve, making everything possible for her, hoping against hope that somehow she would still depend on his advice and good offices.

Not likely, Mr. Greve. The end is almost here.

She could almost taste it, touch it. Everything else was secondary.

Except—she did not know if Trane would take up her invitation to come for her in the morning, and she had to be prepared for that. She awakened early to draw in the contours of her Linnea face, resenting terribly that she had even invited him to come to her, when she was desperate to make her travel arrangements and return to Riveland.

He rapped sharply at the door promptly at nine o'clock, and she wasn't even ready. Or maybe she deliberately wasn't ready; she didn't know. There was just something about the anticipation of expecting the man that excited her beyond all endurance.

It wasn't fair. And it was true.

She opened the door to him and he stalked in, wary as a cat. "Anyone here, Mrs. Wiltshire?"

"Only your suspicions," she retorted. "Sit down, Mr. Taggart."

"No, you lie down, Linnea."

"Oh, really?" This was a new game; he had never gotten quite to the point so fast before. At least not at the Springs.

"Oh? We'll waste time, then, arguing about it? Who has the power, Mrs. Wiltshire. On the other hand, a man can find a willing woman any old place he cares to ask the question. I'm not so sure about what you might find if you pose that same question, Linnea."

She took a deep breath to fight down the anger at his implicit threat. "I'm not worried," she said dismissively.

"No, I didn't think you were," he said. "I wouldn't have knocked on that door this morning otherwise."

She turned to look at him, and the light in his eyes made her catch her breath.

"We don't have much time, widow-lady," he said gently.

"No, we don't," she agreed, and she knew there was the faintest tinge of regret in her tone. Whatever he was,'he had released her, Cassandra, from Jesse Taggart's hell, and he had taught her that she had a sensual life, a consuming life, and she was ready to take the next step. But not with him, not with a man who would stake his pretenses on a lie.

As opposed to her, of course. But she *did* have a sister, and Jesse had never had any sons.

"Linnea . . . ," he said softly. The black widow was a treat, he thought, just standing there and challenging him with her knowing eyes and thinly garbed body. He knew her so well . . . Cassandra, Cassandra, who had known nothing of kisses and caresses, and nothing of love . . . Was this love, or was it pure, plain lust—or was it him, and did it not matter which it was, as long as it *was?*

He wanted to call her name, her real name, he wanted to say he knew, he understood—he thought he understood; but in fact the only thing he really comprehended was his violent need to make love to her.

He was ready. She, by the glowing light in her eyes, was contemplating her response to the obvious rampant evidence of his desire.

And this time, this time, it would be different. Here, at the Springs, for the first time, he had all the time in the world to love her, all the privacy, all the comfort to lay her down and take her in luxury, in tenderness, wholly and completely . . .

She moved slowly to the bed, her mind crowded with sensual images of them together and what her life had been like long before Jesse had died. One more time, once more . . . In this context, where the atmosphere of pretense pervaded the room, it almost didn't matter who they were or what they were.

She could have loved him, she thought, as she knelt on the bed and untied her robe and slipped it off her shoulders. If she had ever known what it was to love. This wasn't love, either. She didn't know what it was. But it wasn't a pretense: the intense desire she felt for him was as real as anything she had experienced in her life.

Such a short life: Cassandra gone and Linnea taking her place, with all the thoughts, dreams, desires, and memories of Cassandra. She couldn't begin to think what might happen after she left this room. She only knew she would be leaving as soon after their tryst as possible.

She lay down on the bed, her head propped up on one arm. "So, Mr. Taggart, interest me in this morning's . . . activities." Amazing how she could say things, had been saying things that Cassandra never would have thought of; it really was a release to pretend to be someone else.

Where did a man start? She was wearing only her pristine white camisole and pantalettes and black stockings fastened just below the knee with a pair of intriguing lace garters. Her hair was in total disarray, wildly curling the way Cassandra habitually wore it, and her eyes deepened with sensual memories as she looked at him.

It was almost enough to have her lying there waiting for him, anticipating what was to come, remembering everything that had been.

She lifted her leg, angling it so that the enticing split in her pantalettes spread open to reveal what awaited his caress.

She watched his face. He never showed anything in his face: it was all in his eyes, and in the obvious elongation of his forceful, lusty manhood.

She felt her power. She was right. The power was all hers, and she could play games with him and tempt him to the breaking point, or she could open her arms to him and surrender completely without demanding anything but the raw power of his masculinity filling her with that pure, incandescent pleasure.

And yet there was pleasure in the chase as well.

She eased herself upright and slanted another provoking look at his bulging groin, and then slowly she slid the straps of her camisole off her shoulders to bare her naked breasts.

His light, bright eyes kindled with that sensuous light that was so entrancing to her. He knelt on the bed behind her and cupped her breasts in his hands, and his hands were so large they covered her breasts completely so that the hard, thrusting points of her nipples pressed tightly against the palms of his hands.

She leaned back against him and twisted her head to demand his kiss, and his possession of her mouth was as intense as if he had penetrated her body.

One of his hands released one breast and slowly slid down her belly to cup her seductive sex, easing into the silken recesses of her moist feminine fold to gently and firmly make himself felt as his fingers explored the lush intimacy of her.

She moved against his fingers, tight against his towering manhood, tight against the pleasure that threatened to inundate her body as he played with her taut nipple and the sweet, sweet spot of capitulation deep within her sultry sex.

She wanted it and she didn't want it — she wanted him, and whatever tumultuous climax he could command with the mere caress of his fingers would be nothing to what she could feel with his ultimate possession of her.

"So . . . interesting," she murmured against his lips, greedy for his kisses in a new and tormenting way because she knew this would be the last time, the last place. "Oh . . . but — don't . . ."

"No . . ." No, he didn't want to pleasure her in just that way, but she had spread her legs, and she was pushing against his fingers, and her kisses were wild with desire and he didn't want to stop; he just didn't want to take that one long moment. . . . "Yes . . ." How could he release her? He eased away from her, from her mouth, her breast, her wanton sex, and he guided her back onto the bed and then let her watch as he undressed himself and in turn watched her.

And there she was, her breasts taut and naked, her body naked and full of seductive promise, her lips swollen with his kisses, waiting for more, waiting for *him,* his caresses, his sex, her eyes blazing with desire as he slowly moved toward her.

She held out her arms, and he reached for her, levering himself down on her body, and he felt the whole sensation of her taking his weight as if this had been the one single thing for which she had been waiting.

She wrapped her arms around him, she wrapped her legs around him and thrust her hips against his hard driving manhood, lifting herself off the bed in a mute demand that was as old as Eve.

"Oh God — C . . . Linnea . . ." Lord, he had almost given the thing away. "Linnea —" He rolled her name around in his mouth as he kissed her, as he loved her body entreating him with its movement, its subtle sensual claim.

She never heard the slip; she was beyond hearing, she could only feel — the tight, hard weight of him, the long, thick, hard slide of his naked maleness against her belly, against her sex.

Oh, she was waiting for him, enthralled by the feel of him, lost in his kisses, in the sensual torment of waiting for him, and waiting.

And he waited to possess her, to draw out every last nuance of her passion until the ultimate moment when he poised himself directly at her velvet cleft, and with one luscious little push, he entered her sultry silken sheath, and came home.

And it was home and it was a promise, and she felt it, too, and as he shifted his body to possess her as deeply and fully as possible, she began to cry.

She felt him lick away her tears, take her lips, delve into her mouth; she felt him kiss her and position himself within her and she felt the roaring desire for completion with him and she began again the rhythmic shimmy of invitation to invite his deep carnal caress.

His world, his, and no one else's; he made a world for them of opulent sensual pleasure centered on the thick, torrid thrusts of his manhood and the deep, luscious, wet possession of his tongue.

She could have stayed that way with him forever. But the tumultuous sensations within her escalated; there was no stopping them, no stopping her body from its fathomless need.

She demanded; he gave, ceaselessly, tirelessly, unendingly. Her hands constricted in pinching little caresses all over his body; her stockinged feet caressed his back, his buttocks, and hooked into the backs of his knees to give her purchase to cant her body with him, against him, to gyrate freely with his forceful thrusts, and still she could not find completion.

She did not want completion: her climax would end everything, and she wanted the sensual slide to go on forever.

Her body told her differently. Her body bore down on his hard heat, seeking the end promise and her fulfillment. Her body wanted, her body gave and demanded in return. Her treacherous body knew when, just when, to give in, to let go, to give to him the mindless tempestuous pleasure his hard, driving body had given to her.

One subtle pumping of his hips and she found it—the keen edge of that elusive luminous rapture. And now there was no stopping her.

He sensed it, she vibrated with it. He drove into her relentlessly again and again and again, heightening the feeling, pulling it from her, compelling her to come, demanding her pleasure as the culmination of his.

And suddenly it was there, a torrent of dazzling sensation gushing from deep inside her, volcanic, devastating, an avalanche of surrender to his potent virility, to his power.

Like nothing she had ever felt before. Like nothing she would ever know after.

His clamoring body needed no other validation than her wild, keening cries, and her complete voluptuous submission to his inexorable masculinity. He couldn't prolong it, not for one second more: with one galvanic thrust, he gave himself up to his churning, explosive surrender to her.

Chapter Twenty-two

It was amazing how her mind immediately shifted into the problem at hand once Trane had removed himself from her presence.

She had time, there had been time to lie in his arms as he held her tightly in the tumultuous aftermath; and time to feel his passionate juices seep away from her body just the way she intended to make him seep out of her life.

But she needed time, too. She had to arrange for her train ticket and a carriage to take her to the station. She had to pack her Linnea-clothes and hide them away so he did not become suspicious, and she needed to find exactly the right ruse to divert him from finding out that she was heading out on her way home.

Home to Riveland . . .

. . . She missed it.

That stunning thought hit her as she was bathing later on that morning, after she had convinced Trane, following about a half hour's argument, that he must give her time to relax and bathe before she received him again. He hadn't wanted to go. She hadn't wanted to let him go. But the fact of Greve's telegram was like a piece of tinder in her pocket, ready to flare up with only her intentions to strike the flame.

She had to strike now. There was nothing in her way. The legalities were done and she could take her rightful place as her own legatee, free from restraints and conventions.

Two weeks in the Springs had opened her eyes to so many possibilities. And she could now take advantage of all of them. A widow of means was a very popular guest at any resort, at any convention. Her pursuit of pleasure would be hampered solely by her own discretion, her own impeccable taste.

She needed to return to Riveland only to set things in order there, to acquire her new overseer, to pretend to learn the basics of crop production so she could set things in motion for the succeeding year, and she would be free as a bird.

Her body tingled at the thought. Free . . . unencumbered, her barrenness a blessing now instead of a curse.

Yes, it was time.

And she would think of a nice, delicate way to delay Trane until she got ahead of him.

She felt she had to sneak out to the station to get a timetable and arrange a ticket, and that really felt like too much. There was a six o'clock train to Atlanta; she could stay overnight with her former landlady, she was sure of that, and continue on to Riveland the following morning.

Anything to get out of the Springs as soon as possible, because she was that close to succumbing to Trane Taggart's sensual aura, just as she had been at Riveland.

She couldn't; she just couldn't. What mattered was her autonomy; she had lived with Jesse Taggart for eight long, abusive years never even envisioning the kind of union possible between two people.

She would store the memories, and that was all.

Easy words, hard to do, with her ticket in her pocket and Trane's glimmering gaze making love to her all over

391

again.

The feelings just seemed never that far from the surface. A word, a look, triggered them instantly, and her swelling desire almost overwhelmed her.

She couldn't let go of sanity. Sanity was Riveland, a home, a base from which she could leave and come back all of her own free will. Sanity was the wherewithal to do the things she wanted to do without limitations. Sanity was burying Cassandra Taggart, who had had a short and miserable life to begin with.

Sanity was *not* falling in love with the sensuality of Trane Taggart.

She met him for high tea, a late afternoon lunch, with half her plot already in hand, her bags safely stored at the desk of the Whitestone Hotel, and the bill fairly paid until the following morning.

"Mr. Taggart."

"Mrs. Wiltshire. Won't you join me?"

His simple, innocent-sounding words were so inciting. "I'd love to," she murmured, taking the chair opposite him that an observant waiter rushed to pull out for her. She meant it, too; the only thing she saw or felt when she looked at his all-knowing eyes was his lusty masculinity. She could hardly concentrate on anything else. It was as if there were some aura around him, drawing all that was potently feminine in her to the towering maleness of him.

It was too overpowering in daylight and in such a small place as a hotel refreshment room.

She couldn't think of having much more than tea or coffee and some thinly sliced toast and scones. He ordered the same, and she lost her appetite completely.

Everything started to turn around on her. She didn't want to leave him. The thought was unbearable. In this neutral place, she could be anything she wanted, and he could be her lover.

He *was* her lover, with all that implied, and life did

not turn on her sensual needs. Beyond the Springs, there was another life, one made up of seasons and work, intentions and ambitions. She had those; she had had them once, and she was almost willing to relinquish everything if she could stay at the Springs and wallow in the sensual maelstrom of his lovemaking.

Almost.

There had to be other men, eligible men somewhere, sometime, and she would meet them when she was fully, formally, and legally Linnea Wiltshire, mistress of Riveland.

Until then, she must not let the likes of Trane Taggart pull her down into the morass of her own repressed feeling. He had tapped something in her she had never been aware of, and she saw that, in gratitude, she might have stayed with him forever.

"Ah, the tea," she said, more in command of herself now. What were words, after all? She could choose whether they affected her or not. She just would not let him stir her up anymore.

But he hadn't said a word. He took his coffee and set it aside and just watched her as she edgily put sugar in her tea and broke apart a small piece of toasted bread and put it in her mouth.

"It's almost time for you to go back to Riveland," he said suddenly.

She jumped. "Why no, Mr. Taggart; whatever gave you that idea? I believe Mr. Greve is going to notify me when all is in readiness."

"Oh, was that the plan?" He stirred the coffee idly without having added anything to it. "I'm happy to have the pleasure of your company, then, Linnea."

Oh, the words . . . Well, she could play too. "You gratify me, Mr. Taggart."

"You don't know how that satisfies *me*," he returned in kind. "Our mutual fulfillment in each other's company is all too rare."

393

"It tempts one to want to explore this fruitful friendship much more deeply, does it not, Mr. Taggart?"

"It is my passionate desire to probe every inch of it, Mrs. Wiltshire."

"What an alluring thought. I'm open to suggestions, Mr. Taggart."

"You understand my thrust exactly, Mrs. Wiltsire."

"I pride myself on grasping the situation immediately, sir."

"And you hold on tightly to the essential point, ma'am."

"And I'm not afraid to bear down on you when necessary."

"A most penetrating observation, ma'am."

"It comes so easily," she murmured.

"I believe you've come right to the point, ma'am."

"I've spread *my* cards on the table, Mr. Taggart," she said, just a little testily now because he was getting to her and he knew it. She didn't know words could be as powerful as caresses—but he did, and she had to put an end to this foolishness before she capitulated again.

"What a ravishing idea, Mrs. Wiltshire. Where would you like me to take you?"

"Dear Mr. Taggart: I don't want to hold you up much longer."

"You could never prolong things too long, ma'am."

There was a note in his voice when he said that, and she looked at him closely; she could detect nothing. His face, as always, was impassive. Only his eyes reflected the living comment of his thoughts. His eyes glittered with enjoyment at their wordplay, and something more.

Something she had to use, and she felt a stabbing pang of regret that everything would end here, now, and with this, because she knew exactly what she had to do, and how she must elude him.

"Till tonight, then?" she whispered, crossing her fingers, hoping perhaps that he would insist they meet sooner because she did want—she did want . . .

No, she wanted other things *more*.

"Are you sure?" Oh, no games now, just wicked need that matched her own. But the waiting, that would be part of the game, too, she thought. And the culmination would be the ultimate surprise.

"I like to draw things out as long as possible," she murmured.

"Then it will give you the deepest satisfaction to know I can fulfill this desire too, Mrs. Wiltshire. When do you want me to come?"

She couldn't bear it any longer. She had to leave him. She stood up almost imperiously. "I would like to see you come at six o'clock, sir."

"I will be pleased to present myself to you then," he said agreeably, and took her hand as she held it out. "Linnea . . ."

"Shhh." If he said another word, she would scream. He knew what he was saying, every last word calculated to titillate and arouse her, and she was.

"Tonight . . ."

She ran—not from the refreshment room—but once she was out in the lobby, she positively fled the hotel altogether and deliberately lost herself in the crowd on the promenade.

She knew what she had to do; she couldn't hesitate a minute, she couldn't let the seductive thought of sensual gratification get in her way. There was only one more step to accomplish and she would be well on her journey home before anyone discovered she had gone.

Trane sat at the table in the refreshment room for a long, long time. He couldn't move, he couldn't stand up, he couldn't assuage anything, especially the gnawing physical hunger that he felt for Cassandra.

Tonight—the thought of it made his blood pound.

What a woman, what a liar, cheat, impostor. So, what had he accomplished by his artful seduction of her? She had wound her coils more tightly around him.

He didn't know if he ever wanted to escape, or if it mattered a damn what she was and what she had done.

Cassandra . . .

Cassandra who touched him, Cassandra who begged for his touch, Cassandra with whom he might make a life in a place where a life with another person had never been possible.

Cassandra alive and writhing with unbridled passion beneath him, wanting him, seeking him, demanding everything from him. Cassandra . . .

He wanted Cassandra. Everything else was secondary to that.

Eventually, he was able to leave the refreshment room, but not until five cups of coffee and two plates of dainty, thin-sliced toast had been added to his bill, and his rampaging manhood finally stopped reacting to the thought of Cassandra.

They would have a long, private evening alone, far away from the festivities of the streets and the hotels. They would have a little isolated world of their own, and he would build it around them word by word, caress by caress, kiss by kiss.

He had things to occupy himself until the time arrived that he would go to Cassandra. Another suit at the tailor's, a long, leisurely bath. an hour in his own bed to revitalize his energy.

The room was too small to contain him; the bed was barely large enough.

Cassandra . . . her name throbbed in his thoughts like a primitive drumbeat. Cassandra . . .

At five-thirty he was dressed, impatient to see her, to touch her, to kiss her.

His rooms were a brisk ten-minute walk away from the Whitestone Hotel, and as he handed his key to his concierge, he was handed a note.

From Cassandra.

"I await you. The door is unlocked."

Oh, yes.

He envisioned her waiting, and it heightened his own sense of anticipation as he made his way quickly to her hotel.

The rear garden seemed positively crowded with people this night. He felt the familiar frustration at how hard it was to find a private place and time alone. Everywhere there were couples in the throes of a flirtation, hiding in the discreet shadows of the covered walkway, kissing under the overhang of the doors of the cottage suites.

It seemed as if it took him forever to get to Cassandra's door, and he knocked lightly before he turned the doorknob.

There was no answer. He pushed the door open slowly. He had to remember to call to Linnea — tricky when he had been thinking all day of Cassandra. "Linnea . . ." A whisper. The room was dark, and he wondered at it until he saw the curving form of Cassandra, a dark shadow waiting for him in her bed.

He closed the door behind him carefully and made his way to the bed. She was closest to the window, and he knelt on the opposite edge. "Linnea . . ."

He reached out his hand to touch her hip and he was blasted backwards by an explosive movement. *"What the hell . . . ?"*

A *man's* voice. "What the hell do you think you're doing?"

"Who the hell are you?" Trane ground out, picking himself up from the floor and groping for the kerosene lamp on a nearby dresser. "Where is . . . Mrs. Wiltshire?"

"My dear sir, I was about to ask you the same thing," the indignant male voice retorted as the lamp flared into light.

They stared at each other. "Mr. Upjohn, sir," the stranger said.

"Mr. Taggart. I was to meet Mrs. Wiltshire here to-night."

"As was I, sir, as was I."

"Bloody hell!" Trane exploded, resisting the urge to pick up the incensed little puppy and toss him out on his ear. "Goddamn hell." There weren't enough words in the language for him to vent his rage at this betrayal. He knew with a surety what she had done and where she had gone, and he was smarting because he had been so gullible, so utterly oblivious to anything but her enticing, sensual body.

He was a goddamned fool, but no more so than she: she thought she had gotten away with something, the black-widow bitch. He couldn't wait to see her face when she set foot on Riveland.

It was an easy matter to get there before her. It was imperative that he show up long before she did, and it was no problem to discover which train she had taken and when she would arrive in Atlanta. She had elected the wrong timetable, he thought. He was going to be at Riveland to meet her at the door, and then the fireworks would start.

It was the only thing that kept him going through the anguish of her betrayal.

It kept him going through the unending night as he rode down the turnpikes and highways of Virginia and Tennessee, bedding down only when he was so tired he could not keep his eyes open, or when he needed a fresh mount.

She would have to stay in Atlanta overnight because she would get in too late to hire a carriage to take her down to Carthage.

He could keep traveling straight through; he had nothing to encumber him but his saddle roll in which he had packed the stiff, stuffy suits he had been forced to purchase in the Springs. He wondered bitterly if he would have any reason ever to wear them again.

Maybe he would. Maybe he would need them to attend the funeral of Linnea Wiltshire the first when she walked into Riveland and beheld the existence of the second.

The closer to home she got, the more frenetic she felt. Nothing had gone quite right, and she could only hope that Mr. Upjohn and Trane had not killed each other in the course of discovering that she had cleverly arranged that ruse and eluded them both.

Well, too late for regrets now. The problem was her arrival in Atlanta was so late, she found it almost impossible to find transportation to her former boarding-house, and it was inexcusably late to rouse her landlady and beg her indulgence and a room for the night.

Nonetheless, she did it. It was possible that Trane could have gotten to Atlanta before her and had made the rounds of the hotels, hoping to root her out before she got back to Riveland. Anything was possible.

Unless she was making too much of how much he seemed to want her.

Anything was possible. He surely wouldn't want her now.

Mrs. Waters, once she had got over the irritation of being called from her bed, and having finally recognized her, was most accommodating. "I would not have known you, Mrs. Taggart. You learned your lessons well."

"Yes," she said, taking a deep breath and inhaling the scents and sounds that had become so familiar to her over the course of the several weeks she had spent there. "Money is a great motivator, Mrs. Waters, as you well know. I need a room for one night."

"You have it," Mrs Waters said, mentally extending her own hand.

And after that, it was easy. Easier. She was given a hearty breakfast in the morning, in her room, and she made sure to pay for it handsomely before she left. She was given a luxurious bath and help with dressing, and she paid luxuriously for that, too, but she didn't mind at all. Linnea Wiltshire was generous with old friends who had helped her in the past.

At ten o'clock, a carriage rolled up in front of the boardinghouse door and a deferential driver loaded her trunks and settled her comfortably within; she was willing to pay extravagantly for that service as well.

She sent word, before she left, to Mr. Greve that she would be arriving at Riveland late that afternoon and that she would be pleased to receive him at his convenience.

And the words meant nothing except that she was one step closer to officially taking over Riveland and all it entailed.

She had missed it, and when, later that afternoon, the carriage finally came in view of the boundaries of Riveland, she was surprised at the emotion she felt.

She had always wanted to escape it, and now she willingly came home into its embrace.

Her carriage turned up the drive and she marveled at how different everything looked to her now.

Or perhaps she had never really noticed how everything looked to her when she was so engrossed in trying to run away from it.

Well, now she understood. Now Riveland embodied all of her dreams and the freedom to make them all come true.

But she had to remember things; she had been away

two weeks and she had grown careless. Imagine forgetting her gloves. She could say she had a recurrence of the skin condition she thought the waters had healed. She must remember the accent, and to distance herself from everything and everyone on Riveland. She must remember her pencils and rouge and apply them more carefully and every day; she must remember the color in her hair, to freshen it every several days.

She rooted around for a pair of gloves to put on before she reached the house. It wasn't only Trane's perceptive gaze she was afraid of; Zilpha, too, knew her as well as anyone did, and Zilpha was damned suspicious already.

It was best to carry through all these little details, and then to relinquish them one by one. If anyone ever realized that she was not Linnea, he would find it out way too late to do anything about it.

She had successfully convinced Trane, and he was the one who worried her the most. Everything else should be easy.

As her carriage barreled up the drive, she thought of the coming months and all that lay ahead. In the waning days of summer and the early weeks of September, she and Zilpha would begin taking stock of stores, begin to work on stockings and winter clothes for the workers, and in addition, they would make soap and dip vast supplies of candles. They would scald the beds to get rid of bedbugs, and they would make sure every pot and pan in the kitchen was scrubbed and cleaned. Zilpha attended to making the quilts, a chore for which Elsie as well had an uncommon talent, and they would restuff mattresses and harvest the late potatoes and butcher meat and salt it up to preserve it for winter.

They did not spin their own material; she had put her foot down about that, and so she was sure that among the supplies that should have arrived from Vecsey's on her standard order, she would find the usual food staples and medicinal items as well as a dozen bolts of material from which to cut clothing.

But—she caught herself up—Linnea would not know about these things. Linnea would be asking advice and allowing her servants to teach her the order of maintaining Riveland until she was versed enough to take control.

How was she ever going to remember *not* to lift her hand with the knowledge of how the thing should be done and still remain Linnea?

She bit her lips as she thought of all the ramifications of assuming this new identity. She really had not thought it through as thoroughly as she should have.

She still would have taken Linnea's identity; she just would have done it a little differently, would have planned it a lot better so that she would not get caught in these little traps for which she was not prepared.

Now she must take everything as it came at her and somehow wriggle her way around the fact that she knew things Linnea would not know, or that she had experience which had never been part of Linnea's life.

She absolutely *had* to remember the accent.

And now Riveland came in sight, pristine in the late afternoon sun, columned, balconied, the stuff of her worst nightmares and her most uninhibited dreams.

What would Riveland be to her now?

Riveland would be her sanctuary, true and sweet, and no one could wrest it from her ever again.

Zilpha kept watch at the window all morning.

Linnea was to stay upstairs in Cassandra's refurbished bedroom until Elsie signaled that she was to make herself known.

Trane paced the hallway in a fury that still had not abated after two whole days and nights.

"Carriage comin', Mr. Trane."

"Fine."

"You sure dis be de missus?"

"I'm sure," he said tersely. Oh, he was in a fine rage. He couldn't wait to catch her out, to see the expression on her face when Linnea came down the stairs. He felt like he was living a fairy tale, and he had only to wave his magic wand to transform Linnea into Cassandra and to give Linnea back the life that Cassandra had taken.

She had been living a fairy tale, he thought, and now, as in all good stories, the consequences must be met.

"Carriage done stop, Mr. Trane."

He stopped his pacing and moved to Zilpha's side by the parlor window where she was peering out from behind the lacy curtain. And there was the treacherous Cassandra-Linnea in her smart traveling dress of brown grenadine. There was a little hat jammed down on her smoothed-out curls, and the face was exactly the same as it had been at the Springs: free of care, perfectly content to play the role she had chosen for it.

The conscientious driver who had helped her out of the carriage now lifted her trunks, one at a time, and brought them to the door, and she followed, picking her way daintily up the steps.

"Missus done come," Zilpha said, as the bell sounded loudly in the entrance hallway.

Trane nodded. "Answer the door, Zilpha."

"I don' like it."

"Cassandra has come home, Zilpha."

"Yes sir, Mr. Trane." She was compliant, but her back was stiff as she exited the room.

From beyond the parlor, he heard Cassandra's excited fluty voice exclaiming over how good it was to finally come home.

And he heard Zilpha's voice: "I call Ojim to take yo bags, ma'am."

And Cassandra's voice, urgent and low, and Zilpha's emotionless response: "Yes, ma'am, Mr. Trane done come back, round 'bout two days ago."

Cassandra said, "I see."

"And another visitor done come, ma'am."

"Oh, really? Mr. Greve?" she asked hopefully.

"No, ma'am."

"Well, who is it?" she demanded impatiently. What a time for Zilpha to be playing games with her!

"Yo' visitor comin' now, ma'am," Zilpha said, and turned her eyes up the steps.

Cassandra's gaze followed hers. A woman was walking slowly down the stairs, a woman with long, streaming blond hair, slender, sharp . . .

"Oh my God," she whispered. "Linnea . . ."

And then she whirled to face Trane, lounging in the parlor doorframe, his face grim, and his eyes revealing that he had known everything.

Chapter Twenty-three

"I don't think you make a creditable Linnea," her sister said critically when she reached the bottom step.

"I suppose I don't," Cassandra said tightly. "How are you, Linnea?"

"I don't know, sister dear. How *am* I?" Linnea shot back. She was absolutely nonplussed by Cassandra's appearance and by the rigid stance of the man behind her watching from the parlor door. They were all mad, she thought, even Cassandra. It was all due to years of isolation on a huge plantation with nothing to do but direct slaves to plant and hoe and harvest cotton. It had to be enough to drive anyone to lunacy.

"Not happy," Cassandra retorted; she felt like her brain was divided in two, the one side assessing and understanding that it was her sister standing before her and that Tranc had used her with the full and complete knowledge that she was not Linnea; and the other part of it coolly evaluating her loss in terms of her freedom, her autonomy, her life. She wondered if she wished Linnea had never been born.

No. . . . She reached out her hands toward Linnea. "Linnea . . ."

Her sister grasped her hands. "I'm here."

"I'm glad. Really."

Linnea shook her head.

"We have to talk," Cassandra said, squeezing Linnea's hands for want of something to do. "It's been a long trip. . . ."

"So Mr. Taggart said."

"Oh yes, the duplicitous Mr. Taggart. How are you, Trane?"

"As well as can be expected, dear guileless Cassandra, after my run-in with a deceitful impostor, an irate popinjay, a duplicate sister and a wall of flames. Truly, I think I've come out of this debacle with my sanity intact, and there is something to be said for that."

"Yes," Cassandra murmured, "you would know a lot about impostors and popinjays, wouldn't you?"

"All of us are here under false pretenses, darling Cassandra. I have nothing to hide."

"Oh, there is a challenge if ever I heard one, Trane Taggart."

"I expect you to take it up, Cassandra."

"Yes, it certainly is a different kettle of fish than where you might take *me*," she said tauntingly. "But there is time for that, is there not? There's time for everything now." She turned back to Linnea. "You have to excuse me. This really is a shock, and I need some time to get my thoughts and myself together. Zilpha?"

"Missus?"

"My room?"

"Mr. Trane done ordered fo' to fix it. Ever'thing just as you remember, Missus."

She wheeled around to face Trane once again. *"Why?"*

"It seemed fitting, ma'am," he said tersely, and his tone did not brook any discussion of the matter at all. To him, the fire and the destruction of her room seemed a lifetime ago, and would never be connected with the temptress of the Springs. That was another episode to be relegated to the status of a dream, a hard lesson learned by a man who thought he had learned them all a long time ago.

She shook her head; she felt like her head was about ready to topple off her shoulders, and it wasn't because she had been so just and righteous. Maybe usurping another person's life deserved some kind of retribution, and maybe she would have to pay for the rest of her life.

She would figure it out when she got upstairs to the privacy of her room.

But still, it seemed strange to be climbing the steps to enter the place she had deliberately set to go up in flames.

It was as if nothing had happened there. Everything had been repaired, repainted, restructured and refinished. There wasn't a trace of charring or the scent of the burning.

She threw herself down on her bed and started to cry.

Mr. Greve came the following day. Zilpha knocked on her door to announce his arrival. *She* had not left the room the whole day or night. She hadn't wanted to eat, but she did see Linnea long enough to hear an abbreviated version of her story; she couldn't face Trane. She had enough common sense to realize she despised him for ruining her plans, devious though they were, and she hated him for making love to her and pretending she was Linnea when he had known the truth.

How could she know in a million years that Linnea would turn up on her doorstep, looking like a waif and destitute to boot. How Raylene would have crowed with triumph that Linnea's high-flown marriage had come to nothing and she now had to throw herself on the mercy of her family.

How complicated could things get?

But there was still Mr. Greve and all the explanations attendant on retracting her claim to Linnea's inheritance. And the probable end result of that, she thought dolefully, would be that Linnea would try to kill her to get hold of it.

Why not? Everything else had gone wrong.

"This is really quite astonishing," Mr. Greve said, almost falling into the chair behind him.

"No, it isn't," Cassandra said. "To all intents and purposes, Mr. Greve, I have committed a crime. And now I'm resurrected from the dead and you must withdraw all those papers you filed on Linnea's behalf, and I suppose my sister must decide whether she will have me arrested."

"Cassandra—" Linnea protested.

"Remarkable," Mr. Greve murmured. "How thorough you were, Miz Taggart. I had no doubts."

"No, I wanted to make sure you didn't," she said. "Linnea?"

"I refuse to talk about this, Cassandra. I know nothing about it, and I don't want to know anything about it. All I can see is you changed the color of your hair in some ungodly way, and that is all."

"Mr. Greve?"

"I will withdraw the papers, and all conditions and restrictions will be reinstated as per Mr. Taggart's instructions," he said stiffly. He did not know what else to do: he could not prosecute on any firm ground while the real Linnea was living at Riveland protesting she knew nothing of a conspiracy to defraud Jesse's estate.

But the cleverness of the plain-speaking Miz Taggart was something else to be reckoned with. He never would have dreamed she could concoct such a scheme, *and* take him in with it. He was more annoyed with himself than anyone, for even believing a word of it. He just couldn't understand, seeing them together, how he could have been so completely misled.

That spoke all too clearly to Miz Taggart's deceitfulness, and it was plain to him that she must be carefully watched, lest she attempt something of a like nature to get control of her husband's fortune again.

"I think that is all I have to say," Cassandra told him.

"I suppose there is nothing left to say," Mr. Greve said pettishly. He really wished there were; she should not be allowed to get away with such an impersonation. Nor should she have been allowed to remove all that money from Jesse's accounts merely to satisfy a whim to try to coerce the whole from his hands. He was really put out by her audaciousness. "I don't suppose you have any of that money left," he threw out at her suddenly.

She stiffened. "I have enough, Mr. Greve, although I fail to see why it is any of your business — still."

"We disagree on that point, Miz Taggart, and I see that it is time for me to take my leave."

"I appreciate your coming so promptly, Mr. Greve."

"Miz Taggart — Mrs. Wiltshire." He looked down into the great green eyes of Cassandra's sister, and he thought his heart melted, just a little. She was a sad woman, Mrs. Wiltshire. If she had ever had her sister's spirit, it was gone now.

"What a pompous man," Linnea said when Mr. Greve had exited the room.

"Yes, and he wields his authority like a sledgehammer," Cassandra said. "He will only hold this little incident against me, as he has held everything against me since I took control of Riveland. It is the one thing over which he has no say-so by the terms of Jesse's will, especially now that we are graced with Mr. Trane Taggart's presence. That has been both a bane and a blessing to me. But it has come to the point where I must weigh whether it is more difficult to deal with Mr. Taggart or Mr. Greve, and I do believe Mr. Greve is winning on that score."

"You talk too much," Linnea said. "You never used to."

"No, I never did. I had eight years of imposed silence as Jesse Taggart's wife, and I haven't stopped talking since he died. Now please, Linnea, let me show you Riveland, which is going to be your home."

She did not protest this, because she was more curious than Cassandra would ever know. She felt as though intrigue swirled around her and there were secrets locked behind every door, and while her own life had been open and tragic, Cassandra's was romantic and gothic, and she wanted to share it and be a part of it.

The house was opulently furnished, if not a little worn, and the bedrooms, as she had already seen, were plainly decorated as rooms that would not be seen by company. "And besides," Cassandra elaborated, "Jesse had no family or friends to visit, only the occasional partner in some kind of business, so he didn't need fancy bedrooms to accommodate guests.

"We didn't used to have a garden either here. I just started that. Jesse would not have wasted money on seed for crops he could not sell. So we raised an abundance of corn and potatoes, and I am very happy to have some variety finally in our meals.

"There are a hundred slaves more or less, about three-quarters of them working the fields, and the others in the house or taking care of the grounds. If there is anything you want, you have only to ask Zilpha and she will attend to it.

"Everything else comes under my care and control. The house servants and I take care of everything concerning daily living, and, as you will see later, I keep charge of the stores and dispense medication and the like. You will also see that the work of Riveland is ongoing. We've pulled in the cotton crop that was planted a year and a half ago, and we seeded for the year after next already. And there is another field to be harvested next summer that was planted last year. We've brought in two corn crops, not counting what the slaves have harvested in their gardens. And two crops of potatoes. I've brought in turkeys and have ordered chickens—Jesse never saw the sense of that and I expect to expand next summer, depending on what this year's cotton brings.

"We didn't used to do anything extraneous, and Jesse would put most of the profit from the cotton back into improving the Riveland strain. Of course that left no room for anything else; I have chosen not to live like that, and I guess that is obvious."

"But at least your husband's wealth was his to give," Linnea said.

"Yes, and he tied it up in knots so that no one could untangle it—and no one would want to. I was moved by desperation, Linnea."

She couldn't see it. *She,* Linnea, knew what desperation was: it was being cold and hungry on the London docks with nowhere to go and no money in your pocket. It was being cast aside by your husband's family as if you did not exist, and being told there was nothing for you and your only choice was to leave. It was traveling for a month on a cheap steamer with every man in sight after a glimpse of your drawers and maybe something more, if you would accept payment for your favors. *That* was desperation, and she had no conception of what the wealthy, pampered Mrs. Taggart was talking about.

But she kept quiet. There really was nothing to say that Cassandra had not been as desperate as she, and she didn't even have to make any judgments about that. All she had to do was take in the full prospect of all Cassandra had meant to claim—in *her* name. It stirred something deep inside her, a corrosive abiding resentment, and she didn't even try to clamp down on it: she began to nurture it.

"In any event, we produce a good-quality cotton. I daresay we've shipped about forty or fifty bales so far this season. There are two grades—prime and not prime—and the one of course commands the higher price. After Jesse died, I didn't know how I was going to get the pick out of the field and to market, but we did it. Trane took over and, I must be fair, it got done and in perfect time."

"And he is Jesse's son?"

Cassandra didn't hesitate for a moment. "He is *not* Jesse's son. Jesse couldn't have children, as no one knows better than I. Nor could I, for that matter. I don't know who Mr. Taggart is, but he is *not* Jesse's son."

Linnea knelt by her mother's grave in much the same

411

manner that Cassandra had that long-ago day two weeks before when she had returned to Riveland in the guise of her sister.

"Oh Mother, how you would enjoy the events that have transpired since your death," she murmured. "You would have seen Cassandra triumph and Linnea fall by the wayside, and you would have been so happy that my elopement with Mr. Wiltshire turned into dust. But you lived to enjoy the fruits of Cassandra's marriage to Mr. Taggart, and that must have made you so happy."

"She was never happy," Cassandra said. "She was afraid of losing her youth and beauty, and in the end, all of it was claimed by disease. She was never happy."

"Maybe none of us were," Linnea said, linking her arm with Cassandra's as they walked away from the burial hill. "Maybe none of us is meant to be."

But I was, Cassandra thought, for one long, crazy moment when I thought Trane Taggart was possible.

She didn't say that; she hardly dared think it. Trane was still something to be dealt with, but he was busy running his workers ragged with the tail end of the pick, and harvesting potatoes and still more corn to be sent downriver with the second-grade bales of cotton. He wasn't the least bit interested in the scheming Cassandra Taggart. He had well and truly paid her back for the dastardly trick she had pulled.

"But still, Cassandra, he is a lovely-looking man," Linnea said to her one afternoon when they had gone to the fields to observe the workers harvest the end crop of cotton.

"Is he? I hadn't noticed," Cassandra said with what she hoped was true indifference in her tone.

"You can't fool me," Linnea said, and Cassandra threw up her hands.

"*How* am I trying to fool you?"

"You're telling me that man has been living on Riveland for five months and you haven't *noticed* him?"

Was notice the right word? To the point, as it were?

"Well, now you do sound like the Linnea I remember," Cassandra said evasively.

"Yes, I think you have," Linnea continued, slanting a penetrating look at Cassandra's impassive face. "I hate that hair, my dear. It's going to be red-gold forever until that coloring grows out, and I wager your Mr. Taggart noticed you more when you were blond."

"This discussion has no basis in reality," Cassandra said, refusing to bite at the bait. "I think you have noticed him very well, my dear sister, and I invite you to try to interest him in *your* charms."

"But he's such a hard man," Linnea demurred.

Isn't he though? "He has a softer side," Cassandra said staunchly. *And I wish you would discover it and make him want you and take him away from Riveland.*

No, I don't. . . .

"He will take his meals with us," Cassandra went on, "and you will get to know him better." *And I can keep my eye on him better . . .*

"That isn't usual, is it?"

"No, but the man who claims to be Jesse Taggart's son must have some residual rights, don't you think?"

"Or else you want to know what he is doing every hour of the day."

Cassandra smiled. "Oh no, dear sister, I only want you to have the full experience of our family life."

It wasn't family life—it was daggers drawn, Linnea reflected at dinner that night. Trane Taggart was clearly a very unhappy man, and Cassandra was pretending to be righteous.

Well, he was really quite delicious, with that height and that rich, deep voice and that drawl; formal clothes became him. He looked elegant—an untamed lion in restraints.

Cassandra really must take another good, long, hard look at him. Who would not want a lion in her bedroom,

413

in her bed? Cassandra wouldn't — she would probably read him a book. That much hadn't changed, she had noted.

Cassandra was a good deal more imperious now, however, and she obviously liked to boss people around, but after all, Cassandra had been a child when she, Linnea, had gone to England. Maybe it was true, maybe Cassandra did know what desperation was — or maybe it had been her mother's desperation that had promoted a marriage with the older and presumably imprudent Jesse Taggart. Why would such a man marry someone like Cassandra, with no money and nothing to recommend her but her youth?

She felt a little pang of resentment that her own mother could not have engineered such a match for her, but that was really water over the dam now. Raylene would have said she had made and messed up her own bed. It was pure luck that she was still young enough to take a second chance.

Mr. Taggart looked awfully good from where she sat.

It was the look on his face that was rather disquieting. And he couldn't keep his eyes off Cassandra.

She couldn't tell if he were in thrall or in hate. But did it matter? A man was a man, and if Cassandra didn't want him, she was more than willing to take her place in what she considered was a perfectly fair exchange.

Cassandra was feeling like a soul in limbo. Linnea was like her own ghost haunting her. She didn't quite know what to do with her, and it was simpler just to let her rest and recuperate than to try to find a way to ease her into the ever-ongoing work at Riveland.

As the days wore on, however, Linnea started to become the same bossy older sister that Cassandra remembered. And she had gotten hold of one idea between her teeth and was gnawing it to death: Cassandra needed a man on Riveland, and Mr. Taggart was the ideal candidate.

Cassandra in turn was toying with how she was going to dismiss Trane and hire a new overseer, and she deplored having to discuss all over again the wretched restrictions of Jesse's will.

Except that Linnea kept pushing. "Jesse's son, Cassandra . . . how ideal—he grew up here, he's running things already . . . and you have no proof whatsoever that he is not Jesse's son except that you and Jesse had no children."

And then of course she could not tell Linnea about the strongbox and the piece of paper with the name Cole Trager written on it plain as day.

She began wearing the key to her own double-locked strongbox around her neck. And she began encouraging Linnea to pursue Trane. It was the only solution. Whoever he was, whatever he was, he had to leave Riveland, and soon—and if he could take Linnea with him, she would be a whole lot happier.

"Mr. Taggart has his own secrets, Linnea dear. I would be very happy if you were the one who ferreted them out."

"Would you, dear Cassandra?"

"Truly."

"I'd love to."

No, that didn't make her any happier.

She wasn't even going to pretend that her Trane Taggart had a wife and children anymore. She would just tell him out and out over the dinner table:

"I'm going to ask Vecsey's to hire a new overseer."

She didn't expect his explosive response.

"No you're not."

"I beg your pardon?"

"I said no, you're not."

"And why won't I, Mr. Taggart?"

He smiled at her, that same odd little smile which now infuriated her. "Because I'm doing a damned fine job, ma'am."

"It's so true," Linnea said, and Cassandra shot her a baleful look. But what had she expected, when she herself had validated Linnea's interest? "You want to think about that more carefully, Cassandra dear."

"I'm thinking," Cassandra retorted through gritted teeth; nothing was working out the way she had thought it would. What use was that damned strongbox key if she couldn't even find a reason to use it against him?

Everyone believed he was Jesse's son, and where did that leave her? He had a right to be on Riveland, but it went only so far. Besides, no one else's sense of propriety had to be served. No one was watching to see just how she would treat Trane Taggart. No one cared.

So she would write the letter anyway, and see just how Trane was going to combat her right to have whomever she chose running her plantation.

Linnea, however, was being sympathetic to the extreme — to Trane. Cassandra would find her hanging over fences watching him work, or waylaying him before he entered the dining room, so that he was forced to sit next to her.

If he were a suspicious man, he thought, he would definitely have concluded that it was a plot of Cassandra's to make him crazy so that he would leave of his own volition. Linnea was becoming a pest in the short space of less than a week, and he had never known another woman who had ever made him feel that way.

Damn her, Cassandra was enjoying the whole thing, too. Every night at dinner she just sat there and watched him squirm under Linnea's direct questions and boldly insinuating comments.

Old spider lady just spinning those webs and getting madder and madder because she hadn't caught him yet.

He didn't intend to get caught, either. And he wasn't going to let a little complication like Linnea Wiltshire trip him up along the way. A man had plans, and when things didn't work out one way, he made them work another. A man had to be adaptable, and pitch with whichever way the wind was blowing. A man had to land on his feet — just like a cat.

And a woman who had tricked and deceived a man every which way she could think of should not have been so annoyed to see her sister positively throwing herself at him, Cassandra thought irritatedly. Linnea was man-crazy, always had been. She could not have loved Jonathan Wiltshire so much if she was willing to let an overseer take his place. And all of that at Cassandra's instigation.

She didn't know why she was so annoyed about it. Maybe it was because she had so little to do that wasn't concerned with the usual household tasks. How could a person become interested in cutting patterns and dipping candles when everything was so upset around her?

She went back to riding as a means of breaking up the monotony of her day. At least this way, she could keep an eye on what Linnea was doing, and if she were getting too out of hand, she would just insist that Linnea must undertake some regular chores of her own.

She would insist on it anyway.

She could not let Linnea feel that she was a permanent guest at Riveland. Every indigent relative who came to live with a family understood, without being told, that she was under the obligation to perform some specific duty in the household. How much in debt to her must she be in order to repay Linnea for using her name and usurping her life?

She did suppose she owed Linnea something, but how far did her obligation have to extend? As far as watching Linnea driving alone to the far fields with the express purpose of seeing Trane?

She did love the freedom that riding gave her. She needed no escort to ride the tracks and roads of Riveland once she regained her seat. She could range all over the plantation, slowly at first, without anyone having to drive her or keep watch where she went. Yes, that was the best part—the freedom to go wherever she wanted to.

She hadn't necessarily intended to go where Linnea would turn up. The first time they both shrugged it off as an accident and they both sat and watched Trane at work, stripped to the waist and bronzed from the sun, while he paid no attention whatsoever to either of them.

"There is something to be said for the more earthly delights," Linnea murmured, her eyes fastened on Trane like a limpet who never intended to let go. "But of course, you only know of such things from your books, isn't it so, Cassandra? Surely you did not have a fleshly relationship with Mr. Taggart?"

"My dear Linnea, the marriage bed is the marriage bed, as you yourself well know. Still, those earthly delights cannot compensate for an empty pocket, isn't that so?" Cassandra shot back a trifle disagreeably.

"Why, do you know—one never gave those things equal weight, dear sister. But I see now how it was with you."

"And we know *very* well how it was with you," Cassandra retorted.

"Yes," Linnea sighed. "But things have gotten appreciably better, and if you can't see that, Cassandra dear, I wish you would find someplace else to go where you can be disagreeable and negative. I'm enjoying myself here much too much."

Poor, dear, baffled Linnea had found her own ground wonderfully fast, Cassandra reflected venomously. It made *her* that much more determined to keep an eye on her sister *and* Trane as well.

She hated herself, but the next day, she was out on that horse once again, and she only needed to be a distance away where Linnea could not see her in order to perceive exactly the state of things between Linnea and Trane.

Linnea was talking a lot.

Trane seemed to be listening. A lot.

She hated him.

She had sent the letter to Vecsey's and she was awaiting a reply. She watched for it every day. She *yearned* for it, because she wanted so badly to expose Trane's secrets and get him away from Riveland for once and all.

Impostor against impostor. It seemed only fitting. It seemed exactly right.

Chapter Twenty-four

It was another one of those mornings: the air was thick with portent; everyone was busy—too busy—and Linnea was nowhere to be found.

There was something in the air; Cassandra could not put her finger on it, but it made her vastly uneasy. It was as if everyone were waiting for something, but no one knew quite what it was.

She rode out that morning found nothing unusual. At noon, she heard the plaintive horn that signified a delivery up the river, and she rode down to the docks herself to see to it.

But Trane was there ahead of her—and Linnea, damn her. And the shipmen were off-loading the supplies of her standard post-sale order: all the staples, the coffee, the flour, the grain, bags of it; the material; barrels of whiskey, sugar, molasses—and the mail.

"I'll take that," Cassandra said, holding out her hand, daring anyone to subvert her authority, daring Trane.

The captain handed her the packet and she tucked it away, aware that everyone's eyes were on her.

Trane's light, bright eyes were on her, and she perceived, suddenly, that he knew what she had done. She felt just one moment of panic, and that settled back into vindictiveness. The man had lied: she had to find out why. He was a danger to her, and all that was hers on Riveland.

Slowly, she headed her mount back toward the big house, and when she was in sight of it, she pulled out the packet, dismounted, and leafed through the mail.

The response was there and she ripped it open with trembling hands.

We are pleased to honor your request. Please be aware that this commission will take some time to execute.

She was very well aware of that. Nevertheless, she waded headfirst into raging waters that night at dinner.

"I have commissioned Vecsey's to find a new overseer," she announced, and noted that she had not taken Trane by surprise at all.

"I thought we had discussed that," he said, his voice shifting into that patient drawl he used with her sometimes.

"No, we hadn't discussed it," she said neutrally. "You told me what you wanted me to do. I disagreed with you." As if she had never disagreed before. She wished, for one moment, and not for the first time, that he really was Trane Taggart.

He went silent, his eyes grazing her face, which had lost a lot of its vitality and glow. Her hair was growing in now so that the reddish color tipped the ends of her springy curls. She seemed thinner, lifeless. It was almost as if she ware paying a penance for her sins, and one of her punishments was to quell every sensual particle of her being.

And so she had sent Linnea after him—who hadn't a hundredth of the character or the capacity for love of her sister. Or one hundredth of the imagination for deceit or trickery.

"All well and good, dear Cassandra," he said finally, "but I won't be leaving."

"Of course you will be leaving," Cassandra said, wondering at her reckless drive continually to go head to head with this man.

But then, if she fought with him, she would not have to think about other feelings. If she kept browbeating herself about that piece of paper and his lies, she wouldn't have to remember other moments of intensity.

He just couldn't keep pretending that he was Jesse's son—even if Jesse had had a son—just as she never could have kept pretending that she was Linnea.

"I think not," he said, and nothing in his tone of voice warned her. "I think it might be time to look into Jesse's death—and see just what he really intended after all."

Oh damn, that threat still had the power to scare her even after all these months. But she wasn't stupid.

"You go right ahead and do that, Mr. Taggart. I invite your closest scrutiny."

"Much obliged, Mrs. Taggart. You have nothing to hide."

"No," she said firmly, "I don't, but I wonder whether there isn't someone else at this table who does." There—now she had done it: she had made a subtle threat herself, and she was amazed to see he had no idea what she was talking about.

"You are surely not talking about Miss Linnea," he murmured.

"No, I'm not," she said pointedly. She was plain astonished: in all this time he had not once wanted to gain access to that box. He hadn't checked; he did not know the bank receipt had been removed from its hiding place.

How interesting.

"*I* have something to hide?" The conclusion made him smile. "Oh lady, you *know* I have nothing to hide."

She crooked a skeptical eyebrow at him. "But the question is how one hides, not where one hides."

"What the hell does that mean?" he demanded, just a little off balance because of her surety. Something wasn't right here. Heretofore, the merest mention of an investi-

422

gation into Jesse's death had put her into a panic, and now she was issuing threats of her own, obliquely and confidently.

That made him damned uneasy.

"It means don't try to walk all over me," she shot back. "You do what you have to and I will do what I must, and we will see who wins Riveland. Isn't that the prize, Mr. Taggart?"

That challenge made him positively suspicious.

"I suspect it depends on who wins, Mrs. Taggart, as to what will be the prize," he said calmly.

That answer made her damned uneasy.

She watched him. He watched her.

Linnea became a secondary character in their haste to keep track of what the other was doing. Something was just not right.

Cassandra was too confident. Trane was too cavalier.

Linnea was too much in the way and could not comprehend anything that was going on.

"I don't understand," she complained to Cassandra one day. "You have no interest in the man whatsoever, and you follow him around like the sun follows the earth."

"Don't be nonsensical," Cassandra snapped. "I have no interest in the man whatsoever. My sole occupation is the welfare of Riveland." That at least was no lie. "I meant it — he is yours, if you can get him to want you."

"I can get Trane Taggart to do anything I want."

Cassandra smiled grimly. Really, Linnea gave herself a great deal of credit. "You do that."

"Watch me."

I don't want to.

Besides, her sister's driving desire to prove something with Trane had nothing to do with what was between *them.* She should encourage Linnea still more, solely because Trane would hate it.

He still wasn't aware she knew his secret. She wondered what would happen when he found out.

423

She rode out two mornings later, comfortable now in the saddle, and well conversant with all of Riveland's paths and trails.

She didn't have to go anywhere near Trane Taggart this morning, but there was an absolute devil within her that wanted to know what he was doing and with whom.

No, she didn't; it was just Linnea. Linnea's provocations and the hint of competitiveness in her tone always when she spoke about Trane.

And she wanted to know if he had discovered yet that that piece of paper was missing, and if he had deduced who had it.

How could he not, when she had as good as told him?

The shot rang out with the explosiveness of a cannon. Her horse reacted instinctively, rearing back, almost tumbling her, and then taking off like lightning, with her hanging on to his back.

He headed away from the house, down paths she had explored weeks ago, a month ago; nothing at the speed she rode him looked familiar, and she was scared to death she would topple off, scared she would break something vital, scared she might die.

She was going to die. The horse veered off the track and barreled nose-first into a stand of trees and bushes, and the scraping, lurching branches pulled at her, beat her, beat her down.

She felt herself falling, falling, landing on the ground like a rag doll that had lost all its stuffing.

And so now, she thought in that brief instant before she blacked out, now she knew.

She came to, and she had no sense of how much time had elapsed. She felt battered, bruised, disoriented. She had no idea where she was or how long she had lain there.

She got to her feet slowly and brushed herself off, aware of a faint dizziness, and the fact she had landed on a cushion of new-grown bushes and fallen leaves. Things could be worse. And they could be a whole lot better.

Obviously no one had come after her, and that was a disquieting thought. It was much later than when she had started out, which was obvious by the path of the sun.

She began to walk, unsteadily at first, turning back in the direction from which she had come. She thought.

Nothing looked familiar, but it just might have been her throbbing head and aching body that was changing landmarks into something more threatening, more vicious.

Someone had shot at her.

Oh yes, she remembered now.

She walked and she walked, and just when she thought she had been walking forever, she came in sight of the edge of a familiar field.

Now she was oriented, she knew where she was going.

She just didn't know how long it would take her to get there. She felt as if the scenery were moving and she was not.

By inches, by degrees, she got through the field, which was lying fallow this year, so there were no workers, there was no help for her there, and with a last great effort, she made her way down a known track and through its twisting turns until she made the drive several hundred yards from the house.

All uphill from there, but the end was near: she could see the chimneys and the roof. Any moment the square of outbuildings surrounding the rear garden would come into sight.

Any moment . . .

But what she saw as she trudged past the bushes and fences that demarcated the end of the fields and the entrance to the drive, what she saw seemed like something time out of mind, a dream, something that could not

425

have been planned or engineered solely for her benefit because Linnea could not have known she would be in distress or when she would have returned to the house.

Ahead of her, on a little side porch that was located just outside the small parlor, she saw Linnea wrapped around the long, lean body of Trane Taggart. She saw Linnea kissing him, or maybe he was kissing her—she couldn't tell—but the avidity of the kiss was all too evident.

And then she saw the ground beneath her feet.

"I ain't gonna let you move," Zilpha said from the foot of Cassandra's bed.

"Nonsense, I feel fine now."

"You don' know how you feel, Missus. You ain't been asleep but fo' hours an' dat ain't enough time to tell nothin'."

Zilpha was wrong. It was time enough to tell that nothing was broken, that she still felt bruised, but she also felt rested and whole.

Her mind was still there; she remembered what she had seen. That was the part she did not want to face.

"You gonna stay in bed fo' de rest of de day, Missus. You ain't doin' nothin'; you is just gonna rest."

"All right, all right." No use arguing with Zilpha. She really didn't want to go downstairs yet anyway, but she was sure she would see Linnea long before that. Maybe Linnea had a guilty conscience as well.

On the other hand, Linnea had nothing to feel guilty about. She, Cassandra, had invited Linnea to do the very thing that was causing her so much grief.

No, it wasn't that, either. It was the thought that the man was a liar and an impostor, and now—possibly—a murderer.

"I bring you soup, Missus. You is gonna eat slow and simple till we know whut's whut."

426

"We know already, Zilpha. I am fine. Sore, bruised, feeling a little out of sorts, but otherwise, fine, I promise you."

"You is gonna rest. Cain't hurt."

Later, she was glad that Zilpha insisted she stay in bed. She didn't have to see anyone. Zilpha kept a strict watch outside her door. She didn't have to eat, she didn't have to talk. She just had to rest, and she was surprised at how much sleep she wanted.

Much later that night, Zilpha brought her a tray with a steaming bowl of soup. It smelled blessedly good, and it tasted wonderful for about a moment, and then that was instantly mitigated by her visualizing Trane and Linnea dining by themselves this evening belowstairs.

Her stomach curdled.

"Oh my God!" She jumped out of bed and ran for the washstand.

"Missus . . . !" Zilpha came to her side immediately, towel and water in hand.

"Oh my God . . . ," she moaned, grabbing for the towel. She buried her face in it, and then tossed it aside as she felt another welling of nausea.

"Dis ain't right," Zilpha muttered as she cleaned up after Cassandra and helped her change into a fresh night-gown. "Wasn't nuthin' wrong wif de soup, Missus. Cook done made it up fresh fo' dinner."

"Of course she did," Cassandra said, her voice still a trifle unsteady. "It's me." And how could she ever get back on a horse again? She couldn't, she couldn't. She *would*. Sometime.

"Chickens was fresh, ma'am. Vegetable from de garden. Boilin' up all day. Don' make no sense."

"It's *me*," Cassandra said again. She felt blank, empty, not at all sure it *was* her stomach reacting against the events of the day and the heavy fall she had taken. Nevertheless, there was no other explanation.

"Body don' take care of itself wif no reason, Missus.

427

Got to be a reason fo' relievin' itself."

"It doesn't matter."

Zilpha fussed some more. "Done took fresh water from de well, picked dem vegetable in de shade of day, take de chicken from de shipment whut just come, killed him fresh fo' de soup. Ain't no reason yo' body cain't hold dat soup."

Cassandra rubbed her hands over her eyes. No reason? She had taken a tumble, she was sore and bruised, and she had eaten on an empty stomach. She couldn't even remember when her last meal had been before Zilpha served the soup, but she was sure it was not helping to hear the recipe reiterated over and over. Maybe it wasn't her, maybe something in the ingredients was tainted and Cook had been unaware of it.

. . . tainted . . .

She felt a fierce dart of fear attack her vitals.

Tainted. A chicken? Salt?

Someone had shot her and she was still alive. . . .

Desperation?

A man who had discovered something was missing?

Against a woman who could expose him and ruin his plans? What plans? That he could somehow prove he was Trane Taggart and then somehow discover she had accidentally caused Jesse's death and then *take over Riveland?*

Or would it be simpler to murder her and court and propose to the woman he knew to be her sole legatee.

Oh dear God—and she had handed him the whole plot, flat out given it to him, dumped it right in his lap and invited him to help himself to it.

It was scary. He was obviously a man who was used to thinking on his feet—look at how he had turned that whole thing with Trane Taggart to his own advantage, and embellished her invention to boot. Look at how he had seduced her, kept her off her guard, made her want the things only he could give her, in spite of her own best

428

intentions.

So much for all her newfound strength and self-determination since Jesse's death. In truth, Mr. Cole — "Call me Trane" — Trager had been calling all the shots, and it almost destroyed her to have to face the fact.

She lay awake in the dark room over the long, dark night, brooding over this turn of events, the meshing together of all the parts to form the only conclusive whole. It was there, and she must concede it: Trane Taggart — or whoever he was — was out to take Riveland away from her by fair means or foul.

She was not totally helpless.

This thought came to her just as dawn broke outside her window. She had some alternatives herself. She had the receipt to the strongbox at the bank, and at the very least, she could try to see what was inside it that was so important it must be kept under lock and key.

It was the second thing she wanted to do this very morning; the first was to watch her breakfast being prepared. She could take no chances from now on; there were enemies all around her, and she wasn't sure Linnea herself wasn't one of them.

She called for Elsie to help her dress and instructed her to tell Isaac to prepare to take her into Carthage later on in the morning.

She looked businesslike, she thought, as she surveyed herself in the mirror. Black moiré was always imposing, and three flounces and velvet trim added a touch of sobriety. She couldn't do much with her hair. It was almost back to its warm golden color, but those reddish ends contrasted oddly with the matching bonnet she wore. She only hoped she did not run into Mr. Ward or Mr. Greve on this trip, but that was a chance she had to take.

Zilpha prepared her breakfast for her at the table: fresh coffee, sliced fruit, a slice of buttered biscuit, right from

429

the oven, which Zilpha had mixed up herself.

And then Linnea: "My, my, you are looking much better, Cassandra."

"Why thank you; I'm feeling perfectly fine now, as it happens, I'm driving into town," she added, watching Linnea's face. "Perhaps you would like to come with me." She thought not. She saw the wheels turning in Linnea's mind and she did not like the direction they were veering.

Well, it was true, she would have Riveland all to herself this morning, with only Zilpha to witness her excesses and dalliances, and none of that mattered to her, Cassandra, anyway.

Linnea smiled, and it was one of those self-serving little smirks that immediately put the recipient on guard. "Oh no, oh no. I couldn't bear to travel to town in this heat when I can just relax on the veranda and be cool and comfortable."

. . . And as undressed as I please without you around, dear sister. Everything is fair game.

She could almost read Linnea's thoughts. But Linnea was something to be dealt with at a later time.

Her carriage was waiting with Isaac at the reins. Everything safe, with one hurdle to cross today, one question to be answered.

It was enough for one day.

And it was too little. The bank clerk who served her and who brought out the two boxes that she had rented, looked at her blankly when she presented him with Cole Trager's receipt.

"But you aren't Mr. Trager, ma'am."

She thought fast. "I'm his wife."

He shook his head. "No, it says right here, you are Mrs. Taggart. Can't be both, ma'am."

"I *am* his agent," she insisted.

"Well then, Mr. Trager would've sent a note to that effect."

"What if he were dead?"

"We would open the box to his heirs at the end of the term of his rental, ma'am. Anybody could produce a piece of paper with his name on it, you understand. But you see, this here *is* the original, and the clerk countersigned it, so we know what Mr. Trager's signature looks like. Then again, ma'am, it isn't my business to be asking what you're doing with it."

"He gave it to me," she said, keeping her frustration out of her voice with very great effort, and trying as unobtrusively as possible to tuck the receipt out of his sight. "He didn't know about all your rules and regulations, sir. He wanted a safe place for it in case anything happened to him. He *trusted* me."

"Come back at the end of the term then, ma'am, and we'll see whether he shows to claim his property, or whether you have some entitlement to it."

"I appreciate that," she responded grimly, accepting the fact that he had backed her into a corner. She had made a wasted trip, left Linnea alone with Trane on Riveland doing who knew what, and the end of it was that she was no closer to any truth than she had been before she left.

Worse than that, Mr. Ward, just happening to leave his own office at the moment she exited the bank, caught a glimpse of her, and called after her as she fled down the boarded sidewalks and disappeared around a corner where Isaac held the carriage for her.

"Quick! Get moving," she ordered him, with one foot on the step board and half of her body hanging out of the coach. *"Hurry!"* She swung herself inside as the carriage lurched forward, and she fell back against the seat in a heap of skirts and petticoats.

As Isaac turned the carriage to run back into town, she saw Mr. Ward, standing in perplexity in front of the bank, wondering where the elusive Mrs. Taggart had disappeared to.

Now she was helpless. Without whatever was in the strongbox, she had nothing with which to threaten Mr. Trager-Taggart except the fact that she had the receipt. And that was dangerous. A man could kill for something like that if he had never meant for it to be seen in the first place.

And a man had gone to an awful lot of trouble to hide that one little piece of paper. It wouldn't protect her from anything; it hadn't protected her from his trying to gun her down and possibly poison her.

She had nothing in the way of weapons. And he could attack her on two fronts, possibly three, if she were spineless enough to still welcome his lovemaking after all that had happened. But he would never try that now. It was easier to contest Jesse's death or just kill her altogether.

She had to change that will.

She couldn't do it today. Maybe she could.

"Isaac—to the Riversgate—*please* . . . *please*. . . ." She heard the desperation in her own voice.

And she knew what she would do: she would leave all of Riveland to the *real* Trane Taggart or his heirs. They had said he had existed, those people to whom Mr. Greve had spoken. They had said there really was a Trane Taggart.

Let *him* prove it. Why should she make it easy for him? Why should she hand the whole over to Linnea, now that she was aware of the plot?

The carriage jerked to a halt in front of the hotel.

"You stay, Missus. I fetch Mr. Greve," Isaac said stolidly. "Ain't fittin' you walk in dat place by yo'self."

He disappeared into the crowd of men loitering in front of the hotel, and she squeezed herself back against the side of the cushions. Greve had to be there. He *had* to.

She closed her eyes, just for a moment, and she heard the click of the carriage door opening.

"Mr. Greve."

"Miz Taggart. I'm rather astonished to find you here."

"I have an emergency," she said, trying hard not to sound hysterical; but it was a strange situation, and she felt its urgency. She didn't know whether she could convince him that time *was* of the essence. "I must change the bequest in my will."

He grew quite still. "Well, that is easy, Miz Taggart. I will come to Riveland tomorrow and we'll take care of it," he said easily, placatingly.

"No, I want to do it now."

He perceived her agitation. "You are obviously under duress, Miz Taggart. Surely you do not want to make such an important decision now."

She swallowed hard. She could not let her emotions or her sense of danger closing in on her affect her good common sense. This was the right decision, and she was in town and there was no reason not to do it now.

"I am quite calm, Mr. Greve, and I do have my reasons. Is there a place we may transact this business in privacy?"

He nodded, loath to acquiesce to the urgency he sensed in her. He was sure she would regret it the next week, if not the next day. "I believe we can use an office at the bank."

She groaned inwardly as he directed Isaac to return to the building, but it couldn't be helped. This was more important than anything that had transpired there; she only hoped the officious clerk would be busy elsewhere, or just not recognize her at all.

But then, they went into the building through a private entrance and all her fears were for nothing anyway.

"Mr. Ward permits me the use of one of his rooms the odd times I may have need of it. Come, sit down and I will see to some paper and ink for you."

All this was done with the utmost concern for her, and she wasn't sure she appreciated the fact that Mr. Greve

433

wasn't trying to argue her out of it.

"I am replacing my sister as my heir," she said, as he sat down next to her and began taking notes. "The reason being that she is deriving the full benefit of living on Riveland during my lifetime now. So I think it is only fair to try to rectify a wrong that Mr. Taggart—that is, my husband—actuated. On my death, Riveland is to go to Trane Taggart, or his heirs."

Mr. Greve's pen stopped scratching. "Have you told him?"

She had to make another split-lightning decision. "No." Why elaborate about something that only she—and he—knew. "How soon can that be formally written up and signed by me?"

He shrugged. "An hour, perhaps. Are you staying in town that long? I would be glad to bring the papers out to Riveland. And in fact I *am* glad that you are ensuring that you won't be playing any tricks to gain control of the estate in the future."

But wills can be changed, Mr. Greve, again and again. "Oh no," she dissembled, "Riveland is the most important thing now."

That satisfied him, but it was ashes in her mouth. She had taken a good positive step: she had removed the possession of Riveland as a motive for murder.

Oh really? But he won't know the end result until after he kills me.

But at least he won't get what he's after. . . .

Except you won't be around to see whether he does or doesn't.

She really wasn't thinking clearly. She hadn't taken any weapons away from him; she had only changed the probable outcome.

And wouldn't Linnea get a nice, nasty surprise, especially now she knew all the complications about her, Cassandra's, impersonation. She wouldn't put it past Linnea to connive with Trane, now that she was chasing that impostor with such ferocious intensity. They could be conspiring against her even at that very moment.

Oh Lord . . . Her bequest would shock them out of their minds and she wouldn't be around to see the tables turned.

A clerk came into the room to transcribe the conditions of her bequest and she dictated the terms, thinking furiously.

She would sign some more papers and the deed would be done, and then what? She had to go back to Riveland.

Had to?

In fact, if she were not on Riveland, nothing could happen to her. But she would be leaving it all in the hands of the man who was not Trane Taggart. She would be running away.

Damn, there was just no right way to save herself. No way to prove anything. Nothing, unless he hauled her into court — or killed her.

Chapter Twenty-five

She read the true and the fine copies of her last testament very carefully, and when she had finished, she found herself hesitating to sign.

"Miz Taggart?" Mr. Greve prompted.

"I had a thought . . . ," she said, rather oddly, but she did not air it. What if Mr. Greve handed Riveland over to this impostor without requiring he prove who he was? Greve already believed he was Trane Taggart because it had been verified by people who knew *of* Trane Taggart, but who wouldn't recognize him, surely, after all these years. It wasn't proof if you had witnesses that a man had once existed and lived a long time ago in your town.

What was proof of anything? Somewhere in a little town ten miles inland from Galveston, there might be proof that someone named Cole Trager had stolen another man's identity, the same way she had intended to steal Linnea's. . . .

And that proof could never come to her.

But *she* could go to *it*.

Absurd. She didn't even know what it would require to go to Texas from inland on the coast of Georgia. She didn't know a thing about trains or stagecoaches or any kind of travel. She knew how to go to the Springs, was what she knew, and only because the exigency of the moment had compelled her to travel there.

Was this not as urgent? How else could she expose the

man everyone thought was Jesse's son?

Jesse's son. She had yet to be presented with anyone who had ever known him.

Unless Greve were in on this conspiracy, too?

She slanted a look at him. He wore the same faintly patronizing look on his face as he always did, and he waited, with grave patience, for her to sign the document she so urgently requested he prepare.

Yes, she had been rather precipitate about it, but there was no other choice, and no one else. She dipped the pen into the inkwell and slowly and carefully signed her name.

"To the depot, Isaac," she directed as she stepped back into her carriage, and without a word, Isaac drove her exactly where she requested.

Here there was an atmosphere of bustling people with places to go, for whom a small town like Carthage held no attraction whatsoever as they awaited the next coach out to Atlanta and places beyond.

The stationmaster was amenable and full of information. "Two ways to go, ma'am, was you to leave in the week. Can take the Savannah-Albany down to Glenmore where it meets the Brunswick, and then coach to Albany to catch the Southwestern through to Eufala. Then trunk line goes through to Mobile, and if you're lucky you can catch a schooner off a week's sailing over to Galveston. Or you could coach straight across to Watsonville, Stephens, and Columbus to Albany and get the train from there."

"Which is fastest?"

"Them old trains beat those coaches every time, ma'am. They go straight through with sleepers. You'd be roadhousing was you to take the straight-line coach, but it's a little longer trip from Glenmore station to Albany."

Everything he said was meaningless to her. "Can I buy my ticket here?"

"I can help you, ma'am. When you going to be ready to go?"

Even she didn't know that. She paid the fare for coach and train, tucked the tickets away in her reticule, and walked back to Isaac with resolution in her step.

Now there was something she could do — if she wanted to, if events warranted it. If things spun so completely out of control, she had no choice.

"I came through Carthage on my way to Riveland," Linnea said at dinner. "So different from the small farm town near Jonathan's home. Much more to offer. Everything there had to be imported from London. The Wiltshires lived deep in the country, Cassandra, although Jonathan and I did like to spend most of our time at the London townhouse. The months I spent on the estate were pure torture for me. You can't have any idea what isolation is until you've lived for several months in England away from everything. Oh well. I will take my turn in Carthage one of these days. Do tell us what you did."

"This and that," Cassandra said, pushing her meat around on her plate. She couldn't eat. She felt choked by a cloying atmosphere of suspicion and discontent she felt in the room, in the house. "And what did you do all day?"

"Oh — this and that," Linnea said airily, attacking her food with the enjoyment of someone who had not eaten a good meal in a long time.

"And where is Trane?"

"Down at the docks again. We're expecting the barges for the last shipment of bales."

"The two-grade cotton," Cassandra confirmed. She knew about that. It was the press of the end bolls, the less superior grade, the plants that grew low to the ground where they were more susceptible to moisture, dirt, infestation. Still, a quality-grade press could be gotten from the pick, and that had been the previous weeks'

438

finishing work.

All to market now. The winter season of storing and refurbishing was about to begin, the perfect time to begin a sojourn to find a man's past.

"I can't eat any more," Cassandra said. "I'm going outside."

"I'll come with you," Linnea said promptly. "We haven't talked enough, Cassandra. I haven't nearly thanked you enough for taking me in."

Cassandra slanted a skeptical look at her sister. *No, you haven't,* she thought, *especially since you found out you could possibly inherit the place. And didn't I hand you Trane on a silver platter so the two of you could scheme and plot against me?* What a stupid mistake that had been!

And she especially had made the mistake of allowing the wrong man too much latitude in her too circumscribed life.

They walked down the hallway together from the dining room to the entrance foyer, in harmony for a brief sympathetic moment.

Sully got to the door before them and opened it deferentially, and they walked out onto the veranda.

"It's beautiful here," Linnea said. "I could stay here forever."

Oh, I just know you could. "You will always have a home here," Cassandra said insincerely, gritting her teeth as she uttered the words.

"I knew that. That's why I came to you."

She knew that. And now she knew everything else, and Linnea was surely a woman who knew how to make pie from a handful of measly pecans.

"Everything is so lovely here at this time of the year," Linnea went on. "The fragrance of the air, the sense of things humming behind the scenes where you can't see them but only know they get done. Oh, and the sunsets. Do you know, I just love the sunsets."

She pointed to her left where the drive circled around

the house and led to the track down to the fields and the Little Midway River beyond.

There was a glow in the sky, as there usually was at this hour, but it seemed brighter, more phosphorescent, almost unreal in its intensity.

And there was a wafting thickness in the air, as if something momentous were being carried back to them on the wind.

Cassandra smelled the smoke first, concurrent with the first cries of alarm from down in the fields.

"Missus . . . oh Missus . . ."

Two, three, four boys came running up the track. "They's fire, Missus. Mr. Trane done said come git you."

But she had dashed off the veranda before they could even finish the message, and she was heading toward the stables, shouting as she ran: "Isaac—saddle Decatur. . . . Hurry!" forgetting utterly that she had not been back up on a horse since she had fallen.

But what did details matter when the smell of smoke pervaded the whole upper fields of Riveland?

Isaac pulled the cinch and helped her up in an instant, mounting her sidesaddle before she had a moment's hesitation. He slapped Decatur's rump, and she had no time to think about falling or anything else, because the moment her horse pulled onto the track, she saw the flames snaking up to the sky.

Oh my God . . . the field . . .

No—she rode Decatur hard down the track, and she saw no sign of fire, not anywhere, and yet the flames shot higher and higher and she didn't know until she came in sight of the far sward by the river that it was the barges that burned, the barges and the cotton all ablaze in one roaring inferno, being moved out into the river by the tide, and the helplessness of the men on the docks who were dark shadows against the fury of the fire.

And Trane . . . where was he? Who had done this—to her—to Riveland?

Who was hurt, when had it started? A thousand questions, none of which could be answered immediately. Her most pressing chore was to ascertain injuries, provide medicaments for those who had been hurt, offer shelter for the night, and maybe then she would find answers to the suspicions that crowded her mind.

She dismounted a hundred yards above the docks and ran down to the pier. There were two dozen field workers milling around helplessly, a dozen shipmen from the barges, several women, Eli and Ojim.

"Where's Trane?" she demanded of Ojim.

"Oh, Mr. Trane. He right dere, Missus, out on de dinghy; he been pushin' dem flatboats out to de center so dey can burn deyselves out. See 'im? See 'im, Missus?"

A moment later she saw him, long and lean, silhouetted against the flames, maneuvering with two barge poles precariously from the center of a frail little wooden boat in the center of the river, drenched with sweat and determination, a man who would not let the flames or a simple woman defeat him.

Ojim had called for lanterns and torches, and a dozen men now ringed Trane and Cassandra and Ojim and the shipmen who stood watching their barges go down in the river like butter melting on a flapjack.

"What did we lose?" Cassandra said finally.

"About three hundredweight of low grade," Trane said, running a wet towel over his sooty face. "Two barges. Six men on each, all ashore, but we're liable for pay and insurance. Damned bad luck, Cassandra."

"Was it?" Her question sounded particularly sharp in the dusky, smoky twilight.

Trane swung on her. "What would you call it, Mrs. Taggart?"

"Coincidence?" she retorted, moving her gaze from his to the smoke-streaming ruin settling deeper into the fathomless river. *Why?*

"Was a accident," Ojim said. "Dey done brung de

441

barges up to de pier and we was ready fo' loadin'. And we start, and we got 'im done, Missus, and she just went right up in flame and no one know whut happen. Mr. Trane only want to save de docks; we got to save de fields is all we care 'bout. So dat's whut we did."

"I see," she said coolly, but she didn't feel strongly that that exonerated Trane from any treachery, especially if he had been first out on the water—before or after someone sighted the flames?

Oh, he was so dangerous. This was a crime against her as surely as if someone had shot at her or tainted her food. This was money lost, time and effort wasted, compensation to be paid. This was a very firm way of telling her who was really in control, who could take everything away from her.

This was the challenge, the one she swore she was going to meet.

She was going to Galveston, and she was leaving as soon as she could sneak out the back door.

Sneaking out the back door wasn't as easy as she had thought it might be. Everyone came back to the house. Zilpha sent Elsie, Leola, and Sarah scurrying to make up beds to accommodate the unexpected guests. The men wanted baths and dinner; they wanted to sit around and discuss every detail of what had happened and they didn't mind drinking Riveland whiskey while they recapitulated each particular of the devastating conflagration.

It was boring beyond belief to listen to a brood of grown men recounting their heroics against insurmountable odds.

But she was the hostess, and she and Linnea had to attend to their duties at dinner and thankfully leave the men to Trane for the post-dinner colloquy.

She and Linnea sat in the small parlor, staring at each other.

"You lost a lot of money," Linnea said finally.

442

"Riveland lost a lot of money," Cassandra corrected, none too gently. "But there are so many factors that can affect a crop. If it hadn't been a fire, it could have been an infestation, or too much rain. There is no solid income on a plantation, I'll tell you. You are always taking credit against the coming year's crop and sometimes you never catch up." Yes, it was good to let Linnea know that there was work and impoverishment on the wealthiest-looking plantation. It would curb her greed, but it wouldn't do anything to restrain her own impatience.

Did she really have to bid these strangers good night? Couldn't she just race upstairs and . . . Her imagination was running away with her, but it seemed suddenly very urgent that she get on the road to finding out the truth about Trane Taggart. There was nothing more for her to do here. And she couldn't risk anything else happening, either to her or to Riveland.

What if she said, "I'm tired, Linnea. Just thinking of the consequences of this fire exhausts me."

"Oh," Linnea said, as if she had been startled by the sound of her sister's voice, "why, I'll be glad to stay until everyone has gone up for the night, Cassandra. Don't think a thing about it. I can see you would rather not do it, and I don't mind."

No, she didn't, did she? Cassandra would have bet the whole doused and drowned bargeloads of cotton on it.

She walked upstairs slowly, listening at the library door to the sound of the deep hearty male voices within.

This was an aspect of being Jesse's wife she did not know at all. Jesse had never entertained, and apart from a business associate now and again, he never brought anyone to the house, not a relative, not a friend. Whatever he wanted, he sought it elsewhere, and she had never been a part of anything else but the day-to-day survival of Riveland.

She felt a pained little pang that in all those eight years she had not entertained nor put up relatives or friends who had come for long, sociable visits. She had missed

443

the companionship of other women, the hospitable sound of people enjoying one another's company.

Too late for that.

Too late for a lot of things.

Not too late to sneak out the back door.

Somewhere in a trunk in the back of her closet, she had hidden the forbidden clothing in which she had effected so many escapes over the years. In there, she found the costume of the groom that had served Linnea so well one fateful afternoon when she had cornered Mr. Wiltshire and forced him to propose.

That would do perfectly. She needed a shirt with that, boots, a hat and a lightweight jacket. She needed to roll up into a heavy cape a serviceable dress, another cape, some underthings, a brush, a towel, some grooming items—oh damn, the thing was too bulky already—and not as thick or containing as a woolen blanket. . . .

She needed water. She needed a place to stash her money and tickets. She needed her thick grease pencil to darken her eyebrows and add some subtle aging to her face. Oh Lord, she could even use a mirror, but she couldn't chance taking one now.

And what did she know? She knew he had said Galveston, ten miles inland from Galveston, which could be ten miles anywhere along its coast, but she had to reckon he had come from near the boat landing to make such a long journey on such short notice for so little gain. A man wouldn't travel hundreds of miles in his own county unless he really felt he had something to gain. And people knew people. Someone along the way would have heard of Cole Trager. Someone somewhere would point her in the right direction.

It was so chancy—

She turned herself this way and that in the light of her mirror, and she was distressed to see how much she had filled out since she had last worn those trousers. She could barely squeeze herself into them and close them, so her shirt and her midriff bulged out slightly above the waistband. The jacket would cover that, she thought, pulling it on impatiently, and it was indeed the one item that fit with the same precision as before. Even the boots—her feet had grown a half size. She slicked back her hair with water—no time for color, but perhaps a dusting of ash if she could find some.

She bit her lips and jammed her hat onto her head.

Now what did she see? A slightly effete young person who could be either male or female, but with that mouth, she was sure she would never pass muster. She went to work on her face, adding depth again to her eyes by penciling around the socket, and smudging a dark circle underneath her lower lid. She darkened her lipline, too, lowering it a little so it looked less inviting and more petulant.

Did she have to be petulant, too? She might; she didn't think she could get away with anything else.

All right, then. She had her cape laid out on the bed with everything in it she meant to take. She rolled that up and tied it with a piece of leather strap she cut from her trunk.

Now . . . final check. She needed to bind her breasts—they were too obvious under her shirt. She found a length of material and wound it around her bosom down to her waist, and in this mummy wrapping, she put most of her money for safekeeping. And she fashioned an underarm pouch to contain her tickets and money she would need for her immediate use.

There now—

She surveyed herself again as she heard the stamp of footsteps coming up the stairs. Passable—risky—she heard all the words in her mind, and then she heard Trane: "Gentlemen, a pleasure in spite of the circumstances."

Her guests—or were they his guests?—concurred.

"We don't need to trouble Mrs. Taggart with the details

any further."

A rumble of assent to that statement, and she found herself steaming with resentment. Trouble her about *what?*

"Good night, gentlemen."

A chorus of good-nights wafted down the hallway, and then she heard the sound of his boots receding down the stairs. She heard Zilpha pointing the way to this one and that which room he was to occupy, and then, at long last, there was silence.

And where was Linnea?

Oh, she could only guess, but she hoped and prayed Linnea was keeping dear Mr. Call Me Trane very, very busy because she, Cassandra, was going to be very busy herself.

If she had not ridden that afternoon, she thought dolefully, she might never have been able to climb into a saddle again, especially in the dead of night with only a lantern to light her way.

What providence had sent her running to the stables! She marveled at it, and the ease with which she was able to saddle up and appropriate a blanket roll and finally make her way down the dawn-lit drive of Riveland to the turnpike toward Watsonville.

After that, pure grit carried her through. The ride was long, debilitating, sapping her strength and energy, boring as she hunched low on her mount to get the most comfortable position with the least amount of strain.

No one took notice of her in Watsonville, but the coach was going to follow in another four or five hours from Carthage, and she felt that she couldn't wait, she had to push on, she had to get *there.*

She was beginning to feel like a fool.

Who in her right mind dressed in trousers and hared off looking for a man's past on as sketchy a number of clues as she had? Who in her saner moments would ever think she was getting away with anything?

Southerners were obviously too polite to even look at her, let alone notice whether she was a callow youth or a dangerously reckless young woman. But what would happen in Mobile? What would happen anywhere else at all?

She kept pushing. The thought of Cole Trager successfully taking over the identity of Trane Taggart drove her obsessively toward Mobile every time she wanted to turn back.

It took a week of day-long hard-riding travel until she reached Albany and her first connection southward. She stabled her horse and stored the saddle, and wearily and thankfully, she boarded the first train that came on the first leg of her trip to Alabama.

Trane started out for Carthage the next morning with the barge men long before anyone in the house was awake. He counted this trip as a respite, not only from the disaster of the night before, but from the cloying presence of Linnea Wiltshire. He never in his life thought he would long for Cassandra's artful impersonation, but he almost felt like he had to run for his life from the hunger of the voracious Linnea, lest she devour him at thirty paces.

He had a fleeting thought that there was something to be said about the separation of the spheres of men and women, because if it were a fact, Linnea would not be following him all over Riveland and leaving all the house chores to Cassandra and the servants.

And Cassandra had been restive the last few days. Suspicious. Not well. Things that tore at him because she would not let anyone come near her, let alone him, and he was damned afraid of sticking one foot in the spider lady's web.

She was back to that again, plots and plans weaving around in her head. She had lost a lot when Linnea had reappeared.

So had he.

Damn.

There was too much riding on this to have it all thrown to the wolves by the likes of Linnea Wiltshire. And hadn't she gone from impoverished widow to salivating wolverine in the space of only a few days?

But why think of her? He could only take care of today's problems today, and this aftermath of the fire was a singular enough complication without adding to it the dilemma of Cassandra.

He couldn't begin to envision all the papers that would have to be filled out, but he figured if he notified Greve and the bank, he would be spared any unnecessary steps in between.

But when they arrived, they found only the telegraph office open, and so he notified Vecsey's before he even spoke with Greve. Later, he found he had missed Greve, and so at nine o'clock, he headed to the bank.

Ward knew about it already, and he wondered which tom-toms had passed the word along the river.

"It was a mighty sight, Mr. Taggart. I expect there were a few dozen people who had seen it up and down the river."

"I expect so," he said noncommittally. "Anything more you need now?"

"No sir, Vecsey's will prepare the papers and we'll take care of the rest. But next time Mrs. Taggart is in town, tell her she must come countersign the drafts."

And that was that.

Or was it?

"Mr. Trager, Mr. Trager . . ." An eager clerk waved him over from behind the counter, and he almost turned and walked out the door rather than acknowledge the name. He had almost forgotten about the damned thing.

"Yes? What is it?" A man could be abrupt when someone was about to expose a secret to the light of day.

"Hear tell someone was in here yesterday, asking to see in your box. Thought you ought to know."

"My box?" And how could that be?

"Had the receipt and all. Said she was your wife . . ."

His . . . *wife*—had the *receipt*?

"Said she was your agent, Mr. Trager. . . ."

Receipt?

"Said you might be dead . . ."

Dead? Planning something?

"Of course we couldn't turn it over, not till it was proved or she had something that said she was entitled, like some kind of notification from you. . . ."

She had the receipt . . . ?!

"Thought you ought to know," the clerk finished.

Trane hauled out a coin. "Much obliged."

"Any time."

She had the receipt.

Crazy. *He* had the receipt.

He took a deep breath. Where could a man check out a thing like that?

Wasn't much open but . . . the public baths—

Hell . . . two bits for a tub and five minutes of privacy to find out if a man could have any secrets at all—

Goddamn hell . . .

She had the goddamned receipt, the goddamned black widow spinning away . . .

And he couldn't think of one fool goddamned way she could have gotten her hands on it.

He was in a simmering rage when he got back to Riveland; the miles had just been eaten up by his trying to devise some story to account for how Cassandra had gotten hold of that bank receipt, and he couldn't come up with a single damned thing to account for it.

And things went from bad to worse.

"Missus ain't slep' in her bed," Zilpha told him in greeting as he burst into the house and before he could demand to see Cassandra.

"I mean Missus ain't been to bed. Ain't been slep' in

449

and she ain't no place around nohow. I done looked."

Damn. "Did you touch anything in her room?"

"No, Mr. Trane, I come lookin' fo' you."

He took the steps two at a time, with Zilpha tracking behind him as quickly as she could. The door to Cassandra's room was open, and sunlight streamed in through the parted curtains. The quilt was still spread on the bed, but her moiré dress had been discarded in a heap by the closet, almost as if she had been in some kind of hurry.

He scanned the closet. It didn't look like anything was missing.

But wait — shoved hastily into it against a wall of dresses was a small leather-bound trunk.

He pulled it out curiously.

"Oh, dat Missus's from when she come wif Mr. Jesse all dem years past, Mr. Trane."

He fingered a strap that had been cut, and then turned it upright and opened the lid. He didn't know what he expected to find, but he was damned nonplussed by what he saw. In the top tray there was a box, empty now, but it obviously had contained something gray and flaky. He ran his finger around the inside of it and rubbed it and smelled it. It smelled smoky, like ash . . .

There was a bottle of reddish liquid next to it, and a length of plain flowered material that could have been a stock tie or a sash, but he had the feeling it wasn't.

Underneath this tray, he found a dress of the same flowered material neatly folded on top of a blanket that was made of a rough dun-colored wool.

And that was all. It was a pure mystery to him, along with the one about how she had found that piece of paper. He closed the trunk lid, bound up the one uncut strap and put the trunk back in her closet.

"Miss Linnea awake yet?"

"No, sir. She sleepin' sound and she always sleep late, Mr. Trane. Where you think Missus got to?"

"I don't know, Zilpha. But I'll find her."

"Yes, sir. I can't do nothin' mo' fo' you now?"

"No, I don't think so." He stared at the four walls of the room as if they could give up her secrets, and Zilpha backed out of the room to leave him alone.

No spider webs on the ceiling either. No trace of a fire or the anguish he had suffered believing her dead. And now it all came down to the fact that she knew something about him he had not meant for anyone to ever find out.

Where the hell was she?

He had to get out of that room. Her scent pervaded the place—and all her lies. He would never understand what Jesse had been thinking of when he plucked an innocent, untrained, untutored young girl from an impoverished family to be his bride.

But then, he didn't have to understand anything about Jesse Taggart. The bastard was dead and only the living suffered his sins.

So . . . a horse was missing. Cassandra was gone on the heels of a fire and the fact she had tried to get access to his strongbox at the bank.

Well, well . . .

"How would I know where Cassandra is?" Linnea asked irritably, her hand reaching for the sugar to add to her coffee.

"She sat with you last night?"

"No, no, she went up to bed before me. She was upset about the fire."

"Who wouldn't be?" he muttered, cupping his own coffee in his hands and trying to focus on Cassandra's state of mind and what she had been thinking.

"You remember—I was the only one in the small parlor when you and your guests finally left the library. . . ."

Well, he hadn't wanted to remember that. Linnea had been gracious, but each and every one of those strangers knew exactly what was on her mind that night.

He had gone out the back way. He wondered how long she had waited for him, and he was amazed she would even speak to him this morning.

"Where would she have gone?" Linnea asked plaintively.

"Don't know. There's a horse missing, so Isaac tells me, and a lantern in the barn, a saddle gone, and her bed hasn't been slept in. Slim clues, I have to tell you. She might just have gone for a ride somewhere, but surely she would be back by now."

"Oh surely . . . ," Linnea murmured, bending her head to hide the thought that flashed into her mind. What if she didn't . . . ?

Slim clues, *hell*, Trane thought. *No* clues. A missing horse, for God's sake, a curious woman poking her nose where she had no right to poke it—but that was Cassandra anyway . . . damn . . . An accident—

What made him think of that?

Cassandra was missing . . . and so was a horse. Yes, that connection was plain. She had only ridden again because of the fire. The accident . . . she had been thrown—what had she thought?

The fire—a coincidence, she had said.

He rubbed his face, feeling the stubble where he hadn't shaved in a couple of days, feeling futile that he couldn't make sense of Cassandra's having his receipt and her seeming disappearance.

He wondered how long he could categorize it as probable until he decided to search for her. And where the hell would he start?

Where would a woman like Cassandra start—sheltered, never having gone anywhere in all the years she had been married to Jesse until she picked up one day and went to Carthage, and then subsequently went to the Springs.

If she had done that, she could do anything, he thought. It must have been hard enough, a woman alone. And he mustn't forget the little space of time between her "death" and her resurrection as Linnea. Where had she been then?

Oh no, Cassandra wasn't the sheltered little flower

452

everyone thought. Cassandra had resources beyond all of them. She had proved that over and over again.

It was just that no one had noticed.

Somehow she had gotten away with every impersonation she had dreamt up—including Linnea—without any redress demanded of her whatsoever.

Clever, clever Cassandra.

Clever enough to find her way anywhere she chose to go.

Where would she have gone?

He felt time slipping away from him. Cassandra had been gone hours and hours. On horseback, he was almost sure of it. To some point. She couldn't be traveling light and hard and not have some destination in mind.

She could have been in Carthage the same time as he, and he never would have known it. She could have gone to the depot and taken a coach right out of town under his very nose. . . .

The thought was a spur to action.

He had to do something, and Carthage was a place to start.

Chapter Twenty-six

He was a day behind her, maybe less.

"Tell you the same thing I told the lady," the station-master said. "You go by train, you're not going quite so direct. You go by coach or ride up by way of Watsonville, you're going straight line. You want to know which way she went, I can't tell you, stranger. Don't even know if she used the tickets. Just said she wanted to get to Galveston."

Hell and goddamn . . .

Wasn't that just like the spider lady, trying to catch every damned thing in her goddamned web. You couldn't hide a thing from a woman like Cassandra. Damn, damn and *damn*. And there wasn't much he could do about it with her having the day's gain on him. About all he could do was follow and make sure some secrets just stayed buried where they belonged. They didn't make no never-mind now. Couldn't change a thing.

Couldn't change Cassandra, either. Blight of his life. Black widow forever. Nothing could change because of a promise he never could keep.

Hell and damn.

He didn't think there was room on this earth together for him and Cassandra Taggart and the goddamn gall it took for her to go tearing off to pry into things she would be better off not knowing.

How the hell was he going to hold her back now she

454

had the bit between her teeth?

How the hell was he going to restrain himself once he caught up with her?

Cassandra was seasick.

It was the last thing she expected to have happen to her after she had gotten as far as Mobile without incident, and it began to look as if she would spend the two weeks of her voyage lying in her cabin with a bowl by her side. Thank heavens she was not the only woman aboard; there was a friendly Mrs. Worth going to join her husband in a place called Brazoria, somewhere along the Texas coast, who took a motherly interest in the youthful Mrs. Taggart, who was not taking her first boat trip too well.

Mrs. Worth actually thought there was another reason she was so uncomfortable on this voyage, and Cassandra saw no use in disabusing her of that notion. A woman who was thought to be in a family way was a woman untouchable by virtue of her delicate condition. And that suited Cassandra just fine.

Mrs. Worth's plain round face appeared with cheerful regularity at Mrs. Taggart's cabin door, cautioning her to keep her head down, offering to bring her anything she required, and occasionally staying to talk with her when she felt able to chat.

But Mrs. Worth's one drawback was, she was curious as sin, and she wanted to know everything about Cassandra Taggart, including why she was traveling to Galveston from so far away as Georgia.

There was only one correct answer: "My husband. My husband is to meet me in Galveston, and he has purchased some land and has built us a home. . . ."

Mrs. Worth understood this explanation very well. There were a half dozen women aboard who were going to Texas for just that reason: a husband—or to find one. She knew well the availability of an eligible man in untamed places like Texas. Hadn't she met her own husband in just that way?

"Does he know?" she whispered.

"Does he know . . . what?" Cassandra asked cautiously.

"About—that." Mrs. Worth pointed to Cassandra's midsection.

Cassandra bit her lip. Why not? What would Mrs. Worth ever know about her inability to bear children? She was never going to see the woman again, and besides, she felt a little grateful to her for adding this interesting little detail to the story of her journey westward. She even saw herself using it once she got on the trail of Cole Trager. She could say she was his wife, and he had abandoned her when he found out she was going to have a baby.

What a reason for tracking him all over the Texas wilderness!

"No," she answered, "he doesn't know. . . . He always wanted—he'll be so happy . . ." She felt a little tear starting. She *could* imagine being so happy over the advent of a child.

An actress. There was no other word for what she was, lying there sick to her stomach and convincing poor, good-natured Mrs. Worth that she was expecting a child, just as Mrs. Worth had suspected.

"Oh dearie, how wonderful. What luck. Where did you say you're going?"

Uh-oh. "Do you know? The name of the place totally escapes me," she said apologetically. "But—well, you'll meet him, I'm sure, when we get to Galveston. He said—he said . . ." *Oh, what an opportunity*—"it was a little town about ten miles inland from Galveston. . . .'"

"*Ten* miles?" Mrs. Worth gave it a moment's hard thought. "Well, that could be any number of places. There's Concha and Red Mesa, Deadman, Bitter Creek, Alamosa . . . Any of those names strike you?"

She shook her head. "I'm sorry. I think everything's

plain gone out of my head."

But Mrs. Worth understood that as well. She patted Mrs. Taggart's hand and bid her good-day and promised to stop back later with some soup and perhaps some bicarbonate and maybe Mrs. Taggart would feel better by then.

Mrs. Taggart felt wonderful just at the moment. She had the names of five likely places where she could pursue the elusive Cole Trager. Surely one of them would yield a clue.

She turned herself over onto her back and contemplated the names Mrs. Worth had given her. *Concha* . . . *Deadman*. Tough-sounding names, places where a woman alone might be seen as an invitation to something else, but a woman in a delicate condition might be respected.

Just like Mobile, where it had become evident to her that she would make a more successful trip southward as a women rather than an effeminate youth. There were too many pitfalls, and she had almost fallen into them unwittingly; there were things she knew nothing about, men who liked the companionship of younger men, women on the prowl for any man they could get. There were thieves and sharps, and there had been times on the journey when she thought she was wandering through a world totally made up of people out to cheat anyone they could bamboozle with their quick talk, confident eyes and knowledgeable hands.

She had learned; her natural suspicion and native wit prevented her from becoming an easy mark, but still, it was a world out of time, one she never could have envisioned on Riveland.

And she didn't like acting the part of a man. She found herself studying young men along the way for indications as to how to behave. She had to learn the swagger, the gestures; she had to exaggerate everything in herself and her memories of Jesse to put forward the appearance of an innocent youth.

It was so much better to have the leeway to be a

women. In Mobile, the shipping office paired her up with two of the women who were taking the voyage, and with them it had been an easy matter to acquire accommodations and to attend to the necessities.

But that would all change again once she arrived in Galveston. She hadn't even thought one minute past getting there, and—damn it—her body-wrenching nausea wouldn't allow her to do anything else.

The schooner *Southcross* arrived in Galveston on a mid-September day, and one day later, the steamer *Artesia* labored into port, discharging barrels of stores and supplies, and a handful of hard-traveling passengers, among them Trane Taggart, who hadn't given a damn how he got to Texas as long as he damned got there.

Getting there wasn't fun, either, but that was beside the point. Finding Cassandra would be like looking for a needle on the floor of the barn, but he was bound to find her. She would leave a trail of questions from Galveston right on to San Angelo, but he was willing to bet she would find what she wanted—or something of what she wanted—and relatively soon, too.

It all depended on whether she got lucky and started out in the right direction. It meant he had a choice of whether to go around asking questions or just plain go where he knew she would eventually wind up.

Wasted time.

He wanted to catch up with her before she got there. There were too many things that could get in the way afterward.

He couldn't take chances. He was going to go around to the most likely spots in town and ask if someone had been asking directions to Bitter Creek.

It sounded insane.

And he was a desperate man. He was dealing with the worst kind of feminine personality—a creative woman.

And the worst of all female traits—tenaciousness.

How the hell had she gotten to Texas and no one had seen or heard of her?

He had ridden the Watsonville to Albany route, and had checked every way station along the road, and not a man, not a stationmaster or coach driver, had seen anyone resembling Cassandra Taggart.

And, it seemed, neither had anyone in any hotel or any boarding place in the whole of Galveston. She had come and gone and no one had noticed one feisty green-eyed blonde with blood lust in her eye.

"Get dozens of travelers a week," one hotel clerk told him. "What do you expect? They stay one night and they're on a boat going inland . . . and you expect to find *one* woman—from how many we get coming here, man?"

He had even forgotten exactly what he had told her back those many months ago. He had mentioned Galveston, he had mentioned Texas, he had said . . . He could have said the whole damned place and every damned woman. What the hell had he told her?

. . . a little town, ten miles inland . . .

He heard himself saying it. For God's sake, whoever would have thought she'd be on her way down there four months later? And he knew she was going to hit Bitter Creek sooner than later, because he had stupidly given her the parameters.

And there wasn't anyone who had seen her go on either of the two yawls that sailed emigrants over to the mainland across Galveston Bay.

He didn't know what to make of it. Either he was so far behind her or she was so far ahead of him, he would never catch up to her; but she might just altogether catch him.

Well, by God, a man had to try, and if the wind didn't quite catch his sails, he would just go arrange for another boat.

She called herself "Case"; it sounded like a good,

strong, male kind of name, and she was going to need something muscular for protection, because she had had no idea that Galveston Bay was like a little horsehoe of water and that the place she was looking for might be anywhere ten miles from its perimeter.

Clever, clever Mr. Trager; of course he had never for once thought she would ever come looking for him here, but oh, how devious of him to characterize his home place as "ten miles inland."

How infuriating: she was so close and so far and she had not yet devised a strategy for asking the questions she needed to ask in order to track him down.

The easiest thing, once she was on the opposite shore, was to dive back into being a callow youth in transit and to pretend the Tragers were his family, and expecting him. Of course then he probably would have had instructions on where to find them. But maybe he had lost them. Maybe their last letter had fallen in the water as he was coming over from the island.

No, that didn't sound too likely.

In fact, the only story that seemed even remotely possible as a ploy was the very thing Mrs. Worth inferred on her voyage from Mobile: that she was going to have a child and that Cole Trager had finally sent for her.

Hmmm . . . It really went against the grain to use such a fabrication. There was something unholy about it, even to her, who had never shrunk from using anything at hand to accomplish her ends.

But it became increasingly clear to her, as she jolted down the little backroads from the coastal docking point of Port Landing, that her only recourse was to tell a plausible story, no matter how farfetched it really was.

The other caution was not to travel alone as a woman. She had in her pocket a crude little map drawn up for her by the captain of the sailing boat; he had been very firm and fatherly about where she should travel and how she should proceed, and she really was quite grateful to him for his interest.

He was worried about her; *she* was worried about her. This place was wholly unlike anything she had ever experienced before. This was a wild, raw place and, although the two coastal towns seemed generally civilized, she knew she had no preparation as to what to expect when she ventured inland.

How absolutely reckless could a woman be, tearing off to places unknown without some kind of protection other than a name and a pair of trousers? It boggled her mind that she had come this far without any major catastrophe.

Well . . . unless you counted — but she wasn't going to think about that.

She had her map, she got herself a horse and saddle, she managed to get back into her guise as a naive youth, and now, as she cantered cautiously along one route mapped out by her kindly captain, she wondered why she hadn't been smart enough to think of secreting a weapon as well, when she had packed up so hurriedly at Riveland, and she swore she would never do anything by the seat of her pants ever again.

"I'm looking for a family name of Trager." That was her voice, deep and gruff — and *young*-sounding. Those were her knees, knocking together in utter fear. And here she stood, in the doorway of what loosely might be called the general store in the small town of Deadman, and every last man within was looking at her as if he would like to see her dead, too.

"What fer?" This was a cranky-looking elderly man with wire glasses and a beard that reached midway down his chest.

"I — I'm kin," she said firmly, keeping her voice low and her eyes down.

"Ain't no one got kin in Deadman," the man said, turning to his mangy-looking companions. "Anyone know any Trager folk?"

There was an ominous muttering of negation.

"So, sonny . . ." The man in the wire frame glasses started walking toward her.

Oh, Lord, oh no . . . She backed away from him, feeling behind her for anything that blocked her way to the door. She almost stumbled as she crossed the threshold, and she turned and tripped down the three little steps to the porch, and she *ran*.

. . . Her *horse*—hitched right by the store . . . She ran; she didn't care where she got to, as long as it was as far away from that man with glasses as possible.

And Deadman consisted of one long main street with log cabins—maybe about twenty—laid out on quarter-acre plots, sited every which way. At one end of the main street was the plain clapboarded church, and at the other was the saloon and the general store, and that was all of Deadman.

She had to sneak back and get her horse, and she wondered how she could have been so stupid as to have left him anywhere near a place that predictably could have been a problem.

She pulled up by the church, wondering what to do next. The church looked deserted, as if no one in town ever got there on a Sunday. It looked like the symbol of something that had never happened: a growing, thriving town. There had to be a reason the place was called Deadman, she thought, but it had sounded to her just like a place a man like Cole Trager would come from.

She edged her way around the back of the church. Maybe, just maybe, it would be safe to go into the sanctuary and try to plan what to do next.

"Can I help you?"

She jumped. "Reverend—" *Oh God, lower that voice . . .*

"Come in, child." He had a sumptuous voice, the kind that would ring out from the pulpit and bring every last sinner to his knees. But he obviously had not had any success in Deadman.

She entered the church behind him, and he motioned

462

her to sit in one of the pews in back of the church. It was the simplest of all interiors, with plain benches lined up meticulously front to back, a two-step dais on which there was a lectern and a plain wooden cross appended to the wall behind.

"Who are you?" What a commanding voice the man had. She could have confessed anything to him. She decided not to.

"I'm looking for a family called Trager," she said.

"There are no families here," he said, and there was a sadness in his voice. "There are only men who want to tame a wilderness or tame Lady Luck. You won't find any families here."

"Then I'll keep searching," she said resolutely.

"Best not do it got up like a man, young lady," the minister said, so softly she almost did not catch his words. "You can't fool a man in this town," he added for good measure, and she looked up at him, startled. "This is one of them towns where men come to hide and let things slide. There's a reason they call it Deadman."

"That's what I was afraid of," she murmured. "I just had to start somewhere."

"You're lucky you had sense enough to come here," the minister said. "I'll help you, but you must get out of town today."

"I'll be happy to leave *right now*," Cassandra said emphatically.

"Good. Now tell me exactly what you're looking for, and I will do everything I can to aid you."

"My horse . . ."

"I'll get him."

"A map of some sort? I'm searching for this family, just as I said, and the only thing I know is, they're from a town inland from Galveston, about ten miles."

"Such urgency to come as far as you have—I can hear by the way you speak, my dear—I wonder if you would tell me why."

Oh, that old question *why*. She thought of a dozen explanations in the lingering moment between his asking the question and her answering it. But only one made that peculiar kind of sense.

"I'm looking for a man called Cole Trager. He's the father of my child."

It hit him finally, as the yawl sailed into the calm waters of Port Landing: no one had seen Cassandra because Cassandra had been impersonating someone else.

Darling Cassandra—she could have been anyone from an old lady to a ghost, and no one would have noticed her, she was that skillful.

Hell. What *would* she have been? How did a *man* try to emulate the thinking of a Cassandra?

Or . . . how did a Cassandra go about thinking like a man?

He played with that interesting thought for a moment. It went hand in hand with the meager clues she had left behind: she had taken no clothing, she had departed Riveland on horseback, at night. Wearing something that—it could be inferred—had been in that trunk with the cutaway leather strap.

Something she had brought with her to Riveland when she had came as a bride.

A woman who liked to don diguises to fight her way out of uncontrollable situations.

There had been some kind of disguise in that trunk.

And she had left in the deep of the night, on horseback, with little or nothing to hand to sustain her over a long trip except . . . what?

Money? Had there been something about money? If she had money, she could have purchased anything she needed along the way. All she had to do was take the most minimum of necessities.

But a woman couldn't travel light wearing a dress. It was too dangerous, as well as too cumbersome. She couldn't travel fast, either.

Yet she had gone, and she had gotten a day's gain on him—on horseback, and no one had noticed her.

There was only one conclusion he could draw from all those indications, and he was absolutely sure it was the right one: she hadn't traveled dressed as a woman. She had taken off from Riveland dressed as a man.

She was back in skirts again, this time with horse and buggy, courtesy of the minister of Deadman, and a more detailed but still rudimentary map of the towns in that ten-mile radius.

But she was still a woman alone, and she was beginning to think that vengeance and guts were the only things propelling her forward. What she was doing was sheer insanity, and she had no idea what to expect anywhere along the line.

She could run right into another town like Deadman. And it could be the very place where she would find out about Cole Trager, and she might be hung before she could even ask a question.

This was a place made up of savages, she thought; nothing was sure, not even that she would come away with her life.

They had mapped it all out, she and the minister, sitting on the dais, a piece of paper and his memory all that lay between her and any chance of success.

He had figured she had better start going north rather than west. After all, ten miles from Port Landing was a lot different from ten miles from Deadman, or even Anahuac on the other side of the bay.

He named the towns as he plotted them out on the map, and she recognized them as the very ones suggested by Mrs. Worth aboard the boat. Concha, Red Mesa, Alamosa, Bitter Creek, with Bitter Creek located about ten miles up from the outer curve of the Bay, and Alamosa down the other side, toward Anahuac.

She had a long ride ahead of her with no protection,

and only the kindness of strangers on which to depend.

"Can you handle a gun?" the minister asked her.

It had been so long ago, in another life, when a man had wanted to kill her so he could make another life. "Yes, I can," she said firmly, and he left her for a few minutes and returned with an old Colt revolver.

"You take that, ma'am. You might have need of it. But then again, maybe you won't. Now, I'm going to go see to your horse, and find you a buggy, and you'd best be on your way as soon as possible."

She was on her way sooner than that, and he rode with her a far piece to be sure that no one had followed her and no one molested her. She had changed into her dress, and he made sure that the bonnet of the rickety vehicle was securely fixed over her head to afford her the most protection possible. She offered to pay him, and he refused her money, but she forced him to take ten dollars for his collection box anyway.

When he left her, she felt bereft; it was like the good miller leaving the secret fairy-tale princess in the forest, except that the princess always had a charm or an incantation of some kind to rescue her from evil forces.

She had nothing except a will of iron and a determination to see the thing through.

Well, actually she had no choice. It was sheer folly not to turn straight around and head back to Port Landing and just go back where she came from.

But the next town was Red Mesa, and she just couldn't leave before she asked one or two questions *there*.

"You want to know if someone hired or bought a horse from me in the last two days, mister? Are you *crazy?*"

"Reckon I am. What do you say?"

"I say find me one day someone *doesn't* hire or buy a horse from this stable. You know how much trouble we have keeping stock, man? I tell you, if I'd of known when I come here . . . Yeah, someone—a lot of someones—

hired horses in the last two days. I need a little more to go on than that."

"How about someone young, a boy, maybe a little older, a little unsure of himself. Looking to get someplace fast and not knowing how to go. Blondish hair, slight build, real gruff-like voice . . ."

"Oh yeah, that one. Yeah, I remember that one. Had a lot of money, he did, and was just throwing it around. Didn't care what it cost, wanted the best mount, the best saddle, and directions inland. Yeah, I do remember that one. Was gonna head straight out to Deadman and wouldn't listen to nobody's warnings. Got a notion in his head, that one did, and just went for it."

Deadman. Hell. Trane tipped his hat. "Much obliged."

"What's your interest, man? I mean—in case anyone comes lookin' for *you?*"

"It's my brother, son, and a meaner tenderfoot you never met. Appreciate the information."

"No trouble," the stable owner called back. "Stop in and see me on your trip back. Let me know if you found 'im."

"I'll sell you my horse," Trane said grimly, "and maybe the son-of-a-bitching fool's tack." He waved as he rode off, a clutch of desperation grabbing his vitals. *Goddamn—Deadman.* Cassandra was a fool.

But no more than he, for trailing after her there.

It was almost dark when he pulled up on the outskirts of town. There wasn't much town. He knew where he was because of the saloon and the general store, right flat out at the top of the main street. Easy to get to, easy to leave. Free spenders liked that. And the low-life liked a place that staked out the newcomers and gave them a warning when someone appeared whose face wasn't likely to be welcomed.

He dismounted by the store and hitched his horse. Damn, he had a bad feeling already, and he hadn't been too long in the Georgia cotton fields to lose his fine sense of bad atmosphere. You didn't have to walk into the

467

store to feel it. It hung over the long main street like a heavy fog.

It was a place where nothing felt right unless you were doing something wrong. It was a place if you were fool enough to go to, you brought a gun or you were a dead fool.

He stepped into the store. All eyes whipped around to look at him, and one man moved away from the bunch, an elderly man with a long beard and wire-framed glasses.

"Stranger?"

"I'm looking for someone."

"Oh yes?"

"A boy . . . come through here maybe eight, twelve hours ago."

"A boy. You looking for a boy, stranger? A pretty boy?" The man moved closer and Trane tensed up. "You like them pretty boys, stranger? We got a hotbed of 'em here; you don't have to go chasin' after no boys, stranger. Just put your money down like the rest of 'em."

He went cold. "Tell me if you saw the boy."

"Wasn't no boy, stranger, and you and me know that."

"I want the boy," he repeated stonily.

"We ain't got no she-boys here, mister. You want to make somethin' of it?"

Damn hell. "Do you?" He reached for his gun first, pulled and fired just as the beard shot into the air, and knocked down the lantern that hung haphazardly over the center of the room.

The thing fell with a whoosh and immediately the flame caught the straw on the floor.

Trane backed away, and he jumped his horse on a run. He heard bullets whizzing through the air behind him as he galloped crazily down the street, the smell of acrid smoke following him, the sound of hoofbeats as someone came after him.

He barreled through a crowd running toward him as word of the fire spread, and the group parted for him like he was an Old Testament prophet; he rode through them and over them if they got in his way, and he heard the shouts and shots behind him: "Stop that man!" But he was too far ahead, he could feel it.

He just had to keep going and going and he would be out of that hell before someone really gave chase.

But where the hell he was going after *that* was anybody's guess.

He limped into Red Mesa at about eleven the next morning, grateful for the air of civility about the town that greeted him as he dismounted and hitched up and went looking for a two-bit public bath.

Damn, a man could get killed in Texas, that was for sure. He knew there was some reason he had left.

A washdown refreshed him considerably, but there wasn't anything he could do about his clothes, short of putting them on and then finding the mercantile store and purchasing something new.

In fact, that wasn't a half-bad idea. Red Mesa was one of those burgeoning little towns that was starting to grow, just far enough away from the lawless side of the Bay that it actually attracted settlers. So it was a bustling main street that morning, and there was a surprising variety of businesses lining the board sidewalk on the one side of the street, and a nice vista of homes lining the other and ranging westward and north going up toward the hills and right to the horizon.

Bitter Creek wasn't hardly this big. A handful of emigrants had found it over the years, as they became disillusioned with larger towns, and the proximity of places like Deadman. Bitter Creek had been just big enough to be heaven.

But that didn't take away from the sense of vibrancy of this town; he felt it as he rode the main street and searched for the dry goods store in town. These people were building, these people had hope.

469

And they had dreams enough to support a large variety store, which was located right down at the end of the main street; it needed all the space it could get, and it was set hard by the depot so goods and supplies didn't have to be hauled more than a hundred yards to reach their destination.

There was something about Red Mesa he liked very, very much.

He hitched up his horse again, right by a dilapidated little buggy, and stepped up onto the boardwalk.

And he heard a voice, a right-familiar voice, and he stopped dead in his tracks, right by the door to the store.

Was it her? It *had* to be her. . . . The words were right—but there was something very wrong.

"I'm looking for a family named Trager."

Yes, that was Cassandra's voice, all right.

"Don't know of no family in these parts, ma'am. Trager, you say? It don't sound familiar to me."

"I've come a long way," she went on, "all the way from Georgia."

"By yourself, ma'am? I do say . . . Trager?"

"Yes, sir."

He could just see her now. Oh, was that ever Cassandra, playing emigrant woman to the hilt—bonnet, calico dress and all.

And then she turned slightly and he could see her slightly rounded middle. And he heard her words: "I'm looking for their son, sir; his name is Cole Trager," and he felt a cold anger wash over him.

The lying, cheating, deceiving little witch . . .

"He's the father of my baby. . . ."

Chapter Twenty-seven

"Nope, never heard of a family called Trager around here," the storekeeper said, his voice sympathetic. "I wish I could help you, ma'am, but all I can offer is a selection of goods in the store. You just take your time and look around. Now, sir, can I do something for you?"

"I reckon you have," Trane drawled from the doorway, and Cassandra whirled around, her face a study in pure vexation. "You're about to reunite me with my *beloved* wife."

"I've never seen this man before," Cassandra said.

"She . . . wears glasses," Trane interpolated quickly. "Come kiss me, Cassandra. Aren't you happy to see the 'father of your baby'?"

"I'd be very happy to see him if you were he," she snapped.

"I do believe it's possible I'm not he," Trane said smilingly through gritted teeth, "but you *are* my own dear wife, and I'm taking you home with me before you get into any more trouble with those men you habitually attract. Trust me, Cassandra—all is forgiven."

"I'll never forgive you if you don't let me walk out of this store," she hissed.

"I'll go to church. Better still, I'll take you to church. I'm sure you have a lot of praying to do, Cassandra."

"I'm going to pray I never see you again."

"My dear, the glasses—all this talk about not seeing—

471

you really should put aside your vanity."

"Trane . . ."

"No, dear, there are no trains into Red Mesa, not yet."

She bit her lip. "I want to get out of here."

"That's fine. I'm ready to leave myself."

"That *relieves* me, but I don't intend to go anywhere with you."

"You're not going anywhere without me, either."

"I'll just push you out of the way."

"I always said you were pushy, Cassandra. I invite you to try it."

"You try my patience beyond belief," she snapped.

"Yes, I do agree one needs a certain amount of stamina when matching wits with you."

"And you of course have the staying power."

"I think I have proved that already, Cassandra," Trane said gently.

She stamped her foot and turned her back on him and looked right into the interested gaze of the storekeeper. "Best you go with him, ma'am. He looks like he's fixing to stay, and I don't know what that's going to do for business."

"I wish I could give him the business," she retorted.

"Not a very businesslike proposition, Cassandra, when I'm so much stronger than you," Trane said, coming up behind her, putting his arms around her and just turning her and hoisting her up over his shoulder. "Much obliged, mister. She can be the very devil when she gets a bee in her bonnet. A woman gets like that when she's carrying, I guess. I could tell you how a man feels when he's carrying—but I reckon that's another conversation for another day. Thanks again."

He shook the man's hand, ignoring Cassandra's kicking feet and the fists that pummeled his back with the rhythm of a tom-tom.

And then he turned to face a positive ground swell of interested onlookers. "Well, I'm damned. Look at that, Cassandra. This is a town that has your very welfare at heart."

"I'd like to have a knife at your heart, Trane Taggart."

"You do keep going on about trains, Cassandra. Far as I know, there's no trunk line to Red Mesa. I take it that's your buggy?"

"Yes."

He carried her down the sidewalk and set her down in the seat. "Room for two. Good planning."

"I wasn't planning—"

"No, that was damned evident," he growled, unhitching his horse and tying it behind the buggy.

"Well, who the hell gave me directions, for God's sake: ten miles inland from Galveston. Who expected a damned wilderness?"

"And who the hell had to track you clear across three states and set fire to a whole town in the process?"

"Who?" she demanded nastily.

He swung into the buggy next to her and picked up the reins. "Why it was old Cole Trager, honey. The man who is going to save your virtue."

"Trane—"

"No, Cassandra, we are not going to a train, either. I'm taking you back to Riveland."

She ground her teeth. "No, you're not. I'm going to find out what I came to find out, because I know damned well you're not going to tell me."

"No, I don't think I am."

"Fine . . . I've got the whole picture anyway. All I need are the details."

"You're never going to find them. You don't even know where to look."

"I'm going to do just what I started out to do: I'm going to canvass every town until I find . . . Cole Trager."

"You won't find him, Cassandra."

"That won't deter me. I'll find *something*."

"God, you are a handful."

"But you know that already, whatever your name is. And you're not getting Riveland away from me."

Goddamn hell.

There wasn't anything he could tell her now.

"You won't find Cole Trager," he said again.

"What *will* I find?" she asked sweetly.

"You've found it already, black widow—the legacy of Jesse's lies."

"And Trane Taggart is the biggest lie of all."

He didn't like that, and he couldn't refute it.

"Where are we going?" she asked after a moment.

"Up toward Concha. There's a boat from there back down to Port Landing, and that's how we're going."

"Really." She thought furiously for a moment. Concha was several miles farther to the north of Red Mesa. She didn't feel any tension in him at the thought of going there. There was nothing there, then. It wasn't the place where she would find the family Trager. It was just a place. So beyond that, there was just Bitter Creek and then Alamosa. Two more towns, one of which perhaps hid the secrets she had come to uncover.

She had to get there without him. She had to try.

It was more imperative than ever now, especially since he had come chasing after her. It meant something was on the line. And it was just possible he was feeling rash enough to do something desperate to prevent her from finding out the truth.

Concha was a smaller town, a settlement, really, the gateway to western Texas, the townspeople liked to say. A man had to travel a long way to get in, but he had an easy way out. The ferries ran once a day, early in the morning, and got a man to Port Landing in time to catch the first boat to Galveston.

They had to spend the evening, and Trane wasn't about to give Cassandra her head and let her do what she wanted.

474

"Oh, really? But where could I go?"

"Who knows what you would dream up to do," he said grimly. "Damn, if I had a pair of handcuffs, I'd snap them right on your wrist so I'd know where you were every minute."

But the best he could do was a hotel room; registering them as Mr. and Mrs. Cole Trager—out of spite, she thought, because obviously no one in town knew the name, and he meant to make it very clear to her just what folly her search had come to.

She refused to give up. There were two more towns, Bitter Creek and Alamosa, and if nothing turned up in Alamosa, she would give up and go back to Riveland.

Riveland . . . God, it was like a dream. She had spent too much time in travel, too much energy combatting unseen enemies. She had to find the truth.

She settled herself down in the bed, and sent him a challenging look. He pulled up a sagging upholstered chair and folded his long legs against the edge of the mattress.

"Tell me about this 'father of the baby' business."

She didn't see any harm in that. "I made it up. It seemed like a good way to get information out of people. Who wouldn't tell a woman who was going to have a baby where her husband's family was?"

She just utterly amazed him. "You are something, black widow. You just spin away all those little plots and schemes. And look at where you are: far and away from where you belong, letting other people run your business. I don't know what kind of sense that makes."

"There is no sense," she said tiredly. "There's nothing. There's not even you. You'd save me a lot of trouble if you told me who you really were."

"You choose, Cassandra. I'll be whoever you need me to be."

"Be Cole Trager, because then at least I can understand what you did and where you came from."

"Then you understand *nothing,*" he grated. "And you're

475

better off not even talking about it."

"Or you are," she retorted.

"I definitely am," he agreed silkily. "Go to sleep, Cassandra. There's nothing more to say."

She did think there was, but he was looking adamant and so angry that she couldn't trust herself not to make him erupt.

She concentrated instead on the room, and how she could escape him. It didn't look too promising, unless she could somehow manage to incapacitate him; but her gun was rolled up with the rest of her possessions in the back of the buggy, which he had stabled. She could only think of one other way to put him flat on his back and she wasn't sure she wanted to go that far.

She felt tired suddenly, drained by her emotions, queasy, and not for the first time this past night and day. Maybe she needed to sleep, but she could not bear to close her eyes and give herself over to him.

Maybe she needed something to eat: her stomach was rumbling and lurching, but she didn't want to ask him for anything—not *anything*.

"I asked the desk clerk to get us some food," Trane said after a while, taking pity on her tormented expression.

"Did you?" she murmured. How convenient. He would take the food, do something to it, offer it to her, and they would play the same scenario as had happened after her accident on Riveland. "How thoughtful." She had to get *out of there*.

She wound her hands around her roiling stomach. It was a large square room they were in, with one window, which was a straight drop three stories down: she had checked. There was one closet, one bed, one dresser, the bedraggled chair which could barely hold Trane's weight. A pair of worn curtains surrounding the window with which, in a pinch, she could try to tie him up.

But this wasn't like that first time at Riveland. He wasn't going to sleep one minute this night, for suspicion

476

of her devious nature.

Well, he had dealt enough times with that. She had to think of something totally outside the realm of anything she had ever done before in order to escape him this time, and her brain was too tired to even consider anything but the most mundane ideas.

It would come. Some opportunity would present itself. She had only to wait and be patient, and she would be on her way to Bitter Creek.

It was the coffee the next morning; just the scent of it sent her stomach reeling, and she wasn't sure she could even drink it after the long fraught night of keeping herself awake.

She could smell it even beyond the door, and when Trane brought in the tray, she could see there wasn't much choice. The clerk had sent up two cups, a battered pot filled to the brim with steaming brew, some sugar, and a small plate of biscuits, with no butter to accompany it.

But it really was the coffee. There was something about the smell of it: it was like the soup and fried meat the previous night. They had looked good, smelled good, and tasted like water and shoe leather. She could hardly eat last night; she was sure she couldn't take anything in her stomach this morning.

Trane put the tray down on the small stand next to her bed, and she felt that sensation coursing through her stomach once again.

Or maybe it was the mornings. Ever since that two-week trip on the *Southcross,* she had never been right in the mornings.

She wasn't right this morning.

She almost felt as if . . .

No, no . . .

But if it happened—it was something over which she had no control—and if he happened to be right

477

nearby . . .

Oh no, oh no, not even she could be plotting and planning something like that while her stomach was revolting against everything on the tray in front of her.

He poured the coffee. "Sugar, I remember?"

"Trane —"

"Something hot. It will wake you up."

"I'm awake," she said desperately, because there was no stopping events now. "I have to —"

But she didn't have time; as she levered herself out of bed, her body took care of the rest — and he was just leaning forward to hand her the cup. It went crashing to the floor, and the liquid poured all over him along with something else, and he was so startled, she had a moment, just a moment, to relieve herself and then push him — *push* him so hard that he fell backward heavily, and she made a mad dash to the door.

Down the steps, holding her stomach, how stupid was that? She was in no shape to travel, not now. No, she could finish this little episode somewhere along the way, she would — Anything was worth getting that extra chance to hunt down Cole Trager, even this monumental distress, even the murderous anger that she could hear in his voice all the way down the steps after her.

She raced past the hotel clerk, who called after her, and she fell heaving into a little side garden bound by bushes where her travail was obscured, if not unnoticed.

After that it was a small matter to repossess her buggy, pay the stablemaster, hitch up her horse, ask directions, and triumphantly start on her way to Bitter Creek.

A man could get bitter, he thought, as he sat up in that stifling room drowning himself in coffee while the hotel clerk hunted up a laundress to wash out his clothes. A man wasn't prepared for exigencies like this: a man just didn't think something like this would happen.

A man got in trouble when he came to care for a devi-

478

ous woman.

The fat was in the fire now. He wouldn't be able to get a mile near Bitter Creek before her, and there was nothing he could do about it.

He didn't know if it were better or worse if she confronted what awaited her there without him. But she had made the choice and she owned it. She wanted the end of the story, and she sure as hell was going to find that.

He wondered, at the end, what she might find in her heart.

He wondered if he would get there in time to find out.

And then she heard the last words she expected to hear:

"Never heard of no family named Trager here and about, ma'am."

She thought she would die. She had been so sure.

She had spent the whole morning's journey in anticipation of coming right to the truth the moment she asked the question.

Bitter Creek was the same kind of little settlers' town, deeper into the wilderness, with only a trading post, saloon and hotel on its modest main street.

"Creek's down yonder," the post keeper told her. "Got some good grazing land back beyond, big ranches. They start to run cattle around and about here, got those big spreads. Bitter Creek ain't a highly populated town. I been here a few years, I run the whole thing from here; I get the supplies and the post, and I'm telling you there's never been no Trager in these here parts."

She felt a nauseating wallop of disappointment.

But she tried again. "I'm looking for a man named Cole Trager."

"Now, ma'am, if there ain't no Tragers in Bitter Creek, how is there gonna be someone named Cole Trager?"

"Only Cole we got around here," another man put in, "is Col*trane* — "

"WHAT?!"

"—but you ain't lookin' for the likes of him, I don't expect."

"What did you say?" she demanded.

"I said we got a Col-*trane*, ma'am, but he ain't no Trager."

"What *is* he?" she asked faintly, her heart throbbing so hard she was sure it would burst right out of her body.

"He's a Taggart, ma'am, what did you think?"

God, what did she think? What did she think? She didn't know what to think.

He's a Taggart, ma'am . . .

She moistened her lips, but no sound came out.

We got a Col-trane, ma'am, but he ain't no Trager . . .

She just couldn't believe this. She couldn't comprehend it at all.

"Does . . . does Coltrane Taggart live around here?" she managed to ask finally.

"Did, down the road a ways before the creek. Why do you think, ma'am?"

"Well . . ." Well, *why?* Where was her inventive mind now? She knew right well—it was all tumbled upside down and she couldn't get it rightside up and *thinking* again. "Well—maybe he is the man I'm looking for."

"Doubt it, ma'am. Ol' Trane's been gone 'bout five months now, don't know where."

"But still—"

"Ma'am, you just don't pry into a man's life around here 'less you got a real good reason."

Back to the lies, and now who was the impostor? she castigated herself. But—God, she had to do it, she had to *know.* "I'm . . ." She took a deep breath. "I'm his wife."

"Stands to reason you know where he is, ma'am."

Damn the man. Now what? She didn't want to say it, but he had left her no choice. "He left me and our baby . . . our baby to be . . . and he promised to send for us and . . ."

"Don't sound like Trane Taggart, ma'am."

Oh, the man had a gimlet eye and a fine-honed sense of the truth, or else he was a damned close friend of Trane's. Or whoever he was.

"I came to appeal to his family," she said, in a last-ditch effort to sway him.

"He didn't tell you nothin' about his family?" the post keeper asked in disbelief.

"He *told* me his name was Cole Trager," she retorted, reaching deep down in her bag of tricks for something to keep the lies alive. "Don't tell me that doesn't sound like Trane Taggart. Just tell me where . . . where I can find his family."

The post keeper's face softened just the barest bit. "I'll have Jimmy here take you there. Jim?"

"Hey—McNeil—I . . ."

"You just do what the lady wants. You take her to Trane's family. You know where they are."

"Whyn't you do it, and I'll stay by," Jimmy said.

McNeil eyed him speculatively. "All right. Maybe that would be better. Now . . . Mrs.—?"

"Trager," she said sharply. The lies, the lies—

"You got a buggy here. Good. Real good. It's all right, Mrs. Trager. There isn't any mystery. I'm going to take you to Trane's family is all, just like you want. You have no enemies here in Bitter Creek."

But I do, she thought, as he cracked the whip and her horse moved forward.

It was not a short trip; it wasn't a long trip. After a while she could see the glittering water of the creek beyond the green of the wilderness where it merged with the sky. They seemed to be climbing upward to some plateau; already she could look down and see landmarks, places they had passed, the creekbed, circumscribed and whole, and far in the distance, the three or four buildings that made up the town.

"Trane's spread starts about here," McNeil told her at a place where the ground leveled out and there was a gate and the start of a split-rail fence.

There was a road hacked out of this wilderness that was fenced and deeply ridged from wagons and horse hooves, and McNeil opened the gate and drove through and along this road deeper and deeper away from anywhere, deeper into the woods and the silence, and Cassandra became queasy and uneasy once again.

"I wish you would tell me," she said fretfully.

"Can't tell you what a man didn't want you to know, ma'am. I can show you, though. Doesn't violate nothing to *show* you."

Show her?

Show her?

She saw it first, a small square area that was chained off to the side of the road, and she turned an angry green questioning gaze on Mr. McNeil.

"Taggart's family," he said succinctly.

She swung her legs out of the buggy and walked slowly to the little cemetery.

There were two graves, both well markered with names, one of which she recognized immediately; the other — she wasn't sure . . .

Jackman Taggart, she read. *Died December 1858 . . .*

Jesse's mysterious brother. Jesse's *brother . . . ?*

And the other grave marker: *Marigrace Sheffield Taggart,* she read. *Died January 1859 . . .*

"Mr. Taggart's wife?" she asked, pointing to the grave, her back still turned to Mr. McNeil.

"No, Cassandra," Trane's voice said behind her. "My mother, and Jesse's first wife."

Chapter Twenty-eight

She fainted.

All this and nothing . . .

She thought she had died.

Somebody had died. A lot of people had died and she had got caught in the middle somehow.

Nothing was what it seemed.

She didn't want to know what things really were. If she knew that, she might explode.

Something in her felt like exploding anyway.

When she awakened the next morning, she felt the queasiness again, and she didn't know where she was or what had happened. She was in somebody's bed in a cold room and the light of dawn was snaking through a window.

Someone knocked on the door.

"Go away."

"Cassandra."

She didn't answer him, and he pushed the door open anyway.

"I hate you," she said stormily, and turned her head away. He had no right, no right at all to be Trane Taggart. She couldn't even look at him. She wondered if she could even look at herself.

"This is Jackman's place," he said easily, ignoring her little tantrum.

"You could have told me." And she didn't know if she

could ever forgive him for that.

"Told you *what*—that Jesse was never married to you? Forgive me, Cassandra. I wanted to find an easier way around that one. It kind of negates a lot of things—like Jesse's will."

"Oh God," she groaned, and clutched her stomach. She felt like an avalanche of unbearable facts was sliding down all over her, burying her, suffocating her . . . "Oh, God . . ." She was going to die. A human being could not stand to have the ground ripped out from under her in one crashing torrent.

She really felt like she couldn't breathe.

"Cassandra . . ."

"I can't talk. I'm going to . . . I'm going to . . ." She jumped out of bed and raced for the door, frantically looking for an exit outside. Outside . . . yes . . . outside was the truth—outside—

She wrenched open the door and ran, ran as far as she could until she had to stop, had to relieve her heaving stomach, had to lie on the grass, exhausted, until he came and picked her up.

"I don't believe it," she said defiantly. "I don't believe any of it. You set it up."

"Oh, I'm one fast worker, spider lady. Ain't nobody faster than *you*, ma'am. I can't keep one damn foot ahead of you. You just tell me how I flew in here last night and got up this little cemetery and then got back to Concha in time for your little performance this morning."

"I still don't believe it."

"That's fine, Mrs. Taggart. You just don't believe it."

She buried her face in his shoulder. A strong shoulder, muscular, flexed with the effort of carrying her. She hated him. She couldn't believe him. She couldn't believe the events.

Everything came to an end in Bitter Creek.

She really would have been better off had she let him take her back home to Riveland.

* * *

In the night it came to her that Trane really was Jesse's son, and the reality of what that meant to her was like a lead weight straight to her stomach. After all this time, it was true: she was the barren one, the one who would never conceive, the one who had to live forever with that knowledge. She mourned; she knew she mourned: her pillow was wet with tears and the sense of something gone so intense it was almost like having lost the child itself.

And what was left were the questions, and even the questions couldn't explain why the fates had chosen to deprive her, and her alone.

But the questions . . . Jesse's wife had been dead—he could not have married her otherwise . . . and yet she was dead and buried here in the very year that Jesse himself had died. . . . How did that make sense? Nothing made sense.

The emptiness overwhelmed her; she couldn't sleep.

He was really Coltrane Taggart; she hadn't made him up. He was really Jesse's son. There really was a brother named Jackman. And what were they all doing in Bitter Creek, Texas, twenty years after Trane had run away from Riveland?

It made no sense.

She refused to ask him.

The following morning, she trekked up to the cemetery again and examined the grave markers. They were thick blocks of wood, neatly incised by the burning end of a pointed branding iron.

Jackman Taggart. Died December 1858.

Marigrace Sheffield Taggart. Died January 1859.

A month later?

"I buried them both," Trane said behind her. "They wanted to be buried together. They loved each other, always had. She took sick after he died, and never recovered. Made me promise, though. I had to promise to go back and see Jesse and tell him she had died, and his

485

brother had gone, and make him do what was right. I didn't have a hope in hell of doing that, but I figured why not? I didn't have anywhere else of my own and I was damned tired and drained after they both died."

"So you came . . ."

"I grant you, I took the long way around. I didn't want to face Jesse after all those years, not really. But I promised."

"I see." She didn't see. She saw Jesse's wife's grave on the hill, and she saw that she had never been married to Jesse, and that was all.

"So she was living here, all those years I thought I was Jesse's wife." The words did come out, calmly, reasonably; she stated the case exactly right.

"I reckon so," Trane said, "but I swear nobody knew Jesse had taken another wife. Jackman would have called him on it, I swear to you he would have."

"But all those years . . . ," she whispered.

"I know."

"And you knew," she added, as that tormenting thought heaped itself on the dungheap of everything else.

"How could I tell you?"

She shook her head. "I don't know . . . I don't know."

But he should have.

Except—then what would have happened? She would have lost everything.

No, maybe he had been right—

She never would have known if she hadn't come tearing out to Bitter Creek to find another man's memories.

"I can't bear this."

"No . . ." He made no move to touch her, and he wanted to so desperately.

"How much worse does it get?" she asked finally.

"You know the worst already."

"Oh good," she murmured.

"Maybe it is good."

"Will you tell me the rest?" she asked.

"I'm not exactly sure what you mean."

"I mean all of it. I mean that we—that is, my mother and I, thought Jesse's first wife was dead."

"I would doubt if you ever heard him say it. He might have said she was gone or he was alone or something. He was a crafty old bastard, and I'll tell you, he was treating my mother about the same as I imagine he treated you after you had been married for several years."

"Yes . . . ," she whispered.

"So I ran away, just like you heard, and I came straightaway to Bitter Creek to my Uncle Jackman, and I told him what Jesse was doing, and I'll tell you what he did . . ."

"Yes . . . ?"

"He stole her away from Jesse, just like he had done all those years ago, and Jesse never knew—though I bet he suspicioned—where she got to, and he probably didn't care anyway, because he had an opportunity to get himself a fine *young* girl in his bed—"

"Yes . . ."

"And so he made it seem like my mother had died, because he couldn't goddamn bear to think she was happy finally. . . ."

"Yes . . . "

"And he tried to get himself a son, didn't he?"

"Yes . . ."

"And he couldn't . . ."

"No—and it was my fault, my fault . . ."

"And he couldn't," Trane said again, "and he started to hate you just like he hated my mother, because he couldn't get a son. . . ."

"But he had one," she whispered.

"He couldn't get a son, Cassandra, not from my mother, not from you, not from anyone. You know it. *You know it.*"

"But you—"

"She loved Jackman first," he said tautly. "Did you know he and Jesse worked Riveland in those first years? You know what an animal Jesse was, and there was his brother—refined, caring, hardworking, a month too late to court her. What do you think, Cassandra? What do you think?"

"Oh God . . ."

"You think she could stop loving him—even after she had his child and pretended it was Jesse's? You think Jesse didn't know? Or didn't find out? I never got which. I never cared. When he started beating on her, I made sure Jackman got her out of there. She was Mrs. Taggart till the day she died, Cassandra, but she was the *right* Mrs. Taggart. The only thing she didn't have was the paper, and who the hell needed that in the wilderness."

"His son?" she whispered.

"Not Jesse's," he said stonily. "Thank God, not Jesse's, but it took me years to work over that one. I went away from them, too, and God, I wished I hadn't, after I got through understanding it. That's why I promised her. I wanted to kill him with the knowledge that he had committed a crime before God and man, and the son of a bitch died before I got there, and only because I couldn't get up the guts to face him sooner. I'll never forgive myself for that, either. I wanted to spit in the bastard's face."

"Not his son," Cassandra repeated. Not, not, not; it was a drumbeat in her heart. Not, not, not . . . It was Jesse, it had always been Jesse—She started to cry. "Oh God . . ." The tears streamed down her face. *Not his son.* What it meant to her . . . not his son—she felt like she was coming apart, like she was breaking into fragments, like she was a character in a children's rhyme, all coming to pieces, and the pieces were drowning in a flood of tears that she could never stop.

And then she felt herself being gathered up in someone's arms, someone strong and warm who held her tightly, as if he would never let her go, as if his power and desire alone could make her whole.

Nothing could heal the wound. She had been the only one living a lie and now she had to come to terms with that.

"I can't even go back to Riveland," she told Trane later on that evening.

"You have no choice," he said. "This is Jackman's house, as I said, but after my mother died, I made arrangements to sell it as he required in his will. *We* have to go back."

"You don't need to to anything, Mr. Taggart. You can do whatever you want. How lovely it is to be a man, free from those kinds of encumbrances."

"Whoever said I was free?" he asked obliquely.

"Who owns this house?"

"McNeil, as it happens."

She shook her head in disbelief. Layers upon layers. The man who would introduce her to Trane's family had bought the house. . . .

"I don't want to go back," she said.

"If you don't go back, you can't go forward."

"And where have *I* got to go any which way?" she demanded furiously. "I have nothing, *nothing.*"

"Nobody knows that, Cassandra, except you and me."

"Oh yes, and what were you planning to do with it, Mr. Taggart, with all your little secrets?"

"I *wasn't* planning to fall in love with you," he ground out.

"That's rich, Trane. You sure you don't want to amend that, now that I may not have possession of Riveland?"

"Did you ever think who would?"

"No, I never got that far, Trane, but it's obvious you did."

"*If* I ever did, I don't want to speculate now, Mrs. Taggart. You are in no fit state to discuss this anyway."

"What am I in a fit state for, Mr. Patronizing Taggart?"

"Spinning your webs, black widow. You'll figure it out; I don't doubt you will. But we are guests here by the grace of the kind and extremely patient Donald McNeil,

489

who never has liked spending autumn evenings in the loft over his store. We vacate tomorrow morning, Cassandra, and there's nowhere to go but back to Riveland."

Nowhere to go, and she wasn't even sure about Riveland. For someone who had wanted to get away from it so hard, she was allowing Trane to push her back there faster than she would have dreamt possible. And even then, she might have to leave it all over again.

All those weeks of travel to come to this end, and to turn around in another week and go back again. Something in there seemed irrelevant and futile, and she didn't quite know what it was.

She didn't know what to expect of their journey home either, but the first surprise he handed her was that they would be traveling together.

"As husband and wife?"

"It's the only way, ma'am."

"Well, I won't go."

"I'll carry you up on deck myself."

"And we know how efficient you are at carrying things around."

"Never dropped anything yet, Mrs. Taggart."

"Don't I know it, sir. Not even a secret."

"Let it go, Cassandra."

"Oh, I don't think I can, Trane. I just don't think I can."

Secrets . . . They overlaid the moments she had of tender feeling toward him, especially back on the *Southcross* on its second return trip to Mobile, when she was laid up in her bunk again, exactly the same as before, with the debilitating seasickness.

He nursed her, and he stayed with her. He wiped her brow and he talked to her. He held her and he scolded her, and there was something so sweet about it, she wished there were no secrets and that they really were going back to something real, something they were building

490

together.

It was on the train, somewhere between Mobile and the first stop of the southwestern trunk of the line they were traveling, that she first understood with clarity what he meant when he had asked if she had ever thought who would gain possession of Riveland.

And it was so very simple. If Jesse's will were invalid, his next of kin would inherit . . . not her, not his first wife. His brother, the mysterious Jackman. And if Jackman were dead, then his heirs, because Jesse had no other kin that she knew of. And that meant . . .

Trane.

And that meant—he had been using her all along and everything was a lie and a ruse solely to get hold of Riveland—exactly what he had said he did not want to do.

She was sick with it. Even his story about promising to confront Jesse had probably been a lie. Why not? Who stood to gain the most no matter what happened, but the convenient Mr. Taggart.

If she could have run from that train and escaped into oblivion, she would have done it.

She watched the endless stretches of flatland and towns roll by and she watched Trane's face, impassive and secretive, watching the scenery, watching her when she wasn't looking.

She had figured it out—he could see it in her eyes, and he didn't know whether he was glad or sorry about that.

She looked at him differently now; she would never look at him again with that seductive green gaze that gave no quarter and begged no mercy.

He had lost her, and he had known the risks when he followed her to Bitter Creek.

It was all bitter; the whole story was like bile in his mouth, in his gut. And he didn't know what they were going back to.

They had been gone—she had been gone—almost two

months, maybe more, by calculation—too much time to leave Riveland in the hands of a man like Mr. Greve.

He felt an urgency about it that was not mitigated by Cassandra's voice coming at him in the darkness one night.

"Do you want to know the irony of it?" she said scathingly. "You'll enjoy this, Trane, I know. I remade my own will before I left Carthage. Yes, I did. I didn't want Linnea to get her hands on Riveland after all that had happened. I didn't want her getting any ideas, so I changed things. I made the whole thing over to you. Now tell me *that* isn't funny, Trane."

"Ma'am, I think it's tragic," he said, and he meant it. She had only been to town that one day; she must have done it then, and she had no inkling at all, no assurance that Greve had ever filed the papers.

He had a bad feeling, a real bad feeling, and he didn't know how to tell her that, either.

They were doomed, he thought, because he couldn't tell her anything at all.

She was lying on her side on the bed in the hotel in Watsonville, and they were so close to home.

"Cassandra . . ."

"What?" she said rigidly.

"We have to talk."

"I can't talk. My stomach won't let me talk, or eat, or ride—or damned anything."

"You've been sick to your stomach almost every morning."

"You know I have." She turned her head away. "I hate it."

He didn't know if he hated it—he rather liked the idea, but it was the wrong time, damn it; it was just the wrong time.

"Cassandra . . ."

"What?"

"Listen to me."

"Must I? I have, and I don't like what I've heard."

"You're going to like the rest a lot less. But you have to hear me out."

"I have no choice."

"I guess you don't, black widow. Here is how it goes: I'm going into Carthage today to get a fix on things."

That made her sit up. "What do you mean?"

"Frankly, ma'am, I don't know what I mean. I just have a feeling, is all, and I like to know the lay of the land before I commit my gunfire."

"I see—I have to trust you because you're leaving me here?"

"That's about the size of it, ma'am."

"Well, I'll tell you, Trane Taggart, the suit doesn't fit. I go too."

"Sure, we just waltz into Carthage together after almost two months. That doesn't make too much sense, either."

"Right, and next you'll tell me you can move faster without being encumbered with a *woman*."

"And next you'll tell me you have a handy pair of trousers and you can move faster than lightning."

"You got that right, Mr. Taggart. That's exactly what it is."

"Spider lady's up to her old tricks again, eh?"

"I don't know what you're talking about, Mr. Taggart."

"I damn bet you don't, lady. Fine, get yourself trousered up, Mrs. Taggart. Let's see what kind of a man you really are."

She made a short, slender man, with a six-shooter in her pocket, her hair greased up and under her hat, and that seductive mouth hidden under the shadow of its brim.

She just might make it, he thought, as they unhitched their horses and mounted up for the ride into Carthage.

493

It was rounding on noon, and they weren't going to speed on in there; he set the pace because he wanted them to look like casual travelers to the ninety percent of the casual population that would be abroad on the main street in the afternoon.

Come to that, he didn't even know what he expected to discover on this little foray. He didn't expect to find that Riveland was the sole topic of conversation on the street corners in Carthage.

It was a busy, bustling day in Carthage, and no one took notice of them, just as he had reckoned.

"Well, this is just fine," Cassandra said dourly. "What next?"

"I don't know . . . I just don't know—" He was thinking hard, thinking fast. They had been gone two months. A lot could happen in two months. "I've got two thoughts. I think I'm going to go on over to the Riversgate and ask after Mr. Greve. I think that would be a very wise thing to do. And you are just going to keep your head down, Mrs. Taggart, and mind them horses."

The hotel was farther along toward the river, and they had to nose their horses through a swarm of carriages, wagons and riders. "We'll hitch up across the street here, Cassandra, and I swear, if you make a move, there's going to be hell to pay."

"I can't move," she said, her voice muffled. She felt just godawful. She felt like a stuffed and trussed turkey. She should have stayed at the hotel, she thought; she could have slept the morning away and felt better later. Or maybe she just could have made her way back to Riveland and left him in Watsonville, and that would have been a much better ending to the story.

He wouldn't have had the nerve to follow her there and make claims he probably couldn't substantiate. He would have just gone away, and she wished he would. If he could just walk through the door at the Riversgate and disappear into another realm somehow, her nightmare would be over.

She turned her head slightly to watch him as he deftly skirted the street traffic and mounted the boardwalk in front of the hotel.

He turned to look at her for a moment before he entered: he didn't trust the spider lady, not one damned bit. She was hunched over, looking every bit like she was going to take off at a high gallop at any moment. Damn it.

"Where's Greve?" he demanded as he pushed in the door.

The concierge looked at him with a raised eyebrow. "Excuse me, *sir*."

"Where's Greve?" Trane said again, reining in his temper and the real bad feeling he had about Mr. Greve's whereabouts.

"Who wants to know?" the concierge asked aggressively. He had orders from Mr. Greve, very specific orders, and a bundle of money to back it up. Mr. Greve wanted things very quiet. Mr. Greve was a very private man.

"Trane Taggart wants to know," Trane said with an edge in his voice.

"Mr. Taggart." The clerk knew that name for sure. Taggart was the former owner of Riveland, and the name of the sister of the woman who lived there now. "Mr. Taggart." He was rolling the name around on his lips, as if he were weighing it, trying to decide whether this were someone Mr. Greve would want to know his business.

Trane tossed a bill on the desk.

The concierge didn't even look at it, but he knew very well it was there, and he even knew the amount. "Mr. Greve is preparing for his wedding this evening to Mrs. Wiltshire."

Goddamn hell.

He had to get out of there, *fast*. "Much obliged," he said, and he walked—he *walked* out of that hotel lobby, and he made it across that street calmly and purposefully, and he swung up into the saddle next to Cassandra, who looked like she had not moved one muscle since he had

495

left her.

"We're going to Riveland, Cassandra."

"Of course we are," she agreed instantly. Her wish hadn't come true; he was going with her, and it was the last thing in the world she wanted.

He hesitated a moment. "I wish I had the goddamned receipt to the strongbox."

"Why is that, Mr. Taggart?"

"You have to trust me, Cassandra."

"Really, now—the man who will take over Riveland if I hand him whatever is in that box so he can prove he is the rightful heir. Please, Mr. Taggart, that really strains the imagination."

"And God knows you have one, spider lady. Well, I'll tell you what. You just stand by here and let good old Mr. Greve hitch up with your sister and then see where Riveland is going to be."

She caught her breath. "What do you mean?"

"Hell, I don't know what I mean, Cassandra. I don't know anything except Greve is getting married tonight, and you—you've been gone from Riveland for two months, and I don't suppose you've even thought about the consequences of *that*."

She hadn't. "Oh my God . . ."

"You have to make a choice, spider lady, and a damned quick one. It's me—or you, and I don't rightly think you're in a position to win here."

"But you wouldn't," she said tightly.

"And we don't have time to discuss every angle of the damned thing, either."

"How convenient for you."

Hell. He felt time slipping away from him by his own carelessness, by her inordinate stubbornness.

"I want *us* to win, Cassandra."

"That's not possible, Mr. Taggart. There is no us."

"I want to reclaim Riveland for my son," he went on doggedly.

"You have no son."

"Maybe I do, spider lady."

She felt a wave of heat work its way down her body, corrosive, hateful. A son somewhere—

"Don't you know you're going to have a baby, Cassandra?" God, what a way to tell her—in the middle of a hot, dusty town, surrounded by motion and emotion and everything going to hell. Maybe it was the only important thing, and maybe, in the end, Riveland was meaningless . . . to both of them.

"I? How would I know that?" she said, plainly not believing him.

"By the way you're feeling these mornings, Mrs. Taggart. You don't believe me. How could you not know that?"

A baby? *She*—was going to have a baby? She felt the earth move, she swore she did, and it wasn't because she was going to faint, either. It was just so—shattering that she was nurturing a *life*, and that he knew it, and she didn't . . .

. . . and it had to be *his*.

"There were never any women with babies on Riveland," she said, after a long, long moment when she repressed the urge to touch her stomach. "When a woman got with child, Jesse sold her away. He didn't want to see it, he didn't want to know about it. When he needed stock, he bought boys about thirteen years of age right off the breeding farms. He didn't care. I never saw a woman who was carrying a child." And Raylene, damn her, had never told her a thing about what to expect, either. And after a while, it hadn't seemed necessary to know.

He wanted to take her in his arms right then and there. Hell—goddamn that bastard. Goddamn everything.

"Cassandra—we have got to get to Riveland, and I have to have something in my hand to fight Greve if I need to. He's got everything on his side because of Jesse's will. No matter what happens, you violated the terms, and he'll come get you with that."

"A baby," she whispered, not even hearing him.

"Cassandra!"

She rubbed her face. "All right. I violated the terms I agreed to with him. So what?"

"I don't know. We can't assume you have a position of strength anymore as Jesse's widow. You understand me, Cassandra? We have to have more ammunition."

"And I'm to give it to *you?*"

"To our future, Cassandra."

She bit her lip. She didn't know what that meant. He was talking in riddles, and the worst one was that Mr. Greve was set to marry Linnea.

"Trust me, Cassandra."

"I don't know how I can." But who else was there? He was the father of her child, just as she had told everyone for nearly fifty miles all along the Galveston Bay border. The irony of it was staggering.

"You *have* to."

She hesitated again. He could take everything from her, and she didn't know if she could survive that.

"I'm trusting you," he said, "after everything you've done to me."

That brought her head up.

"You are a piece of work, spider lady. You could trap a man and leave him hanging while you put on one of your little disguises and go out after other prey. We have to trust each other." He felt like he was dangling on one of her threads and she could either cut him off or reel him in.

"You weren't fooled for a moment," she said scathingly.

"It made things very interesting, Cassandra."

"Yes, and I can see you're *very* interested now," she retorted.

He gave up. "You are goddamned blinded without those glasses you need, lady. You better get yourself a pair right fast, because you're going to miss the end of the story." He felt on the edge of fury. She had the one thing in her possession that could help them defeat Greve, and she had nothing to hand to save Riveland for herself.

"Tell me the end of the story, Trane."

"I'll tell you, all right, spider lady. It turns out the man was a goddamned fool. He came to fight his father and instead he found a very dangerous black widow, and he goddamn fell in love with her. And she goddamn wove her little webs until someone bigger and stronger came along and just cut her down from the ceiling. And she got stepped on and she never damn knew what happened to her."

"Trane—"

"Trust me, Cassandra. I love you."

Oh God. He loved Riveland more. But she was tired of fighting with him, tired of arguing. His desperation was real, deep, urgent. She couldn't even think about it, because she hadn't even assessed the fact that she had his seed growing within her.

She drew out the old six-shooter that she had taken from the minister in Deadman, and she picked delicately at the barrel. "I took it with me," she said, as she pulled the tightly rolled piece of paper from the gun. "I was going to confront you with it."

He took it and unrolled it. "I made up the name because I didn't want anyone to know Jesse's son was back in town putting things in a storage box that someone might get curious about."

"What's in there, Trane?"

"I would have thought you'd have guessed, Cassandra. I was bringing him Mother's death certificate."

499

Chapter Twenty-nine

It was not an easy matter getting onto Riveland in broad daylight. They could not approach it from the river, nor was there much leeway to skirt around the long, tree-lined drive.

They had to pick their way past the entry road and go beyond the house, beyond the slave cabins to a point where they could walk, with their mounts, through the undergrowth until they came in view of the potato patch and the gardens.

Riveland loomed in the distance, ominous now, concealing secrets, so many secrets.

They crawled through the undergrowth and into the garden, and around the little trellis of vines that hid them for a moment from the house.

"This is so risky," Cassandra whispered. "This is my house, my sister."

"You are the last person she wants to see, lady. Believe me. Come on." He led the way now, still on hands and knees, all his bad feelings escalating like a hot-air balloon as they got closer to the house.

It was the activity, the frenzied, unusual activity that caught their eye as they hunkered down behind a small gazebo at the edge of the long, sweeping side lawn.

"How are we going to get past that?" Cassandra groaned. "There isn't a door or window that someone isn't hanging out of."

"All we have to do is find Zilpha. Where is she most likely to be?"

"She doesn't have a most likely; she's all over the place. Maybe—maybe we can get in through the little porch off the small parlor."

"I'd rather climb in a window. They're probably dusting down the whole main floor if there's going to be a wedding tonight."

"I can't believe this. All right, maybe if we got into the square near the kitchen garden—I think the dairy has a back entrance."

They crept through the bushes along the back of the house to the ell of outbuildings that formed a square around the garden.

There were servants everywhere, working on the garden, beating at carpets, hanging out laundry. There didn't seem to be an inch of Riveland that wasn't occupied by someone.

"I wonder where Linnea is," Cassandra murmured, as they eased themselves up against the rear brick wall of the dairy.

"You don't want to know," Trane said, as he reached for the doorknob and twisted it. "Locked, Cassandra."

"That's not usual. I guess we have no choice—we have to get into the house."

"Get down. . . ."

They ducked into the bushes, and not a moment too soon. A phalanx of servants marched across the lawn, carrying a small sofa they intended to beat and wax down.

"Oh my, right from the small parlor," Cassandra groaned.

"I told you."

They waited a moment until a servant spread a blanket and the sofa was set down on it, and then they made a run for it, around the square of outbuildings to the side of the house facing the stables.

"Isaac might help us," Cassandra suggested.

501

"We've got to find Zilpha," Trane said adamantly.

"How?"

"I don't know. We'll wait. She's bound to come out here sometime."

They hunched down in the bushes again and watched the hive of activity that had been set in motion by the planning of a wedding.

"It is an awful sudden wedding," Cassandra said at length.

"Isn't it?" Trane agreed drily.

"It has nothing to do with me."

"Maybe not."

"If I forfeited my right to Riveland, Jackman was to inherit everything."

"I know."

"I don't understand. You get everything anyway."

"Stop talking like that, Cassandra. I didn't arrange this damned wedding, I'll tell you. Wait—there she is. . . ."

"Zilpha!" Cassandra called her, her voice low, sharp, urgent.

"Who dat?" Zilpha demanded, her ears pricking. "Who dere?"

"Zilpha!"

"Where you at?"

"Here."

Zilpha started walking along the bushes by the house. "Where?" And then she stopped short. "Oh Lawd almighty, *Missus.* Oh Lawd . . ."

"We have to get in the house," Cassandra whispered urgently.

"You do, you do. I get dose lazy gals away from de porch and parlor. You just keep quiet, Missus; I get you inside."

It took five minutes before she came out on the porch and motioned to them, and they cautiously crept up to the house and up onto the porch and into the small parlor.

The place was empty, denuded of furniture.

"Missus Wiltshire done took it all away, Missus. Want to have de space big fo' de wedding, fo' de party."

"Tell me about that," Cassandra demanded.

"Ain't much to tell, Missus. When you ain't come back in a week, dat Greve done declare you daid, and he done put de will fo' Missus Wiltshire fo' to take over just like you writ, and he come tell us dat Missus Wiltshire is de new Missus on Riveland and Miz Taggart ain't never gonna return."

"Oh dear God."

"Den he sets to courtin' Miz Wiltshire and dey is marryin' up tonight, and he plannin' to move right in and run Riveland, along wif dat Mr. Daggett he done hired back."

"Jesus," Trane swore.

"And you ain't even daid."

Trane rubbed his hand over his face. "Well, I'll tell you, Zilpha—tonight Miss Cassandra is going to come back from the grave."

"Missus Wiltshire usin' de big bedroom whut was Miz Coburne's fo' she died; ain't no one usin' Missus's room now, Mr. Trane."

"Good. Get us up there."

She did it, too. She hid them in the back stairwell until she could clear away the workers who were cleaning the upstairs, and she brought them to the room by the servants' staircase. "Dat Mr. Greve, he plannin' one big party wif all dem fancy businessmen he done met at dat big hotel in town. He gonna show 'em who de boss on Riveland," Zilpha told them in a whisper, as she unlocked the door to Cassandra's old room.

"You just let us know when the ceremony is about to start," Trane told her.

"I watch de door, I watch fo' de ceremony," Zilpha promised, closing them into the room.

"How is she going to do that?" Trane wondered.

"She'll do it," Cassandra said confidently. She walked

over to the window. The bustle was evident here too: Greve meant to put the most extravagant face on this travesty, she thought.

Trane watched her. It was still daylight, very late afternoon, and her face was in shadow beneath the hat she still wore. He wondered what she was thinking.

But then he thought maybe he knew.

"Greve never filed that change of legatee," she said after a long contemplative moment.

"No," Trane said, "I don't expect he did, and I hesitate to suggest who gave him the idea."

She grimaced. "It was a stupid idea. And I brought this whole thing down on myself."

"No," Trane said sharply, "Jesse brought it down on *you,* giving that man so much power over you. A man gets crazy when that kind of wealth is just within his grasp. You know it — you saw it. What was between him and Riveland, really, Cassandra? One lone uppity female, and an unexpected son who couldn't prove his identity. You think a man wouldn't kill for a chance like that?"

His words fell on her ears, stark, damning. Hadn't she always thought he had too much of a proprietory interest in Riveland?

"I think he engineered everything," Trane said grimly, thinking out loud, everything taking on a blinding coherence with the advent of this precipitate marriage. "I think he was the one who shot at you both times, and me. I think he tampered with the gig and maybe even started the fire . . . or paid someone to start the fire . . . I think . . . Someone who knew Riveland, and knew the fields — Daggett, maybe . . . I think . . . if he could have chased me off and gotten rid of you, and pretended to search for Jackman and never found him . . . How much effort would that have taken? How could a court disprove that he had initiated a search? They would have handed him the whole, lock, stock and barrel, since he was the one Jesse had trusted to administer the estate."

"So instead, I handed him Linnea."

504

"No, you took a risk, and you never knew she would turn up at your door. You like to take risks, Cassandra. You're taking one now."

"Yes I am, aren't I?"

"So am I," he said, taking off his hat and tossing it on the bed.

"He could have killed us," she whispered.

"We'll murder his ambition."

"How?"

"We're going to 'speak now' before anyone can forever hold his peace. We're going to disrupt the wedding and we're going to haul Mr. Greve into court for stealing your legacy and my birthright, and between the two of us, we have a case so strong the only thing he will be able to do is leave Carthage in disgrace, and take your disreputable sister with him."

"You sound so sure. The courts are not almighty favorable to a woman—ever," she said edgily as she turned from the window and began pacing in front of him. "And how many years will it take, and—"

He caught her on her second go-round and toppled her on the bed beside him.

"We're coming at him from two fronts," he said roughly, shifting his left leg over hers so that she couldn't get up again without a struggle, "just like I'm coming at you. We've got the widow, and we've got the son who is by right the next of kin if the will proves invalid. And we could have"—and he shifted his body onto hers, gently now so that she didn't feel threatened or suffocated—"one more invincible item to present to a court."

"Truly?" She didn't struggle, she didn't move. This was the Trane Taggart against whom she had to fight her hardest battle. The minute his weight settled on her, she remembered everything as if it were yesterday, and her body craved him again. It had been two months, and it had been a union built on lies and deceit, and she still didn't quite trust him, and his ready declaration of love jangled all over her body as his pressed tightly against

505

her.

"There *is* something to build on, Cassandra."

"Yes, I feel it building," she said tartly.

"We have one thing in common," he said obdurately, ignoring her jibe.

"It comes between us every time."

"Cassandra—" He heard the patience seeping from his voice like a bucket leaking water.

"Trane—I *can't* . . ."

"Kiss me, Cassandra, and then tell me what you can't."

"No."

"Oh yes," he murmured, slanting his mouth over hers. "Remember, Cassandra . . ."

"I remember too well," she sighed, as his mouth covered hers commandingly. She did; she remembered everything, the kisses, the bed, the night she conceded he was Trane Taggart when she didn't believe a word of it; every capitulation and every sensual demand was in that kiss, his and hers.

It was the first kiss between two people who had nothing to hide.

It was so sweet, so seeking, so arousing, that she had to believe that they did, they had one thing in common.

"The lies are finished," he whispered against her lips. "We've made a new life, and we make a new life from here, from right here."

"What do we do?"

"We reclaim Riveland for the future of our children, Cassandra. We get Greve and your sister out of our lives forever; and then, Cassandra, we marry and we make a life for ourselves and our children on Riveland."

"We—marry? Are you *crazy?*"

He smoothed back her hair, and he touched her face, her mouth, his finger tracing the line of her lower lip as if he never seen it before. "Maybe I am," he murmured, that odd little smile settling on his lips. "But you play good games, Cassandra, and that could be a very good thing once you come to love me."

506

Once I come to love him . . .

Maybe she loved him already, she thought; she didn't even know: it all got knotted up in that other business of Jesse's will and keeping control. Who had control now, she wondered. She couldn't tell; she could hardly see. The sun had gone down, and shadows filled the room.

And she was filled with the pervasive sense that they were the only people in the world who existed at that very moment, and she felt as if she were on the brink of an ineffable discovery.

Maybe, she thought as she responded to his light, seeking, little kisses, when you stripped away all the deceit, all the games, all the stories, maybe what was left was a man who had stumbled onto something he wasn't prepared for and didn't know what to do about; and maybe he had ultimately come to care for her, and everything happened just as he said, and for the reason he said, and he really meant to save Riveland for her, and to make a life with her and the child.

Maybe the thing that scared her most was that he truly was for real.

Oh, but she needed that now. *She* needed to learn how to be real. She had always been made up of the sum of her resentments and her lies. What was she, balanced against everything that he was.

And still he had told her he loved her, and he had risked everything by doing so.

She had to find him, she had to find their love; she had finally found herself.

"Dear God, do I want you," Trane murmured against her eager lips.

Yes, and she had found him. "It would be a lovely way to pass the time," she agreed softly, her lips a breath away from his.

He took her invitation, he took her willing lips, he crushed her willing body tightly against his, he savored the taste of her burgeoning love, her ardent capitulation.

This was Cassandra, smooth and silky, real and want-

507

ing, the woman no man else had ever known. And he wanted—real, rocking, thrusting, intense—he wanted her.

"Cassandra . . ." His voice was an ache against her ear.

"Love me," she begged, lifting her hips to invite him to remove the all-impeding trousers.

He shifted himself upward to remove her garment just enough so he could get to her, and his own. "You know I swear I don't know what to put where," he muttered, settling himself down on her body again where she could feel the massive proof of his need for her right then, right there.

"Oh . . . I just know you'll figure it out," she whispered, opening herself to the joy of receiving him once again, as her lover this time, as the man whose seed had spawned the child within her, as the mentor of her future, all these things encompassed in the slow, heated slide of his towering manhood deep within her velvet sheath.

And he stayed there, the center of her world, bound to her as surely as if they had spoken the words, pledged to her forever by the very act of possessing her in this carnal and complete way.

There was no other way; he filled her and completed her, and she felt that erotic, keen sense of connection once again that bonded her to him as she surrounded him totally with her feminine heat.

They were one and they rocked back and forth gently with the extravagant sensation of it, and he began, ever so gently, the long, slow thrusts to bring her to culmination.

She let herself feel it in all its dimensions, for its power and its fertility and for its prowess in creating that fulminating pleasure deep within her. She gave herself up to it as she had never done before. It was coming, it was the beginning and the hope, everything she had ever dreamt of embodied in the man who possessed her with such all-consuming passion. She was his, entwined with him, growing with him, creating with him . . . coming to love with him, coming to the soft, glissading peak of desire with him, cresting in an enfolding wave of radiant sensation, sliding deep into the tumultuous thrust of his triumphant, wrenching release that spent itself at the very moment they heard the urgent knock at the door.

"Zilpha!" she whispered, as he slowly eased himself away from her.

"It's time, Cassandra. *Hurry.*"

He righted his clothing first and whipped off the bed to open the door.

"Dey's in de parlor," Zilpha whispered, a wraith outside their door.

"We're coming," Trane whispered back.

"Got to be soon."

"In a minute. Cassandra . . ."

"I'm here."

"Dat Missus Wiltshire, she gettin' ready to come down de aisle," Zilpha cautioned. "Hear dat music?"

They heard it, wafting faintly from belowstairs.

"We'll wait until the minute that minister asks if there is any impediment to their marriage."

"I understand," Cassandra assured him in an undertone.

"Are you ready?"

She drew in a sharp breath. "I can't wait."

He opened the door wider and she slipped out before him and past Zilpha, who waited patiently at the threshold.

He waited a moment, thinking to close the door behind him, but there were no secrets now; there would never be any secrets, ever again.

"Leave the door open, Zilpha," he told her, as he swung it wide and held out his hand to Cassandra. She took it joyously, and together, to the resonant strains of the wedding march, they ran down the stairs.

HEART SOARING ROMANCE BY LA REE BRYANT

FIERY ROMANCE

CALIFORNIA CARESS   (2771, $3.75)
by Rebecca Sinclair

Hope Bennett was determined to save her brother's life. And if that meant paying notorious gunslinger Drake Frazier to take his place in a fight, she'd barter her last gold nugget. But Hope soon discovered she'd have to give the handsome rattlesnake more than riches if she wanted his help. His improper demands infuriated her; even as she luxuriated in the tantalizing heat of his embrace, she refused to yield to her desires.

ARIZONA CAPTIVE   (2718, $3.75)
by Laree Bryant

Logan Powers had always taken his role as a lady-killer very seriously and no woman was going to change that. Not even the breathtakingly beautiful Callie Nolan with her luxuriant black hair and startling blue eyes. Logan might have considered a lusty romp with her but it was apparent she was a lady, through and through. Hard as he tried, Logan couldn't resist wanting to take her warm slender body in his arms and hold her close to his heart forever.

DECEPTION'S EMBRACE   (2720, $3.75)
by Jeanne Hansen

Terrified heiress Katrina Montgomery fled Memphis with what little she could carry and headed west, hiding in a freight car. By the time she reached Kansas City, she was feeling almost safe . . . until the handsomest man she'd ever seen entered the car and swept her into his embrace. She didn't know who he was or why he refused to let her go, but when she gazed into his eyes, she somehow knew she could trust him with her life . . . and her heart.